# A Pigeon and a Boy

# A Pigeon and a Boy

## MEIR SHALEV

*Translated from the Hebrew*
*by Evan Fallenberg*

Schocken Books · New York · 2007

Translation copyright © 2007 by Meir Shalev

All rights reserved. Published in the United States by Pantheon Books, a division of Random House, Inc., New York, and in Canada by Random House of Canada Limited, Toronto. Originally published in Israel as *Yona V'naar* by Am Oved Publishers Ltd., Tel Aviv, in 2006. Copyright © 2006 by Am Oved Publishers Ltd., Tel Aviv.

Schocken Books and colophon are registered trademarks of Random House, Inc.

Library of Congress Cataloging-in-Publication Data

Shalev, Meir.
[Yonah ve-na'ar. English]
A pigeon and a boy / Meir Shalev ; translated from the Hebrew by Evan Fallenberg.
p.   cm.
ISBN 978-0-8052-4251-5
I. Fallenberg, Evan.  II.  Title.
PJ5054.S384Y6613 2007
892.4'36 — dc22      2007000843

*6642*

www.schocken.com

Printed in the United States of America

First American Edition

2  4  6  8  9  7  5  3  1

*To Zohar and Michael*

# A Pigeon and a Boy

# Chapter One

## I

"AND SUDDENLY," said the elderly American man in the white shirt, "suddenly, a pigeon flew overhead, above that hell."

Everyone fell silent. His unexpected Hebrew and the pigeon that had alighted from his mouth surprised all present, even those who could not understand what he was saying.

"A pigeon? What pigeon?"

The man—stout and suntanned as only Americans can be, with moccasins on his feet and a mane of white hair on his head—pointed to the turret of the monastery. Many years had passed, but there were a few things he still remembered about the terrible battle that had taken place here. "And forgetting them," he declared, "is something I'll never be able to do." Not only the fatigue and the horror, not only the victory—"A victory that took both sides by surprise," he noted—but also the minor details, the ones whose importance becomes apparent only later: for one, the stray bullets—or perhaps they were intentional—that struck the bell of the monastery on occasion—"Right here, this very bell"—and then the bell would ring sharply, an odd sound that sank, then abated, but continued to resound in the darkness for a long while.

"And the pigeon?"

"A strange sound. Sharp at first, and high-pitched, like even the bell was surprised; then it got weaker, in pain but not dead, until the next shot hit it. One of our wounded guys said, 'Bells are used to getting hit from the inside, not the outside.'"

He smiled to himself as though he had only just understood. His

3

teeth were bared, and even those were terribly white, as only elderly American teeth can be.

"But what about the pigeon? What kind of a pigeon was it?"

"I'm ninety-nine percent sure it was a homing pigeon, a Palmach carrier pigeon. We'd been fighting all night, and in the morning, two or three hours after sunrise, we saw it suddenly lifting off."

This Hebrew he had unleashed, without prior warning, was good—in spite of his accent—but his use of the term *homing pigeon* in English sounded more pleasant and proper than its Hebrew equivalent, even if the bird in question did belong to the Palmach.

"How could you be sure?"

"A pigeon handler was assigned to us, a pigeon expert with a little dovecote—that's what it was called—on his back. Maybe he managed to dispatch the bird before he was killed, or maybe the dovecote busted and the bird flew away."

"He was killed? How?"

"How? There was no lack of how to get killed here—all you had to do was choose: by a bullet or shrapnel, in the head or the stomach or that major artery in your thigh. Sometimes it was right away and sometimes it was real slow, a few hours after you got hit."

His yellow eyes pierced me. "Amazing, isn't it?" he said, chuckling. "We went to battle with homing pigeons, like in ancient Greece."

# 2

AND SUDDENLY, above that hell, the fighters saw a pigeon. Born from bulbs of smoke, delivered from shrouds of dust, the pigeon rose, she soared. Above the grunts and the shouts, above the whisper of shrapnel in the chill of the air, above the invisible paths of bullets, above the exploding grenades and the barking rifles and the pounding cannons.

A plain-looking pigeon: bluish-gray with scarlet legs and two dark stripes like those of a prayer shawl adorning the wings. A pigeon like a thousand others, like any other pigeon. Only an expert's ears could pick up on the power of those beating wings, double that of normal pigeons; only an expert's eyes could discern the width and the depth of the bird's breast, or the beak that carries forth the slant of the forehead in a straight line, or the characteristic light-colored swelling where it meets the head. Only the heart of a pigeon fancier could grasp and contain the longing that has collected inside such a bird and determined its course and forged its strength. But already his eyes had grown dim, his ears had fallen deaf, his heart had emptied and was still. Only she remained—the pigeon—her yearning for home, his final wish.

Up. First and foremost, up. Above the blood, above the fire and the columns of smoke. Above the wounded, their flesh riddled, torn, burnt, silent. Above those whose bodies will remain intact but whose souls have been extinguished. Above those who have died and who, with the passing of many days, will die once again with the deaths of those who remembered them.

Up. Aloft and distant, to where the gunfire will become a faint ticking and the shouts will fall mute and the smell will dissipate and the smoke will clear, and the dead will appear one like the other as if cast from a single mold, and the living will take their leave of them, each man to his destiny, wondering what they did right to deserve to live, and what their comrades—lying now before them—did wrong that they deserved to die. And then a quick look to the sides, and homeward, in a straight line, as homing pigeons fly. Homeward, her heart fluttering but courageous, golden eyes frightened but fully open, missing no helpful topographical detail, a transparent, auxiliary set of eyelids pulled taut over them against blinding light and dust. Another thin stripe embellishes the short, curved tail, a hint at the bird's ancient Damascene pedigree. The small, rounded head, full of yearning and memories: the loft, the pigeonhole, the cooing of a mate, the warm scent of the nest and brooding. The hand of a young woman passing over the feeding trough, the tinkling of seeds in the young woman's box calls her, the woman's gaze scans the heavens awaiting her, and her words—"Come, come, come"—invite and comfort.

"Not only me. We all saw it," the elderly American said. "They must have, too, because all the weapons fell silent for a moment. Ours and theirs. Not a single gun fired, no grenades exploded, and all the mouths stopped shouting. It was so quiet that we heard the bird's wings beating the air. For a single moment every eye and every finger was following that bird as she did what we all wanted to do: make her way home."

By now he was quite agitated; he paced to and fro, his fingers plunged deep into the snowy-white thickness of his leonine hair. "After all, that's what she was: a homing pigeon. That's all she wants and all she knows. She took off, didn't make that big circle in the air you always read about in books, the one that homing pigeons make before they figure out the right direction to take. She just flew straight out of there, no delay, like an arrow shot in that direction—northwest, if I'm not mistaken; yes, according to the time of day and the sun, I'm correct. Right in that direction. You wouldn't believe how fast she disappeared."

A matter of seconds. With the greatest of longing and speed. She was there, then she faded. The hand that dispatched her fell to the ground; the gaze still followed her, the bell still resounded, refusing to die out, a few final notes spilling forth, gathering toward that distant sea of silence, while the blue-gray of the pigeon was swallowed into its twin on the horizon, and was gone. And below, the fingers returned to their triggers and the eyes to their scopes, and the gun barrels resumed their thunder and the mouths their groaning and gaping and gulping of air, their bellowing, their gasping of last breaths.

Now the man turned to his friends, reverted to American English, explaining and describing and pointing: "Over there somewhere, behind the pine trees," or "Right here." He told of an Iraqi armored vehicle equipped with a machine gun and a cannon that "was running around here like it owned the place." With the gestures of a generous host he motioned to "right there, that's where I lay with my gun, at the corner of the roof. But over on that building there was a sniper and he put a bullet in me."

With dexterity uncommon in a man his age, he bent over and rolled up his trousers, exposing two pale scars between his knee and ankle. "See? Right there. The little one's where the bullet went in, and the big one's where it came out. Our sapper carried me down on his back, went back up to take my place, and got hit by a mortar shell." He reverted to Hebrew, meant only for me. "A bigger and stronger guy even than me, poor sucker. Torn right in half, died in a split second."

He talked and recounted, freeing memories that had been imprisoned inside him for so long. He let them breathe a little air, stretch their bones, see the place where they were formed; he let them argue, compare: Which had changed? Which hadn't even been there in the first place? Which were worthy of being preserved, and which no longer?

"And the guy who brought the pigeons?" I asked, pursuing my own agenda. "The pigeon handler? You said he was killed. Did you see where exactly?"

Those eyes settled on me again, the yellow eyes of a lion. One large, tanned hand wrapped itself around my shoulders; another large, tanned hand rose in the air and pointed. Age spots on the back of it, its fingernails buffed, a silver sailor's watch beautifying its wrist, a white shirt-sleeve pressed and rolled to the elbow. It was a hand easy to imagine clutching a rifle, patting the head of a grandchild, pounding on a table, knowing waists and thighs.

"There."

A good and pleasant vigor coursed through me suddenly, as if those were the eyes of a father gazing upon his son, as if this were the hand of a father slipping from head to shoulder—guiding, offering strength and support.

"Where? Show me exactly."

He tilted his aged head downward to mine, just as all the tall people in my life do when speaking to short ones. "There. Between the edge of the grass and the children on the swings. You see? There was a small stone shack there, no more than six or seven feet on either side, a kind of gardener's toolshed. We were all positioned in the courtyard and the rooms of the monastery while the guys who stayed on from the other company were holed up in that building, on the other side of this alley. The armored vehicle blasted anybody who so much as stuck his nose outside one of the buildings. But the pigeon handler—God knows why or how—made it out and got himself over there, which is where we found him when it was all over."

# 3

I COULDN'T STAY there any longer. I shepherded them into Behemoth—that's the name my wife gave the huge Chevy Suburban she bought for me—and we departed for the German Colony neighborhood of Jerusalem.

Now I felt the full force of my fatigue; a small group can be more demanding and bothersome than a whole busload of tourists. The day had risen on us in Tel Aviv, after which we'd continued to Kibbutz Hulda and the story of the convoy named for it, been detained for a light meal of sandwiches at the Harel observation point, and jounced about on the Burma Road on the way to Hamasrek and the stronghold at Sha'ar Hagai for more explanations and more lookouts.

From there I took them to the Palmach cemetery at Kiryat Anavim, then into Jerusalem, to the monastery and this surprise: that the eldest of the six Americans I was ferrying about and guiding—a senator, his aide, his adviser, and three businessmen, all of them guests of the Foreign Ministry—had once been a member of the Palmach and had fought in the battle that had taken place there, which I was attempting to describe for them. And from there to the even bigger surprise of the homing pigeon that had suddenly taken wing from the pigeonholes of his memory.

"Did you know him?" I asked.

"Who?"

"The pigeon handler you told us about earlier."

His face filled the rearview mirror of Behemoth. "Not really. He wasn't one of the fighting gang—he'd come to our brigade to set up an operational pigeon loft. They said he was a top-class professional, that he'd been handling pigeons since he was a boy."

His eyes did not let up their vigil; they continued to pin me down like the hooked spines of a caper bush. "I don't even remember his name anymore. A lot of other friends of mine were killed, and it's been so many years."

At the stoplight facing the German Colony cemetery I turned left. I took advantage of the crowds of people and the cars that slowed us to a crawl to spread my wares: the Rephaim and the Philistines, the British and the Germans. "Gentlemen, please note the verses from the Bible inscribed on the portals. And over there is the old Jerusalem train station. It's no longer in use, but when I was a child I would travel from here to Tel Aviv with my mother. In a steam engine, can you believe it?"

The train would rumble its way slowly, creaking along the metallic curves of the ravine. I remember the tiny, well-tended vegetable beds of the Arabs on the far side of the border, the soapy froth amassed by sewer water. The wind would set aloft bits of ash from the steam engine and you would brush them from your hair, happy: we were going home, to Tel Aviv . . .

I am revisited by the scent of bread, hard-boiled egg, and tomato, the provisions you always brought with us. My forehead would shudder—just as it is shuddering now, as I write these words—in antici-pation of the egg you would rap on it, your favorite game. *"Plaff!"* you would shout, laughing. Each time I was taken by surprise; each time you laughed. And the rustling of your fingers in the wax paper as they pinched salt and sprinkled it. And that little song you would sing with a child's inflections: *The engine's sounding, choo, choo, choo / Now take your seat, and that means you!* And the smile that spread across your face the farther we got from Jerusalem, a smile of joy and contentment: home, to Tel Aviv.

Yes, of course they believe it. Why wouldn't they? The tour has been meticulously planned; the sandwiches, coffee, and juice have awaited them at the appointed hours and places, lending reliability and validity to the tour guide's memories and explanations. At the café of the Cinemathèque, the reserved table appears as promised, as do the sunset and the view. That's Mount Zion, and over there is David's Tomb, if anyone's interested in those kinds of sites and stories; and down below, Sultan's Pool, and the ancient spigot "that waters the parched and weary."

And over there—the hills of Moab turning gold in the last light of day. "Yes, they're so close you can reach out your hand and touch them. That's where Moses stood on Mount Nebo and gazed at the Promised Land. He thought it was pretty close, too, but from the other side."

"Maybe that's the real problem for you people," observed one of the businessmen in the group. He was wearing a ridiculous safari vest full of pockets, the kind that tourists and foreign correspondents love to sport while in the Middle East. "Everything's so small and close and crowded over here, so that from every place you see more and *more* places."

The tour guide—that is I, Mother; make no mistake, do not forget—responded with an "Absolutely" and a compliment of "That's right." Indeed, small and close and crowded with people and events and memories. "In such a Jewish manner, I might add," he said, and then he mixed in history and etymology, truths and fables, and pointed out the Valley of Hinnom, or Hell, and he told about the film festival held there and the graves of the Karaites and the awful child sacrifices of Moloch, and who'd ordered iced coffee? The tiny victims cry out from the altars.

With nightfall I delivered my small and distinguished group to the King David Hotel, where an important member of Knesset—"From the opposition, in fact," I was told by the Foreign Ministry staff member who had set up the visit—would be dining with them. Afterward he would make a speech and answer the delegation's questions about current affairs, "because the foreign minister not only agrees they should hear differing opinions, he *insists* on it."

I went up to the room assigned to me—not all groups are as generous as this one—and I showered and phoned home. Six rings and a sigh of relief: no answer; Liora is not at home. Or maybe she is at home and she knows it's me and has decided not to pick up the phone. Or perhaps it's the telephone itself, once again identifying the caller and once again choosing to ignore me and remain silent.

"Hello," I said. "Hello . . ." and then: "Liora? It's me. If you're there, would you be kind enough to pick up?"

But it was my own voice—matter-of-fact and polite—that responded: "You have reached the home of Liora and Yair Mendelsohn. We can't come to the phone right now," and after my voice, hers—impatient and enthralling in its Americanness, its hoarseness: "Leave your message after the beep."

I hung up and phoned Tirzah on her mobile. Tirzah never answers with "Hello." Sometimes it's "Yes," and sometimes "Just a moment, please," and then I can hear her giving instructions to people, and I listen with pleasure.

"All right," she said, "I'm with you now."

"Why don't you come up to Jerusalem, Tiraleh? They gave me a bed that's too big and a full moon and a window overlooking the walls of the Old City."

"It's you, luvey? I thought it was that pest of an engineer from the Public Works Department."

Tirzah doesn't use my name. Sometimes she calls me Iraleh, the way her father did when we were kids—"Here are Iraleh and Tiraleh," he would proclaim whenever he saw us together—and sometimes, affectionately, she calls me "luvey."

"It's me. A different pest."

She laughed. Now she's finally convinced: not *that* pest, but *this* pest. When Tirzah laughs, I'm happy. I can take it as a compliment; she laughs because of me.

"Where are you?"

"At the King David. So, are you coming?"

She laughed again. Certainly a nice proposition, absolutely, she and I and the bed and the window with the moon and the walls of the Old City, a very tempting proposition, but the next morning they would be pouring the concrete at a project in Haifa Bay and she had two meetings with people from the Defense Ministry—one with the jerk from the Building Department and one with the nice guy from Finance—"and I was hoping we'd have a chance to meet at our house, because there are a few decisions we have to make."

I ignored the "our house" and asked what decisions she was talking about.

"The usual: floor tiles, window frames, what colors to paint the walls. Don't worry, I'll decide; you just have to be there."

"Tomorrow. I finish up with these Americans and then I can come."

"How are they?"

"You won't believe it: one of them was in the Palmach."

"You love me?" she asked playfully.

"Yes. And yes," I answered, preempting her next question, which would be, as always, "And you miss me?"

"Do you want to hear what else we've managed with the renovations?"

"I've got to tell you something this guy suddenly told me."

"Stories are for bedtime."

"I'm in bed."

"For when we're both in bed, not just you. Tomorrow night. We'll inaugurate the full moon and you'll tell me everything. And bring me one of those fried-egg "samwiches" from Glick's kiosk—have them go heavy on the salt and tell them to sear the hot pepper on the grill. Tell them it's for me. Don't forget to tell them: It's for Meshulam Fried's daughter!"

I got dressed, looked at myself in the mirror, and decided to skip the dinner and the important member of Knesset from the opposition and his differing opinions. I stripped off my clothes, climbed back into my large bed, and napped fitfully, annoyingly, facing the full moon and the walls of the Old City, and awakened more tired than before, then got dressed and went down to the bar.

# 4

THE OLD LION was lying in wait on an armchair in the corner of the lobby, alert and smelling of aftershave. His eyes and his watch glowed in the dim light, his white mane coiffed, his wrinkles deep, his silver eyebrows standing on end.

"I've been waiting for you," he said as he rose to greet me, though it was not clear whether from politesse or to remind me of his advantage over me—in years, in height, in knowledge. His eyes had seen, while mine had not. His ears had heard, while mine had merely imagined. His mind was shelves of memory, while mine was rolls of conjectures.

"I was promised an important delegation from America," I told him.

"They never mentioned anything about a guy who served in the Palmach."

"I wanted to thank you," he said. "I hadn't been back to most of those places since then, and I thought it was going to be tough for me."

"Well, certainly not as tough as back then, during the war."

"You'd be surprised, but in some ways it was easier then. I was a colt, really eager to see battle, ready to take on anything and quick to heal. I was just what a war wants its soldiers to be: a guy without a potbelly or a brain or kids or memories."

"So where was it most difficult for you today? At the cemetery or the monastery?"

"The monastery. At least at the cemetery there was one good thing: they're dead but I'm still alive. Once upon a time I felt guilty about that, but not anymore."

"He's buried there too," I said.

"Who is?"

"The guy you told me about today, the pigeon handler who went to battle with you guys and got killed."

"The Baby!" he cried. "That's the reason I've been waiting for you here. To tell you I remembered: we all called him the Baby."

"And when you recall his name, can you picture him, too?"

"His face? Not really. More the image—kind of blurry, without all the features. But it's him all right. He was called the Baby because he was short and chubby, and someone from the Jordan Valley told us that's what he was called at school and on his kibbutz. He was always busy with his birds, and he never let anyone get near the loft because he didn't want to frighten them. He explained to us that pigeons need to love their home; otherwise they won't return to it. Will you look at this! When I talk to you, more and more memories come back, but I can't for the life of me recall his real name."

He leaned over me as he had at the monastery, and in spite of his eighty years the scent of a predator filled the air: a breath of chocolate and mint, a whiff of alcohol, faint aftershave, rare meat—bloody on the inside, seared on the outside—a nonsmoker. My nostrils informed me that his shirt had been laundered with Ivory, like my wife's undies, and underneath it all was battle smoke, dust from roads that never settles, embers from a bonfire.

"It's remarkable, you know: the older and denser I get, the more things rise to the surface. We never had a single night when we weren't busy, and there was a division of labor: whoever didn't go out to battle dug graves for the ones who didn't return. I can still hear the sound of the pickaxes in the valley, metal on rock, even more than the sound of gunfire. You just dig and dig, you don't even dare think about who exactly it's going to be this time. Incidentally, he was one of the regular grave diggers."

"Who was?"

"The Baby. After all, until the battle at the monastery he didn't fight with us. So he dug graves for the ones who did. The graves were supposed to be ready when the guys came back in the morning with the bodies. The dead hate to wait."

How strange, I thought to myself: the man doesn't seem the talkative type. But now he appears to be purging himself of everything that has piled up inside him and been waiting for release since then. I recalled a story you told me when I was a teenager. You said that words are born and multiply in lots of ways: some subdivide like amoebas; others send out shoots and branches. With this guy, the letters were mating with memories.

"And what about you? Did you join the war as a volunteer from America?"

"What?! You're insulting my Hebrew! I'm originally from Petah-Tikva; I still have family there. I'm a product of Mikveh Israel, agricultural training school, and the reserves and Haportzim, the fourth battalion of the Palmach. Judging by the tour you gave us today, you know these places just as well as I do: the Castel, Colonia, Bab-el-Wad, and Katamon, of course. And then the war ended and I wasn't accepted at the Technion, so I went to study engineering in America instead. I met a girl there, got a job with her father—"

"He really *was* called the Baby," I said, putting a stop to his prattle. "And the pigeon you were talking about this afternoon really *was* one of his."

"I see you've taken a great interest in that pigeon handler," said the elderly American Palmachnik. "Did you know him?"

"How could I? I wasn't even born then."

"So what's your connection to him?"

"I'm interested in homing pigeons," I told him. "Maybe because I've taken visiting bird-watchers around the country in search of migrating birds."

The gold in his eyes faded to blue, his wrinkles softened, his expression grew friendlier, as if he wished to recount more and, without knowing it, to offer consolation as well—to explain and to heal.

"We won the battle at the monastery by a hair," he said, "and with major casualties and wounded. Even a few poor nuns got killed. Among the living there was a kind of a joke about it: like us, the nuns died for Jerusalem; like us, they died virgins. We fought right through the night, and when the sun rose, instead of encouraging us it filled us with despair. In the light of day we could see they had more and more reinforcements, and an armored vehicle with a machine gun and a cannon, and worst of all, we could see the true color of our wounded and we knew who might live and who was sure to die. We had so many down that we'd already begun to wonder what would happen if the order was given to retreat: who would we take with us and what would we do with the ones we couldn't. And then, like some heaven-sent miracle, the transmitter started working again and announced that the Arabs had started beating a hasty retreat from the whole area, with their commander at the lead, and we should just hold on a little longer. What can I tell you? In the end we won, but it was one of those victories where the winner is more surprised than the loser."

"Well, at least you were happy about it, right?"

"We didn't have the time or energy for rejoicing. We got up, started organizing the evacuation, and suddenly a little door opens up and three nuns step outside. Two of them dragged the bodies of their sister nuns inside, while the third—she was old and short, a dwarf almost, in a black habit that reached the ground—walked among us with a bottle of water and a few drinking glasses. What a picture that was: us, all those wounded and dead, and this nun wandering around like we're at some cocktail party and she's handing out drinks. The whole time she's saying, *"Nero, nero,"* and we didn't know what this *nero* was, but we knew we'd won because she'd come out to give water to the victors. You get it? If we'd lost, she'd have served water to the Arabs instead."

"*Nero* is water," I told him, "in Greek."

"If you say so," the man chuckled. "A tour guide has to know how to say 'water' in all kinds of languages. Maybe one day you'll get some Greek bird-watchers and they'll be thirsty."

"Bird-watchers don't come here from Greece," I said. "They come from England and Germany and Scandinavia and Holland, and sometimes as far away as the U.S."

But the man flashed me a look of reproach and sent me back to the place and time to which I had led him and which I wished to avoid. "We left the monastery and went looking around; we thought we might find one of our own among all the bodies outside. First we found a dead platoon commander, his guts spilled out on the ground, and then we found him. Someone shouted, 'Hey look, the Baby is dead.' God, just saying 'the Baby is dead' makes me shake all over."

"Did you see him, too?"

"Yes, I just told you that, and I told you that earlier, too, but you don't want to hear it, or else you want to hear it again and again. I saw him lying in that shed near the monastery, between where the grass and the swings are today."

"Inside the shed?"

"Half in, half out."

Apparently he saw the horror in my eyes and hastened to make himself clear. "I mean, don't misunderstand me. His body was whole, not like that just sounded. The wall of the shed was half destroyed and he was lying with his legs inside it, but from the waist up he was outside. There was a machine gun lying next to him—a tommy gun—and lots of gardening tools, and if you're interested, then I'll tell you his face was whole and at peace, and his eyes were open and looking upward. That was the worst part of it: they were full of life, and they were watching. You know what I was thinking about then? Not what I'm thinking about now. I thought, Where the hell did the Baby get a tommy gun! We were fighting with shitty old Stens that never stopped jamming, and *he'd* been given a tommy gun? Forty-five caliber—a bullet that no matter where it hits you, you're dead! Now do you understand why it was easier for me back then than it is now? That's the way it is when you're young. I couldn't figure out how it was that he'd been given a tommy gun and we hadn't."

I could no longer be sure what had brought this on, what had given birth to this outpouring: the words, the drink, me, the images in his mind. What had really happened there and what had been conceived in his memory?

"We'd been given green American battle dress, leftovers from World War II. Where the insignias and ranks had once been, the green was darker. Do you believe the bullshit I can still remember, and yet I can't remember some of the important stuff? Anyway, he was lying there in battle dress that had once belonged to an American sergeant about twice his size, and when we picked him up his arms fell to the sides and the battle dress opened and we saw that his pants—excuse me for telling you this—his pants had been cut open from the belt to almost the knee and peeled back to both sides, and everything was bloody and wounded and hanging out."

Suddenly the American thrust out his arm. "Here," he said as his hand grasped my right hip, then slipped around to my lower back and remained there. "The bullet went in here and came out here . . ." His hand slid to the front and pressed lightly, and I did not know what to do with the strength of the repulsion, and the pleasantness, I was feeling.

"Maybe there was more than one bullet, maybe it was a whole round, because his, his . . . what do you call it, I've forgotten the word in Hebrew . . . his hip, yes, his hip was just gone, completely exposed, and there were such quantities of blood, and his thigh was shredded, all the bones jutting out. I think he managed to cut open his pants but didn't get a chance to treat his wounds and so he wound up lying there like that until he died."

"What about the pigeons?" I asked.

He removed his hand. Grief and relief mingled one with the other. "The little dovecote he carried on his back had been shattered to pieces, and there were two dead pigeons on the floor. The third one was gone; that was apparently the one I told you about when we were there today." To my great distress, he began to hum the tune to a song I had heard my mother sing many times: *To silence the cannon yields / In abandoned killing fields.* He said, "And it was a beautiful, special kind of a day; only later we realized it was the First of May, and there was this bird rising up above all that hell, that valley of death. She'd been lucky the dovecote got smashed—that's how she managed to escape."

"She didn't escape," I told him. "He dispatched her. He did manage to do something before he died."

The man was astonished. "Who told you such a thing?"

"There's no other possibility. That's the only way the facts fit together."

"What do you mean he sent her? With a letter to headquarters?"

"He didn't send her," I corrected him. "He dispatched her. 'Dispatch' is the correct word for pigeons, and that is precisely what he did, like Noah in the ark: 'And he dispatched a dove, and the dove found no rest for the sole of her foot, and she returned to him into the ark.'"

"And what about that pigeon? What happened to her?"

"He sent it to his girlfriend in Tel Aviv."

All at once I felt that feeling I'd known from long ago: the wings beating inside my body, up and down, from the vibration in my knees to the emptiness in my loins to the ache in my breast to the spasms in my gullet. Home, Odysseus of the Feathered Creatures, in a straight line. The great magnetic forces of the earth are guiding her flight, longing pushes her from behind, love is signaling to her, switching on the landing lights: come, come, come, return from afar. That was the reason why the Baby had taken her, the purpose for her domestication, her training, her heredity. "Strong muscles, featherweight body, hollow bones, the lungs and heart of an athlete, the ability to navigate, a sense of direction."

And the three desires that become one: the desire of the Baby, who at that moment had died; the desire of his beloved, who at that moment already sensed what lay ahead; and the desire of the bird to reach home. Home. Home to Tel Aviv, to the gold of the sand, to the blue of the water, to the pink tiles of the roofs.

Home. To the upraised, joyful eyes awaiting her. To the heart beating on her behalf. To the hand that will greet her with seeds of hashish, the traditional gift that pigeon handlers present to their birds returning from afar. To the other hand, which will remove the message capsule from her leg. And then the terrible scream of comprehension, his name spattered from mouth to heavens, the slamming of the door to the pigeon loft and the footsteps receding in great haste.

"God," the elderly American Palmachnik from Petah-Tikva said. "What are you trying to tell me? That that's what he managed to do with the last moments of his life? To send a pigeon to his girlfriend in Tel Aviv?"

I said nothing, and he grew agitated. "And what exactly did he write her from there: Hello, I'm dead?"

# Chapter Two

## I

I WENT TO FIND myself a home. Some people shoot—themselves or others—but I went to find myself a home. A home that would heal, and soothe, and build me as I built it, and we would be grateful for each other.

Off I went, armed with the surprising gift my mother had given me: to carry out her will, the command she'd issued with a note of regret threaded through her words: "Take this, Yair. Go find yourself a home. A place to rest the soles of your feet. A place of your very own."

"A home that has been lived in," she instructed me, "small and old. Fix it up a bit . . ." She stopped talking for a moment, gulping air and coughing. "And make sure it's in an old village and the trees nearby have matured—cypress trees are best, but an old carob tree is good too, and there should be weeds poking through the cracks in the sidewalk."

She explained: in an old village the scores have been settled and the old enmities have grown accustomed to one another and the truly great loves—not the small bothersome ones—have settled down and there is no longer a need for guesswork or the strength for experimentation.

"Rest awhile, Mother," I said. "It's not good for you to talk a lot and exert yourself."

You were lying in your sickbed, winded and impatient, several gladioluses in a pitcher on top of the cabinet, a blue kerchief covering your bald head. "Large trees, Yair, don't forget. The wind in a big tree is different from that of young trees. Here, take this . . . and build yourself a little outdoor shower, too. It is pleasant to shower facing the wind and the view."

My body trembled, my hand reached out and took it, my eyes looked and read. "Where did all this money come from?" my mouth asked.

"From Mother."

You coughed, you drank the air in spasms. "Take it while my hand is warm and I am still alive to give it to you. And tell no one about it. Not your brother, not Yordad, not your wife."

Those were truly the words: "go" and "find" and "a place of your very own." And between your coughing fits I was reminded of that place that is not mine, the house that Liora bought us on Spinoza Street in Tel Aviv. The house and its mistress; she and her abode. The large, light-colored rooms just like her, and the proper angles just like hers; she of her wealth, of the whitewashed walls of her body, of the marvelous distance between the windows of her eyes.

# 2

BEFORE SHE FELL ILL, my mother was tall of stature, with fair curls and a single dimple. After she fell ill her stature bowed, her curls fell out, and her dimple was effaced. At the first memorial service we held in her honor, my brother, Benjamin, and I were still standing next to her grave when a dispute arose between us: on which cheek was that dimple? Benjamin said it was the right one, while I stood firm for the left. At first we joked about it, exchanging slaps and stinging remarks, and then my slaps grew heavier and his words became as snakebites.

After betting—we used to argue often; later we made bets, always on the very same lunch at the very same Romanian restaurant—we began interrogating anyone we could about the placement of that dimple. At once additional disputes awakened and additional brows wrinkled and additional bets were made. And when we came to investigating old photographs—with childish excitement and the sweet pain common to adult orphans—we discovered, with great disappointment and the thin, unavoidable feeling of having been cheated, that her dimple did not appear in any of them. Not on her left cheek and not on her right.

Could it be that we remembered a dimple that had never existed? Perhaps we had imagined ourselves a mother, her smile and her height and her dimple and her curls? No! We did have a mother, but it turned out that in photographs—we only learned this after her death—she did not smile. Thus, the pictures never show her large, identical teeth or the slant of the sneer on her upper lip or her dimple or the look that took up residence in her eyes during the first year of her marriage to Yordad.

When she spoke to us of him she did not say "Father" or "Dad" but "your dad": Tell your dad that I am waiting for him. Recount to your dad what we saw in the street today. You want to own a dog? Ask your dad, but do not forget to tell him that I do not approve. And because we were little and she continued to call him "your dad," we thought his name was Yordad and we called him this when we spoke to him or about him. It has remained his nickname to this very day. He did not protest, but he did demand that we not call him this around strangers.

"Call Yordad upstairs for lunch," my mother told us each day at her punctiliously German one-thirty, and we would charge down the stairwell to his ground-floor pediatric clinic—Benjamin at three already skipping while I, five years old, still stumbled—pushing each other and shouting, "Yordad, Yordad! Mother says you should come eat . . ."

They both smiled, she laughing aloud in the kitchen, he while silently hanging up his smock. Occasionally he would scold us: "Children, don't run in the stairwell—you will disturb the neighbors," his fair head hovering at the top of his great height. And occasionally he would lean down and turn on his "color lamp" for us, a large and shiny flashlight that shone red and yellow and green and that he would use to capture and soothe the hearts of the young patients who came to his clinic.

Now my mother is dead and Yordad has retired and turned his small clinic into his apartment. But then he was a pediatrician, four years older than my mother and twenty years more aged than she. More than once did he gaze at her as though she were a child, too, sometimes adding a gentle rebuke as well, and with the years, as happens with husbands whose wives do not age with them, he began making up useless rules, instructing her about what to wear because it was cold outside and what to eat because it was hot and pointing out "Once again you've forgotten!" about that which had slipped from his own memory.

On occasion the need to establish rules and regulations arose in her as well, though these were very different from his. "What does a person need?" she proclaimed one day after the first spoonful of dessert. "Not much: something sweet to eat, and a story to tell, and time and space, and gladioluses in a vase, and two friends, and two hilltops, one on which to stand and the other upon which to gaze. And two eyes for watching the heavens and waiting. Do you understand what I mean, Yair?"

And another time, when we were already living in Jerusalem, you suddenly closed the book you were immersed in reading—a small, chubby book with a light blue cover, though my brother, Benjamin, believes it was gray—you closed your book and made another pronouncement: "I can't take it anymore."

"I can't take it anymore." I heard you then just as I do now. "I can't take it anymore," you said; and fell silent, so that all those listening could be properly unsettled by what you had said; then you opened your small, chubby book and I—though this past February turned forty-nine, a sluggish, aging bull—I grow sad once again recalling that distant moment, for the colors of that book's cover and the edges of its pages and its silk bookmark—the bright blue, the soft pink, the deep gold—I remember well. Your eyes, your skin, your hair were precisely the same colors. But I no longer recall the name of the book, nor will I ever read from it, to search out and find and know what was the sentence that so agitated you, that caused you to utter those words. To clarify for myself whether the idea that eventually led you to leave home sprouted then.

My mother left home in the manner that characterized everything she did: with a decision that swelled and ripened slowly and once made could be rescinded by no one. She would sit at the kitchen table with a large sheet of paper that she would divide into two columns. At the top of one she would write FOR and at the top of the other AGAINST. For and against painting the stairwell white, for and against chemotherapy and radiation, for and against committing suicide, for and against veal schnitzel with potatoes boiled in salt water and sprinkled with *schnittlauch*—chopped chives—and drowned in butter, or Sabbath afternoon meat pies with bay leaves. She made her lists, counted on her fingers, and made her decision only after tabulating and weighing. Sometimes I try to guess what you wrote there before you left home— and I am overcome with dread of the FOR and AGAINST of curiosity.

That is what she would say to us, to me and my brother, Benjamin: "I am for going to the sea, but Yordad is against!" That is also the way she would shop or exile books she did not like from our home, the ones in which "the writer enjoyed himself too much or suffered too much while he was writing." And with that very same decisiveness she composed our Family Constitution, over which Benjamin and I can no longer make bets, for it—unlike that blue-bound book—is still in existence and in my possession, and can be opened and viewed.

There are times when I am capable of astonishing speed and resolve, in contrast to my personality and my shape. So it was that day, the day of her death. While the news was just spreading, taking root, showing no signs of change or remorse, and while the doorbell and the telephone rang incessantly and Yordad wandered aimlessly, banging into the walls, and Benjamin, as always, was late or busy, I rushed to take that Family Constitution of ours and I hid it away in one of the equipment compartments of Behemoth. It has been in my possession ever since. Here it is: written on thin, light blue letter paper, with your distinctive Hebrew lettering: the potbellied *pe,* the dandified *beth.* Here, your cranelike *kaph-sophit,* the *samekh* so tiny it looks like a dot.

Here, I say to myself over my small treasure each time I remove it from its hiding place—here, over this light blue, your hand hovered, hovered and wrote: "The children will tidy their rooms, dry the dishes, and take out the rubbish." "The children will tell their mother stories and on Saturday mornings will shine the shoes of all members of the family." "The children will see to watering Mother's parsley plant in the kitchen." "The parents will clothe, feed, teach, caress, and hug the children and will bring no more of them into the world."

And on and on, here. Right over this very paper. Your hand. Hovering, almost landing, warm and alive.

# 3

SHE WAS AN EASYGOING, pleasant mother and her anger seldom flared: only when Yordad called her Mother instead of Raya, her name, or when her sons referred to her as "she" instead of "Mother," or when they disturbed her as she painted the house, or when we answered "Not true!" to something she said.

Once, however, she did something that I understood only years later. It happened on the Day of Atonement, Yom Kippur, five years after we had moved from Tel Aviv to Jerusalem. Benjamin was eleven and I was thirteen. On the eve of the holiday we put on white shirts and sneakers and went to the neighborhood synagogue. Usually Yordad did not permit us to wear sneakers, specifically because he was worried about the development of our feet and generally about all our bones. But for some reason the holiday customs, including the prohibition against wearing leather shoes, touched his heart. He even fasted, despite the fact that he normally did not keep a single one of the Jewish laws.

"In my father's memory," he announced, the expression on his face sanctimoniously festive, a look we never saw on any other day of the year.

My mother, brother, and I did not fast, but according to his wish we refrained from eating anything that would waft aromas through the window, outside. "This is Jerusalem," he said, "not Tel Aviv. We must be considerate of our neighbors."

After breakfast my mother wished to listen to music on our gramophone, but Yordad restated his demand.

"We'll listen quietly," my mother said. "And you needn't remind me all the time that this is Jerusalem and not Tel Aviv; I'm only too aware of that."

"I beg you, Raya," Yordad said, "do not listen to music on Yom Kippur here." He pronounced her name the proper, official way, Ra-a-ya, instead of *Ra*ya, the way everyone—including him—called her on the nonatonement days of the year.

My mother buckled her sandals and put on her wide-brimmed straw hat, the yellow weave blending with her hair, the blue ribbon crowning the angry blush on her face.

"Come," she said, "let's go breathe some air outside, because suddenly we've sprouted a pope. A person could choke on all the righteousness and incense around here."

Astonished and obedient—when referring to us and her, "astonished and obedient" was the way to describe our ongoing situation, apart from a few controlled mutinies staged by Benjamin—we followed her. We took Bialik Street down to the little garden planted by residents of the Beit Hakerem neighborhood to commemorate their sons who had fallen in the War of Independence, and at Halutz Street we turned left. Next to the plot of land used for growing crops adjacent to our school— to our relief, this time she did not jump over the fence to steal parsley from the vegetable beds—we descended to the valley, emerging on the other side, where today there stands an ugly row of hotels. Sometimes I pick up visiting bird-watchers from the doorways of these hotels, and sometimes Liora's brother, Emmanuel. When her extended family comes to visit from America they stay at the King David, but Emmanuel is tightfisted, so that when he comes alone he stays at one of these hotels, near the entrance to the city.

Back then an old pathway ascended from the valley, a remnant from the days of the Arab farmers and the peddlers and the mule drivers who passed from Malkha to Lifta and from Sheikh Bader to Dir Yassin. Benjamin, as usual, skipped and jumped from rock to rock while I plodded along, my eyes glued to my mother's heels, my nose enjoying the scent of hot dust and my ears the crackle of leaves and stems of the end of summer.

Next to the large garage for buses belonging to the Mekasher company there was a small abandoned fruit orchard: a pair of pomegranate trees, a few grapevines and fig trees enclosed by a row of prickly-pear cacti. The pomegranates were not yet ripe, the prickly pears were already rotten, and the young grapes had turned to raisins, but the fig trees were bearing fruit. My mother loved figs. She explained that they should be plucked, not picked, so we plucked and ate until a passerby fainting from righteousness and heat and the fast shouted at us. "Shame on you for eating figs! Today is Yom Kippur!"

My brother, bolstered with the strength and courage of sinners by my mother's presence and the sweetness of the fruit, shouted back at him, "Pious shmious!"

My mother said, "Stop that, Benjamin. There is no need to answer."

The man cursed and went on his way and we entered the large bus garage, where we crossed a dirt path and came to the lot with the old buses waiting to be sold or dismantled. My mother sat on a boulder and, as though distracted, began juggling three stones. I, as usual, went looking for crabs and beetles. Benjamin leapt from boulder to boulder without looking ahead or to the sides or backward, as though he had eyes in the soles of his feet.

Suddenly, after her surprisingly successful tossing and catching of stones, my mother stood up and, without prior warning, flung them quickly, forcefully, one-two-three at one of the buses.

The silence shattered into a thousand resounding shards. Benjamin, close by her, and I, a little farther off, watched her anxiously, astonished. She bent down, picked up two larger stones, then two more, and smashed two more windows.

"What are you doing, Ra-a-*ya?*" my brother said, imitating Yordad.

"Go on—you two give it a try, too," my mother advised us. "It's very pleasant."

"Shame on you, busting up buses," Benjamin said. "Today's Yom Kippur." But I bent down like you, collecting, then pitching two stones.

"It really takes talent," Benjamin mocked, "to miss hitting a bus from seven feet away."

My mother laughed and I, hurt and angry, stooped to pick up a stone as large as a loaf of bread. I moved around to the front of one of the buses and, with both hands raised over my head, hurled the stone against the windshield. The thick glass cracked but did not shatter while I, in the throes of rage and delight, cast about for an even larger stone to throw.

"Wait, Yair," my mother said. "I'll show you how."

Over at the side stood the frames of several rusting seats that had been removed from one of the buses. She grabbed hold of one of them, a bench seat from the back of the bus that was nearly ten feet long. I lifted the other end and we carried it over our heads like an iron battering ram, she in the lead shouting, "This is Jerusalem, not Tel Aviv!" while I, head bent, pushed from behind, and we cracked the windshields of two other buses, and we were suddenly overcome with a wild and excellent lust for revenge and destruction that was thwarted only by Benjamin's cry of "Stop! Stop! The guard is coming!"

We tossed the bus bench aside, crouched behind one of the buses, and glanced at one another, red-faced and smiling. From the far side of the lot the old guard rushed in. He was tall, with dirty hands and a look of permanent sweat on his face. We had seen him more than once at Glick's kiosk ordering a fried-egg "samwich" with hot pepper.

Huffing and puffing, a filthy cap on his head and tattered shoes on his feet, the guard ducked in and out between the buses until he caught sight of us. He was amazed: a blue-eyed, golden-haired mother and her two pleasant sons were not in the mug shots of his assumptions.

"What's going on here? What you are doing?"

"We are sitting here in the shade and resting," my mother said.

"Tired from fasting," Benjamin added.

"I heard breaking here. I heard metal and glass falling down."

"There were some riffraff here before," my mother said. "They were throwing stones. But when we came they ran away. Isn't that right, boys?"

My face was burning. I bowed my head.

"They went that way," Benjamin said, pointing.

The guard went off to have a look around, and when he saw nothing but a silent city—Jerusalem during the days of awe, grumbling and righteous—he returned to us, crestfallen.

"I know who you are. You are the missus of Dr. Mendelsohn, the kiddie doctor here."

"That is right."

"My brother showed me you once. Me and him, we were at the Iraqi market, sitting at the tavern next to the chicken seller, and you walked up with him"—the guard pointed at me—"to do shopping. My brother says to me, 'You see this one, this lady here? She is the missus of Dr. Mendelsohn from Hadassah Hospital. Her husband is a good doctor. He told me to bring my daughter to his clinic at his home and didn't take any money at the end.' Maybe those riffraff wanted to beat you up, Missus Mendelsohn? If only I catch them, I break their bones here."

"No, no, everything is fine; the children are looking out for me, thank you," my mother said. "Everything is fine here. We had a wonderful Yom Kippur here and we wish you, too, to be inscribed in the Book of Life here."

She rose to her feet. "Come boys, let's go home to Yordad."

We followed, Benjamin in the lead, jumping from rock to rock, I trailing after them. On the street you took his hand in one of yours and mine in the other and you said, "It doesn't matter what happens, you will always be mine here."

We all laughed. Three years later you left home. Were you already considering it on that day? Benjamin says of course you were and I say perhaps, but we can no longer make bets over that.

# 4

"Abandoned her sons . . . ," "another man . . . ," "no strength left in her . . ."—these conjectures and denunciations wafted through the corridors of Hadassah Hospital and among acquaintances, at school and at Violette and Ovadia's neighborhood grocery. One only thing was true and clear: if there was another man or if there was not, if he had appeared on the scene before her departure or after, my mother never returned to our home. She remained in her new place, her own, a rented flat on the outskirts of the Kiryat Moshe neighborhood, in an apartment block facing the flour mill and the bakery. It was a tiny apartment, but from her window there opened up an endless view to the edge of the west.

Benjamin and I were adolescents then, I in the tenth grade and he in the eighth. He was already taller than I. I remember that year not only because my mother left but also because it was then that Benjamin adopted the loathsome habit of tilting his head downward to mine when we spoke to each other. We both opted to remain with Yordad at home in Beit Hakerem because at his place we each had a bedroom, whereas at Mother's there was only the single room that was hers. Still, we came to her every day, always at the same hour. We loved sitting in her kitchenette. At home in Beit Hakerem she had had a *küche* — "a real kitchen," Yordad said, amazed, as he contemplated the logic of her departure—while in Kiryat Moshe she had only a *küchlein,* a tiny, crowded kitchenette.

Sometimes we went together and sometimes separately. She was always alone and always received us cheerfully, with embraces and caresses, the scents of soap, fresh and plain, and coffee and brandy and talcum powder upon her. She would shut off her small gramophone — she listened to music extensively, mostly Purcell's opera *Dido and Aeneas* — and move aside the vase with her beloved gladioluses, which now appear from time to time on her grave. Who brought them to her back then? And who now? She would serve us caraway-seed biscuits and tea with lots of lemon and sugar.

More than once I wondered what would happen if I came at some other hour. Would I meet the other man, even though there was no such man? A man trying to entertain her, please her, someone who would tell stories and dry the dishes and shine the shoes and take out the rubbish?

I would imagine him in my heart sitting at the small table, or even on the sofa that opened and became her bed in the evening, his eyes fixed on her, his hands lustful, his lips encircling strong teeth. But I never saw anyone there, other than one time when two men showed up. One was broad, dark-skinned, and bald and leaned on a cane, the other tall and elderly and thin as a shoelace. The one who limped hummed a funny tune about King Ahasuerus of the Purim story and drank black coffee that he prepared himself. The elderly gentleman regarded me, curious and friendly, and asked me about my major in school and whether I knew what I wanted to be in the future. I answered that I did not know and he said, "Very good. No need to rush."

Only a year ago, on the occasion of that surprising meeting when she gave me the money to purchase and build myself a new home, did I dare ask my mother about her leaving us, and for what reason.

"It was not you I left," she said, "it was Yordad and his house. After all, I stayed in his Jerusalem to be near you two."

And when I did not respond, you continued. "Why do you ask? You know the reason; I never hid a thing from you, I explained it all to you when you were still a young man, but perhaps you did not understand or did not wish to understand, or maybe you simply want to hear the story again and again." And she reached over and patted me just like she did then, when I would visit her in her tiny flat. Not with the same strength but with the same motions.

Your fingers were cool and pleasant. When you drew them lightly through my brother's fair curls they were spread wide. "What a beautiful child you are, Benjamin . . ." you told him, and you would reiterate: "What a beautiful child . . ." and your single dimple would bloom on your left cheek. As for the dense black bristles of my scalp, however, you scraped them with the vigor of a cattle breeder, leaning over me from your great height. "You little calf! What choice beef you are!" And I, with a heart both jealous and crushed, exchanged your love for him with those three-dot ellipses above.

After telling her about what was happening at school and at home, and about the nurse Yordad had hired to help him in the clinic—a small, apprehensive woman who was afraid of him and the patients and the ringing of the telephone and her own shadow—my mother would serve us two thick slices of her poppy-seed cake and pack a third in a paper bag. "Give this one to Yordad so that he will be happy, too."

We left her house and returned home, our heads still sensing the touch of her fingers, which had grown stronger and rougher, and suddenly Benjamin said what I had only dared think, that this was a sign of the difficult labor she was obliged to engage in now that "she no longer works in our clinic."

And Yordad, playing a role in the next act of that very same play, opened the paper bag and burrowed his mouth and nose inside it. His eyelids fluttered and shut after a short, tender struggle. I recall the long breath, and his hand, which was miraculously decisive and slack at the same time. He gave us the slice of cake because he was not strong enough to pitch it into the rubbish bin. "Take it. It is enough that she left—I do not need any more happiness than that."

"I can't take it anymore!" Sometimes in her voice, sometimes in my own, sometimes in the wind that blows through the large trees that she insisted be outside my new home. She made her decision, then made it known; she took her clothing and her gramophone and her recording of *Dido and Aeneas*—the opera she loved so well with the beautiful swan song; to myself I called it "Remember Me" because those were the only two words I could grasp—and she departed.

When she made up her mind about the FOR and AGAINST of our household expenses she added sums, counted coins and savings. When she decided about food she listed the diners, the potatoes, the plates and knives. But what did you count then, Mother? What does one count before leaving one's home?

# 5

I DO NOT REMEMBER much from Tel Aviv. We lived on Ben Yehuda Street not far from the Mugrabi cinema, which at the time was still standing. A small brass nameplate that read DR. YAACOV MENDELSOHN, PEDIATRICIAN was affixed to the door of Yordad's ground-floor clinic, and another small brass nameplate—Y. MENDELSOHN, PRIVATE—was affixed to the door of our apartment on the second floor.

Also near our apartment was the cemetery on Trumpeldor Street, and you brought us there to show us the names of poets engraved on the tombstones. Benjamin played among the graves while I cast my eyes upon you and repeated the names. On occasion we traveled to the north end of the street and from there to the Yarkon River, which was not yet built up, and Yordad would find perfect spots for picnics or, in his words, "A pretty place with shade." We went, too, to the zoo, but only the two of us—you and I—and only once. Near the entrance to the zoo there was, at the time, a fenced area with huge tortoises, and I remember the names of the lion and two lionesses: Hero and Tamar and Dolly.

A peacock appeared suddenly, its tail fanned in the dirt, and it shrieked in a frightful voice. I wanted to see the monkeys but you said, "Let's move on, Yair, I can't stand them." We walked up the path. Beyond the pigeon loft and the fenced-in elephant and the pool of the waterfowl there was some playground equipment, a tiny, shabby, amusement park. You stood there looking around, and when we were about to leave, a very fat man appeared and said hello to you. I could not stop looking at his enormous belly. I said, "Mother, Mother, look what a fat man . . ." and he removed the cap he was wearing, bowed, and told me, "I'm not just any fat man, I'm the fat man of the zoo."

The peacock shrieked again. Shouts of joy were coming from the other side of the fence, where people were swimming in a pool adjacent to the zoo. You told me, "This was once the watering hole of an orchard." And when we left there a small parade of men and women carrying red flags passed by. You said, "Today is the First of May. Come, Yair, let's go home."

Many a time I return to visit there, even today, in the rambles I am accustomed to taking. From the house that Liora purchased for us on Spinoza Street I set out for Ben-Gurion Boulevard, where I pass by young couples spending time together at the juice bar, and I am always surprised by how similar they are to one another. They all have handsome dogs and children, each man looks like the next, each woman like the other, each man identical to his woman, each woman to her mate.

I head right, toward the memory of the visit to the zoo. Sometimes I enter through the what-was-once-the-gate and sometimes I stroll along the no-longer-a-fence. Then I take another right and walk the length of the large square, the sycamores and citrus trees of which have long since been chopped down and whose sands are choked under the paving stones. I cross Frishman Street and pass by the French bookstore and reach Masaryk Square and the small and pleasant playground where a few young women are always sitting with their children and I wonder who among all these little ones will grow up and write about his mother; who will refer to her as *she* and who as *you*, who will call her *Mother* and who *my mother.*

From here King George Street leads me in a straight line to Dizengoff Center. I enter and paddle along in a sea of screaming children and short, dumpy women with exposed bellies and clear plastic bra straps, and I make my way up to the third floor, to the Traveler shop, my destination. Whoever situated the shop particularly in this spot did so wisely. A few minutes in that vacuous space suffice to awaken a desire to travel as quickly and as far away as possible from there.

In the shop I purchase hiking equipment I will never put to use, listen to lectures about trips I will never take and places I will never visit. I observe with a gaze of jealous longing the young people making travel plans, and they observe with a gaze of jealous longing the expensive sleeping bag, lightweight and especially warm, that I carry to the cash register, and the alpine camping stove that burns for eight hours straight even in gale-force winds. I scan the notes pinned to the notice board by anxious young ladies with modern names and modern spellings, like Tal and Nufar and Noa and Stav and Ayelet, looking for companions to share a soft landing and perhaps even a trek in the dangerous, distant East.

Overwhelmed with no less dangerous and distant delusions, I leave there, taking Bograshov Street toward the sea, plowing through the sidewalk cafés filled with people, and at Ben Yehuda Street I turn left and proceed southward to the head of the street, past the house in which I spent my first years and which has been razed. A few years ago it was torched by one of the many religious fanatics our land is blessed with because, after we moved out and relocated in Jerusalem, the place changed hands and roles until, eventually, it became a brothel.

Back in those days Ben Yehuda Street was far more pleasant. I recall that there were many German-speaking neighbors, a language that my mother and Yordad understood but did not speak, except on rare occasions. We took our evening meals on a balcony overlooking the street. I remember the kiosk that stood underneath, and the royal poinciana tree that reddened the back garden, and the morning glory that climbed the balcony wall and that opened what she called "one thousand blue eyes" every day.

"That's that," she would say at the end of every meal. "The plant is already closing its eyes, so let us, too, go to sleep."

She loved that house very much. Whenever we returned to it, from far or near, she grew excited, filled with high spirits. "Soon we'll be home!" she would say, and once arrived she would add, "Here we are, we're home!" and sometimes she would even ceremoniously recite the lines of a poem that repeated itself as well: "Home is the sailor, home from the sea / And the hunter home from the hill."

The keyhole of our apartment door was the height of a person's head. You would lift me in your arms and say, "You open it."

I would thrust the key in and turn it. You would press on the handle and open the door and say, "Hello, house . . ." to the cool dimness. "You two, say hello to the house, too," she would instruct us. "And listen closely, because it will answer back."

Benjamin said, "But it's a house. How can a house answer?" And I said, "Hello, house," and I fell silent and listened like you asked me to.

"Be quiet, Benjamin," you said. "And both of you, listen closely."

The house was happy, too, at our return, and it breathed and it answered just as you promised. We crossed the threshold and you said, "Let's have a bite to eat," which meant a few slices of bread topped with soft cheese "spread oh so thin" and a hard-boiled egg — *Plaff!* — and anchovy substitute in a yellow tube and chopped parsley and tomato sliced so thin it was nearly transparent. Because that was what one did at home. One returned home, and said hello, and heard the answer, and entered. And then one had a bite to eat and was overcome with joy: we are home. From the hill, from the sea, from far away. That is what we love and what we know how to do.

# 6

MY MOTHER and Yordad taught us many things even before we went to school. He would sit with us in front of the big German atlas and show us continents and islands and faraway lands, would send us sailing over oceans, crossing rivers, scaling mountain ranges and descending on the other side. She taught us to read and write.

"The little dots and dashes under Hebrew letters tell the letters which way to go. An *aleph* with a single dot underneath is read *ee*, a *mem* that has a dash with a tail is *mah*," she told us, using the letters that spelled *mother.* I giggled with pleasure, because the little dots changed the shape of her lips and the expression on her face, and also with relief, for now the letter knew which way to go and what to do.

I was five years old then, and Benjamin would join the reading lessons. Even though he was only three, he picked it up faster than I. Within weeks he was already reading aloud the names of the poets, his legs skipping from grave to grave and his eyes skipping from the graves to my mother's bright eyes. I remember how he even astonished and enchanted the passengers on the No. 4 bus: a very young boy with golden hair reading the shop signs on Ben Yehuda Street in a precocious voice, in spite of the speed at which they passed by the window of the bus.

And I remember the dinner on the balcony when my mother announced, "Soon we shall have a baby girl. Your little sister."

"How do you know it will be a girl?" I asked with apprehension. "Maybe we'll have another brother."

"It will be a girl because that is what Mother wants," Yordad explained. "She has done her FOR and AGAINST and decided that after wishing for and receiving two sons, now we shall have a daughter."

Then she teased us: "The FOR is she and the AGAINST is you two."

Within several weeks' time she began to retch every morning, and I would retch along with her. Yordad said that pediatrics had never seen or heard of such identification between sons and their mothers and that this new phenomenon should be named for me. When he said this his lips smiled, but his eyes did not. A dull anger skittered across them, as though he were a witness to an intimacy he had never known.

Every day we would sit, he and I, shelling almonds on the balcony. "A pregnant woman must take care to eat properly," he informed us, "and since there is not enough meat or eggs or cheese in the market, these almonds are a good and nutritious substitute. This way Mother will have plenty of milk and the baby girl will be large and healthy and her teeth will be white."

He permitted me to eat every seventh almond. "Whoever does not work does not get any."

"But I'm working," I boasted, expecting a compliment, too.

"I am referring to your brother," Yordad said in a loud, stern voice, to ensure that Benjamin would hear.

Benjamin was playing off to the side and did not react. I gathered up my seventh almonds and chewed them until they were pulp, then swallowed them with deep purpose and conviction. I felt the whiteness of the almonds create a whiteness of milk and teeth inside me and you. I hoped that the sister you would give birth to would be small and thick and dark, but she was born before term and died straightaway, so that it was impossible to determine what her height or coloring would have been.

A few days passed before my mother returned from the hospital. That night we heard Yordad talking while Mother said nothing.

"You see," Benjamin whispered to me in the darkness of our room, "you shelled those almonds for her for nothing."

I grew angry in place of you. "Why do you say 'her'? Say 'shelled those almonds for Mother,' not for 'her'!"

# 7

MORE THAN ONCE you sent me shopping, sometimes across Ben
Yehuda Street at Zolti's greengrocery and sometimes at the local kiosk.
"There is no kiosk like this one anywhere else," you said. "He stocks lol-
lipops, clothespins, sardines, chewing gum, ice cream, and, if you order
in advance, shoes, refrigerators, and bridal gowns."

I remember one day when the owner of the kiosk ascended the
stairs to our flat and said, "Dr. Mendelsohn, your son has been stealing
money from me, and apparently from you, too."

I tugged at your dress and you tilted your ear downward to my
mouth. I whispered my question: how was it that at his kiosk this man
was tall but in our house he was short? You whispered your answer back
at me: in his kiosk he stands on a wooden platform, while in our house
he is standing on the normal floor. Your lips were so close and so pleasant to me that it took several seconds for me to notice Yordad's stern
and piercing glare, and when I did notice it my heart stood still inside
me from shame and fear. Not due to the undeserved punishment for a
theft I did not commit but because the possibility that it was Benjamin
who had stolen did not even cross his mind.

The owner of the kiosk understood what was happening at once.
"It's not the dark one, the one that looks like a thug," he said. "It's the
little one who steals, the one with the Goldilocks curls and the face of
an angel."

He descended the stairs and returned to his kiosk and became tall
once again, and you rested a hand on my shoulder and cast a scowl at
Yordad that spun him around and drove him away, so that he sought
refuge in the clinic.

And I recall the daily trek to the seashore to take exercise and swim.
These days I no longer go to the beach; Liora prefers the swimming
pool and, anyway, the flying paddleballs and the young women's bathing
suits make me nervous. The sun's rays frighten me too, a fear instilled in
me by Yordad that I have never overcome. Way back then Dr. Yaacov
Mendelsohn warned parents against the dangerous effects of the
Middle Eastern sun, but no one listened; suntans were considered to be
a sign of health and the fulfillment of the Zionist dream. That's the reason everyone went to the beach before noon and only the Mendelsohn
family went late in the afternoon, when the heat of the sun had abated,

marching against the families returning home, a joyful caravan of irresponsible parents and seared and happy children with reddened noses and backs.

Many people would greet us, and some added requests and questions. In spite of his youth, Yordad already had a reputation as an excellent pediatrician, and these people wished to take advantage of the opportunity for some on-the-street advice. He would tell them, "I am in a hurry; come walk with me and we shall speak." And he would extend his long legs into a quick stride so that the pestering party soon became befuddled and winded. But one day my mother said to him, "Be nice to them, Yaacov, it's easier that way." And when he complained she explained, "It saves time. Try and you'll see." After trying, he saw, and admitted it. "You were right," he said. "At least thirty percent less time . . ."

She told us that once upon a time, when she was a girl, before there were so many sidewalks in Tel Aviv, there were places where wooden planks were placed atop the sand. She loved the feel of these, the way they rocked and sank beneath one's footstep and weight. I loved the spot between the end of the street and the start of the beach, that elusive space between two times and two places, where the city ends and the shore begins, where the asphalt and concrete end and the sand and sea begin. One leg still on the solid of the sidewalk, the other already in the soft and yielding sand.

We played with a small medicine ball, weighted according to our ages, and this was the sole sport at which I was better than my brother. I stood rooted, straining, while Benjamin was hurled backward time and again, falling in the sand and laughing, enjoying himself in spite of his failure. Yordad scolded him, "Stand firm!" Then, restraining himself—he never raised his voice, and when he was angry he whispered—he said, "Stand firm, Benjamin! How is it that Yairi can do it and you can't?" A wave of pleasantness arose inside me: my mother called me Yair, Meshulam Fried, Tirza's father, calls me Iraleh—"Iraleh and Tiraleh, alike as a pair of doves"—and until this very day Yordad is careful to call me Yairi, *my* Yair, as if reminding the world that I am his.

Benjamin grinned, sighed, and fell on purpose. Yordad grew angry. He yanked Benjamin to his feet and sent us to run on the beach, with "knees high, Yairi, don't drag your feet in the sand." So we ran and sweated and breathed deeply, rhythmically. We swam a little, exercised a little. We ate grapes while the sun dropped and the beach emptied, we gathered our belongings and retraced our steps home. I liked coming home better than going there and preferred the transition from sand to sidewalk too, one foot still feeling its way and sinking, the other already finding its resting place, the answer to its needs.

Yordad marched at the head, erect, I followed behind, and my mother and brother were behind me or ahead of me or next to me playing skipping games on the paving stones, "because if you step upon the crack, you will break your mother's back." A benign sun, soft and low, lengthened our shadows. There's mine, wider and shorter than the others and, like its owner, darker, wrapped inside a long terry-cloth robe. That shadow was sullen and enraged and stepped on the cracks on purpose, and its robe was an old robe of my mother's that she had tailored for me after much pleading. That robe drew a large share of mockery and teasing, but it filled its role—to conceal the strangeness of my body—quite successfully.

So fair and tall and slender were the three of them, their tans so golden and burnished, and I was so dark and thick and coarse. More than once I had feared I was adopted, and Benjamin, who perceived every chink and impaled every foible, made me angry with a little song he wrote. "They sent you in a package, / They found you in the trash / They took you from an orphanage, / To Gypsies we paid cash . . ."

My mother was angry. "That's enough of your nonsense, Benjamin," she said, but her dimple glinted, giving away a smile. Sometimes even she would joke about that very same matter. "What's going to be with you, Yair? One day your real parents will come and take you for their own and we'll miss you terribly."

I would turn to stone; Benjamin would join in her laughter. Yordad reprimanded them. "Do not be offended by them, Yairi, and as for the two of you—please stop this immediately!"

Adopted or not, I shall write here what I felt but never dared to state back then: that I was not turning out well and that my brother was the correction of the mistake.

# 8

ON THE FIRST DAY of summer vacation in 1957, we moved to Jerusalem. Yordad had been promised a position at the new Hadassah Hospital, which was just being built west of the city, and the opportunity to engage in what he had been prevented from doing in Tel Aviv: research and teaching, as well as maintaining a clinic in which he could see private patients.

I was eight years old and Benjamin was six. Two trucks draped with tarps, one small and one medium-sized, were hired to transport our belongings. We stood by the kiosk, eagerly awaiting their arrival. My mother said one large truck would have sufficed, but Yordad decreed that it was "forbidden to mix the clinic with the family."

Dr. Mendelsohn was in the habit of classifying and separating and isolating elements. He instructed us to return the blocks we played with to their box according to their colors and sizes. He sorted his clothing not only by season and type but also by time of day worn, shades of color, and fabric. He did not drink while eating nor eat while drinking, and he moved from food to food on his plate: first the schnitzel and only afterward the potatoes; first the fish and only afterward the rice; first the omelette and only afterward the salad. My mother said that if he had the time he would eat each component of the salad in turn: first he would gather bits of cucumber, then the peppers, and at the end, the tomatoes. But his prohibition against mixing extended far beyond food: he did not mingle one matter with another, or alcohol with secrets, or types of medications. He assigned each its own importance, and each brought that small smile to your face along with that single dimple in your left cheek and the asymmetry of your upper lip, which mocked Yordad openly whenever he was overly strict with us in the matter of table manners. Sometimes he would ask—and I do not know if he was being serious or joking—"What would happen if the queen of England were to invite you for supper?" And you would retort, "Exactly the same as would happen if we were to invite her."

Yordad prepared the salad for all of us himself. He cut the vegetables with great expertise, seasoned them with oil and salt and pepper and lemon; then, when he had taken his share, he announced, "Now you people cut the onion and add it to your own salad."

Years later, when Benjamin brought home Zohar, the woman he would marry, to present her to his parents, she said, "Dr. Mendelsohn, in my house we call the salad you prepare 'children's salad.'"

Yordad sized her up with his eyes. "Interesting," he said. "And what kind of salad does one eat in your house?"

She laughed. Her laughter roused me because it reminded me of Tirzah Fried's. "Salad in our house is made with meat and potatoes," she said. "But if we do use vegetables, then we add soft cheese and warm slices of hard-boiled egg and black olives and chopped cloves of garlic." Her description was so simple and true that I felt the need to taste it right away. Zohar smiled at me, and I was flooded with an affection for her that has not ended to this very day. She is a large woman—full-bodied, full of life—who loves to eat and read: "Abadi's Oriental cookies and fat novels." In the Beit She'an Valley kibbutz she hails from she has three brothers as big as she and some dozen nieces and nephews, "all the same size: extra-, extra-, extra-large."

Like many other affections, this one, too, stems from similarity. Not the similarity between us—we are not similar at all—but the similarity between our spouses, between her husband and my wife, and as Zohar herself said to me many years later, in a moment that mingled alcohol with embarrassment, laughter with loneliness, "Our troubles are very similar. It's just that your trouble is crappier than mine and my trouble is shittier than yours." I felt a covenant had been established between us, that of two interlopers who had been appended to the same eminent family.

I love her twins, too—Yoav and Yariv—in spite of the jealousy I felt when they were born, and I am proud to say that I am the one who coined their nickname, the Y-Team, which stuck at once and has even undergone a number of improvements: Liora turned them into the Double-Ys, while Zohar decreed separate nicknames for each of her boys. Yoav, the firstborn, became Y-1, while Yariv, born several minutes later, was Y-2.

The family lust for eating made its appearance in the twins during their very first days of life. More than once Zohar said she planned to nurse them for years and years because their nursing was so hardy that it brought her to the verge of losing consciousness and she was addicted to these moments when her "boobs emptied and her boys filled up" and everything blurred and her body was light and bent on flying, while her boys grew full and heavy, becoming the sandbags that weighted her to the ground.

Indeed, at two years of age the Y-Team was taller and broader than any children their age, presenting round and solid potbellies at the front of their bodies. Like me and like their father, they learned the skill of reading before they entered the first grade, not from the tombstones of poets but from the cereal boxes their mother placed in front of their constantly emptying bowls.

At every family gathering they asked whether their kibbutz uncles had been invited, then hurried to find them, shouting joyfully, "Save us a place!" and "We want to sit with you," taking pleasure in the hearty backslaps their uncles planted on them from behind. The uncles always showed up in a band of pressed blue trousers, their sturdy potbellies ensconced in white, tentlike shirts, each one with a large spoon gleaming from a pocket. "We brought our own utensils — that way we manage to eat more."

They paid no heed to the waitresses passing through the crowd and serving tiny hors d'oeuvres. "'Those are just trivial distractions,'" Zohar quoted from one of her fat novels. They took plates from the tower of dishes at the head of the table and, while the nuptials were still under way, they stood, silent and patient, by the closed pots and serving dishes, only the tiny movements of the flaps of their nostrils and the particular angle of their cocked heads indicative of their efforts to ascertain what was under each lid.

"Have some salad," Liora suggested to one of Zohar's nephews, astonished by the mountain of goulash he had amassed on his plate.

The boy smiled. "Salad? You mean lettuce and stuff?"

"Why not? Vegetables are good for you."

"What are you talking about, Aunt Liora? Don't you know how the world works? Cows eat vegetables, and we eat cows."

"It would help you move the food into your stomach."

"Do I look like someone who needs help moving food into his stomach?"

"You see," Liora whispered to Benjamin, "it was on account of these relatives of yours that I named the Chevy I gave Yair 'Behemoth,'" to which Benjamin complained, "I don't like for the children to sit with them. Why don't they sit at our table?" But their mother had already smiled her slow, serene smile and said, "Because these are their type. With them they feel at home, they're accepted as they are. They aren't scolded or corrected, and nobody tries to make them into what they are not."

"One day they'll wind up looking like them, too. No girl will be interested in them."

"They already do look like them," Zohar said, reveling in the fact. "A little small yet, but coming along nicely. Don't worry. And as for girls," she added, "let's wait and see, Benjamin. I know quite a few girls — in fact, I'm one of them — who like boys just like these. Large and kindhearted, boys you can lean on and be carried off in their arms, boys you can slug when you need to and call on for help when you need to."

"If that's what you like, why didn't you pick a big brute like that?" Liora inquired.

"I chose a brute like you."

So you see, our family is small but full of affection. My wife is fond of Yordad and my brother, my brother is fond of Liora and himself, and I am fond of his wife and her sons, and I am jealous of him.

# 9

ALL THE FURNISHINGS in the apartment and the clinic were removed, and replaced with echoes. The movers pulled the last knots tight. With concentration and effort, the tip of his tongue moving in rhythm with the screwdriver, Yordad removed the DR. YAACOV MENDELSOHN, PEDIATRICIAN and Y. MENDELSOHN, PRIVATE name-plates from the doors. He put them, along with the screws, into his pocket and said, "Let's go."

My mother's face turned red. She had two kinds of blushes: one that descended from her forehead and signified embarrassment and another that climbed from her chest and indicated anger. This time the blush came from below. She turned and walked briskly up the stairs and into the empty house. We waited until she returned and announced that she wished to ride in the back of the truck, sitting on the clinic's waiting room sofa. Benjamin rushed to say that he, too, wanted to ride in the back, but Yordad said it was dangerous. There would be sudden stops and winding roads and "If I know you two," he said, "you'll be leaning out over the side of the truck."

She did not argue. We drove ahead of the trucks in our small Ford Anglia. "Watch behind us, boys," Yordad joked. "Make sure that the movers don't run off with the stethoscope and the otoscope and the color lamp."

On the way, I suppose in Ramla, we stopped. Yordad bought a drink called *barad* and Arab ice cream, sticky and delicious, for us and the drivers and the movers. My mother did not want to join us. Yordad told a story about Napoleon, who shot a poor muezzin to death for disturbing his sleep right over there, next to that white tower, and farther on, between yellowing knolls and hills that came into view shimmering to the east, he lectured us on Samson from the Bible as we drove past the village of his birth.

We began our ascent into the hills. Yordad told us about the War of Independence, pointing out the remnants of armed vehicles and recounting stories of convoys and battles, some on the way to Jerusalem and some inside the city itself. My mother shut her eyes, and I did as she did, though I opened mine every few seconds to make sure hers were still closed.

We finished our ascent. The air had cooled; the weather was dry and pleasant. The engine had ceased its groaning and Yordad said, "She handled it like a Mercedes-Benz, our little Ford Anglia."

My mother woke up. Young pine trees emitted a refreshing scent. Yordad praised the Jewish National Fund for its reforestation program and prophesied that there would be "many pretty places with shade here too in the hills of Jerusalem." The road dipped and snaked through an Arab village and Yordad said, "This is Abu Ghosh, and over there is Kiryat Anavim, and now," he announced gaily, "we'll ascend Mount Castel."

My mother said nothing. Our little car climbed to the peak of the hill and descended steeply on the other side. Yordad said, "Khuseini" and "the murderers of Colonia" and "Soreq Creek," and then he pointed: "This is the border, so very close, and over there is Nebi Samuel, our very own Samuel the Prophet from the Bible, and why is it that those Moslems couldn't make themselves a new religion with new prophets instead of taking Moses and Jesus and David and Samuel from other people and calling them Moussa and Issa and Daoud and Samuel?"

He talked and he lectured while you remained silent, and after one more ascent we found ourselves at the Gateway of Jerusalem—that's what he called it. There was no gateway, but the city began there suddenly, around a bend in the road that did not herald its existence. "Jerusalem is like a house, boys. It has a doorway and all at once you are inside. Not like Tel Aviv, which starts a little here and a little there and has a thousand ways to enter and leave, wherever you wish."

He fell silent and smiled, expecting a response, but Benjamin showed no interest and I was waiting for some utterance from you that did not come.

"Do you feel how wonderful the air is here? That's Jerusalem air. Breathe it in, children; you too, Raya, breathe it in. Think about the terrible heat and humidity we left behind in Tel Aviv . . ."

Our small Ford Anglia turned right onto a long street, on the bald and rocky left side of which was a bus terminal and garage and on the right side of which stood a housing project. We passed a small stone house surrounded by grapevines. For a moment I had hopes that this would be our new home, but we turned left onto a short street that was narrow and verdant.

"This is our new neighborhood," Yordad said. "Beit Hakerem. Up here on the right is your new school. Here we'll turn left again—this is our new street, Bialik, and our new house, directly in front of us."

We stopped in front of a building that had one entrance and three stories, two small apartments on the ground floor and four more spacious flats on the upper floors. I asked you, "Is that the Bialik from the cemetery in Tel Aviv?" and you answered, "Yes."

We got out of the car and walked up the stairs to the second floor. Yordad opened the door on the left side of the hallway. We stood in the entrance to a large and empty apartment flooded with bright light and good Jerusalem air. I waited for you to say, "Hello, house . . ." so that we could enter, but you did not. Benjamin and Yordad marched into the flat; your hand lingered, hovering on my neck and shoulder. For one precious moment we remained, the two of us, outside; then your hand signaled me to step inside with you.

Yordad said, "Here, each one of you children will have a room of his own. This one is yours, Yairi, and this one is Benjamin's."

We did not argue. We rushed outside because the trucks had arrived, stopping with a great sigh of sound, and the movers were rolling up the tarp flaps. Residents of the neighborhood started to gather, for all our furniture was on display outside. The adults paid careful attention, wishing to ascertain the means and the taste of the new family, while the children watched the movers, who had already unfurled the straps they would use to carry the furniture and were binding them to their shoulders and foreheads. After all, it was not every day that one could watch a man load a refrigerator or sofa onto his back, reddening like a beet and climbing the stairs.

And when the unloading was finished and the trucks had departed and the curious neighbors had scattered, Yordad removed the brass nameplates and the tiny screws from his pocket—the tip of his tongue sticking out here, too, moving with exertion—and affixed them to the new doors: first, the Y. MENDELSOHN, PRIVATE on the door of the apartment and then the DR. YAACOV MENDELSOHN, PEDIATRICIAN on the small ground-floor flat.

"There we go, Raya," he said, taking a small step backward to review his handiwork. "You see? Just like in Tel Aviv. Exactly. The clinic is downstairs and we are on the second floor."

He gave each of the screws a final tightening. "Now," he said, "you children go find some friends. And we, Raya, shall drink our first cup of coffee in our new home. The kettle has not yet been unpacked, but I remembered to bring an immersion heater and two cups, and there are some cookies, and perhaps we will chat a bit. There is even a cypress tree growing here, which you love so well, and here is a surprise!"

A boy rode up on a bicycle, winded and sweating, then sprinted up the stairs clutching a bouquet of gladioluses. "These are for Mrs. Mendelsohn," he said. "Sign here, please." Yordad smiled broadly, tensely, and signed, saying, "To celebrate our new home."

My mother filled the kitchen sink with water and plunged the stems of the gladioluses into it. "Thank you, Yaacov," she said. "They are very beautiful, and this was very nice of you. Later, when we open the boxes, I'll move them to a vase."

Benjamin and I went outside. Waiting for us on the street were a band of children and the Jerusalem summer, which did not cease demanding to be compared to its Tel Aviv brother, and praised. I said to Benjamin, "Let's go back home and help set things up," to which he responded, "You go back. I want to play."

It took very little time for my brother to learn the Jerusalem names and rules of children's games. He continued to steal from the kiosk, which here was known as Dov's kiosk, and when summer vacation was over he started first grade and did not have to join a class that had been formed several years earlier and fight for his status. He was swift and cunning, charming and golden, and with ease he captured a place for himself. I was sent to the third grade and, as expected, came up against a closed and suspicious pack of children. At first they poked fun at me, for a slow, thick, new child with bristly hair and a low forehead is always made fun of, but shortly they began to invite me to their homes as well, because the rumor was spreading among the parents that not only Benjamin but I, too, was the son of Dr. Mendelsohn, the famous pediatrician who had come from Tel Aviv.

# 10

At that time, the Jerusalem neighborhood of Beit Hakerem was bordered by open land. The shallow valley that descends from the entrance to the city—the very one we would ascend several years later to the pogrom my mother inflicted on the buses—continues southward and spills into the Refaim Creek. This was where my mother took what she called "our big trek," the place from which she plundered the bulbs of cyclamen and anemones and brought them to her garden. Another valley, known for the oversized rock called the "elephant boulder" that lay in its course, descended to the Soreq Creek. "Our little trek" was carried out there, on the back of the ridge that ran above this valley, and its sole purpose was to be able to gaze in a straight line all the way home, westward, to the distant Mediterranean. From this ridge, you commanded us to believe, we could see Tel Aviv.

"Come, let's take our little trek," you would say, and we knew that once again we would take in the pale and distant strip of shoreline, the great expanse of blue-gray beyond, the ever-present mists inside which you repeatedly claimed lay Tel Aviv. I could not see Tel Aviv, but I believed you that it was there: Tel Aviv and the sea and the house with the balcony and the morning glory that climbed and turned blue there and the royal poinciana tree growing redder in the garden, a tree that loves heat and provides shade and that has never managed to take up residency in cold Jerusalem.

"A tree with brains," my mother proclaimed at the end of every song of longing or praise that waxed poetic about the royal poinciana and its flowers. "It is a fact that there is not one single royal poinciana tree in all of Jerusalem. And anyone who plants one is condemning it to death, because trees can't run away when they're unhappy. They stay put until the end."

She and my brother, light as gazelles, skipped from boulder to boulder—in Jerusalem, terrible and evil things happen if you step on the ground, not on cracks—while I lagged behind them, my head bent, my eyes scouting the earth. At the place where the incline steepened, we stopped. The view to the far distance opened up before us. "That is where we come from, Tel Aviv," my mother said, just as she had said in that very spot many times before.

"Not true," Benjamin said. "We're from Jerusalem now."

She flushed. "You don't say 'Not true' to your mother!"

When Benjamin failed to answer, even casting a cheeky gaze at her, she grew angry. "Did you understand me, Benjamin?"

Benjamin maintained his silence.

"Did you understand that, Benjamin? I want to hear a 'yes' from you!"

"Yes," Benjamin said.

A large flock of pigeons passed by overhead on their way to the flour mill, which supplied them with residual grains of wheat. My mother tented her hand over her eyes and squinted to follow their progress with a gaze that only years later, when I had begun leading groups of bird-watchers around Israel, I came to learn was the gaze of one accustomed to observing birds as they migrate, fly to distant places, return. Then she pointed once again to the two strips of sea and shore far to the west, the one narrow, of golden sea sand, the other turning blue then gray, wide and melting into the endless heavens.

"Over there," she said. Then suddenly she thrust two fingers into her mouth and whistled loudly. "You two whistle too—let them know we're here."

Benjamin and I were taken by surprise. Such whistles were not part of the repertoire of virtues we credited her as having. But the moment she whistled, it seemed she had always been doing just that. Quickly she taught us to whistle: with two fingers from one hand, with one finger from each hand, and with one single finger. "Louder," she said, "so they'll hear us down there."

On occasion I still make that little trek of ours today, because even in Jerusalem I have my loitering walk, a very different loitering walk from the one I take in Tel Aviv, but just as fixed. I visit Yordad in his home, then my mother—first the home in which she lived, then her grave on the Mount of Repose—and then I try to re-create our two treks. At that lookout point, from where we glanced westward with my mother, new housing has been erected, so in order to take in the two distant strips, one narrow and golden, the other bluish-gray, I must stand between the buildings, on a rise that has become a road, and then descend the slope slightly, stop, whistle, and look out. A cloud of pollution has been added to the haze and the distance, crouching there and obscuring the coastal plane. Now, however, I have an excellent and expensive pair of Swarovski 10 × 40 binoculars, bought for me— naturally—by my wife, Liora, which proves the truth of my mother's statement and Benjamin's error. After seeing them in the hands of bird-watchers from Munich who could not praise their merits enough, I told Liora about them, then found a pair on my bed, wrapped with festive wrapping paper and a bow. At the time I thought how nice it would have been to find Liora herself in my bed, with no wrapping at all (if I may be permitted one additional, humble request), but that is the way things are and a man of my age and position must run his life wisely, and with resignation.

# Chapter Three

## I

I MET Tirzah Fried—Tiraleh, luvey, the contractor who renovated
my new house for me—when I was eleven years old. I remember the
day well. Summer vacation. An afternoon. Suddenly a hush fell on the
street. Boys lifted their heads from games of marbles. Girls skipping
rope froze in mid-twirl. Men fell silent, licking their lips. Women
became Lot's wife, pillars of salt. From around the bend in the road
there appeared the American car, the white convertible with the red
interior that every person in Jerusalem knew: the Ford Thunderbird
belonging to the contractor Meshulam Fried, a large and spacious car
that would stand out in any place and at any time, but especially in the
lightly automobiled Jerusalem of those years.

The car parked next to our building. A short, thick man with black
hair extricated himself from behind the wheel. Two children about my
age, a boy and a girl, both looking very much like him, sat in the back
seat. By chance I was standing at the window of our flat, and when I saw
them I was overcome with trepidation. For a moment I thought my
mother's stories and Benjamin's scorn were true: my real father and my
real brother and my real sister had come to return me to my family.

The man took the boy in his arms and carried him into our clinic. I
was surprised to watch Yordad come out to him, something he had
never done for any other patient.

"This way, please, Mr. Fried," he said. "Come in this way."

The man and the boy disappeared inside the clinic and I stood
watching the girl, who had moved up to the front seat. My astonishment turned to pleasantness, my dread to curiosity. But just then

47

Benjamin and his gang of friends gathered to ogle the car. Benjamin told them, "It came to my house!" as he drew close, encircling the car, examining the dimensions of the round rear lights, the convertible top, the chrome plating that distorted reflections of the children's faces, the red leather bucket seats.

"Do you know what kind of car you're sitting in?" he asked the girl.

"My father's car."

A small smile flickered at the corner of her mouth. For a brief moment she was beautiful; then just as quickly she went back to being my look-alike.

"It's a Ford Thunderbird," Benjamin said, regaining his composure. "V-8 engine, three hundred horsepower. There's only one of these in all of Jerusalem, maybe the whole country!" And because the girl was not impressed he added, importantly: "It's an American car from the United States."

The girl waved at me and smiled. I left the window, came down the stairs, and stood next to the car with the others. Her eyes lit up. "Want to sit next to me?"

I sat in the driver's seat. Benjamin was quick to announce, "I'm his brother!" and scrambled to climb into the back seat, but the girl said, "I didn't invite you!" and so, stunned, he stood riveted in his place.

"I'm Tirzah Fried," she said to me. I said nothing. I had never before heard a child introduce herself that way. "And you are who?" she asked.

"I'm Yair Mendelsohn," I answered in a rush. "I'm the doctor's son."

"You don't look like him," she said. "You don't look like that kid, either, who says he's your brother."

Benjamin and his friends sauntered off, and Tirzah added what I already knew myself: "You look like me and Meshulam and my brother Gershon."

"Who's Meshulam?"

"Meshulam Fried. He's my father, and Gershon's."

"What's wrong with your brother?" I asked.

"He has rheumatism. He swelled up and my parents are afraid something's going to happen to his heart and he'll die."

"Don't worry," I said, full of importance, "my father will save him. He's a very good doctor."

And that is what happened. Tirzah Fried's brother did not have arthritis but was allergic to penicillin. The doctor who made the diagnosis had ordered more and more penicillin for him, and his condition had worsened rapidly. Meshulam Fried, who had built a whole wing of the Hadassah Hospital, had decided to turn to Dr. Mendelsohn, the new pediatrician from Tel Aviv.

Dr. Mendelsohn grasped the mistake at once. "If you continue to give him penicillin," he said, "your son will die."

"Thank you very much," the contractor said. And to his son he whispered, "You say thanks to the doctor, too, Gershon, say thank you that Professor Mendelsohn his very selfness is taking care of you."

Gershon said thank you, and in the weeks following the white Thunderbird convertible continued to visit. Sometimes it was to bring Gershon to Dr. Mendelsohn and sometimes it was to bring Yordad to the Fried home. On occasion it was the contractor himself who would chauffeur Yordad, and at other times one of his foremen. And when Yordad said he could forgo the privilege, preferring to come in our own little Ford Anglia "instead of traversing Jerusalem in the car of the president of the United States," Meshulam said, "It is not to make you feel privileged, Professor Mendelsohn, that Meshulam Fried sends his car. It is to make sure you will come."

Meshulam Fried was capacious of hand and heart, amusing, emotional, and eruptive. All those traits were spread before us then in the stunning fan of a peacock's tail and have remained so to this very day, some forty years later. He was unfamiliar with the music to which Yordad listened, he drank libations from which Yordad abstained, he spoke loudly and with ridiculous mistakes and on occasion even spluttered obscenities. But Dr. Mendelsohn, who in general stayed away from people, found in him a good friend, a male friend, something every man needs, and something that I, for one, have never been prudent enough to find.

From every such visit Yordad returned with a small basket of chilled figs in hand. "They have a whole orchard," he said, telling us of the contractor's garden, and his fruit trees, and of the garden shed he'd built with a tin roof so that he could sit and enjoy listening to the pounding rain.

"And he put another sheet of tin outside the bedroom window," Yordad said, "so that he can hear the sound of the rain at night, too. And by the way, Yairi, the patient's sister asked why you haven't come along for a visit."

Two days later I joined him. Benjamin was beside himself with jealousy. He remained at home, trying to digest the unfathomable: that someone could prefer me to him, and that the convertible top on the Thunderbird exposed me to the gazes of all the neighborhood children.

The Fried family lived in Arnona, at the southeast corner of the city. The distance between our houses, the sudden appearance of an endless desert landscape, the sweet, far-off singing of two muezzins, heard but not seen, their voices entwined and competing with each other, the close and distant chiming of herds and churches—all these gave me the feeling that I was traveling to the other side of the world.

"This is the border," Yordad told me, confirming my feelings. "You see, Yairi, right there on the other side of those cypress trees, that's the kingdom of Jordan! And over there," he added solemnly, "are the hills of Moab. Look how beautiful they are in the light from the setting sun and how close they appear to be. If you reach out your hand perhaps you'll be able to touch them. Right there is where Moses stood on Mount Nebo and looked in this direction, and he also thought it was very close, but from the other side."

The trip made together, the conversation, the warmth of his nickname for me—Yairi—and his hand on my shoulder, the compliance of the setting sun, which illuminated whatever he wished lit up—all these bolstered my stature. I was overwhelmed with love for him, and the anticipation of more such excursions with him.

The Fried home astonished me: large-windowed and built of pink Jerusalem stone, it managed, in spite of its immensity, to project a feeling of humility and simplicity on its surroundings. Fruit trees encircled it, and Tirzah, who was waiting for me by the front gate, invited me to pick pomegranates in the front and prickly pears in the back, and to pluck figs of all kinds—yellow and green and purple and black. Her mother, Goldie Fried, a quiet redheaded woman, served us fresh lemonade with thick slabs of bread slathered in butter, along with a jar of her homemade pickles; then she disappeared. Her pickles were so delicious that on subsequent visits I would already begin to salivate when we neared the train station, a distance of three kilometers from the pickle jar and the Fried home, just as I am salivating now from a distance of nearly forty years.

"Look, look at this guy," Meshulam would say, holding one of these pickles over his plate. "Even Caesar's table didn't know from pickles like my Goldie's."

He was terribly proud of his Goldie and loved everything she did. "A woman of valor! The cherry in the crown! She runs the house and the family and the money in the bank, and I'm in charge of the workers and the trees in the garden."

Meshulam Fried's contracting business was large and complex, but his garden was simple — not the garden of a rich man, like the one I saw years ago in America, my in-laws' garden, all fertilized and coiffed and styled and irrigated, and cared for by two gardeners, but, rather, an unkempt garden whose owners refused to employ a gardener ("That confuses the plants!") and who colored it only with wildflowers and bushes.

Meshulam told me their names in order, for once without making any errors or mutilating any words: autumn crocuses and saffron, anemones and priest's hood, narcissus, wild garlic, rockrose, star thistles, buttercups, Spanish broom and cassia, strawflower, wild snapdragons, poppies, mandrakes. In summer the last shoots of the rose mallow, the hollyhock, the pink bindweed, and, finally, in fall, the squill. Here there was no fishpond with a small copper fountain, as there was in Liora's parents' garden, and anyway there were no goldfish here. Still, among the rocks darted green lizards and large skinks and two tortoises that moved so quickly, as Tirzah used to recount, making me laugh, that they chased after cats.

Tirzah split each fig and gave one half to me while she bit into the other half. She explained that every fig tastes different from the next, even if they grew on the same tree. "Meshulam told me it isn't nice if someone gets a good fig and someone else gets a rotten one, so you have to split every fig between the people eating them."

"And what if there are three people?" Benjamin asked derisively when I recounted what she had told me.

"And what if there are three people?" I asked Tirzah.

"Tell your brother that figs should be eaten only by couples," Tirzah said, and she told me that her mother and father trickled arak on their half figs; then, she whispered, they shut the door and ate them in bed, "and after that they giggle."

"It's really delicious," she said. "Sometimes they let me and Gershon taste figs with arak, but only a little. Meshulam says, 'Arak is arak and kids are kids. So just one such fig with arak, and only on the Sabbath.'"

"Why do you call him Meshulam?"

"Just because. Gershon calls him Father and I call him Meshulam. That's what Meshulam calls himself. Didn't you ever notice that?"

After that she announced, "And my mother calls him Shulam, and me she calls Tiraleh, and Gershon she calls Geraleh, and she told my father to call you Iraleh. She likes giving names. She even made up the word *peepot* for a girl's sex and for a boy's, too."

Tirzah swatted the prickly pears with the branch of a pine tree to get rid of their prickles, then climbed a tree like a small and sturdy bear cub and laughed heartily. Gershon, on the mend, sat pale and weak on the verandah, and waved to us with Yordad's color lamp in his hand. "He's alive, but how he looks," Meshulam had grumbled. "Preventive measurements I should have taken on that doctor."

Like Tirzah and me, Gershon had the short, thick body and the flattened fingernails and the thick, bristly hair, but unlike ours, his scalp sported a double crown, two small whorls of hair. Yordad, who had spotted them immediately, told me that with identical twins the crown always spirals in opposite directions and that there are some twins that are so identical that this is the only way to tell them apart.

Years later, when Benjamin's giant twins were born, I waited for their hair to grow and saw that Yordad had been right. The two are absolutely identical, but the crown of Yariv's hair spirals clockwise while Yoav's spirals counterclockwise.

"That's how my girlfriend knows which of us has come home for the weekend," Yariv said on one of his last leaves from the army. "But Yoav's girlfriend gets mixed up sometimes, and that's really nice."

# 2

"THAT'S THAT, Mr. Fried," Yordad said. "Your son needs to exercise and eat well, but he's healthy. There is no need for me to pay any more house calls."

Meshulam was overcome with emotion and reacted in the manner in which he was accustomed to expressing his emotions: he rushed to the large safe in the cellar and returned with a thick wad of bills in his hand.

"This is for you, Professor Mendelsohn," he said. "This is for making cured Meshulam's son for him. I thank you."

"Mr. Fried, please," Yordad said, refusing the money and restraining himself from laughing. "You've already given me a check and I've given you a receipt. That's quite enough."

Meshulam was offended. "The check was for the work—the cash is something different altogether. It's my thanks, and thanks don't have no receipt. To Meshulam Fried there's no saying no."

"Here, I'm quite capable, Mr. Fried," Yordad said. "You have already paid my fee, so no, I am unable to accept such gifts."

Meshulam lifted his eyes to Yordad's face, held his pale, delicate hand in both his own dark, thick ones, and said, "Professor Mendelsohn, today you saved not one but two people: my boy and that doctor, who nearly killed him. You earned a gift from me, whatever you want."

"If that's the case," Yordad said, "I would like a few more figs from your orchard, and perhaps three or four pomegranates—the dark kind. My wife and I are particularly fond of them."

Meshulam was even more overwhelmed with emotion. He removed a large blue handkerchief from his pocket and said, "I need to cry a little," a remark we shall all hear again. And after he had cried a little he hung the handkerchief to dry on a branch and spread his hands wide. "Not just fruit, for you, Professor Mendelsohn—a whole tree I'm gonna bring you! Tomorrow morning a tractor and a truck are gonna come to your house. Tell me now which fig tree you want. This one? Maybe this one? Maybe that pomegranate? Whatever you need, just ask. If you need to move a wall in your house or put in a new kitchen, if you got something heavy to move from one place to another, if something in your house breaks down. If some neighbor in your building is making trouble and needs to calm down a little, I got a fighter from Bielski's partisan battalion who does scaffolding work for me now. He can put a nail through a plank in one hit—not with a hammer, with his fist! Just say what you need and Meshulam comes and does it."

"Truly, no," Yordad said. "Please Meshulam, there is no need."

The tears returned to Meshulam's eyes. A new blue handkerchief was produced from his pocket. "You even need a story told to your kids before bedtime and you and the missus are too tired—Meshulam will come. Right, Gershon? Right, Tirzah? Tell them what beautiful stories we got."

Once again Yordad said it would not be necessary, but Meshulam was not giving up. "No good for a professor like you to drive around in a little Ford Anglia like that. I'm gonna give you my car—you drive around in that and you can show off to the other docs at Hadassah and to your relations. Anyway, I was gonna change cars in honor of Gershon getting better. I'll give you my Ford for yours."

Yordad chuckled. "I don't have the money to buy gasoline for a car like yours."

"No need for money with my car. You fill the gas with coupons from Meshulam Fried, Inc. And what's this you were saying before about not needing to come to visit us anymore?"

"I meant that Gershon is well."

"So you don't come as a doctor, you come now as a friend. And Iraleh comes, too," he said, pointing at me. "Look how nice Tiraleh and him play together. I'm putting already a little something aside for her dowry."

And indeed, Yordad—who in general did not like paying visits—brought me to the Frieds a number of times, and Meshulam brought Tirzah and Gershon to my house, and in spite of Yordad's protestations, Meshulam would check and examine electrical switches and hinges and faucets in the apartment and the clinic—"This guy's dripping, we'll have to give him a new gasket soon"—just like he still does today, with my mother dead and Gershon too, the child Yordad saved, who grew up and was killed in the army, and Yordad himself is old and weak and lives in the ground-floor apartment that was once the clinic. Meshulam renovated it for him: he turned the waiting room into a living room and kitchen, the treatment room into a bedroom. He managed to expunge the smell that every clinic has, but he left the diplomas and certificates and citations on the walls, and moved the nameplate Y. MENDELSOHN, PRIVATE from the upstairs apartment door.

"It's good like this," Meshulam told him. "Down here you won't have to put up with so many rooms and stairs and memories as upstairs. Everything's small and easy to reach, and you can even go out and sit in the garden."

He found "good, quiet people who will pay on time and won't make trouble" and rented them the large flat on the second floor, and at every opportunity he shows up, prepares tea for the two of them, and they sit and chat. Yordad, whose old age has made him more pleasant to be around—"Not all the time," Benjamin notes, "but at least some of the time, which is very kind of him"—tells Meshulam jokes and lets him win at chess. And when he tires and falls asleep—Yordad dozes off like a child, all at once—Meshulam gets up and scans the apartment once again "to make sure everything in the professor's house is okay, no breakdowns, no troubles."

And later he leans for one short and concentrated moment next to the living room wall, where today there stands a pretty chest of drawers in place of the examination table where so many children, including his own son, were examined. He extracts the large blue handkerchief from the depths of his pocket and uses it to wipe his eyes. Sometimes he removes the handkerchief from his pocket because his eyes are tearing and sometimes his eyes tear because he has removed the handkerchief from his pocket. Either way, Meshulam cries a little and remembers that time when his son was saved from death, and another time when he was not.

# 3

YORDAD'S HANDS were stable and sure when he took care of his little patients, but for everything else, especially home maintenance, they were terribly clumsy. Even the brass nameplates he screwed to the doors of the apartment and the clinic were, according to my mother, crooked, and with every other kind of job, from changing a light bulb to unclogging a drain, he had neither the will nor the time. She did not hesitate to contact Meshulam from time to time to ask for his help, and his workers paid occasional visits to our house. They fixed everything that needed fixing, brought a truckload of earth to the garden, took our Ford Anglia to the garage for repairs.

Only the spring house-painting she kept for herself. Yordad would rush off to the clinic, Benjamin would pack a bag and announce that he was "going to stay with friends," and I remained with her. Together we would go to the store to purchase whitewash and paintbrushes, together we would drag the paint cans up the stairs—"You're so strong, Yair, a real ox-rocks!"—and together we would move the furniture and cover it with newspapers and old sheets. She would climb the ladder and begin painting—swiftly, her arms moving expansively, a kerchief folded over her golden head—and she was so skilled that she could walk the ladder from corner to corner of the room like a clown on stilts.

"Maybe you want to work for me?" Meshulam teased her. Then once, while Yordad was in the clinic and Benjamin was playing outside and I was helping with the painting, he came and sat whispering with her in the kitchen. In spite of my best efforts I was unable to hear a word, but two days later Meshulam said to Yordad, "The big kid and the missus are coming with me for an hour or two to meet Goldie and the kids and to pick a few green almonds from the garden."

We took the same route we always did, from Beit Hakerem to the entrance to the city; then just a little before the Mekasher bus company garage Meshulam turned right onto Rupin Street, which was then just a narrow road that passed between open, rocky hills. He told my mother that soon he would begin building "something big here, for the government and for the Hebrew University," and she patted him on the shoulder and said, "Who would have believed that something would come of you, Meshulam? Good for you."

We made a curving descent into the Valley of the Cross and a curving ascent into the Rehavia neighborhood, but this time we did not continue toward the train station and from there to the Fried home in Arnona. Instead, Meshulam suddenly veered off his usual course, and we entered a neighborhood I had never seen before.

A parade was marching down the street. People were carrying red flags and signs. Meshulam snorted several times; he derided "those good-for-nothing Socialist *machers*," and their habit of organizing work holidays whether they were necessary or not. We drove up hills and down until the pavement ended; then we turned right and climbed a dirt road. The large, soft tires of the Thunderbird made a pleasant sound on the gravel. A mound of dirt suddenly scraped the bottom of the car, and Meshulam said, "Don't worry—this guy isn't just any old car and Meshulam isn't just any old driver."

"We're not worried," my mother said. "You're the best driver in the world."

A large stone building and another, smaller stone building topped by a bell tower stood at the crest of the hill nearby, both encircled by tall pine trees. We got out of the car and walked around and my mother said a lot of people had been killed there during the war, young people who hadn't had time to make a child or build a home or plant a tree.

"Or tell a story," she added. Suddenly a small door in the stone wall opened and a tiny woman, nearly a dwarf, dressed head to toe in black, emerged from the courtyard and poured us water from a bottle dewy with cold.

"Nero . . . nero . . ." she said, and Meshulam, who had been walking wordlessly behind us the whole time, explained to us that *nero* meant "water" in Greek, and to her he said, "*Efharisto*" and bowed. The nun returned his bow and reentered the courtyard, closing the door in the stone wall behind her. I was overcome with worry: what would we do now with the glasses?

"That's all right," my mother said. "We'll put them next to the door before we leave."

"But what if somebody takes them? She'll think we stole them."

"Don't worry, Yair; nobody will take them, so she won't think we stole them."

And when we returned home Meshulam removed a small basket of green almonds from the trunk of his car and handed it to my mother. "Here. So you have something to bring home and show."

# Chapter Four

## I

THAT DAY BEGAN as many others in the Baby's life, with his eyes opening as always before those of the other children. With his skin feeling the coolness and warmth of the air, so pleasant to the senses in the early morning hours as they chase one another, mixing and separating. With his ears listening to the male pigeons squabbling on the roof, their nails scraping the drainpipes, the hands of the woman in charge of the kibbutz children's house toiling in the small kitchen. With his nose smelling that the porridge is already cooking in there, the margarine softening, the jam reddening in little dishes. With his heart constricting with images that visited him in his dreams but whose identities he cannot recall on awakening.

The Baby covered his head: a small darkness. The blanket swallowed the sounds. For a kibbutz child there are few moments like these that are solely his. "On a kibbutz, even time is shared collectively," I was once told by my sister-in-law, Zohar, who grew up in a children's house "exactly the same." And lying in ambush behind those few short private moments is everything that is about to take place and cannot be prevented or postponed: the morning cry of "Good morning, children, everyone wake up!" and the parting of the curtains and the tumult of the awakening and the uproar of washing and dressing. And after the meal, the collective departure to the road to wait for the collective ride to the collective schools of the Jordan Valley kibbutzim.

"He was what we called 'an external,'" I was told years later by an old man from that kibbutz, someone who would have been the Baby's own age if he had not been killed in battle. "We didn't pick on him like other externals because he had an aunt and uncle here. But an external is an external. That's just the way it is."

"Just like you in your family," Zohar said, chuckling. "You're kind of an external, too."

The Baby had a mother and father, but the mother could not bear life in the Land of Israel—not the people, not the heat, not the poverty, and not the demands. She left him in the hands of his father and returned to the country of her birth, where she was greeted by the theater and music she loved and had missed, by the language and climate, and by the death that claimed her early, her punishment several years later.

The father married another woman, who kept him apart from his friends and demanded that his son be sent away. "You have an older brother on a kibbutz," she said. "A little old, but a good man. He can take him in. The kibbutz is a good place and the people are good. It will be good for us and good for him."

And so, surrounded by all that goodness, he was exiled to his new home. He was seven years old, and the backs of his hands—still dimpled like an infant's—and his dark, chubby cheeks earned him the nickname "the Baby." I know nothing of his feelings at that time, and there is a limit to what I can guess or verify, particularly since everyone from the Baby's early life is long dead: he himself in the War of Independence, his aunt and uncle in the same year from the same illness in the same old-age home. His father in his bed, next to his third wife, about whom, apart from the fact of her existence, I know absolutely nothing. His mother in a concentration camp, from hunger and cold, pondering both the child she had left behind and that unbearable sun and the possibility that the entire Second World War had broken out for the sole purpose of paying her back for what she had done to him. And his stepmother in a traffic accident on Gaza Street in Jerusalem: for her punishment, fate brought together rain, a bus, and a motorcycle with a sidecar full of flowers, which ended up scattered on the pavement.

But at that time, all these people were still alive, and the Baby's aunt and uncle took him in and raised him with love. They were elderly, their only son already married and living on another kibbutz. The stepmother was right: they were good people and enjoyed a certain status on the kibbutz. The aunt was the first woman in the country to head an entire branch of production on a kibbutz—a cowshed of milking

cows—and the uncle ran hither and thither on kibbutz movement matters, always returning with a report for the general assembly and "a little
something" for his wife and nephew.

Visits by his father grew shorter and less frequent, and the Baby
began to call his aunt and uncle "Mother" and "Father." Every afternoon, when he came to visit them in the family apartment, they hugged
him and kissed him and told him a story. They asked him what he had
learned that day at school, and they taught him to stick two cookies
together with jam and dip them in tea and to play checkers at the same
time. The uncle knew how to imitate the galloping of horses by rapid
drumming of his fingertips on the tabletop, and the aunt taught him
tongue twisters. When he tried repeating them, the words clogged in
his throat and made him laugh.

After that he would ask to leaf through the Album, a French picture book they kept in the cabinet of their bookshelves. He did not
understand the words—truth be told, neither did they—but there were
beautiful photographs and pictures there of castles and mountains, of
butterflies and reptiles, of flowers and crystals and winged creatures,
and the uncle thought to himself that they should take care, that this
album was just as likely to awaken in the heart of the young reader a welcome passion for learning as it was a dangerous passion for collecting.

Indeed, as he walked about the kibbutz, the Baby's eyes were always
cast downward, not from fear or embarrassment but because they were
on the lookout for a shiny beetle or a glittering stone or the darting
green lightning of a lizard. And sometimes he would notice a coin or a
key that had fallen from someone's pocket. Then he would rush to his
aunt and hand over, quite officially, the new find, and she would pat him
on his neck and say, "What a nice little *kelbeleh* you are." Then she would
give him a note to pin to the notice board in the dining hall: the lost
item could be retrieved from her at the cowshed by providing identifying marks. The Baby had been certain that a *kelbeleh* was a puppy, and it
was only years later, after joining the Palmach, that he discovered it
meant "calf," and he did not know if he should be happy or irritated.
One way or the other, this virtue of his became known around the kibbutz, and more than once he was called upon to find something important that had gone missing, because his eyes were quick at searching
and scanning and finding that which was lost, just as in the future they
would know how to identify each returning pigeon while it was still
high in the sky and far off.

So it was one morning that he was standing with the other children who were waiting for their ride to the collective school when suddenly a strange truck appeared and stopped at the edge of the road. Everyone regarded it with curiosity. Vehicles were not at that time a common sight, each and every car arousing the interest of children, and thus an unknown truck even more so.

A man in work clothes and boots—the kind of thin man whose age could be anywhere from thirty to sixty, the kind of man who seems both very familiar and completely unfamiliar at the same time— alighted from the truck. He shouted, "Thank you very much, driver-comrade!" and "Good morning, children-comrades!" as he began walking with long strides. He was very tall, in his hand a woven wicker basket with a handle and a lid, his nose slightly hooked, his freckles plentiful and densely scattered, his thick red hair parted precisely in the middle of his head.

The visitor made straight for the tent camp of the Palmach, pre-sented himself to the platoon commander, and the two headed pur-posefully for the kibbutz carpentry shop. In the carpentry shop they were met by planks, nails, screens, a carping carpenter, and tools. In those days every kibbutz had a carpentry shop, and every carpentry shop had a carping carpenter, and every such carping carpenter, when asked to carpenter some thing, even if he was told that this thing was important for the nation soon to be born and the war drawing near, would grow even surlier. But this visitor was accustomed to carping car-penters, was familiar with their habits and manners, and even knew the best way to draw out their patience: he showed them "top secret" sketches. He whispered, "You may not reveal this!" He gestured with freckled hands that explained and requested, and, most important, he asked questions that gave his cohort the impression that he was not issuing orders but, rather, asking for advice.

The two began toiling over something that at first appeared to be a giant box or a tiny shed, the walls of which sported openings of various heights and sizes; a person could move about erect in this space, his arms spread. A short time later, internal compartments were added, and shelves on the outside, and screened windows covered with wooden slats, and double doors, the inner one with screens.

For two whole days the sounds of pounding and sawing and argu-ments and instructions in Yiddish, German, and Hebrew could be heard. On the third day the platoon commander sent several young men from the Palmach tent camp around to the carpentry shop. They loaded the small screened-in shed onto a cart, pulled it to the petting farm of the kibbutz children, and set it up there, facing east. The visitor checked to make sure that no nail or splinter was sticking out, and when he was satisfied he said, several times, "That is good," and "That is very good." Then he opened the lid of the wicker basket he had brought with him and removed from it a pigeon. It was a pigeon like any other: bluish-gray, similar to a thousand other pigeons, but broad-winged and short-tailed, a light-colored swelling where the beak met the head. The visitor placed the pigeon in the small shed, and while everyone understood that this was a pigeon loft, they had no idea for what purpose it had been built and why only one pigeon had taken up residence there.

The visitor served his pigeon a dish of water and some seeds, then went to the dining hall but did not eat a full meal there. At first he pecked at his plate, then began dunking an endless series of cookies into an endless series of cups of tea with lemon, an act observed by many eyes and interrupted only when the Baby's aunt approached his table.

"Hello, Doctor," she said, and added, "how are you?" Then she invited him to pay a visit to the cowshed to see a calf leaning toward death.

Thus everyone learned what only the dairy-farmer aunt knew: that this was not just any redhead who builds pigeon lofts and places in them a single pigeon, but a veterinarian. And not just any cattle curer from some nearby town or kibbutz but a real doctor, with a diploma! The visitor examined the calf, collected ingredients from various women—the dairy farmer, the medic, the supplies administrator—as well as from the kitchen of the children's house, and concocted a tepid and putrid remedy, which he siphoned into the calf's mouth from a bucket; after this he went to the room allotted him and, according to the night watchmen, did not extinguish the light in there until dawn.

First thing in the morning, the visitor left his room, hurried to the cowshed, administered more of the remedy he had mixed the day before, and said, "Patience, calf-comrade, soon you will heal and forget." From there he proceeded, limbs flapping, to his pigeon loft, where he removed a small notepad from his shirt pocket, wrote something on a thin slip of paper, tore it out, rolled it up, and placed it inside a capsule he had taken from his trouser pocket. He took hold of the pigeon, attached the capsule to her leg, and let her fly.

There was something pleasant and pleasing in the way his hands dispatched the pigeon, a gesture that contained the granting of freedom and the handing over of power and a wave of good-bye and hope and envy. Everyone present at that moment was stupefied. Their gazes followed the pigeon until she disappeared in the distance. Even the veterinarian was stirred, despite having dispatched thousands of pigeons since he was a boy in the German city of Köln, where he had been born and raised, and where he had dispatched his first pigeon.

For a moment his hands remained outstretched, as if helping the pigeon in her ascent; then he pulled them in and tented them over his eyes. His gaze escorted her as she grew distant, his lips wishing her a safe and swift journey. There is joy and newness in every dispatch, he thought to himself, and when she could no longer be seen he removed a second pad from a different pocket and scribbled something.

The next day a green pickup truck entered the kibbutz laden with metal boxes and wood-frame crates with screens; small, bulging burlap sacks; more woven wicker baskets; troughs; and tin vessels. At the wheel sat a silent young woman, the kind whose knee never stops jiggling when she is seated, and she, too, had brought with her a single bluish-gray pigeon. A certain type of know-it-all began to gabble about female drivers and those who give them licenses, while another type of know-it-all began to argue whether it was the same pigeon the visitor had dispatched the day before.

In the metal boxes there were tools and instruments, the burlap sacks were stuffed with seeds and grain, and from the wooden crates there arose soft noises, an impatient scratching and a dull cooing. It did not take a genius to connect the sounds to the sights and the guesses to the smells, and to understand that inside these crates there were more pigeons. The veterinarian and the silent young woman emptied the truck, put everything in the shade, and went to check that all was in order in the new pigeon loft. Afterward, they gave the carpenter "the trap door," a set of thin metal bars rotating on a common axis that can be set to swing outward only, or inward only, or in both directions, or in neither.

The carpenter affixed the trap door to the opening of the pigeon loft, and the veterinarian brought the troughs and tin vessels inside and secured them. Spying the tip of a nail that was pointed inward and had managed to escape his notice, he said, "You thought we didn't see you!" and pounded it with his hammer. Then the silent young woman smiled a smile that no one had suspected her of harboring and she took out a handsome and colorful sign written in Hebrew lettering and adorned with childish flowers and blossoms and birds. The letters spelled out PIGEON LOFT. She hung the sign over the door of the loft, took two steps back, looked at it, straightened it, then smiled again, while among the onlookers a third type of know-it-all began to wonder whether, after smiling so much to herself, she might not smile at others.

Then she took a hoe and a pickax, moved away from the loft, and dug a large, square pit. She was strong and diligent, she neither stopped work nor straightened up until she had completed the task, and she answered with a shake of her head "all the fighters from the pioneer training program and all the tough guys from the fields and all the big bruisers from the locksmith's workshop"—that is the way the story would be told in the future—who approached her one after another and offered their assistance.

She returned to the pigeon loft, sprinkled seeds, ladled water into the vessels, and brought the screened crates inside. She straightened up and looked to the veterinarian as if waiting for instructions.

"Open them, Miriam, open them," the veterinarian said. "These pigeons are yours."

The young woman opened the crates. Some forty pigeon chicks, most of which were already fully feathered but some of which still sported remnants of down, burst out of them, filling up their new home and falling upon the food and water. She cleaned the empty crates and put them out in the sun to be sterilized; then she took the waste from inside the crates and dumped it in the pit she had dug earlier and covered it with a thin layer of dirt.

# 2

IN THE EVENING the two appeared in the dining hall, and after having dunked cookie after cookie into glass after glass of "lemon with tea"— that is what the kibbutz jokers were already calling it—the redheaded veterinarian stood up and tapped his glass with a fork. A stunned hush ensued: who was it that dared to make such a bourgeois salon sound in the dining hall of a kibbutz?

"Good evening, comrades," he said. "Dr. Laufer here." He presented them next with the silent young woman: "Her name is Miriam, and she is an expert pigeon handler." He asked if there were any strangers among them or if all present were members of the kibbutz or the Palmach, because "we are harboring a secret of sorts."

"Only members here" came the answer from the crowd.

"We shall start with words of gratitude," Dr. Laufer began. "We wish to thank you for agreeing to take in under your roof a pigeon loft for Haganah homing pigeons. The pigeons we have brought here are four weeks old. Soon they will begin their flight training, and at the age of six months they will be yoked to a life of family and work."

People in the crowd began to murmur. Expressions like "yoked to a life of work" were not foreign to their ears, but speaking in the plural, as the doctor did, instigated a quarrel among the veteran kibbutz members: was this the *pluralis majestatis,* the "royal *we,*" primarily the aggrandizement of the speaker, as in the Book of Genesis—"Let us make mankind in our image, after our likeness"—and also the Koran, or was this the *pluralis modestiae,* the amplification of humility?

Dr. Laufer did not wait for this important matter to be clarified; he announced that this pigeon loft was "secret and important" and had been placed in the children's petting farm so as not to arouse suspicion. "Should the English army come to make a search, one must say this is the children's pigeon loft." He explained: "Homing pigeons are very similar to regular pigeons, and only the discerning eye of an expert can tell the difference between them. Still, one must exercise caution. The English are certainly familiar with homing pigeons; they dispatched thousands of them at the front during the Great War. We are telling you all this so that you will know to maintain the secret and the loft and you will not reveal them to anyone."

Now it became clear to the astonished crowd that the *pluralis* used by Dr. Laufer was a new and different kind of "royal *we,*" in fact a *pluralae,* a feminine plural. At once, additional arguments erupted: there were those who said this was nothing more than an erroneous use of Hebrew, just another in the list of errors made by *yekkes,* the German-speaking Jews; there were those who felt they were being presented with a certain sort of humor, the kind of joke of which *yekkes* are particularly fond; and there were those who said that Dr. Laufer spoke thus because he had grown accustomed to living among pigeons and the Hebrew language refers even to male pigeons in the feminine.

"It is impossible to overstate the importance of homing pigeons," Dr. Laufer announced. "From the days of the pharaohs and the first

Olympic games in Athens, pigeons carried out their missions and delivered news on their wings. Many a time has a single pigeon saved an
entire battalion of soldiers or a lost convoy, and on occasion has even
sacrificed her own life for man. The Phoenicians brought the pigeon
with them in their ships. The sultan Nur-ad-Din connected the entire
Muslim empire through a network of pigeon lofts. Homing pigeons
brought the news of Napoleon's defeat at Waterloo to Nathan Rothschild three days before it reached the European capitals and their
rulers, and there are those who claim," said the veterinarian, suddenly
whispering, "that he owes the beginnings of his fortune to them.

"And just last year," he said, raising his voice again, "a homing pigeon
brought along by fishermen saved three boats caught in a storm off the
coast of New England, in the United States of America."

Dr. Laufer recited a line from Ovid, declaimed a florid poem about
pigeons written by a medieval Spanish Jewish poet, and added that the
pigeon is the incarnation of the Holy Spirit in the New Testament,
quoting fluently and precisely two of the four versions: "And straight-
way coming up out of the water, he saw the heavens opened, and the
Spirit like a dove descending upon him," as well as "I saw the Spirit
descending from heaven like a dove, and it abode upon him."

"Of course we do not need to remind you of pigeons in our own
Bible," he said. "From the Song of Songs we have 'my dove who art in
the clefts of rocks' and *yonati tamati,* my undefiled dove of innocence.
And then there is the dove dispatched by Noah from the ark that kept
returning until it found rest for the sole of its foot." Charmingly, invol-
untarily, he waved his long arms as if dispatching a pigeon, raising a vol-
untary smile on the faces of the attentive crowd.

"Indeed," he asked with emphasis, "who but the Jewish people
returning to their homeland can better appreciate the tremendous
yearning of the pigeon for her home and homeland . . ." He lowered his
voice as he neared his conclusion. "For that reason we must plead with
you once again to keep this matter a secret. Do not unwittingly reveal
the existence of this pigeon loft to anyone, and certainly not wittingly,
either."

He had one additional request: that comrades not loiter in the vicinity of the loft, nor open it, nor thrust a hand inside, nor make unneces-
sary noise, nor frighten the pigeons. "A homing pigeon must love her
home; otherwise she will not wish to return to it," he said. Then he
thanked the comrades once again before taking his seat and dunking

more cookies into more glasses of tea. And when he had eaten and drunk to satiation and had amassed in front of him an impressive pile of squeezed half lemons, he took his leave of the carpenter and the district commander and the Palmach platoon commander and the calf that was now recuperated and the Baby's aunt, the dairy farmer, and he went to the room that had been allotted to him and at long last sank into sleep.

Early the next morning he awoke, started the engine of the green pickup truck, and drove off to where he had come from. And all at once everything settled back to the way it had been. The aunt returned to the cowshed and the calf that skipped gaily toward her. The platoon commander returned to his command and his training exercises. The carping carpenter—who only now comprehended how pleasant the veterinarian's company had been—returned to the tediousness of cabinets and beds. And Miriam the silent pigeon handler returned to the new pigeon loft, which was her responsibility. She cleaned up, refilled water, put the wooden crates in the storeroom, reviewed each pigeon's individual file card and the list of band numbers recorded in the flock's log. As the sun set she seated herself on an empty crate and took pleasure in the jiggling of her knee and an evening cigarette.

# 3

THE SPEECH Dr. Laufer made in the dining hall bore fruit. No one mentioned the pigeons, but they certainly did mention the pigeon handler, Miriam. They discussed the cigarette she smoked, wondered about her jiggling knee, pondered, too, the other knee and the distance between the two, the jiggling one and the quiet one, and they came to the conclusion that these were not agitated knees or lazy knees or knees that went out dancing, but rather knees of self-confidence and strength and stability. The cigarette, too, they came to realize, was not something on which to pin their hopes, for Miriam smoked only after completing her daily chores. That is to say, it was a cigarette of unwinding from hard work and not a cigarette of recklessness.

For the first three days, Miriam kept her pigeons enclosed inside the new loft. She fed them at the appointed hours, quarantined two sick pigeons, and broke the neck of a third pigeon, whose throat had become inflamed with an infectious malady, after which she burned its body and buried its ashes in the pit.

She wrote lists in the loft log, shooed away cats that displayed more than the usual feline curiosity, caught with her pickax a tenacious black snake that had tried repeatedly to slip into the loft through gaping loops in the window screens. And, like all the other members of the Palmach training program, she worked at all kinds of jobs demanded of her by the kibbutz. At dusk she would sit down, smoke her lone daily cigarette, and jiggle her knee.

The children, who were not interested in Miriam's knees but in the new pigeons and the new loft that stood in the yard of their very own house, were told that it was forbidden for them to enter the loft or feed its residents and that they might regard the pigeons but only from afar. This was enough to double their curiosity and triple their questions because the new pigeons were plain and simple-looking, but there were too many strangers flocking around them and it was clear to the children that the pigeons were steeped in mystery and secrets. In their petting farm there were already two pairs of pigeons: white ornamental pigeons, their heads pulled tautly backward and their tail feathers spread like those of a peacock. No one knew which were the males and which the females because their primping and preening habits were quite similar one to the other's, and so self-absorbed were they that they failed to bring descendants to the world; thus it was impossible to discern which was being wooed and which was doing the wooing, which was not laying the eggs and which was not doing the mating.

Miriam went to the village of Menahamia and brought back a few more ornamental pigeons, whose job it was to blur the presence of the new homing pigeons. They were housed in an adjacent loft that appeared to be connected to the new loft but in fact was separated by an internal screen. There were dandified French pigeons that looked and acted like small chickens, with feathered necks and enlarged craws and an arrogant gait, and other pigeons that the children dubbed "slipper pigeons" because soft feathers covered their toes and slid across the floor.

The guys from the Palmach, too, tried to add a few pigeons to the new loft—large, meaty birds that one of the boys had brought back from his parents' home in Magdiel—and they claimed it was not for their succulent taste that they had been enlisted but in order to serve as camouflage for the homing pigeons. But then Miriam proved that she was not silent at all, that she was capable of speaking if necessary and even shouting: she did not want these pigeons anywhere near her loft! She knew what the boys were up to, and she was not willing for someone to go poking about, sticking his hands into the loft and pulling out some hapless pigeon for slaughter.

"It's likely to frighten them. Let them fly away and find a home somewhere else!" she said, then repeated Dr. Laufer's motto: "A pigeon has to love her home; otherwise she won't want to return to it." And the Baby, who was standing next to the loft just then and hoping that she would take him in and let him help with the work, recalled that day as the one on which she had smoked two cigarettes, one after the other, and even her quiet knee jiggled.

Even the woman in charge of the children's house had an important issue she insisted be raised: she was not willing—so she announced— "for a sign to hang in the petting farm, so near the children's house, with a mistake in the Hebrew!" When asked what all the commotion was about, she said that when vowels were added to the Hebrew letters signifying "loft"—*shin* and *vav* and *kaph*—they would make the word *shovakh* and never *shovekh*, as Dr. Laufer's sign had it spelled. Miriam responded by telling her that anyone who knew Dr. Laufer knew that this was not the only mistake pigeon handlers made in Hebrew.

For example, she explained, the trap door at the entrance to the loft is called a *loked,* and not a *lokhed,* as would be grammatically correct. Even she, Miriam, called it a *loked,* although she knew this to be a mistake, and she would not take down the sign with the word *shovekh* instead of *shovakh* because not only must the homing pigeon love her home, the pigeon handler must as well.

Lo and behold, not long ago I found such a *shovekh,* not in the petting farm of some out-of-the-way kibbutz but in a poem written by Natan Alterman his very selfness (I've adopted an error or two of Meshulam Fried's):

> *Fields that have paled and trees trailing veils*
> *Left open to your white light.*
> *Cherry trees for you illumined while up over the* shovekh
> *Doves make dizzy the Night.*

I was really excited. Miriam the pigeon handler had been right. After all, no one can claim that Alterman—Alterman!—wrote in erroneous Hebrew. Still, the poet made a mistake of a different nature: pigeons do not fly at night. I wanted to tell this to my mother, and to ask if she knew which came first, the *shovekh* in the poem or the *shovekh* on a kibbutz in the Jordan Valley. But my mother had already died, and Benjamin, whom I phoned to ask, told me that the time had come for me to stop this nonsense of mine, that my reliance on the riches of my wife and the memory of my dead mother were turning me into a bum and an idiot.

"*Shovakh, shovekh,* it's all the same. Poets will do anything to make their rhymes and meters fit!" he said before hanging up, adding that if I have trouble falling asleep at two in the morning that is no reason to wake up him too. That's what God made woman for. Wake her up.

# 4

ON THE FOURTH DAY, after all the new pigeons had become familiar with the look of the loft and its scents and sounds and setup, Miriam took them out for a flight, the first in a series of morning and late afternoon flights designed to make clear to them that, unlike their wild counterparts—the rock pigeons—who leave home to search for food, homing pigeons return home for that very purpose.

From that time on, the regularity of training exercises continued. Every morning Miriam awakened early, made a thorough search of the loft and its surroundings, and then, several minutes after sunrise, she opened wide the windows and shooed the pigeons outside by waving a white flag and clapping her hands. For a moment they would perch on the landing boards and then, happy to spread their wings, they lifted off and circled their new home overhead.

Several minutes later, when they were ready to return, Miriam waved the white flag at them again; after a quarter hour she exchanged it for a blue flag, reversed the latch on the trap door so that it could only be entered, and whistled loudly. To the children she said, "Go away, they want to come home." And when the pigeons came close she sang to them, "Come, come, come to eat," and she rattled the seeds noisily inside the tin vessels.

The pigeons landed, at first hesitantly and later willfully, and Miriam recorded which pigeons had landed first and which last, which had managed to pass easily through the bars of the trap door and which had not. Miriam moved those that tarried or even refused to enter again and again to a different section of the loft, where they would not set a bad example for the others.

During the first two days, the returning pigeons found seeds scattered on the ground, but after that Miriam was careful to serve them only from the troughs. Pigeon food is very dry, and pigeons finish off every meal with water. When the first pigeon finished eating and began to drink, Miriam cleaned up all the leftover grains, leaving nothing for the laggards or the tardy, and certainly nothing for those who remained on the roof of the loft. After the meal she went to do her kibbutz chores as required of her as a member of the Palmach, and the pigeons remained incarcerated. In the late afternoon she returned, opened the windows, and waved the white flag to announce the second flight. Upon return the pigeons received their main meal of the day. Miriam then finished her work and sat down to smoke her evening cigarette and jiggle her knee, and then she went to sleep in the Palmach tent camp.

Very quickly the pigeons learned the white of takeoff and the blue of landing and the shrillness of fingers whistling and the various locked and unlocked positions of the trap door and the magical promise of the rattling of seeds in a tin vessel. Within a few days Miriam had lengthened the flights to half an hour in the morning and an hour in the late afternoon, and during the time the pigeons spent airborne she cleaned the loft, changed the water, and threw out the waste.

The children drew near, stared, asked questions. But Miriam kept silent and signaled to them to keep away. She exchanged flags, and the hungry flock descended as one. The pigeons all entered the loft, and the pigeon handler was satisfied. She checked them one by one, made records in a number of pads and on various cards, and she gave thought to making successful matches among them. And so it was, day after day: the feeding, the watering, the flight, the whistle, the cleaning, the waving of flags, and she did not answer the children's questions, nor even bestow a glance in their direction.

Quickly, the children grew accustomed to these sights and they stopped drawing near and peeping—all except one, the short, chubby boy they all called the Baby. That was his nickname back then, and when he was an adolescent, and when he joined the Palmach; and thus spread the cry down the footpaths of the kibbutz nine years later: "The Baby has been killed," "The Baby fell in battle," and all the others, which contained not only grief and pain but also the shock created when those two such opposing words are joined: "baby" and "dead."

# 5

THE PIGEON LOFT drew him in. The contrast between the humble appearance of the homing pigeons and their lofty title jolted him. Miriam's work awakened thoughts in him. The hour of his rising grew earlier as if by itself, and, unlike his custom until then, he no longer remained in bed, savoring those moments of the day that were entirely his own. Instead he rose, dressed quickly, grabbed two slices of bread from the bread box in the kitchen of the children's house, and ran to watch as the pigeons were released for their morning flight. Miriam gestured to him to keep his distance and he moved back, behind a nearby palm tree. Without meaning to, he imitated her movements: he waved imaginary flags, tented his hand over his eyes, adopted the habit of raising his gaze skyward, at times following the birds until they disappeared from view and at times awaiting their reappearance, the gaze of all pigeon handlers in every place and at every time.

Miriam smiled to herself, though she turned only an angry expression in the Baby's direction. Her eyelids narrowed. "Go away!" Her brow darkened. "You're frightening the pigeons!" The Baby withdrew even farther and watched from afar, but after several days he began to draw closer again, until one day he dared offer to help her. He was prepared, he said, to do any kind of work. He was small, he admitted, but industrious and strong—"Look at these muscles, touch right here, don't be afraid, push hard," he said as he thrust out his bent arm and his face reddened—and he would not drive her crazy or disturb her in any way, he would come straight from school and would accept and carry out every instruction, no questions asked.

Miriam said, "I don't need help!" but on that very day there appeared a crack in a joint of the water pipe serving the pigeon loft, and Miriam needed someone to open and close the main valve until she managed to fix and tighten one side. The Baby carried out the task nicely, and she was pleased with his work and allowed him to clean the troughs. She watched him, fairly captivated, much as Dr. Laufer had watched her when she was his age and her mother had brought her to the zoo in Tel Aviv and she had paid no heed to the leopard or the lion or the monkeys, standing and looking only at the pigeons, never leaving the loft, until the exceedingly tall, redheaded man invited her to enter. Now she stood watching the Baby, who was industrious, thorough, and, most important, moved inside the loft with a natural tranquillity and soft, fluid movements that did not cause the pigeons to be frightened of his presence.

She instructed him to sweep the floor of the loft and sent him to bury the waste in the pit, and, several days later, when she had stubbed out her evening cigarette, she asked him suddenly how old he was.

"Eleven," he told her.

"That's a good age. Do you want to keep on pestering the pigeons and me or do you want to learn to be a real pigeon handler?"

"What's a pigeon handler?" the Baby asked.

"A pigeon handler is the person who looks after homing pigeons," she said. "I'm one, for example." Then suddenly she added, "This is my favorite hour of the day. Now the sun's setting in Tel Aviv, too, and the zoo is full of shrieks and roars and growls, and Dr. Laufer is giving his pigeons their evening meal and saying good night to them."

"So these really are homing pigeons?" the Baby asked. "Like he said?"

"Yes."

"So where do they take their messages? Wherever they're told?"

She smiled. "Homing pigeons know how to do only one thing: return home. If you want someone to send you a letter with a pigeon, you have to give him pigeons that were raised in your loft."

"Yes," the Baby said, "I want to learn to be a real pigeon handler."

"So we'll see what we can do," Miriam said as she stood, a sign that she was leaving now and so should he, because it was forbidden for him to be near the loft when she was not around. The pigeons might grow frightened, and we have already stated that pigeons must love their home; otherwise they will not return to it.

# 6

AND NOW, a coincidence that no one understood then but the effect and importance of which will be known hence: on the day that Dr. Laufer left Miriam and her birds in the loft he built on the kibbutz, a wounded pigeon landed on a certain balcony on Ben Yehuda Street in Tel Aviv. Landed or dropped, then convulsed a bit, dripped a few spots of blood on the tiled floor, and collapsed.

On the balcony just then were a boy and a girl. She, an only child of about twelve, lay reading on her stomach, while he, fifteen and a half,

the son of the third-floor neighbors, had come downstairs a few minutes earlier to retrieve a shirt that had fallen from their clothesline onto
this very balcony.

The two knelt quickly near the wounded bird and looked it over. It
was an absolutely normal-looking pigeon, bluish-gray with red feet,
similar to a thousand other pigeons. But its eyes were clouded with pain
and its right wing crooked and dangling. Its thin broken bone could be
seen whitely through the shredded flesh.

The Boy raced upstairs to his apartment to fetch a box upon which
was written VERBANDSKASTEN in beautiful white lettering. Back on
the balcony he removed from the box bandages and sterilizing solution,
cleaned the pigeon's wound with iodine, and used raffia and a twig to
bind the broken right wing. The Girl, wishing to get a better view,
leaned her fair and curly head on him so that a light, pleasant thrum-
ming shook his body in a way he had never dared feel even in the dreams
he dreamt of her.

The Girl, who did not know what she was awakening in his heart,
pointed to the pigeon's tail. "Look," she said. A thin string held two
quills tightly together. "This feather's hers and this one isn't."

And indeed, one of the quills was featherless and not embedded in
the skin and, judging by its thickness, belonged to a chicken or even a
goose. The Boy slit the string with a small pair of scissors, released the
quill, and lifted it up to the light. There was something inside it: a small,
rolled-up slip of paper. He used a matchstick to push it out, then spread
it out and said, "Read it. There's a message here."

There were only three words written on the slip of paper: YES OR
NO? they demanded, or asked. As short as any words can be.

"What does that mean, 'Yes or no?'" he wondered. "'Yes or no' what?"

The Girl's heart pounded. "It's a yes or no of love. Someone wants to
know if someone else gives her consent."

"Why love?" the Boy asked. "It could also be a letter between relatives or businesspeople or some Haganah matter."

But the Girl persisted. "It's a love letter. Now the pigeon is here and
the boy doesn't understand why the girl isn't answering."

From this the reader can grasp that neither earthquakes nor world
wars are necessary to change the course of a person's life and create an
uproar. Sometimes it takes nothing more than a child's slingshot or a
cat's claws or an opportunity that falls in the path of a hawk. Whatever
the reason, because the pigeon needed urgent care and the Boy needed

an opportunity, he took an old wooden crate, lined it with netting, and placed the bird inside. "I know what we'll do!" he said. "There must be a veterinarian in the zoo. If you want we can go there together, and I'll help you carry the crate."

First they walked northward on Ben Yehuda Street; then they turned east and walked down the boulevard until they reached the sandstone hillock familiar to all the people of Tel Aviv. Many of them swam in the pool that had once provided the water for an orchard.

"Tickets!" said a man who stood at the entrance to the zoo. He was very fat and wore khaki, a cap with a visor on his head.

"But we have a wounded pigeon here."

"This isn't a hospital for animals. If you want to enter, you got to pay."

The two skulked off. "What a mean man," said the Girl.

"Don't you know him?" the Boy asked. "He's the fat man of the zoo—that's what everyone calls him. He's not mean, that's just his job. But if you bring him stale bread for the animals, he lets you in."

"So go get some, fast! People always leave bread on fences; you're never supposed to throw it away."

The Boy raced off, and just then a green pickup truck appeared in the street. A long-limbed, thin, extremely tall, redheaded man of undistinguishable age and a narrow, crooked nose alighted from it and turned toward the gate of the zoo. The fat man said, "Hello, Doctor," and the Girl did not hesitate. She approached him and said, "Are you perhaps an animal doctor? I have a wounded pigeon here."

The man glanced at the pigeon. "Come in," he told her. "We'll see what we can do."

The fat man stepped aside from the gate. Dr. Laufer rushed in, his arms and legs flapping, his body bent forward, his freckles skittering along in the air. The Girl followed him on a path her feet would tread thousands of times in the coming years, passing first the turtle pens, then the cages of a few smaller animals whose names she did not yet know—types of ferrets and weasels and martens—and then the lion and lioness and their bitter-souled neighbor, the lone leopard. From there the path curved and the terrain opened up a bit, and in the middle of a clearing stood the pigeon loft, not a round structure on a pedestal as she had imagined, but a shed. A real shed, with a door and screened windows and a roof and walls, and it faced south, a pool for waterfowl and monkey cages next to it, and beyond, the elephant's yard.

Dr. Laufer took the pigeon from the crate, removed the splint, and asked, "Who dressed this?"

"My neighbor," said the Girl.

"He did a nice job," Dr. Laufer said. He removed the bandages, sterilized the pigeon's wound with a brown ointment, reset the bone, and redressed the wound. After that he added, no guile intended, "You surely know that this is a homing pigeon, don't you, young lady?"

"No," said the Girl, feeling her face redden.

"From now on you shall. With a regular pigeon the beak protrudes from the head like the handle on a skillet, but the homing pigeon's beak runs straight from the line of the forehead, and she has a light-colored swelling. Right here, you see? And her build is stronger, her shoulders broader, and inside she has the lungs and heart of an athlete. And if you see her fly, she flies alone, in a straight line, higher than regular pigeons."

"I didn't see her fly. All of a sudden she fell onto my balcony."

"Perhaps she had a band around her leg?" the veterinarian asked. "With a number? That way we can know who she belongs to."

"No," said the Girl.

"Perhaps she had something else attached to her leg? With a letter?" Dr. Laufer removed a small, metal tube with a strap and a tiny push button from his pocket. "This is called a 'message capsule,'" he told her.

"No, not that," said the Girl. Just then the Boy returned, bright red and huffing, with the bread he had found. He opened his mouth but fell silent when she glared at him.

"Or perhaps something like this?" asked Dr. Laufer as he removed from another pocket the severed quill of a goose feather.

The Girl blushed but said nothing.

"You have taken good care of her; she's a good pigeon. She is young and she will heal quickly. If you like we can continue her treatment here."

"I'll take care of her at home," she said.

"I'll help you," the Boy was quick to offer.

"And who might the gentleman be?" the veterinarian asked.

"I'm her neighbor."

"You were the one who dressed the pigeon's wound?" he asked the Boy. "The knot was sloppy indeed, but you have good hands. Maybe one day you will be a professional yourself." He turned back to the Girl. "When this pigeon has been restored to good health, you will have to let her go. This is a homing pigeon. She must return to her home. That is the only thing she knows to do and the only thing she wants to do. 'Odysseus of the Feathered Creatures' — that is what we call her."

"That's the way it is with homing pigeons," said the Boy importantly. "I read about it in the children's newspaper. They fly upward, make a circle in the air, and then they head straight for home."

"But I want her," said the Girl. "She came wounded to me. I'll nurse her and raise her, and my home will be her home."

The doctor's freckles drew closer to one another. "This pigeon will never be yours. Homing pigeons do not belong to human beings; they belong to a place. When she returns home the owner is of course very glad, but it is not to him that she returns but to her home. That is why they are called *home*-ing pigeons in English."

"Maybe," said the Girl, "it's from the Hebrew word *homiyah*."

"'Longing,'" the veterinarian said, regarding her with a look of surprise. "Very clever. I should have thought of it myself, from that Bialik poem: 'Light-colored pigeon of longing, my dove / Wings of the ship she does guide from above.'"

"I'll take care of her," the Girl insisted. "Please just tell me what to give her to eat."

"An injured pigeon receives the same food that a healthy one gets. Most important, you must change her water twice a day. Pigeons like to bathe and drink, and that is quite pleasant to watch. They drink like horses, dipping their beaks in the water and sucking it up, unlike other birds," he said, and he imitated a drinking bird, his head bent backward and his lips protruding and smacking.

The Girl broke out in astonished laughter. Dr. Laufer gave her a bag of mixed seeds that would last, he said, a week, and to this he added a handful of dirt and bits of gravel and basalt, and slivers of eggshell; then he reminded her just how important it was to change the water twice daily and told her to return for more feed in another few days, and that if the fat man at the entrance to the zoo refused to let her enter she should tell him she was Dr. Laufer's guest.

"And if you need to, just shout!" he said. "Call us from the other side of the fence in a loud voice. It's a small zoo. If we ladies are inside, we always hear."

"Why does he talk like that?" the Boy wondered aloud as they left the zoo.

The Girl said, "I actually like it."

In spite of her injury, the pigeon ate with an appetite and drank from the water. Over the course of a few days she grew stronger, spreading and gathering her wings as far as she was able. A week later the Girl returned to the zoo. Dr. Laufer examined the wing of the pigeon and said, "We are making very good progress. This is a pigeon that has already performed some physiotherapy on herself. Leave her here, we'll remove the splint and she will begin to spread her wing and grow strong soon, and it will not be long before she is able to fly."

"But she's already getting used to my house—she can try to fly there!"

"In this crate she cannot exercise. If you set her free she will fly thirty feet and drop. Just like story of Sarah Aharonson's spy pigeon that fell right into the courtyard of the local Turkish officer," he said and he guffawed in the way *yekkes* do, a laugh the Girl would hear so many times henceforth.

"Leave her here in our large pigeon loft and come take care of her every day."

# 7

AND THAT IS PRECISELY what happened. The pigeon remained in the pigeon loft at the zoo and each day, after school, the Girl came to visit her; and although the fat man of the zoo allowed her to enter, she was always careful to please him by bringing stale bread for the animals. The pigeon grew healthier and she tracked her progress as the bird practiced spreading and stretching her wing, and hopping a little higher each time.

A few days later Dr. Laufer called her to "see something interesting" in the laying compartments: a chick had hatched. Then he showed her how its parents fed it with "pigeon milk," which they vomited from their throats. He taught her to rattle the seeds in their tin vessel and sing, "Come, come, come to eat," and the next day he pointed out a pigeon seductress as she enticed another pigeon's mate.

A few days after that he said, "Your pigeon is now healthy. She can fly."

The Girl breathed deeply and said, "I've thought about it, and I consent."

"We hereby thank you in her name," said Dr. Laufer.

The Girl reddened again and said, "But there is one more small thing," and she proceeded to tell him about the quill that had been attached to the pigeon's tail, and the letter inside it.

"So there was, in fact, a pigeongram," he scolded. "Why didn't you tell me when you brought her?"

The Girl said nothing.

"You know what a pigeongram is, don't you?"

"I don't, but I understand."

"And what was written there? Surely you read it."

"It was a love letter."

"Really? That is quite a bit more interesting than the boring pigeongrams we send for the Haganah. But how much love can you write on such a tiny slip of paper?"

"Three words: 'Yes or no?'"

"Yes," Dr. Laufer said. "Absolutely."

The Girl removed the quill from her pocket and handed it to him. Dr. Laufer murmured in surprise. "We know of only two people who put their pigeongrams inside feather quills. One of them studied with us in Germany and remained there when we came to this country, and the other came along with us but has since died."

He removed the slip of paper and read: "YES OR NO?" He smiled. "So that is really what was written . . . we thought you were asking a question." He rolled up the slip of paper and returned it to its place, then sealed the quill and fastened it to the middle feather of the pigeon's tail.

"There," he said. "Just like it was fastened by she who dispatched her."

"Why do you say it like that?"

"Because that is the correct word. You send a letter but you dispatch a pigeon."

"No, why 'she'? How do you know it was a woman that dispatched her?"

"We see it clearly. Look for yourself. That is the handwriting of a young woman."

"A boy sent it, not a girl," said the Girl.

"It was a young woman," Dr. Laufer said. "Regard the handwriting."

It's a boy, thought the Girl in her heart; look at the words. And she surprised herself: how can it be that at the age of twelve I already have such things in mind?

Dr. Laufer handed the pigeon to the Girl. "Here. You dispatch her."

The Girl held the pigeon with two hands, feeling the smoothness of her feathers, her warmth, the beating of her heart, which was faster even than the Girl's own.

"Do not toss her, do not drop her; dispatch her. Like this—" He demonstrated with empty hands. "Your movements must be fluid, and think about what you are doing. It is your first time. You will feel a special sensation. When we arrived here from Germany and we began to tour the Land of Israel and learn its flora and fauna and we saw our first squill and smelled our first dust from a herd of sheep and drank from our first spring and ate our first cracked olives and our first fig from a tree, we had just such a feeling."

The Girl did his bidding, and with a fluid, confident movement she dispatched the pigeon. Three things happened at that exact moment: light shone on her face, a pang of longing filled her heart, and the pigeon, who knew nothing of this, not even the contents of the slip of paper she was carrying, spread her wings, beat them powerfully, and lifted off.

"Beautiful," Dr. Laufer said. "We are rising at a good angle. We have strength. We are healthy at last, and now that we can fly we shall grow stronger. Do not worry about her. She will reach her home. She is a good pigeon and this is a small country and the distances are not great."

The pigeon rose up above the cages, rose and turned to the southeast. "It may just be that she is flying to Jerusalem," the veterinarian explained. "But we hope that her home is closer than that, in Rishon Lezion or Rehovot."

He added, "Or perhaps Serafend, the English army camp. There is a large military pigeon loft there, and even soldiers sometimes feel love. How is it that we did not think of Serafend before? We are sometimes exceedingly stupid."

He tented his hand over his eyes, and when he noticed the Girl doing the same, he smiled. "Do not remove your gaze from her, because she will disappear from your view very quickly, much more quickly than you can imagine."

The Girl said, "She will disappear as soon as she is seen by the person waiting for her."

Dr. Laufer said, "That is not possible. That cannot be."

The Girl said, "But that is how it will be."

Dr. Laufer regarded the expression on her face and felt, in contrast to all logic, that she was right. He said, "Do you know what a *duvejeck* is? I was born in Köln, in Germany, and that is what someone who is crazy about pigeons is called there. That is what you are going to become. A real *duvejeck*."

He removed a notepad from his pocket and recorded in it the new rule: "The pigeon disappears from the view of the dispatcher when she is seen by the person waiting for her." He added, "That is the way it is even if that cannot be!" This he underlined; then he returned the pad to his pocket.

In her heart the Girl wondered whether the pigeon would reach home in time, for the consequences of both the yes and the no were liable to be unpredictable. She also formulated a wayfarer's prayer in her heart, the words of which she believed would lift off behind the pigeon and escort her a short distance on her airborne journey.

"Do you still see her?" asked Dr. Laufer.

"Yes," said the Girl.

"We do not anymore."

"That is because I dispatched her, not you."

Two minutes later she said, "She has arrived."

Dr. Laufer asked, "Do you want to continue to come here and help us in the loft?"

"I will think about it," the Girl said.

"Just now a young woman who worked here six years left us. She also came here as a girl."

"Did she come with a wounded pigeon, too?"

"No. She simply came one day with her mother, to visit the zoo."

"And where did she go?"

"To run a new pigeon loft on a kibbutz in the Jordan Valley. You can begin to learn and work in place of her. And bring that young man who came with you." He leaned over her and smiled. "Yes or no?"

"I will think about it, and I will ask my parents, and I will let you know."

The next three days the Girl spent on the balcony of her home. She lifted her eyes skyward, and every pigeon she saw caused her heart to stop beating. But Dr. Laufer had been right: the pigeon did not return, and on the fourth day the Girl went to the zoo and told him, "Yes, I want to."

"And where is your friend?"

"He can't. He studies English all day long. He has an uncle in Chicago, America, and he wants to go there to study medicine."

"Pity," said Dr. Laufer. "A true pity. But perhaps it is better this way."

"It's because of what you told him," said the Girl. "That he has good hands."

And so it was that at the beginning of 1940 a boy from Tel Aviv began to study Corning's Anatomy and the English dictionary, and two children began to work in two lofts for homing pigeons and learned to become pigeon handlers — the Girl in the Tel Aviv zoo and the Baby on a kibbutz in the Jordan Valley. And because at that time there were few pigeon handlers in the country, and all of them were connected to the Haganah, and all of them met from time to time at professional pigeon handlers' conferences, and mostly because fate wanted it that way — fate had its reasons — the Girl and the Baby were destined to meet and the Boy was destined to travel to America, and study there, and return to Tel Aviv.

# Chapter Five

## I

THERE ARE A FEW character traits that set me apart from my parents and brother and wife. Some I have already mentioned and others I will mention now. They—she included—are well acquainted with the skies above their heads and the earth beneath their feet, while I am a kite whose string has severed. They—particularly she—take risks, while I hesitate. They—especially she—decide and do, while I settle for hopes and wishes, in the manner of the devout in prayer: like a hammer that pounds again and again on the same spot. Always the same words, always toward the same east. Sometimes—with my dark, closely spaced eyes, my desire for wandering and fear of travel, my uttering of prayers and my dread that they will be answered—I feel like the only Jew in my family.

Yordad chose my major in high school—biology, the sciences track—just as he determined in which unit I would serve in the army. On his strong advice I did the course for medics, and thanks to his good connections and my success I stayed on as an instructor. He saw this as a first step toward medical school and taking over his clinic, an idea that surprised me greatly. I had never expressed an interest in becoming a doctor; nor would I have guessed that he had considered me, in particular, to be destined for that future.

"What about Benjamin?" I asked, amazed. "I thought he'd be the one to study medicine and take over your clinic."

Yordad grew serious, his expression clouded. "Benjamin does not have the medical temperament."

And when I asked what Benjamin would get if I received the clinic, he said, "You needn't worry about Benjamin, Yairi. He'll find himself a rich wife."

But Benjamin studied medicine and married a woman whose only goods were her joyful heart and her excellent brain, while I did a course for tour guides sponsored by the Ministry of Tourism. That is what my mother advised me to do. "Don't work in an office," she said. "It's good to be outside, and it is nice to return home from all sorts of places. Anyway," she joked, "maybe on one of those tour buses you'll meet a rich woman. An American tourist. Perhaps it won't be Benjamin who meets her, but you."

"What right does she have? What right does she have to intervene? She leaves us and still tells us what to do!" Yordad rose from his chair, paced back and forth, then lowered his voice. "You could be an excellent doctor, Yairi. Why be a tour guide?" He tilted his head downward to mine. "To tell tales to people and bring them to souvenir shops that sell little camels made from olivewood, and crosses made from seashells? To expect tips? And what's all this nonsense, Yairi, about a rich American tourist? Rich tourists sit in the back seats of chauffeur-driven Mercedes-Benzes, not in buses!"

"It's just one of Mother's jokes," I said. "She didn't mean it for real."

"I don't like those jokes of hers!" Yordad sputtered, fuming. "They don't amuse me in the least."

I did a FOR and AGAINST, became a tour guide, and met my rich wife in the exact manner you joked about: on a tourist bus. If I had the courage I would whine like a baby and say, "It was all your fault!" But instead I will describe things as they were, without pointing an accusatory finger at anyone. I was guiding groups at Christian holy places and Crusader sites and telling them tales and bringing them to souvenir shops, and I had already made a good name for myself and had amassed anecdotes and stories I collected first in my head, then in a small notepad purchased for me by Yordad, that fan of notepads, all of them small and black. And who knows? Maybe I would have continued thus, but one day a beautiful young American tourist climbed into my bus — I did not know then that she was rich as well — and sat in the back. She listened attentively to all my explanations. Sometimes I felt her gaze lingering on me, as though assessing me, weighing me. In the afternoon she approached and told me that her name was Liora Kirschenbaum and that she would like to meet with me after dinner.

Truth be told, that tourist had caught my attention even earlier. Her height and her eyes reminded me of my mother and Yordad and my brother, but she was handsomer than they, albeit in a strange way. Usually, it is not only the contours of the face that make a person beautiful but also what one radiates. My mother's features and her luminescence were one and the same. Tirzah's features are not special, but she is radiant to the point of blinding. And this tourist radiated nothing, but she was exceptionally beautiful. When we sat that evening in the hotel lobby, all those present stared at us in wonder, the way people stare in wonder at such a lady in the company of a dark young man, short and flustered.

The bus driver even made a vulgar crack about tourists who want to get something on with guides, but this tourist was headed in a very different direction. In the fall, she told me, she was supposed to return to Israel with several English friends of hers, young people who had money and time on their hands and were interested in birds. "And we would like you, Mr. Mendelsohn, to take us on a two-week nature tour in search of migrating birds."

"I don't know anything about nature," I told her. "Especially about migrating birds."

She touched my arm. "You won't need to know any birds and you won't need to explain anything to anyone. What you'll have to do is locate and prepare observation points and places for us to eat and sleep, and to equip and drive a car. There will be six of us, including you and me."

At that time Yordad had an acquaintance, an elderly gynecologist who was aggressive, short of temper and stature, and a knowledgeable amateur ornithologist: a *Vogelkundler,* he called it. I went to consult with him and he introduced me to his band of bird-watchers, all old German Jews like him, all far more strange and intriguing to me than the birds that caught their interest.

I told him about the offer I had received from the young American and he invited me to accompany his group on a bird-watching outing.

"She says I don't need to be familiar with the birds," I told him.

"You need to be familiar with the bird-watchers. They'll be your clients, not the birds."

The old *yekke* bird-watchers turned up armed with binoculars, cameras, and a telescope, wearing boots, and khaki trousers that reached their knees, and khaki socks that reached those same knees from the opposite direction. They all wore wide-brimmed straw hats, except for one; his hat was topped with a tuft of feathers, provoking the others to serve him with a sharp, educational rebuke that such a hat was not seemly for someone who loves birds: *"Es gehört sich nicht!"*

They sat on small folding chairs, and almost at once the announcements began: the distance, the direction, the type of bird. And then the arguments: Oriental honey buzzard or black kite? Steppe eagle or greater spotted eagle? The beginners tend to confuse the kestrel with the sparrow hawk, but the wingspan of the sparrow hawk is greater, they told me, and the hawk does not hover. Anyway, a small bird of prey that hovers could only be a kestrel, but a large bird of prey that does this must be a *schlangenadler,* a short-toed eagle.

After several hours, a vote was held and it was decided that we would eat. The men removed sandwiches, fruit, and thermoses of black coffee from their knapsacks. The scent of sausages and boiled eggs wafted through the air.

"We have two people on duty," they told me. "One keeps his eye on the sky in order to alert the members of the group if something interesting appears overhead. As for the other, please meet Professor Freund, on cake duty today." Professor Freund, an expert on Greek history during the week, sliced and served with great ceremony a wonderful apple pastry made by his wife.

"She baked a strudel for us and she stayed at home," he noted with pride. "Bird-watching is a very good hobby for us boys," he said and laughed oddly, something akin to clearing his throat.

They spread before me a map of Israel, explaining which birds I was likely to meet in which locales. It was an important lesson to learn, because even though today I am no expert in identifying birds, I did become adept at knowing where to find them, and spot them, and show them to others. Some places, like the Hula Valley, are known by every bird-watcher, while in certain locations around Jerusalem you can find the resting places of eagles, and in one of the valleys of the Gilboan Hills, those of storks. I have a small ravine where they stay year-round, and a place in the Judean Desert where birds of prey gather to sleep on the ground. I had one eagle owl—the only bird that arouses true affection in me—whose nesting grounds I have visited a number of times; today I show my tourists his descendants. I have one small, isolated pool around which there are all manner of ducks, greenheads and coots, cormorants, egrets, gray herons, black storks, stilts, lapwings. You see, I remember the names even if I don't always know to put them with the right birds.

# 2

SEVERAL MONTHS PASSED. On the appointed day I drove the minibus I had rented to the Haifa port to fetch the rich tourist from America and her English bird-watching friends. Overhead, seagulls and enormous flocks of pigeons circled, landing and alighting at the granaries nearby.

My clients disembarked from a ship arriving from Piraeus. Liora Kirschenbaum called me "darling," tilted her head downward to kiss my cheek, and presented me to the others, a small and amiable group, slightly inebriated and emitting the scents of pleasant colognes, four sunburned noses protected—a little too late—by light-colored straw hats. Four pairs of binoculars hung on four concave chests; four leather-covered flasks were hidden in four back pockets.

We left the port in the direction of the Check Post, and already in the city they began to identify swifts and swallows. We traveled north. Although I was not asked to do so, perhaps out of awkwardness and habit I tried to tell them a few of my often-told tour-guide stories as we drove: Elijah on Mount Carmel, the Crusaders and Napoleon in Acre, the snail that produces the mauve color used by the ancient Phoenicians for dyeing, the invention of glass. Straightaway one of them, a squat and jaundiced fellow, his Adam's apple jutting sharply from his neck, told me they did not want to hear any of the "holy garbage"— that's what he called it—that tour guides pawn off on tourists in the Holy Land.

"We've come to watch the birds, Mr. Mendelsohn," he said. "It's best we make this perfectly clear now so this trip will be a success."

And the trip was, indeed, a success. The organization, the food, the accommodations, the rented minibus—nothing failed. Even the birds did not disappoint. The stork knew the appointed hours, the swift observed the time of her coming, and large flocks of birds of prey passed by overhead as if on command. My new clients were satisfied. They were particularly excited by the sound of a soft crowing they could not locate. It was late in the afternoon and we were eating sandwiches at the edge of a large field in the Beit She'an Valley when suddenly all four raised their eyes skyward. Their gazes scoured the heavens, but the looks on their faces attested only to listening, not seeing.

"What are you looking for?" I asked.

The squat, jaundiced, irascible one signaled me impatiently with his hand to be quiet, and after cocking his head and listening for half a minute he raised his binoculars to his eyes and said, "One o'clock, thirty degrees." His cohorts looked, too, and one said, "The scouts."

"Those are cranes, Yair," Liora whispered to me, her mouth—how pleasant—very close to my ear. "Listen. They make a very soft, quiet sound, but they can be heard at great distances."

I listened to their amicable crowing like conversation and then I saw them, three large fowl with long legs and outstretched necks.

"I thought they flew in large flocks," I said.

"The scouts," said the squat, jaundiced guy, "fly ahead of the flock. They'll find a nice spot to rest, they'll land there, and then signal to the rest of the flock from the ground."

"Pretty soon the sun will set," I noted.

"Cranes fly at night, too."

The stork, the pelican, the birds of prey—all these glide. That is what he explained to me later. The sun heats up the earth, the earth heats the air, and the hot air rises, enabling the birds to rise as well, and glide. That is why they fly exclusively during the day and over land. But the crane is the only large bird that both glides and beats its wings, so that while the stork takes several days of coasting to circumvent the Black Sea, the crane traverses it in one night of wing-flapping flight.

That night they slept at a kibbutz in the Beit She'an Valley. Incidentally, years later it would turn out that this was the kibbutz where Zohar, my future sister-in-law, lived, and that the man who handled the room rental—a tall, stout young man, friendly and efficient—was one of her three brothers. Sometimes I ponder what would have happened if she herself had been working at the desk, or if I had not sat with my guests on the grass but had set out on a walk around the kibbutz and had met her on the sidewalk. I could have warned her against marrying Benjamin. But that evening I sat with my English bird-watchers on the grass until quite late, and my life took its present course.

A full moon was shining. The four of them drank a lot and told stories that amused one another and Liora immensely. I envied them. Their behavior hinted at a certain insouciance and freedom from financial worry that had less to do with monies inherited or earned than with some mysterious heredity.

The squat, jaundiced fellow with the jutting Adam's apple coaxed me to take part in their drinking. I declined. I told them I was not accustomed, that I had never drunk liquor, and that I abstained almost entirely even from drinking wine. But Mr. Jaundice would not give up. "It's high time you tried. Drink it down in one go. This is good Irish whiskey."

Perhaps because of Liora's presence there and perhaps because his words convinced me, I downed the glass he handed me. Was this what my mother felt as she sipped her daily glass of brandy? A snake of fire coiled around my throat. A horse kicked the inside of my brow. I wished to distance myself from them, breathe some air, and get hold of myself, but my body was unable to stand. I crawled to the side on all fours. Everyone laughed and Liora drew near, compassion in her eyes but mirth on her lips.

"I'm sorry," she said. "He didn't know you'd react so strongly."

I was afraid to open my mouth for fear of retching or fainting. I made do with a gesture of "Leave me alone!" and managed to get to my feet, staggering and nauseous. Liora came after me and laid me out— yes, precisely that—on the grass, then sat down next to me and settled my neck onto her thigh, so that my head tilted slightly backward.

After a little while my head cleared. I rose to my feet and stumbled back to my room. Liora followed and made me a cup of Turkish coffee.

"This is the first time I've ever made Turkish coffee," she said. "I hope I'm doing it right."

She held my hand. I responded to her encouraging smile with my own apologetic one. I told her I wanted to return to the grass and breathe the fresh air.

The Englishmen had already turned in. The full moon had risen higher in the sky; it was no longer bathed in a soft yellow light, but was now bluish and metallic. I sat on the grass, Liora at my side, tilting her lovely head toward mine and parting her lips for a kiss. Her body relaxed a bit, announcing its desire to lie next to me. We pressed up against each other. I could not believe what was happening. Her beauty was so near, I could see it in my eyes, feel it over the whole surface of my skin.

Her mouth and tongue surprised me with their heat and vitality, her hands with their daring, my body with its joy, her loins with their ardor.

"You are lovely," the rich tourist I met on the bus told me. "You are small and sweet, just the way men should be. Even without meeting your mother I can tell she's taller than you. I liked that about you right from the first time we met, on the bus."

Suddenly she pulled away from me and lay back in the grass. "Listen," she said.

I listened but heard nothing. I wanted to kiss her again, but she put her hand on my chest. "Wait. Be patient. The moment you first hear them is important."

We lay on our backs next to each other, holding hands. Time passed, measured by the howls of jackals and the dull roar from a distant road. Then a hush fell, a thin silence, followed by a sort of faraway chattering that grew closer and more defined. The world overflowed with wings, the ears with a soft whispering. The full moon blinked and skittered, vanishing, then reappearing from behind passing shadows and uttered words.

I asked, "What is this?"

"Those are the cranes," said the rich young tourist from America. "You remember the three scouts we saw this afternoon? This is the large flock that followed them."

I listened. And wondered: What was it they were discussing? Were they telling one another of experiences from previous journeys? Were they arguing over where to land? Were they comparing this resting place with others? And this rich young woman, who was destined to become my wife at the end of that very year, made me laugh by saying, in three different croaking voices, "Faster! We're landing soon, got to catch a good spot . . ." "Hey, where's Grandma disappeared to now . . . ?" "We're gonna be last *again* and nothing's gonna be left to eat . . ."

The sounds of conversation grew stronger. To this very day I am astounded at the distance to which the voices of cranes carry. They can be heard long before the birds arrive and do not dissipate until after they have departed.

"Geese and cranes talk among themselves when they fly," Liora told me. "Perhaps because they fly at night." She explained that these were voices used by "Mommy Crane" and "Daddy Crane" to calm the little cranes that were just old enough to be making their first journey with the flock.

The rich young tourist you'd prophesied for me had become a flesh-and-blood woman lying at my side. She pleased me. Her conversation was very congenial. She said, "In Japan the crane is a symbol of a long and faithful marriage, but in ancient Egypt it was the raven."

I said, "Really? Here lovebirds are called 'turtledoves.'"

Liora bent my head slightly and planted many soft kisses on my neck.

I felt she was sucking my strength, that any minute I would die from the intensity of the pleasure and feebleness I was feeling. She stripped off her shirt, exposing small and beautiful breasts, then pushed me gently away so that I would remain lying on my back. She laid a long thigh on top of me and said, "Here, Yair, this is going to be our first time."

"Are you a virgin?" I asked, taken aback.

She chuckled. "We'll soon find out."

"Well, I am," I told her. "So you know that right up front and we don't have any misunderstandings."

"I don't believe you."

"Why not?" I said. "My mother was a virgin, and I think my father was, too. It's our family's way."

She drew her face near. Her hands opened, parted, drew out, aimed. Her body climbed, mounted. "I've heard that story before," she said. "Make up a new one."

The beating of wings intensified. The din filled my head. The rich young tourist arched and unfurled and I slipped inside her flesh. It was much easier than I had suspected, more pleasant than I had hoped.

"Shhhh . . . keep quiet. You'll wake up everyone around here," she said as she placed her hand over my mouth.

# 3

APPARENTLY the English bird-watchers told their friends about me upon their return home, because people began to make contact and visit, and my name became known among travel agents as well. I was overcome with the joy of a young man, the joy of financial independence. I felt as though I was taking off, that my wings were spread. And because my mother had no money and my father objected to my choice of profession, reminding me that "it isn't too late, Yairi, to alter this erroneous course," I turned to Meshulam Fried for a loan to enable me to get set up and to purchase the necessary vehicle.

Only a few years had passed since Gershon had fallen in battle, and Meshulam would remove the large blue handkerchief from his pocket every time I came to visit. "Ever since Gershon, it's hard for me to look at you." That is what he has been saying from the time his son fell to this very day. "Ever since Gershon," without the terrible verb that should follow his name.

"I can't look at you, Iraleh," he bellowed into his handkerchief, "without seeing him next to you. Seeing Tiraleh without him is hard too, but it's worse with you." All at once he stopped. "That's enough. I'm done crying this time. What can I do for you?"

I told him about the bird-watchers I guided and the opportunity that had presented itself, and Meshulam said, "I smell the hand of a woman in this. May my right hand cleave to the roof of my mouth if I don't feel her presence."

"That would be my mother's hand," I said. "It was her idea."

"Another woman," Meshulam said. "Not only Mrs. Mendelsohn. It's there on your forehead like the headlights of a newspaper."

I asked him if he could help me find a used minibus and he said he would find one. I asked if he could loan me money and he refused. "For you, the only money I give is a gift."

I told him I would not accept a gift of that magnitude and he said, "So it's not a gift. Meshulam is going to loan you some money and you aren't going to pay it back." He gave me an admonishing look. "Ever since Gershon, you're like a son to me. If he was living, Iraleh, I wouldn't give him the money? If you married Tiraleh, I wouldn't give it to you?"

I refused again. "I'm not Gershon, and Tirzah's already married to someone else."

Meshulam grimaced. "What a wedding we made for her. Good food, good bride, pretty bridesmaids, only the groom should have been somebody else."

I did not react. He said, "Pardon me. With Meshulam, the mouth and the heart are the same thing. What he says in his heart he thinks out loud."

Several days later he phoned. "I found you a car. Come see."

I hurried to his office. "What a shame," he said. "Tiraleh was here fifteen minutes ago. I told her, 'Hold on, your friend Iraleh's on his way,' but she's all the time on tender hooks, running from one job to another. That's what happens when you got a husband like she got herself."

The minibus was standing in the parking lot. I told Meshulam it was exactly what I had been looking for and he told his fleet manager to check everything there was to check and to take care of transferring the title, and apparently he whispered a few more instructions, because after the test the minibus returned with a roof rack and a ladder on top, new tires, and an additional spare.

"How much did all that cost?" I asked, concerned.

"Peanuts. What, I can't buy a little something for the son of Professor Mendelsohn? I wish you every success."

"And where's the seller? I want to talk to him about the price."

Meshulam burst out laughing. "A guy who's got Meshulam needs to talk prices? I already talked to him and I took him down and everything's settled and you're going to give me my money back when you start to earn something."

# 4

A YEAR PASSED. The birds migrated and returned and my minibus—packed with bird-watchers from Scandinavia and Germany, from Holland and America—followed after them, from the Hula Valley to the Dead Sea, the Beit She'an Valley, and the southern Arava. My new business was flourishing and I had already succeeded in paying back a large part of the loan to Meshulam—after much argument.

During that time I corresponded with Liora. Her letters and life were far more interesting and entertaining than mine. We planned another visit. This time she would come alone.

"Now I'm a student of photography," she announced. "Until they bring me into the family business I'm trying out all kinds of other things."

I took her to photograph ibexes at Hever and Mishmar creeks, vultures at David Creek, and some rare owl at Arugot. We drove around a lot. We hiked a lot. We slept in a pup tent that filled up with love. She told me she had missed me, that she thought about and dreamt of that night when cranes had flown overhead and we had lain beneath them.

I told my mother and Yordad that I "had a girlfriend." I told them that I intended to bring her home and present her to them. Yordad gathered his courage, phoned my mother, and told her that in his opinion this was serious and that they should spare me having to do a repeat performance. She agreed, and came for her first visit since she had left home. Benjamin, who was then a medical student, also made an effort and joined us.

"Let's sit in the living room," Yordad said, but we remained in the *küche,* the large kitchen that was once yours. You eyed Liora, while

Yordad only had eyes for you. Afterward he composed himself, apologized, and said, "Liora, you really look like one of the family."

She smiled. "Your son didn't warn us."

Indeed, until that day the similarity between Liora and my mother, brother, and Yordad was known only to me. Now I enjoyed watching it work them over. They regarded one another, looked at her again, grew excited. A small and pleasant cloud rose up above them and blushed near the ceiling.

Benjamin left after an hour, and Liora and I a short while after that. "Why don't you stay awhile, Raya?" Yordad said to my mother, but she left with us and declined my offer to drive her home. "I'll go home on foot," she said. "It's not far."

Liora returned to America, and about two months later I went there—my first and last trip abroad—to meet her parents and her brother Emmanuel. We came back to Israel a married couple. Liora never photographed ibexes again, nor did she go bird-watching. She set up the Israeli branch of the family business, succeeded brilliantly, bought us a home, got pregnant, learned Hebrew quickly, and, with the same speed she amassed money and words, she lost her fetuses. My two children died in the grave of her womb one after the other and at the exact same age, after a pregnancy of twenty-two weeks.

I remember the slap of the doctor's words—that very same old *Vogelkundler* who, several years earlier, had shown me the best birdwatching spots. After the first miscarriage he told us, "It was a boy," and after the second, in monstrously bad Hebrew that mirrored the horror he was describing, he told us, "This boy was a girl," as if hinting at something full of portent but without explaining its meaning.

"Why does he tell us?" I fumed. "Did anyone ask him to? It's a good thing he didn't tell us their names, and where they would have studied, and in which units they would have served in the army."

Liora brushed out her hair slowly in front of the mirror. It was impossible to detect anything in her face but fatigue; her beauty had actually increased. Cascades of copper and gold flowed between the black bristles of her hairbrush. We both regarded her, I in profile, she head-on. And then our reflected gazes met and Liora smiled forgivingly, as mothers smile at the sight of their tiny sons angry for the very first time.

She turned her fair and beautiful face toward me, the face of a queen, I thought. Ivory studded with sapphires and crowned with copper and gold. I felt the mirror's affront, its pain: until that moment it had held the entirety of her beauty, and now, all at once, it had been emptied.

I said, "Maybe you'd like to stay with your parents for two or three weeks?"

She said, "My home is here, and my work and my office are here. You are here, too."

My mother—I ran away from our house in Tel Aviv to see her in Jerusalem for a few hours—said, "Liora is a strong woman, as you already know, but when strong people crack the break is larger and the shards are smaller."

"But maybe something's wrong with her?" I asked.

"Don't blame Liora," she said. "Maybe it's something of mine I passed on to you. Don't forget that we had a miscarriage, too." She put her hand on mine. "Do you remember how we would vomit together every morning, you and I?"

"Sure, I remember," I said, smiling. "And I'm not blaming anyone, Mother, not her, not myself, not you. I just want to try to understand what's happened."

"Go back to her now," she said. "It's not good to leave a woman alone in such a situation."

I went back. Liora had already pieced her tiny shards together so that nothing at all was discernible from the outside. She was as straight-backed and handsome as ever, her skin smooth and pure, her brushed hair whispering like fire, and her clear eyes quiet. She did not ask where I had been and did not scold me for leaving her alone, but when we sat to drink tea she told me she had no intention of getting pregnant again.

I said perhaps she should consult other doctors, but she cut me off. "There's nothing wrong with me," she said.

I asked, "What are you trying to say? That the problem is with me? I mean, you did get pregnant."

Liora grew angry. "I don't ever *try* to say anything, Yair. Whatever I have to say I say without trying."

Later, I lay next to her, put my arms around her, tried to calm her with gentle words. She stood up and leaned over me from her full height. "Each one of us is absolutely fine. It's the two of us together that's the problem." She wrapped herself in the large sheet that until that day had covered us both, took her pillow—Liora uses a particularly soft pillow; mine gives her a neckache—and moved to the bedroom that from that day forth became her own.

I did not protest, and in retrospect I think she was right. Even then she was always right. Once a month she would visit me in my room for her "treatment"—"To keep my complexion looking good," she said—while I, I must admit, was grateful and even happy, then insulted and angry, because afterward she would get out of bed and return to her own room.

"It's not polite," I told her after her next "treatment." "You act like those men that women complain about: you come and then you go."

"I come? Don't flatter yourself."

"So why do you go? Why don't you stay until the morning?"

"It's too hot in bed with you."

Who was this son, who was this daughter that were not born to us? And if they had been born, would they have looked alike? Taking into consideration that spluttering doctor's diagnosis that one was a boy and his brother a girl, and taking into consideration the difference in their ages—exactly two years—I can only surmise and wonder. Even now, sitting on the wooden deck that Tiraleh, my luvey, built for me in my new home, I imagine them as suddenly they take shape from molecules of air and view, becoming real in the transparent void as less transparent images. They do not float in it like fish, nor hover like winged creatures; although there is no solid ground for their feet, they walk as though there were.

About one thing I have no doubts: had they been born, they would have been good friends. It is a fact that they always visit me together, never separately. He is two years older than she, and she—sharper-witted and more mercurial—is exactly those same two years younger than he. They always stand close to each other and are occupied with the same thing, like Siamese twins joined by a shared matter of interest. They argue, gaze at something in the distance, call each other's attention to something with pointed fingers.

I do not give them names. It is enough foolishness that I conjure them before my eyes. Anyway, a name requires a familiar body upon which it can be hung, but these two—they are always changing. Sometimes they are like my parents and my wife and my brother—fair and thin and tall of stature—and sometimes like me, dark and short, though never one of each kind. They never have facial features. I sense all their movements, I hear their voices, but I do not see their faces.

"Why weren't you born?" I ask them, and answer myself: perhaps this is simply happenstance, a case of being thwarted by the hand of fate, or perhaps their mother was right, that any mixture of mine and hers—home, child, work, sleep—was doomed to fail.

# 5

LIORA INHERITED her beauty from her father and her charm from her mother. He is the president of Kirschenbaum Real Estate in New York, and she is the owner of Kirschenbaum Pastries in New Rochelle. Other than parents Liora has an older brother, Emmanuel, whom I have already mentioned, the father of six daughters and the director of business operations for Kirschenbaum Real Estate on the East Coast: Boston, Washington, Long Island, New York City. A long time ago he was a wild young man, fond of sailing and food and drink and expensive clothing. Today he wears the simple black suit and white shirt of a Hasidic Jew, his eyes and shoulders downcast, his voice soft and his gait a hurried shuffle as befitting a repentant Jew. Still, his badgering has remained constant: back then he wore me out with discussions of designer shoes and boat engines, while these days it's contributions to settlers and hidden messages in the Scriptures.

Liora does not believe that a person can change. "It's all a big act," she says about her brother. "He's just as much of a pain in the ass as he ever was, and these ugly new clothes of his are just another way of showing off." She sneered, "Emmanuel is the only Hasidic Jew in the world who wears a tallis made by Versace." In my opinion she is wrong, though. Emmanuel may still be a boring pain in the ass, but his repentance is real.

Two or three times a year he makes an appearance in Israel on one of his business-Judaism-family trips, and whenever he or some other Kirschenbaum comes, Behemoth and I are dispatched to the airport to bring them to their hotel. That is my job, lest we forget that my salary comes from the Israeli branch of the firm.

The automatic door of the arrivals hall opens for me. I enter and wait. Sometimes I even hold up a sign with KIRSCHENBAUM in two languages. I do not have the cap and uniform of a driver but I am good at acting my role, and the sign infuriates Emmanuel to no end.

Here they are. Emmanuel and his father come out first, then the two wives, both dressed modestly but expensively, Emmanuel's wife carrying a round hatbox. Sometimes the arriving group is even larger. I do not know them all, but it is always easy to pick them out. Although they are quite different from one another, the Kirschenbaums—even those related to the family by marriage—radiate an ambience of unity and family identity. "See how beautiful they are?" Liora scolded me when our wedding photos arrived from America. "Only you look different."

"That's the way I am," I told her. "Even with my own family I'm the one who looks different."

And after I am presented to the newest Emmanuel or Liora that has been born or has entered the family, I let them all hug and kiss and chatter while I load the luggage into the back of Behemoth or on the roof rack. I climb up, pull this way and that, load bags, tighten straps. Simple tasks imbue me with energy and diligence. I sit behind the wheel and await instructions.

Several days later, when the family and business meetings have ended, Behemoth and I are asked to take them on trips around the country. Liora's parents are easy tourists, happy everywhere I take them and with every explanation I make. Emmanuel, on the other hand, is interested in visiting only one kind of place: Rachel's Tomb, the Cave of the Machpelah, illegal settlements and outposts in the West Bank. Lately he has also discovered the holy graves of the righteous in the north of the country, which means longer trips for me. I don't mind driving, but it is hard for me to be in his company for so many hours. On those occasions, Behemoth, usually a roomy vehicle, suddenly becomes solitary confinement on wheels and I become a short-tempered and angry prisoner whose sentence carries no parole.

"I can't stand these trips with him," I told Liora.

"That's the nature of the job. Every tour guide gets stuck with annoying tourists now and again. And don't forget that this annoying tourist is the director of the company that pays your salary."

# 6

THE ISRAELI BRANCH of the company that pays my salary is a spacious and elegant office, full of air and sunlight, on Chen Boulevard in Tel Aviv. Liora can make the short walk there from our home on Spinoza Street in her spiked heels. That is how she goes to work each morning: she walks southward on Spinoza, crosses Gordon Street, ignores her admirers on Frishman—the men who wait to watch her firm calves and thighs pass swiftly by each day—then takes a shortcut, turns right, and minces her way up the moderate incline of the shaded boulevard, capping it off with a smooth, quick climb up the twenty-four steps that lead to her office.

Sigal, her stern, pudgy secretary, hands Liora her daily schedule of meetings along with a cup of lukewarm water with lemon juice, tea-hyssop, and honey. Then it is straight to work. After all, someone has to earn a living, bring in the money to buy Yair travel clothes that will never travel and knapsacks that will never be carried and shock absorbers that will never be shocked to their fullest and skid plates for Behemoth's undercarriage that will never get scraped on rocks.

Most of Liora's clients are wealthy American Jews looking for an apartment in Israel, as well as foreign diplomats and, lately, rich Jews from France and Mexico, whom Emmanuel meets at religious conventions. She finds houses and apartments for them in the finest neighborhoods, in Talbieh and Rehavia in Jerusalem, in Caesarea, in Rishpon and Ashdod and Tel Aviv. And since many of them neither live in these homes nor visit them regularly, she handles their maintenance and subletting.

Sometimes Sigal sends me to make one of these houses ready for short-term rental or a visit by the owners. I check the water system, the electricity, the air-conditioning, the kitchen appliances; I hire technicians and cleaners; and on occasion I even buy a few food staples for the owners to find in their refrigerators. For all these services the Israeli branch of Kirschenbaum Real Estate pays me a monthly salary, a sum that enables me to entertain an illusion of independence and my wife to write off a few more expenses.

There are several advantages to being married to a woman of means, but there is a disadvantage, too: I am required to make reports, to be measured, to be itemized into the smallest parts of worthiness. If you wish, my life with the wealthy woman you prophesied for me is a long chain of handing in receipts and proof.

"You're wrong!" Liora protested when she heard me make this claim. "I have never asked you why you need something, and I have never said no. But money is something orderly, and those are Itzik's instructions. You have to know how much is coming in from where and how much is going out to where."

Itzik is her accountant, a Moroccan-born Prussian with a tiny skull-cap in place of a spiked helmet.

"I am a subject, I am a serf, I am a hostage," I told her. "You and Itzik have the barrel of a wallet pointed at my head."

"So quit. You'll get workers' comp from me and you can be self-employed."

"There's not enough work for tour guides these days."

And because Liora reacted by maintaining a scornful silence, I erupted. "You know why I don't have work? Because of people like your brother and his settler friends."

"Don't make excuses. If there's no work in tourism, then change professions. I can set you up with loans and guarantees to get started. Like you were given by that friend of your father's, the contractor who's built half of Israel. I remember how he looked at me when we met at the party back in Israel after our wedding, how he glared at me with snake eyes."

She gave me her own venomous glare. "I've heard he has a very successful daughter who's busy building the other half of Israel. Why don't you go work for them instead of me? Maybe you'll feel more comfortable with her."

"I'll be your driver. On that happy note you can even raise my salary."

"I am willing to raise your salary so that you *won't* be my driver."

That is what she said, but in the weeks following, Sigal began phoning me from time to time to chauffeur Liora around. Sometimes she would sit next to me and sometimes in the back of Behemoth, her wide-set blue-gray eyes perusing papers or the screen of her Mac in preparation for some meeting or deal, while my deep, close-set brown eyes—the eyes of a bull who has guessed his fate—shifted back and forth from the road to the mirror. If I tilted the mirror and my head at the proper angles, the wide space between her eyes and the small one between her knees would reflect back at me inside a single frame.

This new situation awakened new passion in me and, apparently, once, in Liora as well. We were traveling from Jerusalem to Beit Shemesh at Emmanuel's request, to look in on several properties in a development being built there for the ultra-Orthodox community. I suggested we leave the main road and drive through Ein Kerem, Bar Giora, and the Valley of Elah.

So we had done when suddenly my wife ordered me to turn Behemoth onto some dirt side road that I myself was not familiar with, and there, under a large and secretive carob tree, we lay upon a blanket I extracted from the back of the vehicle, a blanket that I had bought and that had already given up all hopes of ever being used. Afterward, happy with the unexpected pleasure my wife had granted me and mournful of its rarity, I fetched from Behemoth the alpine camping stove and a kettle and skillet, so that by the time Liora had awakened and stretched and smiled I had already prepared a field meal for the two of us, seasoned with leaves and herbs I had found between the rocks.

"I had no idea you and Behemoth were so well equipped," she said. "What else have you got in there?"

"Everything you need." And more: a set of tools and recovery equipment and cooking utensils, a large sleeping bag and a thin, self-inflating air mattress, jerricans for gas and water, a headlamp, batteries, a kerosene lamp, a coffee kit, cloves of garlic, instant soup, salty things — that is what my mother would say about Benjamin and me: "Benjamin likes sweets and Yair likes salties"—everything I would need for departure or banishment.

And a spare set of keys for Behemoth kept in a secret, sealed hiding place on the chassis. Thus, if one day Liora informs me that I must leave, I will be able to get up and depart immediately, without the complicated embarrassment of packing and loading, of how many and which clothes to take and of "Did you happen to see my keys anywhere?" I will leave just as banished women once left: bedecked with their gold and jewels. I will leave, I will go, and until some other rich woman takes me in, I will manage to survive for the first few days in the hills.

The next day Itzik informed me that my wife would no longer be in need of my services as a driver but that my salary would continue to be paid in full. Several days later I was summoned to the office, signed a few papers, and went from being a partly employed tour guide to "director of the transportation department" of the Israeli branch of the firm, a department established overnight so that I could head it. Behemoth and I, who once trailed around after migrating birds, now found ourselves ferrying lecturers, singers, and actors and—since we are both capable of departing from paved roads for dirt ones—senior engineers from the Israel Electric Company, foreign television crews, and special guests of the Office of the Prime Minister and the Foreign Ministry. That is how I met the American Palmachnik and his friends, whom I took to the Harel observation point and the Palmach cemetery at Kiryat Anavim and the monastery from which the Baby's final pigeon took flight.

It was during all these trips and all this ferrying that I began to ponder the possibility of not returning. Of finding myself a different home, my own place. My lack of ease in Liora's house had eaten away at me from some years, but now I had an opportunity for scouting and searching. And more than once, when driving a lecturer or singer or sing-along leader to some small village, I took advantage of that opportunity. While my passenger made an appearance in the local clubhouse or community center, I scoured the place, pursued FOR SALE signs and houses bereft of people, homes that wished to be filled with someone new, a place to build me as I built it.

If there was a sign on the house and someone inside, I would knock at the door. If the house was empty, I would draw near and peer in the windows. Sometimes a suspicious neighbor would approach: who was I and what exactly was I doing there?

"I'm the driver of the guest artist appearing this evening in the club-house."

"And what are you looking for?"

"A home."

And at once my mood would improve. There are few people who can define so easily who they are and what they want.

# Chapter Six

## I

I SET OUT to find myself a home. One that would wrap around me, provide a refuge of sorts. I passed down village lanes stippled with light and shadow and the cooing of turtledoves. I peeped and knocked, I entered local grocery stores and inquired of shoppers, I perused bulletin boards studded with thumbtacks and strewn with slips of paper. I paid visits to the village secretariats, all with matching gray desks and people, all with the same aerial photographs: patchwork quilts of orchards and fields, agricultural buildings, pens dotted black and white with cows caught in the amber of the lens.

Like a vulture I soared, scouting after the collapsing, the dying, the dead. I met ruined farmers and couples that had split up. I scoured farmyards of thorns and dust. I drank tea with old people who refused to sell and their children who wished them dead, heard pigeons coo in an abandoned hayloft and winds howl in a breached roof. I saw dreams that had faded away, loves that had been proven false, crumbling cement and cobwebs.

I was a fugitive and a vagabond, my hands on the large, soft steering wheel of Behemoth as I searched throughout the country and, eventually, found it. Here it is, the house you intended for me. Small and decrepit in appearance, it has two old cypress trees that can be seen from the window, just like you loved and told me to look for, and two giant carobs in the corner of the lot, and weeds growing through cracks in the pavement, just as you craved and commanded.

Hello, house. Your walls are peeling plaster, your door is nailed shut to the doorposts, your windows are boarded up, but your rooms beyond

are bereft of people and they echo to me: *Come.* A large spiny-tailed
lizard bolts through the tin drainpipes; its toenails make my skin shudder. Ancient sparrows' nests overflowing with straw poke out from slits
in the roof. I walked round and round it, making my way among angry
thorns as tall as I. A pitiful fig tree, a balding lawn, a lemon tree poised
to die. A sudden noise frightened my feet. A large skink skittered away.

On the other side of the house, the view ambushed me. Wide and
self-assured, feigning nonchalance but here and there making an effort
in green, and, unlike other views in this country, it is unhampered by
roads and electrical wires and other villages. Only hills upon hills, like
the backs of sheep growing distant and paler and topped with small and
stubborn mastic trees, and slopes running yellow. Here there was a lone
carob tree; there, cow pens and cattle fences. And in the shallow wadis
there were low terraces and patches of cultivated land and dirt roads. It
was a simple view but cunning and inviting, a view you could step out of
the house and walk into.

The house was built on a slope, and its western side was supported
by columns. In the space beneath it, junk had collected: an old toilet,
planks, pipes and elbow joints. Someone had used two of the columns
and some chicken wire to make an enclosure that held a tin trough, two
broken egg-laying compartments, and four strange, tiny mounds of
feathers. I examined them with the tip of my shoe and was filled with
revulsion: they were the shriveled corpses of four chickens. Whoever
had lived in this house had left them imprisoned there, to die of hunger
and thirst.

I left. Barring any traffic jams, I would make it in time for dinner
with Liora in Tel Aviv. Several ravens circled overhead in search of a bird
of prey they could tease before settling in for their evening's rest, and
above them feeble, feathery clouds, the sunset pinkening their edges
and pushing them eastward.

I stopped. Behind my back I felt the house I had found for myself.
For one lone moment the entire world was mine. One lone moment,
followed by another in which my foot mashed the pedal and my hands
turned the wheel as far as it would go. Behemoth was surprised; it usually heads home like a cow to its trough, while here it was, driven to the
shoulders of the road in a big, soft leap, then spun around in a spurt of
mud and gravel. I retraced my tracks and returned by way of the fields
to the home I had found for myself.

Behemoth took its time scaling the steep slope behind the house.

I removed the sleeping bag and mattress from the trunk. I inserted a crowbar, pried away a few boards, and climbed up and sat on the sill of the broken window. "When you find your new place," my mother instructed me, "check it in the morning and the evening, at different hours and seasons." One should consider the range of sounds and scents, you explained. Measure the rising heat in the roof and the cold slithering from the walls. Chart the times of sunset and blooming, read the sundials and weather vane at the window.

"Hello, house . . ." I said, my voice loud and clear in the awaiting gloom. I fell silent, inclined my ear. The house breathed and answered. I entered, walked its void without seeing or encountering a thing. I smiled to myself. In Liora's house, rising at nighttime is an adventure on the high seas. First near shore, one hand touching the walls, and only later, with the sudden courage of the explorers, I become more daring. Hands splayed, I feel my way, bump into things, pull back from shoals of furniture and reefs that have sprung up overnight. On several occasions I have even smitten my toes and forehead on thresholds and lintels that have changed position.

Here I marched about with confidence. The air was surprisingly fresh. The floor, which had not felt the touch of feet in a very long time, was glad. I spread upon it the inflated mattress, stripped off my clothes, and slipped into the sleeping bag like an animal in its den. Right away I sensed I was lying precisely on a line of longitude, my feet pointing due north, the south a pillow for my head, and in addition to the pleasantness I was feeling, I had a sense of buoyancy. I shut my eyes and heard the special sound wind makes when it blows in large trees, and the second of three rounds of jackals howling, and then a night bird with a voice that was light and hollow and rhythmic, and precise as a metronome. Before falling asleep I told myself that in the morning I would have a look in the bird-watcher's guide I kept in Behemoth and I would ascertain which bird this was. And then, when I would know this, I would make my decision. I would do a FOR and AGAINST. I would decide the way you did.

# 2

IN THE MORNING, as soon as I opened my eyes I knew where I was. I got up and went out to Behemoth. The night bird turned out to be an owl, *Otus scops,* which is "small, common, and hairy." I chuckled: Liora would say that description suited me as well. I circled the house once again, observing and appraising: the curse of the dead chickens, the forest of thorns in the garden, the water spots on the walls, the insistence of the lizard's nails, the necessity of making decisions and taking action—these said AGAINST. The capacious view, the age of the carob trees in the garden, the placement of the cypress trees in the picture, the breathing of the house, my confident movements inside it—all these said FOR.

I said that I, too, was FOR, and all at once I felt great joy. "For," I repeated, surprised at my newfound ability to decide. I returned the mattress and the sleeping bag to Behemoth and removed the camping stove. I drank my first cup of coffee in the house I had found for myself and went off to make inquiries at the village secretariat.

Between the house and the village secretariat stood five hundred feet, three houses, two tended gardens and one that was dry and balding, four more pairs of cypress trees that would gladden your heart, and a single giant pine that must be home to scores of birds, judging by the quantity of bird dung beneath it.

"For sale? Which house are we talking about?" asked the man in the village secretariat.

"That one," I said, pointing.

As in every other village secretariat, there were aerial photographs hanging on the walls. The short, sharp shadows of cypress trees, like a band of compass pointers, attested to a summer afternoon. A light-colored car—whose?—was parked right up next to the house. Sheets, frozen in the frame, kept their secrets as they hung on a clothesline. The camera had made a single entity of the parked car, the slow movements of the shadows, and the cloth flapping in the wind.

"Sure is," he said.

"Who do I need to talk to?"

"Right here."

"You?"

"You see someone else here?"

"It's your house?"

"No. The house belongs to the community."

"Who lived there until now? It's all boarded up."

"Nobody now. There were renters, but they took off without paying.

Six months of water bills, electricity, and rent. But we'll take care of that. That shouldn't bother you."

"And what's the price?"

"There's a committee—you ought to know that—and a treasurer. We're not some hick town. We have a lawyer. From Tel Aviv. And there'll be a selection process," the man added, "because we've got other bids. But don't worry. We can reach an agreement with you."

"Are you announcing a tender?"

"A tender? What for? Whoever wants to can make a bid, and we'll take the best offer."

I left, returning to the house, and gave it a last look-over, then started Behemoth's engine and slid down the short slope to the field. A flock of pelicans circled high overhead. A Danish bird-watcher had once told me that in autumn pelicans circled clockwise and in spring, counterclockwise. That made me think of the Double-Ys, Yariv and Yoav, and what Yordad had said about the whorls of the hair of identical twins.

There are two more things I recall about that trip. One was the feeling that the house was escorting me from behind as I gained distance. And the other, that when we rejoined the asphalt road, Behemoth turned its nose right instead of left. That was how I came to understand that I was driving to Meshulam Fried's office in Jerusalem and not Liora Mendelsohn's house in Tel Aviv.

# 3

A LONG TIME had passed since my last visit. I see Meshulam fairly often, but only at Yordad's, whom he visits regularly. An extra floor had been added to the company offices and two extra words to the sign out front: AND DAUGHTER. A security guard greeted me, phoned someone, and let me pass.

The door to Meshulam's office stood half open. I knocked and stuck my head in.

"Iraleh!" Meshulam cried as he rose to his feet. He spread his arms and came out from behind his desk specially to welcome me. "You insult me! On the door of Meshulam Fried you knock?"

He gave me a strong embrace, kissed both my cheeks, and smiled happily. "What a guest, what a surprise . . . you used to play jacks here with Tiraleh and Gershon, remember?"

"Yes."

"Ever since Gershon, I'm nothing but memories," he said as he produced his handkerchief. He wiped his eyes and asked to what he owed this visit and how he could help.

I said, "I need you for a couple of hours."

Meshulam said, "I have all the time in the world for you, Iraleh. Something good or something bad?"

I said, "Good. I found myself a house. I want you to come and see it."

"You found yourself a house?" Meshulam beamed. "I didn't know you were looking for one. Congratulations! What's it for?"

"So that I can have a place of my own," I said, quoting you.

"What does that mean, 'a place of my own'? You have a big, beautiful home in Tel Aviv. Professor Mendelsohn told me about the fancy things you got there. And what about Mrs. Liora? She know about this new house?"

"Not yet."

"You win the lottery?"

"The lottery?"

"If your wife isn't part of this and you didn't win the lottery, then where'd the money come from?"

"I've got it. Never mind from where. When will you have a little time to come have a look?"

Meshulam went to the door. "Now. Let's go."

Quick decisions startle me. "Now? It'll take some time, it's a little far—"

"Don't worry about the time. I got enough of that. Meshulam Fried isn't as rich in money as people think, but he's awful rich in time. So he decides when he's going to spend it and when he's going to save it." He smiled. "I got so much time that I'll probably die before I use it all up."

He went to the next office, gave a few instructions there, then marched down the corridor with me in tow. With a glare he repelled someone who wanted a word with him, put a calming hand on the shoulder of another man, turned to me and thundered, "That's true freedom for a person. Not money, but time."

I went out to the parking lot. For a moment Meshulam vacillated. His hands, like two independent creatures, made a little gesture of yes and no. "We'll take your car," he decided at last. "We'll make a little trip and you'll tell me on the way all the tales you sell to the tourists. Where Muhammed flew in the air and where Jesus walked on water and where the angels got Abraham's wife Sarah pregnant."

He slapped my thigh. "But first to Glick's kiosk—we'll take some samwiches for the road."

We left the city. I was planning to tell him about the Roman road we would be meeting up with soon and perhaps even stop for a short walk, during which I could tell him about the gift my mother had given me, but Meshulam had already started in on his own stories. First he pointed out buildings he had erected, then others that he had razed, and after that, hills he had fought on during the War of Independence as a member of the Palmach. "What did you think?" he said. "That everyone in the Palmach was tall and blond like your mother? Well, there were guys like me there, too." And then he got to the heart of matters, his Tiraleh. Tirzah.

"You remember, Iraleh, when you were kids, how every summer Gershon went to camp at the Weizmann Institute and she would come to the office with me? You know what a big-time contractor she is now? You know she's in charge of every one of Meshulam Fried's projects?"

"I knew she worked with you, but I didn't know she'd already tossed you off the board of directors."

Meshulam beamed. "Not me. Her husband. She threw that Yossi out and came to work with me."

He laughed. "Meshulam Fried and Daughter, Incorporated." Then he sighed. "Even if my Gershon was alive I wouldn't bring him into the business. Only her." He smiled. "Him, I'd let him go to the university. She should bring honor from money and he should bring honor from knowledge and together they're the revenge on dear Goldie's brothers and sisters and mine too, how they always looked down at me, especially when they came asking for a loan."

When he saw the look on my face, he continued talking. "You think Meshulam wasn't thinking about you and her all these years? You think Meshulam didn't know you and her is a couple made in heaven? I saw it way back when, on that day I brought my Gershon to your father. There's me, running with my half-dead kid in my arms to the door of the clinic, and Professor Mendelsohn comes out and says, 'This way, Mr. Fried, come in from here,' and he brings me in from his own private entrance, and from the corner of my eye I see you two, as identical as two drops of water and you're eyeing one another."

He fixed me with his gaze. "A woman like my Tiraleh needs a man like her, and a man like my Tiraleh needs a woman like him. And that's that. She threw her husband out and you're leaving home. Now's the time. You've got to strike while the iron's churning!"

"That's enough, Meshulam. I'm not leaving any home," I said.

"You're not? Excuse me, Iraleh, 'I found myself a house,' you said. 'A place of my own,' you said. What does that mean if not that you're leaving home?"

"Anyway, I'm not Tirzah; I only look like her from the outside. On the inside she's a mensch and I'm not."

"Well, now you're talking. But how many mensches you need in one house?"

"We dated in high school," I said. "We had our chance. But it didn't work. And it's not as bad with Liora as you think. That's what married life is like. Sometimes it's not great, but all in all it isn't bad."

Meshulam regarded me scornfully. "What, you been reading *Ladies' Home Journalism* or something? You never even said you love her. Something so simple as love, and that's what's supposed to hold people together. But you didn't even say you love her."

"Meshulam," I said, "since when did you become an expert on love?"

"Since when does it take an expert to say what I just said? It only takes someone who's not a complete fool."

"Apart from love there are a few other things that keep people together."

"So why don't you explain it to me? What are those few other things keeping you two together?" When I did not answer, he answered himself. "It's either her money or your fear, or both. That's what's keeping you together."

"Why are you so preoccupied with this?" I asked. "And what business is it of yours, anyway?"

"It's my business because I want to see you and Tiraleh together again."

I fell silent for several minutes. Suddenly, Meshulam chuckled. "You remember my dear late wife? My Goldie, the woman I loved?"

"Sure," I said. "I remember her very well."

"What do you remember about her?" The scorn had fallen from his eyes; they were pleading now.

"Her pickles," I said, swallowing the saliva that the memory of them secreted in my mouth. "And the nice smell from her hands, and her calm. My mother said she was sure that when you were at work with all those workers and trucks and machines, you must be missing your wife's calm."

"Your mother was a very smart woman," Meshulam said. "And she had a wound on her heart. But you already know about that. Otherwise, why would she pick up and leave home like that all of a sudden? But me, not only my Goldie's calm I miss, also that smell from her hands—like lemons she smelled. Other ladies have to spend a fortune on perfume but her—it came from her flesh. But all that's in heaven now. Just for that I'm going to hell, because if I get up there I'll just ruin heaven for her."

The handkerchief reappeared. Meshulam cleared his throat. "Two I got up there." He folded the handkerchief and returned it to his pocket. "Now you listen. Me and Goldie, we didn't like Tirzah's Yossi as a person and not as a husband for her. You can tell on a man right away if he's an idiot. It's the smart guys you can't always figure out right away. But with idiots, it's smeared all over their faces. Now, you know Tiraleh—just because we told her that, she went and married the guy. To spite us. But sometimes, when I'd ask my Goldie, 'What do you think, Goldie? What keeps those two together?' Listen to what she'd say, that calm, gentle woman, like you said: 'In those matters, Meshulam, it all has to do with what happens in bed.' Would you believe my calm, gentle Goldie could say such a thing?"

"I can believe anything about anyone, Meshulam."

"She had all kinds of smart things she used to say. Here's another one: 'A woman has to look good, but a man—a little bit nicer looking than a monkey is enough.'"

We swapped smiles. "It's the luck of people like us that there are women who think like that. Otherwise, what would be with us guys? We'd only get the girls from the bottom of the barrel. Believe me, Iraleh, Meshulam can tell from one look how a couple is in bed."

I chose not to react to these last observations, and Meshulam continued. "What's more, Tiraleh decides and acts. Not like you. She got up and got herself divorced. I told you that before, but you didn't even ask how or what."

"I didn't ask," I told him, "because I don't stick my nose into other people's business."

"What's that supposed to mean? That I do?"

I said nothing.

"You know what? You're right. Yeah, I stick my nose in, sure I do. If you sit on the sidelines and wait for things to happen, well, nothing's going to happen. Sometimes you have to stick your nose in. And not just your nose. Your hand, and then your other hand, and then, if the door opens just a little, you poke your shoe in, and your shoulder, and even your dick you have to stick in sometimes, and stick it proper! What the thigh doesn't see, the heart doesn't grieve over."

Meshulam checked to see that I was smiling, then carried on. "So just know this, Iraleh. Tiraleh, she's free. And she isn't Tirzah Weiss anymore, she's back to being Tirzah Fried. I paid a lot of money for that fat, stupid piece of shit to give her a divorce, but now she's earning it all back for me with interest."

"So now why don't you tell me," I dared to say. "If you know how every woman is in bed, then what about your Tirzah?"

A small cloud passed over Meshulam's brow, fluttered in his jaw muscles, then was pushed away and expelled. "Tiraleh in bed is like her papa in bed. She knows what needs to be done, she's warm, she's good. You know what? Give it a try. See how she is and show her how you are."

His lips drooped suddenly and trembled. The blue handkerchief was produced once again. "Try, Iraleh . . . try . . ." He pressed my thigh with his hand. "You won't be sorry, I promise you." His voice cracked and broke. "Try, both of you. Try. And make me a grandson. I want my Gershon back."

Meshulam, like other men among whom I do not count myself, is both tough and soft, decisive and emotional, and when such a rod strikes such a rock—all his waters go gushing forth.

"Stop the car," he moaned. "I need a good cry."

I braked. Meshulam got out of the car and leaned against the back door. I could feel his aged body—not large, but compact and strong—shaking Behemoth. Then the shaking abated and Meshulam moved away from the car a bit to stomp his feet at the side of the road in the manner of sturdy, thick people trying to calm themselves.

He folded the handkerchief and climbed back into the car. "We're lucky," he said, "that we lose some of our memory when we get old. Otherwise, we'd have an even heavier load to carry just when we don't have the strength. Enough talk now. Let's go."

# 4

WE ENTERED the village and turned right at the center of town. Five hundred feet. Three houses, two pleasant gardens and one that was dry and neglected, and here are the cypress trees that would gladden your heart, here is the single giant pine, here is the house. Thorns surrounding it. Windows boarded. Meshulam eyed it through the car window and said nothing.

"So. What do you say? How does it look to you?"

"Fine."

"You don't want to see it up close?"

"First let's eat. The smell of the samwiches is making me hungry, and I need to calm down."

I removed the food and the beer from the cooler and we sat on the stairs leading up from the sidewalk, weeds poking through the cracks just as you said there should be, and Meshulam ate and drank with great appetite, his chewing clearly that of a man deep in thought. At last he said, "What's there to check here, Iraleh? It's all clear at first glance. Look for yourself: the location is great. But the house? It doesn't have a chicken leg to stand on! You've got to knock it down and build a new one."

"I like this house. I don't want to knock it down."

"Look what it's built on: the support beams are too thin, there's rusted iron poking through the cement walls."

"How much do you think I should pay for it?"

"Are you buying it as an investment? Are you buying it because you don't have a roof over your head? It's a gift to yourself, so what does it matter how much it costs? Bargain them down a little, just to make your soul feel good, but definitely take it."

"My funds are limited."

"For this dump you've got enough. And if you need a little more, you got someone to borrow it from, thank God. Just remember, what's important in a house is what you can't change. By that I mean the location and the view. Even Rothschild, with all his money, can't arrange to have a view of the sea from a window in Jerusalem. So this house, it's got a great view, but the house itself needs to be knocked down, and if you don't believe me, get Tiraleh out here. Look, I'm calling her right now to get her to see it."

"If this place is so great," I asked him, "then why hasn't anyone bought it?"

"Because they're all stupid, like you. They come and they see the mold on the walls and the cracks and the rust and they get scared. They think about the house and the money and not the time and the place. Here, the location is good and the timing is right. Buy it—Tiraleh will knock it down and build you a new one. That's small change for her."

"No, Meshulam, I like this house. I only want to renovate it."

"I can talk to you until the cows come jumping over the moon, but you won't listen. All right, let's go inside and see what can be done."

# 5

ONCE INSIDE, Meshulam began pounding on the walls and the beams. Sometimes with his fist, sometimes open-palmed, sometimes with his fingertips.

"You hear that? Those are not good sounds. You see these cracks? They've split into littler ones and they're running up and down the walls. This house is a goner, may it rest in peace. One side's sunk further in the ground than the other."

He removed a small screwdriver from his shirt pocket, stuck it into a wall socket, and yanked it from the wall.

"Take a look at this guy," he said. "The wires are insulated with black cloth, back from the days of our forefathers. It's all going to have to be changed. Look," he said, taking hold of a faucet in the kitchen. "Watch carefully." He tugged at it and it came free of the wall, leaving behind a rusted, crumbling stump and dripping brown water.

"You see? It's not because I'm so strong, it's because everything around here is rotted. Look at the ceiling, how it's flaking, look at the walls down near the floor, how they're peeling. Over here, too, see the dampness at the bottom of the doorpost? The leak can be somewhere else and the water creeps under the tiles like sieves in the night. Evil people lived in this house. The way they took care of it, that's how much they hated each other."

"How much will it cost to replace all this?"

"As much as building a new place, and an even bigger headache."

"Still. How much?"

"Why are you always asking about money? Tomorrow morning I'll bring Tiraleh. You can talk money with her. Come on, let's head back." On our way back to Behemoth he said, "Look what's happening with this little lady over here."

Around the fig tree, small unripe fruit lay strewn about, and near the trunk there were mounds of yellowish sawdust. I glanced up into the tree and found that it was falling from holes in the bark.

"This has to be uprooted," Meshulam said. "The trunk's infested and the tree isn't giving fruit. Get it out of here before it falls on someone's head."

"I'll try and save it," I said.

"What's with you?! The house is falling down, the fig tree is disintegrating, and both of them you want to keep? Build a new place! Plant a new tree!"

After bringing Meshulam back to his office in Jerusalem, I left a message for Liora about some trip I was making up north with an Austrian television crew and returned to the house I had found for myself. I drove in silence at a constant high speed. Nothing slowed me down or stopped me; nothing diverted me from my path. All the other cars made way for me. All the intersections I passed through shone green faces at me. After getting off the main road I drove in a straight line through the fields, all the way to the house I had found for myself.

Once again I removed the planks from the boarded-up windows and climbed in through the same window. Once again I said, "Hello, house," and once again the house answered. I took off my clothes and bathed myself in the pleasant April night, the month you loved so well. It's when the first khamsin mixes with the final days of winter "like trilled keys on a piano," that's what you said: "hot and cold." I lay naked on my camping mattress, the sleeping bag rolled up for a pillow. I felt the house surround my body. The man inside it was me.

And one other feeling was inside me as well, a feeling I did not understand at its inception but now I know was the anticipation of Tirzah's arrival, the knowledge that she would come, the realization that a new chapter was opening, different and similar and old and new.

# Chapter Seven

## I

O N   T H E   W A L L  of the loft, Miriam the pigeon handler hung two placards. The title of the first read:

### TEN CHARACTERISTICS OF A GOOD PIGEON HANDLER

And below this it was written:

1. The pigeon handler is moderate in his disposition. A reckless pigeon handler frightens the pigeons.
2. The pigeon handler is loyal and responsible and carries out his tasks in an orderly and punctual fashion.
3. The pigeon handler is kindhearted and cares for each and every pigeon.
4. The pigeon handler is patient and devoted.
5. The pigeon handler is tidy and attentive to cleanliness.
6. The pigeon handler is strong-willed and maintains discipline over the pigeons.
7. The pigeon handler is sensitive in observing and discerning the character and condition of each and every pigeon.
8. The pigeon handler is industrious. There is always work to be done in the pigeon loft.
9. The pigeon handler is considerate of others.
10. The pigeon handler is adept at learning and knows all there is to know with regard to the traits, eating habits, flying exercises,

and care of the pigeon. Further, it is incumbent upon him to know how to compose short, clear pigeongrams.

On the second placard that Miriam hung the title read:

## WORK SCHEDULE IN THE PIGEON LOFT

And below this it was written:

1. Upon entering in the morning: a general overview of the pigeons and the loft.
2. First flight exercise.
3. Scraping and sifting of the floor. Addition of clean sand. Burial of waste in the pit.
4. Cleaning of troughs and drinking vessels and changing of drinking and bathing water.
5. Pigeons return—serving of a light meal.
6. Updating of loft logs.
7. Examination of each pigeon in turn.
8. Special missions: banding, crossbreeding, food testing, long-distance dispatching.
9. Late afternoon flight exercise.
10. Evening meal.
11. General overview.
12. Lights out.

"These two placards you need to learn by heart," Miriam instructed the Baby, and told him what Dr. Laufer had told her when she worked for him as a child: that the first nine characteristics of a good pigeon handler are important for all human beings, even those who do not raise pigeons, but the tenth characteristic is important only for pigeon handlers.

"I don't know how to whistle to them like you do," the Baby said. "I want you to teach me how to whistle with my fingers."

"That's not urgent," Miriam said. "There's time for that."

Several days later he watched as she tied colored ribbons to the legs of three pigeons. She summoned one of the guys from the Palmach, gave him a notepad and a pencil, and explained to him what she wanted him to do. Then she placed the pigeons in a wicker basket, shut the lid, secured the basket to her bicycle, and rode past the cowshed and the fields. The Baby ran after her for a way, but Miriam left the grounds of the kibbutz without looking back.

He returned to the loft and the guy from the Palmach standing there. "You're too close to the trap door," he told him. "The pigeons will be afraid to enter."

The Palmachnik said, "Buzz off, kid."

The Baby fell silent and moved away from him. He looked skyward and waited. After about half an hour he called to the Palmachnik. "Here they are, they're back!"

"Where? Where are they?" the Palmachnik asked, taken aback.

"There. Here. Don't you see them? They're getting closer. What are you waiting for? Raise the flag and whistle."

The Palmachnik, nonplussed by the Baby's surprising aggressiveness and his hawk eyes, raised the wrong flag. The three pigeons were startled and ascended over the loft.

"The blue flag," the Baby called out to him. Then he shouted, "Come, come, come to eat."

The pigeons landed, and the Palmachnik got confused again. He scattered a few seeds on the landing shelf instead of on the other side of the trap door. The pigeons ate a little, then flew off again.

When Miriam returned, sweating and huffing on her bicycle, the Palmachnik announced, "They all returned!" and handed the notepad to her. Miriam looked inside it and said, "You didn't write a thing!" and the Baby could not control himself and shouted, "The blue one came back first!" and "He scattered their food outside."

Miriam was furious. "They have to know they've got to come inside; otherwise you can't remove the message capsules from their legs. Now I'll have to repeat the whole thing."

The next day she tested the Baby to see whether he would manage to fill in her forms legibly and informed him that from then on he would greet the returning pigeons.

"This is very important," she told him. "It is not enough for the pigeon simply to come home. Every rock pigeon knows how to do that. We have to record how long it took her and what she does when she gets back. Does she meander outside or does she come right into the loft through the trap door?"

"So when are you going to take me with you?" the Baby asked several days later, to which Miriam replied that pigeon handling is learned one stage at a time and that now had come the time to move him up from pigeon greeter and trough cleaner to cook.

"You've got a lot to learn before you dispatch a pigeon on your own," she said, placing the notepad and the pencil in his hand.

He wrote: the pea, the lentil, and the vetch provide protein. Sorghum, rice, corn, and wheat—carbohydrates. Linseed, sesame, and sunflower seeds—fats. Miriam taught him the secret to mixing the seeds, and how important it was to sniff them in case they smelled of mold, and to smash one or two of them with a hammer. If the seed was appropriately dry it would crumble, and if it was too moist it would mash.

A hungry pigeon is more attentive, more efficient, she explained to him, and livelier and lighter for flying. That was why they were fed a small meal in the morning and only after their late afternoon flight did they receive their main meal. And don't forget: pigeons like to drink immediately after eating.

She opened the canister containing the mineral mix, which she called "gravel," in which there were crumbs of basalt, which aids the pigeon in grinding the hard seeds she eats, and powdered ferric oxide, which purifies her blood, and coal, which keeps her digestive system clean, and crushed seashells and lime for strengthening her bones and eggshells, "just like they give the laying hens in the kibbutz chicken coops." She added that "homing pigeons need stronger bones than common pigeons. Stronger and lighter."

"And," she said, "this mixture has salt in it, so you cannot give it to the pigeons before a long flight."

"So they won't get thirsty," the Baby said.

"Very good. What happens if a pigeon gets thirsty?"

"She dies on the way."

"No," Miriam laughed. "She'll descend to drink and then in the best of cases, she'll simply be waylaid a bit and in the worst of cases, some-one will catch her or eat her."

The Baby gathered his courage and asked what were the tiny, smooth, dark seeds that she only rarely gave to the returning pigeons, and she told him they were hashish seeds, which the pigeons were wild about. A few were added to their daily meals, but a little more than that became a special treat, a prize.

"And twice a week," she said, "we feed them from our hands." This, she explained, is time-consuming but pleasant and useful, a chance to check on the pigeons and deepen their affection and affability. Animals fear human eyes, the scent of their bodies, the cunning of their fingers. The way to overcome all these is by teaching them to eat from a human hand. That way they grow accustomed and draw near and become loyal friends.

"The pigeon is not intelligent or sensitive or complex, like a dog or horse," she said, "and in spite of what people say about her and how she looks, she has a difficult character. But even she understands loyalty and friendship. You don't need to write that down. With some things it's enough to hear them and remember."

# 2

"You're terrific," she told him a few days later. "One day you'll be a true *duvejeck*."

"What's a *duvejeck*?" the Baby asked, concerned.

"When you're a *duvejeck* you'll know."

"So when are you going to take me to send off the pigeons?"

"Not 'send off'! Dispatch! Before that you have to learn one very important thing: how to catch and hold a pigeon in your hand."

Never catch it in midair, she taught him, and never outside the loft; only after the pigeon has landed and entered. The hands should be visible to the pigeon as they approach her, nothing stealthy and not too fast or hesitant or slow. And always from above, so that if she takes off you can catch her. And lastly, there is the catching itself: palms hold the wings, fingers point downward and grasp the feet. "Gently. Everything gently. Their bodies are not simple like ours; theirs are complex and delicate, built to fly.

"And never look them in the eye!" she said, repeating that to animals, eye contact is an act of aggression. "Pigeons' eyes look sideways, while ours look forward. So to them our gaze seems like that of a predatory animal or a bird of prey."

The Baby's hands drew near a pigeon, lowered to her, grasped her, and felt the quick agitation of her heart. His own throbbed in response. "Not too tight," she said, and he grew anxious. "Very nice," she said, and joy coursed through his body. "Now take hold of another one—they're very different one from the other," she instructed, and he practiced and learned and became familiar with them, cautiously, gently, and with increasing confidence.

Several days later Miriam told him to get hold of a bicycle so that he could accompany her on one of her outings. He was short of stature and had not as yet managed to ride a "comrades" bicycle, so he asked to borrow his aunt's "comradettes" bicycle instead.

His aunt hesitated. "That bicycle belongs to the cowshed," she said.

"Please, Mother, please," the Baby said. And when she heard that "Mother" and saw the hope and the desolation skittering across his brow, she consented, on one condition: that he would not ride too much and that he would practice before going off with "the young woman from the pigeon loft."

He tried and fell, tried again, practiced until he gained his balance. Bruised and scraped, he rushed to the loft and was grateful when Miriam asked no questions, just instructed him to hurry and wash his wounds with soap and water. Then she smeared veterinary ointment on them and told him which three pigeons to catch.

They pedaled first on a dirt lane that ran parallel to the road, she effortlessly, he by pressing his full weight and breathing heavily but forgetful of his wounds and his fear and enjoying the whisper of crunching tires and his excitement at what was about to happen. Near a certain tall electricity pole they turned down a row of cypress trees and cycled toward the fields, bars of light and shadow hitting their eyes, the scent of blooming acacia trees caressing and yellowing their noses.

Several miles on, near the pump house, Miriam stopped, leaned her bicycle against the trunk of a cypress tree, and took the pigeon with a red ribbon on her leg from the basket.

"Take the notepad and the pencil," she said, "so you can write down the color of the ribbon and the date and the hour and the place, each in the proper order."

He wrote in round, childish letters, proud and very anxious.

"First, record the numbers and letters written on her band. Very nice. And where it says PLACE write PUMP HOUSE, and where it says WEATHER write CLEAR, TEMP. 24°C, LIGHT EASTERLY WIND, and where it says TIME write 13:45. That's a quarter to two. Did you write it all down? Did you understand it all? Now watch carefully."

He watched her hands as she dispatched the pigeon forward and upward, her body taut, her breasts suddenly lifting under her gray work shirt, a smile rising on her lips without her thinking about it. The dispatch was so smooth that the pigeon looked like a smile that had detached itself from her body and ascended, and the sight was so lovely and attractive that the Baby did not know why he was ashamed of his excitement.

In the same way, Miriam dispatched the pigeon with the yellow ribbon, and this caused the Baby to worry. Would she let him have the third pigeon or would she dispatch her herself? He filled in the third form and lifted his eyes to her, and Miriam said, "It's your turn."

He took hold of the pigeon and, in spite of what he had learned, briefly stared straight into her eyes like a bird of prey.

"Think about what you are doing," Miriam told him. "This is your first pigeon; don't forget that. Don't just release her, and don't throw her. Think that you're handing her to the heavens. Gently."

Even before he had opened his hands as wide as they would go he felt that his movements were not as successful as hers. But the pigeon had already spread her wings, and his eyes escorted her as she lifted off and his body wished to rise along with her. Her wings were beating, first turning a bluish-gray, then—in an immense, clear sky—blackening and shrinking. The Baby watched her, unaware that this would be the last scene he would witness nine years later as he lay bleeding on his back in the ruined gardener's shed of a monastery, his body riddled with holes and broken and slit open, a pigeon lifting off above him carrying his final wish.

"You're very good," Miriam said. She patted his head with a cool hand, first in small, joyful circular motions, then with two fingers that slipped down to the sides of his neck and delighted his back.

# 3

SEVERAL WEEKS LATER Miriam asked the Baby to ask his aunt to ask the milk-truck driver if he would take a few pigeons for more distant dispatches. First from near the Sea of Galilee, then from Afula and Haifa. Then she told him she knew his uncle traveled to kibbutz movement meetings in Tel Aviv on occasion, and she wanted him to ask the uncle to take three pigeons with him for dispatch from there.

"How will I take them?" the uncle asked.

"There's a special pigeon basket," the Baby answered. "It's made of wicker and it has a handle and a lid."

"And what if they start quarreling on the way, or if they make a mess?"

Miriam did not give up. She went with the Baby to the uncle and said, "The pigeons will not fight. They will make a little mess but nothing terrible. The basket is lined with newspapers."

"And where would I release them?" the uncle grumbled. "Just anywhere? In the middle of the street? Would I just stand there and open the basket?"

"Do you remember Dr. Laufer, who saved your wife's sick calf? I'm sure you'd be happy to do him a favor in return. Take the pigeons to him. You'll find him at our central pigeon loft, in the zoo," Miriam said. "He'll dispatch them and he'll fill in the forms and maybe he'll even give you a few pigeons of his own for us to dispatch from here. That's important. We don't have so many opportunities to dispatch pigeons from great distances."

The uncle looked agitated. His body broadcast his refusal. But then the Baby, to whom the words "central pigeon loft" seemed as magical and important as palaces and temples, called out to his uncle, "I'll come with you. I'll take care of the basket and I'll watch over the pigeons. All you have to do is bring me to the central pigeon loft in the zoo."

"That's a good idea," Miriam said, leaning over him. "I trust you."

"What about afterward?" the uncle said, preoccupied with his own concerns. "Are you going to tag along after me the whole day and come with me to my meetings?"

"You can leave him at the zoo," Miriam said. "Dr. Laufer will find things for him to do. The central loft is large, and there is always work to be done."

At three o'clock in the morning the uncle woke the Baby and led him with his eyes shut and his hands clutching the pigeon basket to the milk truck. The trip deepened his sleep but here and there he snapped awake, and each time he opened his eyes he took in a different landscape, so that the journey came to seem like an interrupted series of dreams. In Haifa they proceeded to the central bus station. The uncle handed him a sandwich from his satchel and bought him a tart drink from an Arab vendor, and when the bus pulled away from the station and headed southward down the coast he told him that it was not enough to look out the window; he should breathe deeply and smell what he was looking at as well, since smells are what we remember best.

The bus stopped at many stations, taking in and discharging passengers. The sea, which was at first nearby and blue and salty-smelling, drew farther away and turned greener. Its scent changed, too: first it weakened, then strengthened; then it took on the smell of an orchard. The pigeons were silent in their basket and the Baby fell asleep again, awakening only when the uncle nudged him and told him to open his eyes and look around. "We're here. This is your first time in Tel Aviv. Look, here's the central bus station."

The Baby was impressed. "There's a central pigeon loft *and* a central bus station here?" he asked.

This made the uncle laugh. "There's a Central Committee for Settlement of the Land of Israel and a Central Department Store for Agricultural Supplies here, too. That's the way it is in Tel Aviv."

From the central bus station the two walked down a scalding, humid street and caught another bus. Again the uncle poked him to look around, and he pointed out shops and cars and men wearing panama hats—things you see in the city but not on the kibbutz—but the Baby was preoccupied with only one thing, and when they were in the vicinity of the zoo and could hear the sounds of the animals and smell their smells, he told the uncle that now he must dispatch the pigeons.

"But Miriam said that Dr. Laufer would dispatch them," the uncle said.

"She trusts me," the Baby said. "And it's the only reason I came all the way here. You'll see, Father. The pigeons will return safely and Miriam will even say that I did a good job dispatching them."

He gave a few seeds to the pigeons—a light meal, nothing to weigh them down but enough to satiate them a bit so that they would not stop to eat on the way—and then he ladled some water into a small bowl and handed the forms to be filled in to his uncle. "Here, write the date," the Baby instructed, and he dictated: "Place of dispatch: gate of Tel Aviv zoo." The uncle recorded the time of day and the weather as well: hot and humid and still and clear. Miriam had entered the numbers on the pigeons' bands ahead of time.

The Baby copied the information onto a slip of paper he would keep with him, inserted the forms into the message capsules, and attached them to the pigeons' legs. He lifted his hands in the air and dispatched them one after the other, first the light-colored one and then, several minutes later, the bluish-gray ones. The uncle watched him. While his lips smiled, his heart—this is the way he would remember it in the future—constricted. He was a kind and loving uncle and he would never forget this moment and would recount it tearfully to all who came to comfort him nine years later, at his nephew's death. As for the Baby, he was sorry that Miriam was not there to see how smooth and right his movements had been and he said, "Now let's go into the zoo and find the central pigeon loft."

However, Dr. Laufer beat them to it. He emerged from the entrance, tall and slightly stooped in his rubber boots, his nose long and his limbs flapping, his hair red and his freckles overflowing, and behind him was a very fat man wearing a cap with a visor.

"Here he is," the Baby whispered. "That's the Dr. Laufer who built the pigeon loft on our kibbutz."

"Well, look who is here!" exclaimed the veterinarian. "The young man sent to us by Miriam, and his uncle. Only the pigeons are not with us."

Crestfallen, the Baby said nothing.

"'And there was no voice, nor any that answered,'" Dr. Laufer said, quoting Scriptures and Bialik, "'and a pigeon with a boy, still knocking at the gate'! You dispatched the pigeons yourself, didn't you? We saw them rising in the air two minutes ago."

"I filled in all the details, too," the Baby boasted, showing the veterinarian the copy he had retained.

Dr. Laufer perused the slip of paper. "Very nice. But we were hoping to add a little pigeongram of our own to Miriam, only now the pigeons have taken off and there is nothing we can do about it."

"She didn't tell me," the Baby said, disconcerted.

"You, uncle-comrade," the veterinarian said, "you are welcome to continue on your way now. We will keep him gainfully employed until your return."

The uncle left and Dr. Laufer said to the fat man, "You see this fine young fellow? He's our guest. Anytime he shows up here, please let him in." And to the Baby he said, "Come!"

The zoo spread out before the Baby's eyes like some enchanted land of first sights. Near the entrance stood several huge turtles, the eye unable to believe they truly existed, in spite of—or perhaps because of—their enormous size. Past the turtle pens were the monkeys, which the Baby suddenly understood were the creatures that visited his nightmares and which he had been able to forget, until now, upon waking. There were a few cages containing smaller animals—cruel and cunning in appearance, the likes of which he had glimpsed more than once in the tangled reeds that grow by the Jordan River, not far from his kibbutz— and a pool for pelicans and all kinds of ducks, all of which were also familiar from the Jordan Valley. Here, however, there was a black bear and a lion and two lionesses, and I amuse myself by wondering whether these were the very same Tamar and Dolly and Hero that I saw years later, when my mother brought me to the very same zoo. There was a leopard, too—Teddy the Great Leopard—which had been hunted in the Galilee. "Would you believe it, Yair? A leopard right here in Israel! Found near the town of Safed . . ."

But the Baby wanted more than anything to reach the central pigeon loft, for it was the central pigeon loft about which he could not stop pondering and wondering. From so much pondering and wondering he imagined it to look like one of the large marble palaces from the fairy tales his uncle would tell him, and like the pictures in the French picture book, filled with hundreds of glittering blue pigeons and shiny white pigeons pecking at golden grains in alabaster troughs and drinking water from ivory basins and taking their naps on beds made of ebony embroidered pillows, with the finest linen beneath their heads.

However, when they reached the central pigeon loft he saw that it was a completely ordinary loft, with the windows and the screens and the pigeon dung and the landing shelves and the trap doors, just a lot larger than the kibbutz pigeon loft, and it had separate compartments for pigeons from other lofts and many laying compartments because here, Dr. Laufer told him, "At the central pigeon loft, we also lay eggs and we raise most of the chicks that are sent out to new lofts around the country."

On the wall of the central loft he saw the same two placards that hung in his own loft—the characteristics of a good pigeon handler and the work schedule in the pigeon loft—and then there appeared in the central loft a girl, a serious girl with fair and curly hair who was older than the Baby by half a year and taller than he by half a head.

Dr. Laufer introduced them to each other. "Just as you are the youngest boy working for us as a pigeon handler," he told the Baby, "so is she the youngest girl. She is very familiar with our work in the loft, and she will tell you what to do."

The Baby glanced at her and felt he would like to extend his stay by many days, so that on every one of those days the girl could tell him what to do, and he was already imagining himself leaving and returning to her, not just there and then but from every time and every place. Because he wished to make a good impression on her, he said, "I was sent all the way from the Jordan Valley specially to dispatch pigeons from here."

"You shouldn't talk about that—it's a secret," the Girl said.

The Baby was perplexed. "I thought I was allowed to tell you."

"It's a secret pigeon loft of the Haganah," the Girl said. "You're not allowed to tell anyone anything."

"So why did you tell me just now?"

They both blushed. "There is no need to argue," Dr. Laufer said. "Among ourselves we can talk freely. It is only forbidden with strangers."

The Baby waited a moment, then asked, "What time do you take them out for their first flight?"

The Girl said, "Just after sunrise. I have to get up really early to make it here in time; then I go straight to school from here."

The Baby said, "I have to get up before sunrise to go to work, because our school is far from the kibbutz. How long do you keep them out for?"

"That depends," said the Girl. "The older ones fly farther away, but the younger ones are frightened."

"Do they let you catch the birds and hold them in your hand already?"

"Sure, for a long time. I even take baskets of pigeons for dispatch on my own. Two days ago from the horse paddock and sometimes from the Yarkon River, too."

"I'm allowed to catch and dispatch, too," the Baby boasted. "And today I dispatched from here all the way to the kibbutz. But sometimes I can't help myself and I look them in the eyes."

"What's the name of the guy who handles the pigeons on your kibbutz?"

"She's a girl, and I don't know if I'm allowed to tell you that, because maybe that's a secret, too."

"I can ask Dr. Laufer," the Girl said. "All the pigeon handlers and all the pigeons in the whole country came from here."

"What do you want me to help you with?" the Baby asked.

"What do you know how to do?"

"Everything. Except whistling with my fingers."

She burst out laughing, then grew serious. "I can't let you touch our pigeons because maybe your loft isn't clean and you've brought diseases. But you can clean up the area."

"And what are you going to do?"

"I'll feed the chicks that are weaning."

The Baby was forced to admit that Miriam had not yet entrusted him with such a delicate job, and the Girl passed victorious into a neighboring compartment where the more mature chicks were housed, the ones deemed ready to be weaned from the "pigeon milk" fed to them by their parents.

The Baby cleaned troughs, his eyes all the while on the Girl through the screen. She mixed seeds that had been left to soften in water for several hours, sprinkled a bit of powdered seashell and ground minerals, then sat down with a chick in her lap. With her left hand she opened its beak, and with a tiny, narrow spoon she placed several seeds inside. She repeated this procedure a number of times, until the baby pigeon's craw was full, and then she added a small amount of water to the spoon and fed it to the chick.

"It's not complicated," Dr. Laufer said behind the Baby's back, "but it is the type of job best left to the regular caregivers and not guests. Don't worry, though—there will be chicks at your loft, too, and you will learn how to do this soon enough."

# 4

JUST BEFORE DUSK the uncle returned to the zoo, peered at the Baby working with a tall, curly-haired girl, and felt a certain something strange: the flock of words that soar about at all times in people's minds, without any order or discipline, suddenly arranged itself in his head into the structure of a sentence. And that sentence whispered itself to him: that in the future these two would be bound in love. Just like that.

He called to the Baby, who turned his glowing, happy face toward him and whispered, so as not to upset the pigeons, "Just a minute, Father. I'm almost finished."

The uncle asked Dr. Laufer if his young guest had not been a nuisance, and the veterinarian said, "On the contrary! He helped us and made himself very useful. You are always welcome to send him to us for a few days. We ladies sometimes need assistance, and he is a professional and eager worker."

The uncle said, "We wouldn't wish to impose" and then "Where would he sleep?" to which the Baby was quick to respond. "I'll be fine," he said, and Dr. Laufer added, "There is space in the monkey cages."

Then he laughed that guttural laugh of his that commanded the attention of his listeners. *Haw haw haw haw!* The Girl suddenly whispered in the Baby's ear. "That's the way *yekkes* laugh. Just so you know."

The warm air from her mouth fluttered at the edge of his ear. Don't stop, don't move away, he called to her in his heart. Stay. And the Girl murmured softly: "That's how my father laughs. It's how *yekkes* announce that what they just said was funny."

"Thank you very much," the uncle said, while the Baby—still woozy from being so near her—prayed that not only Dr. Laufer but the Girl herself would invite him to visit again. She, however, regarded him and said nothing. A reddish tint descended from her brow to her cheeks and the Baby found this mix of hues beautiful—pink and blue and gold: her skin, her eyes, her hair.

"Before you leave, there is just one more small matter to arrange," Dr. Laufer said.

He wrote something on a slip of paper, rolled it up, and inserted it into a narrow cardboard tube, then said to the Baby, "Your hand, please."

The Baby held out his arm. While he tied the tube to the Baby's chubby hand with a thin strip of cloth, the veterinarian chanted to himself an ancient ditty: "'Dispatch a herald dove / And if she recounteth nothing / To her wings a tiny missive do append and place it as a frontlet / Upon your arm, affixed.'"

"Too tight?" he asked.

"No."

"Wriggle your hand a bit. Very good. Now straighten and bend it."

The Baby did as he was told and the veterinarian said, "That's fine. Now you can fly. *Haw haw haw haw!* And what will you do when you reach the loft?"

"I'll give this to Miriam."

"Don't give it to her! Simply enter like this," said the veterinarian as he spread his long arms, "with the letter on your hand. Not too quickly, though, all right? Don't frighten the other birds."

"And then what?"

"Just like every time a pigeon returns to the loft: Miriam will retrieve the letter and give you something good to eat," said Dr. Laufer, and, turning to the uncle, he asked if he could send a few Tel Aviv pigeons back to the kibbutz with him so that Miriam might dispatch them to the zoo.

"I'll dispatch them!" cried the Baby.

This time the uncle agreed willingly, and Dr. Laufer placed three pigeons in the wicker basket the Baby had brought with him, along with a sack of message capsules and ribbons and bands and forms to be given to Miriam.

The sun set. The zoo filled with noises. The Baby understood that these were the shrieks and roars and growls that Miriam had told him about, and the Girl, who escorted them to the entrance of the zoo, smiled at him and said, "I really love this time of day."

The Baby and his uncle parted from her and walked to the central bus station. "That was a very nice girl," the uncle said to the Baby.

The Baby wondered whether he had taken his leave of her properly and whether she had understood that he wished to meet her again, and the uncle said, "Do you know what you can do? Write a little something to her and send it with one of the pigeons that Dr. Laufer gave us for dispatching from the kibbutz. Women love to receive letters, and getting one by way of a pigeon must be very nice indeed."

# 5

MIRIAM HAD ALREADY gathered the pigeons in from their morning flight and had fed them by the time the Baby appeared, his hands waving and his feet raising dust.

She smiled; it seemed she was not unfamiliar with this game. She served him a few shelled sunflower seeds and embraced him warmly from behind and said, "And this is for me, right?" as she removed the cardboard tube from his hand.

"Did the pigeons come back?" the Baby asked.

"The two blue ones returned," Miriam said. "The younger blue one took an hour and a half, very good time. The other blue one took an hour and forty-two minutes."

"And how long did the light-colored one take?"

"She hasn't returned."

The Baby felt disheartened and guilty. Perhaps he should have dispatched her along with the other two and not before them?

"You did an excellent job dispatching them," Miriam said. "Maybe she'll show up in the next few hours."

But the Baby was not appeased. Images of talons piercing and bullets whizzing and feathers flying passed in front of his eyes. He expressed his sorrow to Miriam again, and she said that if this had been a veteran pigeon that had proven herself there would be something to be sorry about, but since this was a young pigeon that had failed to return from her first serious dispatch, this was a sign that she would not have made a good homing pigeon and it was better this way.

And then the uncle appeared, carrying the pigeons that Dr. Laufer had sent them. Miriam transferred them from the wicker basket to a spacious box, served them seeds and water, and said, "We'll dispatch them tomorrow morning, after they've rested from their travels."

The next morning the Baby recorded the details of the dispatch on the appropriate forms. He gave one copy to Miriam to keep and inserted the others into the pigeons' message capsules. Then he and Miriam added two more small messages in separate quills. Miriam had written something to Dr. Laufer, and the Baby had written to the Girl: "I want you to take a pigeon of mine and I want to take a pigeon of yours."

# Chapter Eight

## I

A T SIX O'CLOCK in the morning I was awakened by a loud noise. An old tractor was circling the house, a mower in tow. It lifted and lowered, went round and round mowing the thorns and weeds with great fanfare. I went outside. The tractor operator cut the engine and removed his earmuffs.

"You the owner?" he asked.

"Not yet. And who are you?"

"Me? I'm the guy they hired to clean up the weeds around here."

"Who hired you?"

"Your contractor," the man said, chuckling. "Your contractor's a woman, did you know that?"

I informed him that indeed I was aware of the fact. He returned to his work and I followed after him like a stork following a plowman, my eyes lowered to the damp ground, observing the lizards and insects and centipedes fleeing their ruined home. Even the large skink emerged suddenly, along with two thin and frightened snakes, and scorpions too, their stingers raised in fear and to threaten. There were all sorts of archaeological findings as well, proof and testimony to earlier life: a broken kitchen knife, a doll missing a leg, a faded pair of shoes—the left one a brown work boot, the right a white baby shoe.

The tractor operator finished mowing, lit a cigarette, and remained standing in the yard.

"What are you waiting for?" I asked him.

"My money. She said she'd be showing up here soon."

And that is how I was informed by an anonymous tractor operator that I was about to reencounter the love of my youth. I thought to fetch my shaving and showering equipment from Behemoth, but it was too late: a white pickup truck with the MESHULAM FRIED AND DAUGH-TER, INC. logo in green pulled up, the low, early morning sun silhouetting two images inside it. Meshulam Fried stepped out from behind the wheel and his daughter, inc., from the passenger side. Meshulam let her pass in front of him. Tirzah is short of stature, just like me, but her legs are long and her body erect. Like me and like her, her father, too, knew the charm of her gait.

I tented one hand over my eyes and glanced at her, a cut-out shadow against the low sun. What would I do when her face came into view? What would I call her? Tiraleh? Tirzah? And what would be my first words? "Hello, how's it going?"

And Tiraleh, Tirzah—my love in the distant past and luvey in the near future—took a few steps forward and stopped. I knew that while the sun was darkening her face and making its features disappear, it was lighting up my own and exposing it.

"Good morning," she said.

"Good morning," I said, pouncing on the opportunity. How had I not thought of such a simple opening?

"Here we are again, Iraleh. I knew we'd meet up sooner or later."

I walked toward her and leaned sideways, her face coming into view all at once. Here she was. Her lips were only slightly thinner, her hair shot through with gray. Her eyes had remained yellow-green, a few small lines gathered at their corners: Which of you were etched by time? Which by laughter?

Meshulam moved away, toured the area that had been mowed. Tirzah extended both hands and I took hold of them. We drew our faces close to one another to kiss each cheek, and like former lovers we did not smack the air with our lips but, rather, we allowed ourselves to plant them firmly on the other's cheeks, near the corner of the mouth.

"I'm glad you came," I said.

"Me too," she said, smiling. "Congratulations on the house, and even more on the decision. Show it to me and tell me what you want to do with it."

"I'm sorry," I said, slightly embarrassed.

"What for? The place is nice."

"Not about the house. About us. About all the time that's passed."

"There's nothing to be sorry about. I guess that's the way things were meant to happen." She called to her father: "Meshulam, stop messing with the guy and give him his money."

Meshulam paid the tractor operator but the man remained in the yard, watching what unfolded. Tirzah and I entered the house. "Show it to me," she said. "Explain to me what feels right about it."

"Me," I answered suddenly, surprised at the existence and truth of my diagnosis. "What feels right about this house is me."

Tirzah laughed loudly. The mummified brothers of her laughter awakened in my memory, stretched, and responded with joy. The air filled with hope and excitement. She looked out all the windows and said, "You did a great job with the view." She turned her attention back to me and asked, "So what do you want to do here? Renovate or build from scratch?"

"Renovate."

"Very good."

"But your father already managed to frighten me. He said this place will fall on my head, that it needs to be bulldozed and rebuilt."

She laughed. "Did he only say that or did he give you the whole performance? Did he yank faucets out? Did he pound on things? Did he listen to the walls and interpret what they were telling him?"

"Yes," I said, happy, "he gave me the whole performance. He yanked and he pounded and he listened to the walls."

"Meshulam likes to make an impression on people. And he likes things to be new, right up from the foundations. Who does the house belong to?"

"The village."

"So first of all, buy it from them. It's a good place."

"Your father said so, too."

She turned her face to mine and drew near. "Of course he did. He wants to bring us together again, and I wouldn't be surprised if he's already told you that, too."

"He has."

"You can't take that away from the guy: with Meshulam, his mouth and his heart are one and the same."

Tirzah did not pull pipes from the walls or pound on them. Instead, she tapped my head lightly, mockingly, with the tips of her fingers. People and images jumped from the furrow she had opened in my skull.

"We're still alike," she said, "and we're growing old in the same way. Same hair that will never thin out, same first gray hairs, same asymmetrical laugh lines by our mouths. But my deeper one is on the right side and yours is on the left."

She tapped my belly, too. "And I don't have this little spare tire. Punch me, see how hard my stomach is."

I did not punch her. I prodded her stomach with the open palm of my hand.

"What's this touchy-feely stuff?" Her eyes were laughing. "Hit me."

I made a fist and punched her stomach lightly.

"Harder!" And when I did not respond she said, "I am willing to take on this renovation, but on the condition that I work directly with you. If you bring in an architect or your wife shows up with all kinds of ideas or you sic an interior detonator on me, it's good-bye. Your contractor will leave."

"Okay," I said.

"Because we're not building here, we're just doing a refitting. We'll take it in a little here and let it out a little there, we'll shorten here and lengthen a few stitches there. That's why you don't need a fashion designer; a tailor who knows his stuff is enough."

From the street came the sound of shouting. "What is this? What are you people doing here?" Two men I did not recognize appeared. "Who are you?" they demanded.

"Meshulam," Tirzah called from the window, "will you please see what they want?"

Meshulam walked over to the two and said, "Good morning. And who might you be?"

"We're members of the village secretariat."

"Pleased to meet you. We're the buyers."

"What buyers? Who's buying?"

"This house is for sale, right?" Meshulam pointed at me. "Well, that's the buyer."

"But you can't just start working on the place. You haven't even bought it yet!"

"We're just giving all the thorns a little haircut. We wanted to see what the walls of this place look like, not just the roof. Anyway, it's at our expense—we won't take it off the price. So, good-bye now. Please let us look around in peace and decide."

"Come, Iraleh, let's continue," Tirzah said. "Tell me what you want to do."

"I want the outside walls to stay as they are," I said hastily, almost as if reciting, "and the entrance to stay where it is. I want bigger windows for the view. And mostly I want peace and quiet. No leaks from the roof, no clogs in the drains, no cracks in the walls, faucets that actually open and close. Everything should be strong and tight and working properly."

"That's all? I thought you'd ask for something special. A skylight, maybe? A bidet in the living room?"

"And I want shade and wind where I need them and sunlight when I want it and lots of view should come into the house."

"That sounds better. I suggest that here, instead of a large window, we knock down the whole wall and build you a deck."

"Tiraleh," Meshulam said, "before you start building him decks, are you willing to listen to what a professional has to say? Get rid of this wreck of a house and build him a beautiful new home."

"First of all I want to hear him say he's buying the place, that he's serious," Tirzah said.

"I'm buying it."

"Good job. I'll set up an appointment for you with our lawyer. He can represent you in your dealings with the village and the Israel Lands Authority and anybody else. I'll send an engineer out here to have a look at the foundations and the walls."

"To knock a place down you need a bulldozer, not an engineer," Meshulam said. "I want a new house built here."

"What's this 'I want' stuff, Meshulam?" Tirzah said. "You can want in your own house, not here!"

Meshulam sighed. "You're going to have to replace everything for him. You understand? You can't leave any of the old stuff here. Floor tiles—new; roof tiles—new; windows, doors, solar heater—all new. Get rid of the wiring and the plumbing, put new pipes and wires in. Faucets too, and central fuses and electrical outlets, and everything will need to be scraped down to the cement. Don't let him skimp here."

We went out to the backyard and moved away from the house. The freshly mowed lawn exposed the ground and brought an antique charm back to the house, even a hint of joy and a smile. "Here," Tirzah said, "this area between the carob trees, where the tractor can't reach, should be cleaned out."

She walked in among the trees, raising her knees high above the thicket and trampling weeds with her work boots. "This is just a camp for nettles and snakes, and a real fire hazard. We'll clean here, fix things up a bit, trim the carob trees, and then we'll have a relaxing little haven here."

"You asked me before if there was something special I wanted . . ." I said, feeling my face burn.

"Like what?"

"I want a shower out here, in addition to the one in the house."

"No problem, Iraleh; an outdoor shower is a wonderful thing and very easy to build."

"Something simple: a pipe with a showerhead for the head and a few tiles for the feet and a screen to serve as a shoulder-height wall. That way nobody will be able to see my butt but I'll be able to see the view."

Our gazes locked suddenly, each of us understanding what the other remembered. Me, her, Gershon, spraying water on one another in the garden of the Fried home. Meshulam and his Goldie had gone to visit relatives. Goldie had said, "I left food for you in the kitchen." Meshulam had said, "Behave yourselves, children." The three of us stripping, touching, probing. Our "peepots" and hers, so different and yet so similar. Touching and probing, touching and probing: us boys— her; she and he—me; she and I—him. Holding tight, squeezing, discovering, pressing close, breathing.

"We can build it over here," Tirzah said, "and the water will drain off to the lemon tree. That'll make it happy. Are you still here?" she asked the tractor operator, who had left his equipment behind and trailed after us, keeping at a distance of hope and fear. "Take some money and bring us something to eat from the grocer's. Bread, cottage cheese, anchovies, a few vegetables."

The tractor operator returned a few minutes later, handed her a receipt and change, and announced, "There were no anchovies!"

Tirzah took a Styrofoam cooler filled with cold water from the back of the pickup truck, along with a few plastic cups and plates. I brought the camping stove and the coffeepot from Behemoth. We prepared the first meal in the yard of my new home.

"What are you standing there for?" Meshulam said to the tractor operator. "Come join us."

Tirzah said, "Our engineer will be free in a few days, and then it will take him another couple of days to prepare the plans and quantities."

"Okay," I said. "I'm in no rush."

"And I think it would be nice if you would take a few pictures of the house and show them to your mother."

# 2

THE HOME I have been living in for twenty years, in the neighborhood known as Workers' Lodgings No. 7, between Spinoza and Reines streets in Tel Aviv, belongs to my wife, was created in her image, and is her ally. Once the house was actually two adjacent flats on the same floor, but when Liora found them and purchased them and connected them in a deal that was particularly complicated and successful—and highly enjoyable, according to her—they became one large apartment.

The place obeyed her and gave in to her and allowed itself to be connected and changed, to have appendages added and tissues removed, and in no time it forgot the modest families of workers who'd lived in it once upon a time and became the home of a rich and beautiful woman from the state of New York. Liora installed sanitary fixtures and electrical appliances that had been flown in from America, showers with jet sprays hidden in the walls, silent switches, double glazing. She knocked down and erected, she pried open and sealed, and quickly the house left behind its former life and was reinvented in the image of its mistress. The few things it contained that I liked disappeared: the old cupboards in a niche in the wall were removed and the dish-drying cabinet with the shuttered doors and the wooden slats at the bottom was banished from its place above the sink, just like its netted brother, the vegetable cabinet, was uprooted from the patio. The door between the bedroom and the living room vanished, replaced with bricks and plastered over as though it had never existed. Electric jalousies were brought in to take over for the old wooden blinds.

The doors to both bathrooms, which had nice peepholes that stirred wonder and provoked conjectures, were exchanged for new ones. But when Liora served demolition papers for the sinks that lay behind them, I was spurred into action: "Not those!" I said, and I did not give in. They were spacious sinks, with short, thick pedestals and wide edges, suited to me in shape and character.

"I don't care if they are old and plain!" I cried in a storm of emotion that astonished even me. "Please, not them too!" And because anyway Liora did not unite the bathrooms of the two apartments, as if she knew that one day one would become hers and the other mine, she said, "I had no idea they were so important to you," and she left one intact. That is how I came to have my own bathroom, and in the morning, when I shave with a demarcating string she gave me to tie around my neck—"You need to establish a boundary between your beard and your fur"—I feel that in the alien and hostile place in which I live, deep in enemy territory, if you will, I have an ally. It is only a sink, but when I lay my shaving gear and my soap on it—I like plain soaps, Liora likes them perfumed—it turns into my own private space.

Combining the two flats created seven rooms, and when I wondered aloud what they were for—after all, we have no children and apparently never will, and the few guests that visit us do not tend to sleep over—she reminded me that in her family's home in America there are eight large rooms and two large garages for storage and one large basement, even though only she and Emmanuel grew up there.

I said, "Liora, this is not America and we have no children," to which she responded in anger: Was I blaming her? Were only parents of children permitted to enjoy a spacious apartment with many rooms? Was I trying to hurt her? Was that what I thought of her "after those two miscarriages"?

"There are some people who apportion the rooms of a house according to their functions, or the people who occupy them," she said. "I apportion them according to need and time. Just like we change, so will they. But I don't expect you to understand any of this."

And that is how I found myself in a house that is a sworn and hostile enemy, a house that appears to contain bedrooms and offices and guest rooms but that, in fact, has morning rooms and evening rooms, rooms for solitude, rooms for fun and rooms for splitting up, rooms for arguing and rooms for making up. And between them, small, protean no-man's-lands, border control, and roadblocks.

There are rooms, too, for wandering when Liora is not around, rooms that carry the scent of the changing states of her mood, for investigating the deep gashes made by her fingernails in doors. In spite of her tall, slim figure, she often reminds me of a male bear strolling through the woods of her home, leaving proof of her size on the doorpost-trunks and of her power in her footprints, and on the mirrors she etches testimonies to her beauty.

I, too, have left signs behind. The rooms have become camera obscuras on whose walls are hung a permanent exhibition of my image: shrunken, upside down. I have been documented. I have been photographed. I have been put in storage. I have been copied a thousand times. In copious pictures of arguments, in rare scents of sex, in exten-

sive recordings of silence. My shouts have been absorbed in the walls;
her whispers ricochet.

# 3

WORKERS' LODGINGS NO. 7 is a small and pleasant neighborhood,
but the house itself stirs up a certain malaise in me. At first it seemed as
though someone else were living there with us, just on the other side of
the wall or inside a closet. Later it became a physical malaise: in summer, the walls emit heat, which Liora does not feel, and in winter the
cold wafts off them, which Liora refuses to admit. In the end, my apprehension is palpable, the kind I get from eating food that is not fresh:
undeniable pressure on the diaphragm when I enter the house and
unmistakable relief when I leave it.

Even my morning walk to the local grocer expands my lungs and
straightens my posture. I leave home, place the remains of yesterday's
bread on the fence, and go to buy myself a fresh loaf of rye and day-old
salted white cheese. If you want, my life can be divided not only by
women and places but by four different grocers: these days it's the village grocer, recently it was Shai's grocery on Gordon Street in Tel Aviv,
before that, Violette and Ovadia's place in the Beit Hakerem neighborhood of Jerusalem, and even earlier than that, Zolti's on Ben Yehuda
Street in Tel Aviv. This is the way I return, heavier with each step,
climbing the stairs and thinking, Everyone else descends to hell, only I
ascend to it. I wonder whether this time I will manage to enter the
apartment without incurring the wrath of the front door. When Liora
opens it, the door swivels on its hinges in obedient silence, but with me
it makes itself heard, a groan of sorrow upon my arrival and a clarion call
of joy upon my departure, often accompanied by the shriek of the
alarm.

Even when we had nothing more than a simple lock, before Liora's
art collection and the safe and the surveillance cameras and the sensors
and the alarm sirens, the key would jam, the door would refuse to open.
When that first happened I was confounded. I would wait outside for
her to arrive, for her to listen with amused patience to my grievances;
then she would take the key from my hand and open that obstinate
door. The second time I tried using a little force; for weeks afterward I
could hear her recounting and complaining—to herself, to Benjamin, to

her family during their biweekly phone conversations: "He broke the key in the door. He has no idea how strong he is."

"He is very strong," says Benjamin, always quick to exploit an opportunity. A slow, bright smile flitted between them suddenly, lifting off, arcing over my head, landing, like one of the winged documents on the screen of Yordad's computer. I wondered: could it be that Benjamin and Liora are sleeping together? It is common knowledge that similarity between two people creates mutual desire; if the matter has occurred to me, it has certainly occurred to them.

My brother added, "By eight he was already lugging groceries for our mother, and tins of whitewash up the stairs." He also has a good memory, but why are they my memories? She would skip ahead of me carrying only the paintbrushes or a bouquet of gladioluses or a carton of eggs "so they won't break," while I followed behind, eager to please, making great efforts and turning red in the face, lugging tins of whitewash, oil for the heater, baskets full of vegetables up to the second-floor entrance. "Without stopping, Yair. Let's see you make it all the way to the top in one go . . ." And how you praised my strength: "Such a boy! Small, but so strong, a real ox-rocks!"

Later, too, after she had left us and gone to live in her own place, she would ask me sometimes to come move "something heavy." She and Benjamin would drink tea in her *küchlein* while I dragged the large mattress to the verandah and beat it, wondering whether there actually was another man. I thought, Is my pounding erasing his scent or deepening it, making it penetrate?

I pass through the electric gates at the entrance to the courtyard and climb the stairs. I have already stated that I do not like this house, and the house, I must say, does not like me. It senses me immediately, shines a light on me, fixes its mistrustful electronic eyes on me: Who is this person walking up the stairs? Who is coming to disturb the mistress? I remove the key from my pocket and remind myself of what is to come: open the door, walk in, quickly punch in the secret code and neutralize the alarm. But Liora's home has already aimed a scrutinizing lens at me, has captured my image and compared it to another husband, a better one, who should have taken her for his wife, and it raises a voice of protest and horror.

"You don't punch the code in right," Liora responded to my complaint, patiently inclining her head over mine in the way of *yekke* fathers and tall mothers.

"I don't even get to the stage of punching in the numbers. Don't you understand, it doesn't even let me get near."

"No, I don't."

Once I asked her to stand next to me to see with her own eyes how her house mistreats me. We positioned ourselves in front of the door, I took out my key and said, "See for yourself," and the house behaved as it is supposed to: it waited for me to begin, gave me time to punch in the four-digit code, informed me that I had made a mistake, and granted me time and a chance to correct it, to improve myself, to become a better husband and resident.

"You see?" Liora said.

I said, "The door opened because you're here. It opened for you, not for me."

She said, "You're crazy, Yair."

I said, "What do you mean, crazy? Can't you see that your house hates me?"

She said, "As if you liked it."

But that night she came, opened the wings of the sheet in which she had wrapped herself, and slid in, sprawling next to me.

"Has a month already passed since your last 'treatment'?" I asked.

"Just about," she replied.

A surprise. She had brought along her especially soft pillow.

"Does this mean you're going to stay here and sleep with me?"

"If you don't press up against me too hard."

She has that rare trait that only the luckiest women are granted: her beauty grows with the passing of time. As a young woman she possessed the beauty of a perfect vessel, shapely and cool. Now the thin lines webbing her skin, the bluish hints of her veins, the softening perceivable only to the hand, not the eye, of her belly and breasts—all these have added life and warmth to her. We fell asleep together like we used to, she on her stomach, her cheek on her pillow, one leg extended and the other bent, while I lay behind her. My hand under her breast, my thigh between her thighs, my foot beneath her foot.

When I woke up in the morning I found that she had already risen in the night and returned to her room. I went to the grocer's, returned, awakened the neighborhood with the alarm, and arranged my purchases in the refrigerator. Then I turned to her. "How did you sleep?"

"Very poorly, thank you."

"I actually slept quite well."

"Great. At least there's one thing you know how to do well."

The financial sections of the paper were spread out around her, her laptop, with its illuminated bitten apple, buzzing lightly, her first cup of lukewarm water with lemon juice, tea-hyssop, and honey flowing toward her stomach.

She said, "If you're making breakfast for yourself, I'd like some too, please."

There are two things she hastened to learn and love: the Hebrew language and my breakfasts. I am overcome with pride. I turn on the kettle and the toaster, cut vegetables thin and precise, slice fresh salted cheese, fry an egg. Once I made a hard-boiled egg for her, cracked it open on her forehead, and said, *"Plaff!"* That made her angry. "Stop your silly games, Yair! I'm not your mother!"

I heat the oil in the skillet, turn my back on the rest of her litany of complaints: once again she did not shut her eyes the entire night. Look at these dark circles, they're a gift from you. There is no doubt in her mind: I steal her slumber. That, too.

# Chapter Nine

## I

TIME PASSED. The Baby's uncle became a regular conveyor of pigeons from the kibbutz pigeon loft to the central loft in Tel Aviv. But all the pigeons dispatched from there returned without an answer from the Girl. The Baby also dispatched a pigeongram affixed to one of the pigeons the uncle brought back with him from Tel Aviv, but no response came to that one either.

"It's a bad age," the uncle said to the aunt. "He is old enough to feel love but too young for such a disappointment."

He invited the Baby to come with him again to Tel Aviv—"If you see her and she sees you, everything will be fine," he promised—but the Baby declined. He would wait for her to send him a pigeongram; only then would he come.

Then the green pickup truck returned and Dr. Laufer alighted from it. He had visited the large pigeon lofts of Yagur and Merhavia and Beit Hashita, and later the one at Kibbutz Gesher, and now he had come to Miriam, "last but not least." He brought her pigeons for dispatch and breeding, checked the loft and its residents, the cards and the lists, visited the cowshed, drank tea with lemon in the dining hall, and gave another lecture to the members of the kibbutz.

Before Dr. Laufer left, the Baby gathered his courage and asked whether the Girl had sent a message with him. The veterinarian, dispirited, admitted that she had not, and the uncle, who heard this story, told the Baby: "You are nearly fourteen years old. You must make the matter clear to her. Go to Tel Aviv and bring her your pigeons yourself."

The Baby selected and marked six pigeons that had already matured and began training them specially. His uncle dispatched them for him from Tiberias, Afula, Haifa, and Tel Aviv. One did not return and the Baby disqualified another because, in spite of her speed, she was in no hurry to enter the loft. Four months later he announced, "We ladies are ready" and said that he wanted to set out for Tel Aviv and bring the pigeons to the Girl.

The uncle tried to arrange a place for him with the milk truck, but it had already been promised to someone else. The Baby was unwilling to wait; he had to leave immediately. He was fourteen years and four months of age and there was nothing to worry about, he told his aunt and uncle. The uncle gave him a little money and said, "You'll get to Afula somehow; then buy a ticket and take the train to Haifa. From there, our relatives will put you on the bus."

The Baby put the four pigeons in a woven wicker basket with a handle and a lid, and in his knapsack he took food and water for himself and them. At dawn he went out to the road and caught a ride with a cart driver from Menahamia on his way to Tiberias to sell fruit and buy goods. Near Kibbutz Kinneret the cart driver stopped the car of a man he knew, the principal of the school in Yavniel, and in Yavniel the principal sent him—not before scolding him for being truant from his studies—to the home of a farmer, where he could eat and sleep in exchange for helping sort and package almonds.

"Almonds are the best food for a man on the road and for pregnant women," the farmer told him. "Take some for the road—they'll fill you up and they're easy to carry."

The next morning a Circassian truck driver, an acquaintance of the almond farmer's, gave the Baby a ride the rest of the way. Lean and haggard, he was mostly eyes and a mustache and, to the Baby's relief, tended to speak very little. The shifting expressions on his face were testimony to the fact that he held his conversations with himself. The Baby was free to gaze at the view, to contemplate and comprehend that the longing he was fighting and the thoughts he was thinking and the will to see and hear more, to touch and feel to infinity, were what his elders called love. There was no other option, no other explanation, for if this was not love, then what was? In what other ways did it manifest itself?

The truck exerted itself on the steep curves until it reached the top. Mount Tabor revealed itself in all its roundedness and, farther off and friskier, Hamoreh Hill, too. The Baby felt his body to be a tiny speck moving along the face of the earth, drawing ever closer to his love. The basket shifted suddenly; the pigeons twitched, and he trembled with them. Near Kafr Kana the driver suddenly boomed, "This is my home!" and fell silent again.

From Tabor village the Baby continued on foot, hitching rides from passing wagons filled with fodder or trucks laden with milk and vegetables. In those days the world was empty and the traffic slow and the distances great, and that stretch of road, which I now traverse in Behemoth in twenty minutes, took the Baby half a day. In Afula two boys invited him for a glass of soda and discussed pigeons with him, and after they had left him and he went to the train station he discovered they had stolen from him the pittance he had received from his uncle. He sat for nearly an hour on the bench at the station, the basket on his lap and his heart pounding and frightened; then finally he embarked on a train and traveled in the direction of Haifa without a ticket.

In no time he was caught. The ticket collector demanded two pigeons if he wished to continue his journey. The Baby pleaded, refused, nearly began to cry. The ticket collector grabbed him by the neck and threatened to toss him off the train into the great, empty expanses of the Jezreel Valley. He was terrified. Earlier he had seen a pack of vultures preying on the carcass of a cow, and now he feared for his own fate. In his heart he had already planned how he would send a pigeon to Miriam and his uncle would organize a team to rescue him. But then a strange and foreign woman, a tall, gaunt Dutchwoman sitting nearby and painting watercolors of starlings and goldfinches, was overcome with feelings for him and paid his ticket. Speaking to him in a language he pretended not to understand, she told him she knew what he had in his basket and why he was making this trip.

In Haifa, the Baby went to the home of the relatives, who sent him to an elderly English engineer, a friend of theirs, who was making an overnight trip to Tel Aviv. The man apologized for driving slowly—at night he could not see well—and he asked that the Baby converse with him to keep him awake. The Baby feared the man would ask him about the pigeons, and the old engineer did in fact ask—not only that, he exhibited expertise in two dangerous fields: homing pigeons and the Hebrew language. It would not help the Baby to feign ignorance of English again. He told the man he lived in Haifa and had a loft on the roof of his house and that he was going to "send them flying"—he was careful not to say "dispatch"—in Tel Aviv.

"Very interesting how they find their way home," the Englishman said.

The Baby said, "They have a sense of navigation."

"They do not," the Englishman countered. "They do not know to find the way to anywhere but their own loft. That is not navigation; navigation is the ability to find one's way from any place to any place, especially places with which one is not familiar, while finding one's way home—how shall I put it, young man?—is like obeying the laws of gravity, which we all do anyway. Like a river knows the way to the sea without maps, like a tossed stone is not in need of a compass to return to the earth."

By the time they crossed the Yarkon River, the horizon was lightening and from a distance it was possible to see the first lights shining from Tel Aviv. The car passed by the horse paddock the Girl had told him about, where she would dispatch young pigeons, then continued farther south, where the Baby asked to alight, at a place that would not connect him to any person or matter.

"It's still dark outside," the English engineer said. "Where will you go?" But the Baby replied, "It's fine, it'll be light soon," and he walked to the zoo. He did not know the way, but the roar of the leopard and the monkeys' and birds' early morning chatter could already be heard, and they led him on his way. The gate was locked. The Baby sat beside it, and was awakened half an hour later by the fat man, who had come to open it.

"I remember you—you work in Miriam's loft," he told him. "Your girlfriend hasn't come yet, but come on in, come in, you can wait for her inside."

# 2

ON HIS WAY home two days later, the Baby traveled by bus. Four pigeons, given to him by the Girl, lay in the wicker basket. Dr. Laufer told the two of them, "Pigeongrams of love are very nice, but we have work and training exercises to carry out. With every pigeon you dispatch, add a pigeongram with the information about the time and weather. And do not mix up our message capsules with your goose quills; otherwise we ladies are liable to read what you ladies write to one another, *haw, haw, haw* . . . Now, since you are on duty I am giving you a little money for the trip and your bus ticket."

He thought about her throughout the trip, about the walk they had taken together along the Tel Aviv seashore, about the street where she had removed her hand from his and the alley where she had not. About the kiss she had given him, about the kisses he had given her, about the way in which she had brushed his hand from her breast and exhaled, about their mingling tongues. He asked that she teach him to whistle, and when he failed with one finger and also with two, she said, "So let's try like this," and put her fingers in his mouth.

"Whistle!" she said, but his tongue was stuck between her fingers and his diaphragm filled with desire and his lungs could not inhale.

"Whistle!" she repeated, and his whistle turned into the laughter of surprise and endearment. The Girl said, "Now like this," and she took both his index fingers into her mouth, and when she blew in his face he felt that he was blowing, too. He had never felt such exhilaration before. The sea was churning. Their eyes met, close to the point of blurring, deep to the point of drowning.

"Yes or no?" he asked.

"Yes or no what?"

"Can I take a pigeon of yours? Yes or no?"

He recalled the look on her face as she took his pigeons, as well as her expression when she gave him her own and said, "We ladies agree." And because the country was small and the longings were intense, two pigeons were dispatched the very next morning, one from a loft in the Jordan Valley, the other from the central pigeon loft in the Tel Aviv zoo.

The pigeons, which naturally crossed paths en route, arrived and alighted, their shiny breasts beating powerfully. The Girl and the Baby, each in her or his place, passed along to Dr. Laufer and to Miriam the contents of their message capsules, unlaced the silk strings that held the quill to the pigeons' tails, and stepped aside to read the words meant just for them. Short, numbered words, as was the practice with homing pigeons: Yes and yes and yes and yes. Yes we are in love, yes we miss you, yes we have not forgotten, yes we remember.

Never had they imagined that words so short, so few, and so simple could bring such joy. Never had they known how many times one could read and reread them. Miriam and Dr. Laufer, he in Tel Aviv, she in the kibbutz, regarded the Baby and the Girl with a sigh and a smile. They knew that this was how things would be: after a love letter brought by a pigeon, the sender and the addressee would never again consent to any other type of postman. Nothing would ever compare to the dispatching, the vanishing before escorting eyes, the appearance—at the very same moment—before awaiting eyes.

Here she is: diving, arriving, flying straight as an arrow, the thrum of the beating of her wings mixing with the thrum of blood in the temples, the heart. What can compare to holding her? To the soft feathers of her breast? To removing the letter from the quill? To the beating of her heart? And how does she have the strength to carry so much love? And what is more rousing: the release of the dispatcher or the grasp of the receiver?

Dr. Laufer was satisfied, too. On one of the northbound flights a local record was broken: a pigeon had flown from the Girl to the Baby at an average speed of seventy-four kilometers per hour, just three less than the male pigeon Alphonse, the Belgian record holder for that year.

Every two months the Baby would come to Tel Aviv, bringing and taking new pigeons, and after a year the Girl came to him in the kibbutz.

"This is the girl you've been telling me about? The one that was there when you took him and the pigeons to the zoo?" the Baby's aunt asked her husband.

"She's grown a little since then, but that is absolutely the one," he confirmed.

"Who would have believed," the aunt said, "that the most beautiful and most intelligent girl ever seen around here would come for our little *kelbeleh*? You watch and see how the girls will chase after him now. Girls can smell things like this. I just hope he won't do anything foolish."

# Chapter Ten

## I

EVEN WHEN Meshulam said, "Their price is too high" and "We can bring those slime bags to their knees," I did not argue. The price was set and I was invited to "bring the wife" to a meeting of the membership committee.

"What am I going to do?" I asked him. "Liora will make the wrong impression with her expensive clothes. She'll raise objections and talk in English."

"So bring Tiraleh instead," Meshulam said. "She'll make a great Mrs. Mendelsohn. For the committee, too."

"What do you mean, 'bring Tiraleh.' How?"

"By car, that's how!"

"She's not my wife! They said, 'Bring the wife.'"

"Exactly. They said, 'Bring the wife'; they didn't say 'Bring *your* wife.'"

"And what if she won't agree? How do you know she'll go along with it?"

"That you can leave to me."

The next day I was informed over the phone by Meshulam that his Tiraleh agreed. Not only did she agree, she had broken into one of her big laughs. But her father had yet another idea: "If you two are already going to the village together anyway, why don't you pick her up early, say, ten in the morning, from our Tel Aviv office?"

"But the committee meeting is only at night," I said.

"Summer's not here yet," Meshulam said patiently. "It's still spring. There are anemones and cyclamen in shady places, and a few lupines and cornflowers and buttercups. Even Tiraleh deserves half a day off now and then, no? Take her on a little journey, maybe a nice little picnic with all kinds of goodies. I'll send someone to buy stuff to fill up a cooler for you. Take a trip, eat, enjoy some time together, and then go to the interview."

"What if she doesn't have time? What if she isn't interested? What if she's got a meeting with someone else?"

"She's got time, she doesn't have any meetings, and she's interested!"

# 2

SOUTHWARD IN SILENCE, our first time alone together, we departed from Tel Aviv. Mine is the tongue-tied silence of awkwardness, hers the smiling silence of anticipation, and then we utter inanities to each other, like "Meshulam arranged beautiful weather for us" and "I like these kinds of clouds, like on *The Simpsons*."

I pointed out a high-flying flock of large, soaring birds and told her, "Those are pelicans, heading north." And she asked, "How can you tell what they are from so far away? Maybe they're storks." I informed her that pelicans change colors as they wheel and storks do not.

"Migrating birds have winter homes and summer homes," I continued several minutes later. "But which of the two is the real one, the one they come home to?"

"The whole world's their home," Tirzah said. "When they fly down to Africa all they're really doing is moving from room to room."

I told her about the *yaylas*, the summer residences of shepherds in the mountain ranges of northeast Turkey. In winter they abandon them and descend to the villages in the valleys and the seaside towns; then in spring they return with their flocks.

"I didn't know you'd been there," Tirzah said. "Who did you go with?"

"Nobody," I told her. "I haven't even been there myself. I went to a lecture about the Kaçkar Mountains at the Traveler shop."

"Why don't you go visit the Kaçkar Mountains for real, instead of just listening to other people's stories?"

"I don't like going places—I like coming home," I said, and I recited the other poem I know by heart, the beautiful lines about returning home that are engraved on the tombstone of Robert Louis Stevenson,

about which I also heard at a lecture on Fiji and Samoa and other islands
in the Pacific Ocean:

> *This be the verse you grave for me:*
> *Here he lies where he longed to be;*
> *Home is the sailor, home from the sea,*
> *And the hunter home from the hill.*

The lecturer read them, told about *Treasure Island* and the house that
Stevenson had built for himself in Samoa, noting that he had lived in it
for only three years before dying, and about the natives, who had loved
him and had carried his body for burial at the top of the hill, and suddenly my hearing and memory finished their mutual evaluation and I
understood that Stevenson, and not my mother, had written the lines
she would recite for me outside the door of our home on Ben Yehuda
Street in Tel Aviv—"Home is the sailor, home from the sea / And the
hunter home from the hill"—reciting as she would hand me the key and
lift me up to insert it into the lock, telling me, "Open the door and say,
'Hello, house.'"

# 3

I RECALL HOW PLEASED I was with that childish word *yayla* when I
first heard it at that lecture. Not a *Zimmer,* not a dacha, not a summer
home, but a yayla. I wondered about the owner of such a yayla, denying
the morning frost, ignoring the falling leaves, turning his back on the
first snow flurries until finally he has no choice but to shut the door
behind him and descend to the apartment he has in a small and decrepit
town on the shores of the Black Sea, and for an entire moldy winter that
is all coal smoke, mud, and raki, he misses it, his corner of the world in
the mountains, this place that is his own, until at last, in the spring, he
returns to it, ascends into the mountains, and climbs the wooden stairs
and opens the door and breathes in the air that has been awaiting him
inside, and he says, "Hello, yayla . . ." And the yayla, in the manner of
homes to which one returns, breathes in and answers him.

"What can I tell you," chuckled my contractor who is a woman. "It's a
good thing you bought this house. Just in the nick of time." And she told
me that her engineer had already paid a visit and given orders for thicken-

ing the foundations as well as for the addition of a few beams and girders. "Which means, Iraleh, that we need to start discussing the rooms."

I told her that the division of the rooms—a living room and two small bedrooms—was just fine.

Tirzah said I was a real conservative. "There are no absolute rules in building a house. Everything depends on need and opportunity." She asked, "Anyway, what do you need rooms for? Why don't we knock a few walls down and make the place into one very large room, plus a small one just in case, and a bathroom and toilet?"

"Because that's the way it's supposed to be!" I grumbled, threatened in part by her use of "we." "Because houses need rooms. Bedrooms and workrooms and guestrooms. That's the way everyone's house is. What do you mean, 'What do you need rooms for?'"

"Don't get worked up, Iraleh. That's not why we met today. We met to build you a house, and you'd better thank God that I'm your contractor, because you have no idea what a nightmare renovations like these can be."

"I'm sorry."

"And who is this 'everyone' and what's this 'that's the way it's supposed to be' business? A home is not a department store that you divide up into 'home furnishings' and 'clothing' and 'kitchenware.' A home should be built around people, not functions. In your case, you're not raising children and it doesn't seem like you'll host a lot of guests; there's no need for more than a large room for living and cooking and eating and sleeping and reading, and another smaller room with a bed—just in case—and a bathroom, and there should be large windows and doors open to the view, and a big deck, and I haven't forgotten the shower you requested outside."

"When do I have to decide?"

"As soon as possible. But for now, that's enough about the house. Where are you taking me?"

I was headed for my three hills: every year they begin with anemones and end with buttercups. Tirzah caught sight of them from far away and, like me the first time I saw them, she could not believe that all that redness could possibly be flowers. But Behemoth drew closer and the scarlet blanket came into focus as red petals with black hearts and the light green of buttercup buds not yet opened and the white-gray of anemone seeds floating in the air.

"Stop!" she cried. "It's so beautiful, stop!"

She got out of Behemoth, stood facing the red field, and spread her arms wide. I unfurled the blanket and sat down on it. She leaned over me and kissed my mouth, her lips slightly open, neither gaping nor clenched: an amused, exploratory kiss. Her tongue did not enter my mouth; instead, it moved about between my teeth and my upper lip, scrutinizing me. Had this leopard changed his spots? Had my taste changed? This first kiss since the days of our youth made me tremble, both from its similarity to those wanton, clumsy kisses of old and its dissimilarity.

A good, refreshing scent wafted from the skin of her face, and my lips felt her smile before she pulled away. In contrast to the daring of our youth, I thought how now we were acting in innocence and restraint.

"What are you planning to say at the committee meeting?"

She laughed. "That your lips have remained the same but your soul has become worried and nagging." She brought her head close to mine. "We don't need to plan anything. The first thing they say to you at a membership interview is 'Tell us about yourselves.' It's important that you answer first, without looking at me. They want a normal couple, the man at the head of household with his little woman."

She opened the cooler and burst out laughing. "Papa Fried's aphrodisiacs," she announced as she removed each and placed it on the blanket. "Feta cheese, Swiss cheese with holes, rye bread, cherry tomatoes—he sure knows his daughter well—Hungarian salami, white wine. He really wants us to do it already, even if it means getting to the interview drunk. Radishes with butter, olive oil, pickles . . ." She sniffed them. "Poor thing—he tries to re-create my mother's, but he can't quite manage. While we're sitting here devouring all this he'll be at home devouring his fingernails from worry."

# 4

WE ENTERED the village.

"Lovely," Tirzah said. "Pitch-black streets, huge potholes, and of course they don't sell anchovies in the local grocery."

"What's so lovely about that?"

"It means they don't have a penny. It means they need us more than we need them."

Two cars and several bicycles were parked next to the secretariat. We entered; Tirzah peered into a room in which several people were sitting and said, graciously, "Hello. We're the Mendelsohns."

"We'll be with you in just a few minutes," said a voice.

"Three men," she whispered, "and two women. How predictable. Those are exactly the faces I expected to see here."

We looked at the aerial photographs hanging on the walls. The village: its homes, its chicken coops, its cowsheds, its fields.

"Nothing much happens here," Tirzah said. "That's very good."

"How do you know that?"

"Because nothing's changed from the black-and-white photos to the color ones. Same public buildings, a bit of construction on the farms. Look at this place: in the black and whites there are still a few cows, but not in the color photos. The houses have stayed the same, too."

"All the secretariats in all the villages have the same photos," I informed her.

She told me she had not imagined I could be familiar with so many village secretariats, and I told her I had searched a lot of places for our house before finally finding it here.

She smiled. "You don't have to call it our house yet, Iraleh."

I said, "I'm just practicing for the interview, Tiraleh."

"It's not easy to come and live in a place like this," she said. "Small and old. You'll never know its little secrets, the language of the place, who hates who and why, who is a tree that bears fruit and who is a tree that does not. You're liable to make friends with the village outcast, or praise one man to another when he's actually sleeping with the guy's wife. You have to be careful."

Two more men arrived and entered the room; right away a voice called, "Come in, please."

Tirzah was right. At once I had them figured out: Mr. All-Is-Lost, Mr. How-Shall-This-Man-Save-Us, the birdman, the old maid, the maiden of hopes, the deputy battalion commander in army reserves, and the self-appointed watchdog. Thirteen eyes—the birdman wore a patch over his left eye—scrutinized us with a mixture of mercy and authority.

Tirzah apologized for the muck stuck to our shoes. "We didn't want to be late," she explained. "We left home early, and when we got here we took a little walk around."

"Tell us about yourselves," the deputy battalion commander and All-Is-Lost said at the same time. They exchanged angry looks. Tirzah smiled to herself.

"My name is Yair Mendelsohn," I said, the manly head of the household, "and this is my wife, Liora. I was born in 1949, I'm a tour guide, and now, with the economic situation the way it is, I'm in transportation. As for Liora—"

"Where would you bring tourists in this area?"

"In my field, which is bird-watching and history, there aren't a lot of attractions around here."

"Why is that?" said the birdman, fixing his one good eye on me. "Pelicans and storks pass overhead regularly. Sometimes cranes, too, and we have a system of ancient wells on the other side of the hill, and secret caves dating back to the Bar-Kochva rebellion."

"Indeed," said the maiden of hopes. "Every year thousands of tourists from around the world come looking for the system of wells on the other side of the hill, and we need someone to lead them and explain, and policemen to direct the heavy traffic."

"Where did you serve in the army?" the old maid asked, surprising me.

"I was a medic. I wound up as an instructor in the course."

"It says here, Yair, that you don't have any children," the deputy battalion commander said in a friendly but aggressive manner.

"Excuse me for butting in," Tirzah said congenially, "but since you've mentioned children, well, I'm the wife you asked him to bring and it seems that's sort of in my sphere."

"Excuse me."

"Well, I actually have children from a previous marriage. My son is in the U.S. and my daughter is trekking around the Far East."

"And what do you do, Liora?"

"A number of things. I have experience with growing things—flowers, children—and I'm a nurse, and in the army I was a medic, like Yair. In fact, we met in the course, but afterward we went our separate ways until we met up again."

She smiled at me and I blanched. I am not good at improvisations, and most certainly not the rapid-fire spinning of tall tales.

"And now?"

"Now? We're blowing air on old coals."

One of the women laughed. Mr. All-Is-Lost persisted. "I understand, Mrs. Mendelsohn, that you have many talents, but I still wish to know what it is that you do."

"I'm a jack-of-all-trades," Tirzah said. "But I've always earned a living, never been dependent on anyone. I worked for a catering firm and I designed and marketed wooden toys. I teach folk dancing, too, but he won't dance," she said, pointing at me. "Two left feet."

"And why is it that you want to live here?"

So that I won't shoot you people or myself, I said to myself. So that I'll calm down, have a place that's my own. Because large trees are growing in the yard and weeds from cracks in the sidewalks.

"The area is beautiful," Tirzah said. "The village, too. And we like the house. We're nature people, and we've saved up some money and we're looking for a new environment, a new atmosphere."

"And what will you two do here?"

"I hope the situation will improve and I'll be able to keep on in my profession," I said. "Maybe I'll even specialize in tourism for this area. And Liora—"

"First of all, I plan to renovate the house as my own contractor. And if I enjoy myself I'll make it into my profession."

"In your opinion," asked the watchdog, who, until that moment, had been silently scribbling, "what sort of contribution will you be able to make here?"

"I believe in good neighborly relations," I said. "With pleasure I'll help anyone who needs it."

"I'm talking about organized commitment to the community."

"Perhaps the culture committee," I said. "And Liora, as you can see, will be able to help in a number of areas, organizing—"

"I can sit on the membership-committee interviews of other potential candidates," Tirzah said. "I'm enjoying this."

"You two are a bit old," said the watchdog. "We were hoping for younger couples with small children and plans for more."

"We were hoping to stay young, too," Tirzah said, "and to have more and more babies. But since we've come back to reality, let's get serious here. That house has been standing empty and locked up for quite a while and nobody has shown an interest in it, and here you have buyers. So there's no sense in dealing in irrelevant matters. We're just like all of you: decent, normal people with no criminal record who want to live in peace. We'll contribute to the community just like all the rest of you. No less and no more."

Several minutes later we parted company with them and took a short, dark walk around the village. We stopped for a few minutes near the house. Tirzah said she needed to get back; she had to be in the south of the country the next day. She made a phone call, gave directions, and I brought her down to the main road. One of the MESHULAM FRIED AND DAUGHTER, INC. pickup trucks was already waiting for her there, shining whitely in the dark, its parking lights lit.

She kissed me good-bye on the mouth. I felt her lips smiling.

I could not resist telling her what the tractor operator that had come to mow the yard had said about her, and she laughed. "That's really what he said? Your contractor is a woman? He got the order of the words a bit mixed up, but never mind."

"Good night, Tiraleh. Thanks for your help with the committee."

"Thank you for the trip. And don't worry, we passed."

"You did. I was awful."

"We both passed. It's clear to them that we're not Mrs. Ideal and Mr. Perfect, but they have debts, they don't have any other candidates, and nobody else is going to make an offer like the one you did. Start making decisions about the rooms because we've got to get the plans prepared."

"I go along with your idea of one large room and one small one."

"Good choice. Give my regards to Meshulam—I'm sure he'll phone you in a few minutes. And tomorrow start cleaning up all the creepers and parasites around the carob trees, and cut back all the weeds. The tractor can't get in there with the mower."

"Don't you want to hear from the committee first?"

"There's no need to wait. We passed. And if not, then they got a nice cleanup for free." From the back of the pickup truck that had come to fetch her she took a scythe, a sickle, a pair of work gloves, shears, and a saw. "Here, take these. You should have them."

# 5

A FEW WEEKS LATER, again, I stayed over in the new house. I even received a gift from it, in the form of a dream. In the dream, a telephone rang. I lifted the receiver; at first I heard only silence, then my name. You were calling me, the first time since your death. You said, "Yair . . ." And again: "Yair . . ." Your voice was softer than your normal voice, but I recognized its pleasantness, and in my heart I had no doubt. "Yair . . . Yair . . ." you called, with that tiny question mark you sometimes added to my name, a question mark so small that it was nearly impossible to hear and absolutely impossible to write. And it meant, Is that you? Are you there? Answer me, my son . . .

By the time I had gathered my wits and answered, my mother had returned the receiver to its cradle. The dream ended. Silence prevailed. Only that small, common, and hairy owl was hooting rhythmically outside. I woke up shaken. Why had I not answered? "Here I am, Mother." Why had I not said, "I am in the house you bought me"? Why had I not asked, "Where are you? When will you return?"

I am here, the insides of my chest told me. She is no longer, responded the wall. Yair . . . ? Yair . . . ? Yairi, Yairi, my son, my son, echoed my dream. It is he, my senses confirmed. He is with us, let him in, my memories told me. All at once the knowledge of my place and existence grew stronger and I felt the house my mother bought for me and my luvey is building for me, and it was growing and encircling me like a new and healthy skin, and the feeling was pleasant and decisive to the point that I could no longer be certain whether it was growing within me or rebounding like a warm-cool echo on my brow.

I covered my head with the blanket. A small darkness all my own. I am here, in my place, wrapped up in your gift. I am the void between the walls. I am the man and his home. I am my house and its insides. I am the foot and the step, the span between the doorposts, the space between the floor and the head.

The paleness of the end of night awaits my open eyes—how much time has passed?—like the songs of the bulbuls in my ears, like the continuation of the dream in my heart. Let me go, for day has dawned, you said. Let me go, my son.

# 6

MY HAND RISES and reaches toward the light switch. In Liora's house it would always run into a lampshade and make noise, and back when we slept in the same bed it would cause a long hiss of protest to escape her lips. But here my hand is confident and the finger finds its way and lights the lamp without hesitation or groping. That's the way it was that night with a flashlight and that's the way it is today with a lamp, in the very same house, which is new and renovated, and once again Tirzah is no longer with me. She finished building it and left. Sometimes I read a book, waiting for sleep to return, and sometimes I calm myself by perusing a topographical map, departing at last on a journey.

It's good like this: hiking clothes and walking shoes and knapsacks and storm tents and sleeping bags are piled in the closet and in Behemoth, my feet are up on the bed, resting, my lungs fill up and empty quietly, and only my eyes step between the altitudinal lines and guess the view, expanding the two dimensions of the map to the three of reality: here is a ravine, here is a hilltop, here is a tributary; here it is steep and here is it level; here is a cliff. Here I climb and here I slide and here I pitch my tent and light a fire.

Sometimes I even set out for real. From the house to the garden, and from there to the view from the hills. I discover walking trails that people have trampled, and cow trails, and narrow trails made by ants and hedgehogs, hunting trails made by porcupines and jackals and wild boar. This is what I do everywhere and with every opportunity: I make myself known to the system of tracks and dirt roads, to the possibilities of escape, detour, flight.

"Where is this paranoia of yours from? Why does an Israeli guy have the fears of Jews abroad?" Liora asked on my first and last trip overseas, to marry her in her parents' home in New Rochelle. I had gone off on a morning walk and returned after an absence that had worried the entire family.

"What happened? Where were you?" everyone asked, frightened.

"I went out to get familiar with the surroundings."

Her father, her mother, her brother, her sister-in-law, uncles, aunts, their sons and daughters—all the Kirschenbaums who had come to observe the groom Liora had brought back from Israel—they all looked from one to the other and shook their heads.

"You don't just go walking around here," they told me. "Around here you go by car, or you run in a jogging suit, or you go out walking in a track suit on special walking trails. People who simply walk around the streets get picked up for loitering."

"What for?" Liora asks every time I drive off the asphalt to check out a new dirt path. "There are roads. They were paved with taxes that I pay. When we travel on them we get part of our money back."

On one of my treks I even found the wells that had been mentioned in the membership-committee interview. They were large and deep, and dry stone troughs had been placed near their openings. Once this place had been settled and populated with people, sheep, and homes, and now the only reminder of that were rope marks etched in the limestone edges of the well's mouth. Who among you dug here first? The Canaanites? The Philistines? The Arabs? My forefathers from the days of the Bible?

Not far from there is a large thicket of trees, called the Woods by the villagers, an odd mixture of oaks, carobs, and terebinths alongside test groups of pine, eucalyptus, and cypress trees, the remnants of a temporary nursery fostered here by the Jewish Agency for Israel in the 1950s. There are wild shrubs, too, of a number of varieties, and aged almond trees, and among them I found ancient winepresses, and graves, signs of excavation in the soft boulders already black and gray from lichen. This is not a woods in which wolves and bears move about, but its scent is that of a forest and its shadows are those of a forest and its stillness is that of a forest—a stillness that is not silence but, rather, the murmur and rustle of falling leaves and passing winds, the sprouting of seeds, the fluttering of wings.

And in the heart of this forest there are several small and shaded clearings good for being alone or committing suicide, but usually populated by large families of new immigrants. The longing for Russian forests forces them to suffice with the local thicket. They drink and eat, play musical instruments and chess, roast meat on tiny fires, gather mushrooms. Once I came upon an elderly woman sobbing here. She had stepped in between the trees and lost her way. I had her climb into Behemoth, and we spent an hour scouring the area, she speaking an emotional Russian whose consonants were stuck together with tears while I contemplated the possibility of kidnapping her so that I could have a mother instead of you. In the end we heard her real children running about shouting, "Mama!" Their suspicion turned to gratitude, their anxiety to joy, and I accepted their invitation to eat with them, and even drank a bit, and I felt envy and closeness.

On occasion I come across another kind of sojourner, not the weekend reveler but the weekday refugee: the seekers of solitude, the returnees to adolescence, the not-quite-proper couples in search of a hiding place—or perhaps they are proper couples in search of renewal; unlike Tirzah or Liora, who would know immediately, I am incapable of discerning which are which. Among them are men my age, and we make do with a nod and an exchange of glances of "we've identified you." Many things have happened to us, our eyes say to each other: we walk a straight line, we hurt, we are lacking, fading away, being forgotten, departing, disappearing into the underbrush.

# 7

First I took hold of the scythe, my back stooped, hands thrashing, sawing, initially wary of the angry thistles, then finding shelter in the new work gloves. One hand grasped the handle while the other tightened around the victim's neck. Later, when my back began to ache and my heart had filled with confidence, I tried my hand at the sickle. I felt my movements were wrong but I did not know how to correct them. Just when I had decided to return to the scythe, someone touched my shoulder. It was the tractor operator.

"Slower," he said, "and not so firm." Already I could feel his two hands behind me, the left on my shoulder and the right on my waist, like a puppeteer. My spine became the pivot for a sail, a mast turning on itself. The rough strength of my thighs rose inside it, split and spread to the space between my shoulders, grew softer and flowed to my hands, converging finally in the moving blade. The sickle, too, felt all this and began circling on its own, whispering near the ground, so sharp and precise that even the driest and most delicate plants did not bend or break but were decapitated and fell as it passed.

The tractor operator disappeared, but the touch of his hands on my body remained and I worked that way for more than an hour. Even though I am unaccustomed to physical labor I possess—as my mother often said—something of the strength and purposefulness of a beast of burden: the thick, low back, the protruding brow, the short thighs. "Yair's body rises from his bottom," I heard you say once to Yordad when we were little, "and Benjamin's descends from his neck."

Sweat dripped down my forehead, passed my eyebrows, gliding and searing. Pain glowed in my vertebrae, but my muscles were not fatigued. The thorns and weeds had been shorn, all of them. I raked and piled them up at the side and began to tackle the creepers, which had wound themselves around the branches of the carob trees like boa constrictors. They had sprouted shoots and leaves, had climbed to the treetops in their quest for sunlight and air. I climbed after them, first on a ladder and then on the branches themselves, cutting them, prying them free, casting them to the ground. The tractor operator reappeared, hauling an empty rubbish cart behind him. I piled everything inside with a pitchfork and he drove off to unload the cart at the village dump.

As I was drinking cold water from the cooler in Behemoth,

Meshulam arrived. He looked around and said, "Look how these little gals love you now."

"Why gals?"

"They're female carob trees."

"How do you know that?"

"Don't you see all this fruit? Carobs are like us: the males stink and the females make fruit. What's with these crappy shears and saw? This is what you're going to use to prune?"

"It's what your daughter gave me."

"Let Tiraleh deal with buildings. She doesn't know the first thing about gardens. Go over to my car for a minute—I happen to have a few tools that are just right for you."

On the back seat I found two pairs of long-handled shears and two Japanese saws, all in their original packaging. A pair of scary-looking treetop shears, too, with a string and pulley and pole, and a container filled with a thick green liquid for smearing on the stumps of branches just severed.

Meshulam was beaming. "What luck I happened to have all this with me today, right? First we'll take down the low branches so that the trees will have trunks and a person can stand up straight underneath them."

We hacked away and cleared up the branches, piling them to the side, and Meshulam began teaching me the art of pruning from inside the tree. "Every branch that grows inward—take it down. The ones growing outward you just need to thin out. And every once in a while take a few steps backward and have a look, like an artist observing his painting. Make sure the top and sides look like a roof and walls because a carob tree is like a house. The leaves don't fall off it in the fall, and if you prune it back right it keeps the rain out in winter and the sun out in summer, like a roof."

We continued working for three hours or so, Meshulam below, giving instructions and directions, me on the ladder or on the branches themselves. Tirzah showed up twice. The first time she said, "You're still here, Meshulam? Who's minding the store?" The second time she laughed and quipped, "Very nice, boys, really very nice."

Now the carob trees looked like two large, thick umbrellas. It was possible to stand erect beneath them and look upward and see airy, refreshing spaces and a dense green roof.

The tractor operator returned with the rubbish cart. Meshulam asked if I knew how to back up a tractor with the rubbish cart attached and I told him I had never tried.

"Backing up with a cart isn't exactly playing a violin or something," he joked. "If you've never tried, then you don't know."

He sat in the driver's seat of the tractor and maneuvered it skillfully backward. "Once I was the best driver in the whole Palmach," he said. "Me, the son of Fried the tinsmith of Herzl Street in Haifa. Better than all the kibbutz boys and moshav boys that looked down on me. Now load up the rubbish and I'll go have a rest. I'm only allowed to work as much as I want to, not as much as I need to anymore."

He removed a bottle of beer and a folding chair from his car, sat down, and sipped. He told me, "Once, when Tiraleh was little, I liked that she called me 'Meshulam.' But ever since Gershon, I keep begging her to call me 'Father.' A person can't suddenly not hear himself being called 'Father.' There are enough people who call me 'Meshulam' or 'Mr. Fried.'" Then he shouted to her: "You call me 'Father.' You hear me? Call me 'Father!'"

Tirzah was in the house. She heard him but did not appear or answer.

"If it's so important to you, Meshulam," I said, "I can call you 'Father' every once in a while."

"How about once a week," he said.

He dozed on the chair for a while, awakened, and left.

# Chapter Eleven

## I

FROM TIME TO TIME the Haganah pigeon handlers would gather for in-service training sessions. They listened to lectures on message capsules, parasites, illnesses, and foods, related anecdotes to one another, and traded opinions and pedigree pigeons too old for flight but still good for mating.

These conferences were usually held at one of several kibbutzim in the center of the country, but Dr. Laufer decided to hold the 1945 conference in Tel Aviv. Since it was summer and school was no longer in session, he was given a classroom in the Ahad Ha'am School, in which he had previously run a petting zoo for the pupils. The participants visited the central pigeon loft in the zoo, but not as one large group, rather "in dribs and drabs"—said Dr. Laufer with unusual eloquence—"so as not to draw attention." They were housed with families active in the Haganah in Tel Aviv, and the Girl's mother recommended "a certain honest and decent housewife" who would prepare a modest dinner for all at a discounted price.

Miriam departed for Tel Aviv two days before the Baby in order to help Dr. Laufer prepare for the conference, and he, before leaving the kibbutz, made certain that his replacement—a veteran chicken breeder, not just some youngster from the Palmach—had recorded everything and understood what he was meant to do. Over his right shoulder the Baby hung a small satchel that contained a few toiletries, writing implements, a shirt, and a change of underwear. In his left hand he carried a basket with pigeons for the Girl and in his pocket, a bus ticket that one of Miriam's pigeons had brought him from Tel Aviv.

By the time he arrived at the Ahad Ha'am School there were several participants already there, all of them adults; they all eyed him, curious. Dr. Laufer looked favorably upon the Baby and introduced him to all present as "the future generation" and as "Baby-Comrade." The Girl was not there, occupied with all kinds of last-minute matters. Just before the opening lecture she entered and sat in the place he had saved for her next to him, and at once she pressed her arm against his. He was sixteen years old, and his body stirred.

The walls had been hung with anatomical diagrams of the body of a pigeon—inside and out—and a number of quotations, like "Who are these who fly as a cloud, and as the doves to their windows?" and "When the pigeons go abenting / Then the farmers lie lamenting," as well as sayings made up by Dr. Laufer himself: "PIGEON = PARTNER, PAL, POETRY-IN-MOTION" and "IN RAIN OR SLEET OR WIND OR HAIL, OUR FRIEND THE PIGEON SHALL ALWAYS PREVAIL." This year a new motto had been added, too: "PIGEONS OF A FEATHER DOCK TOGETHER," which provoked discussion. Was this yet another *yekke* error or was one expected to add a *Haw, haw, haw* after it?

Between the diagrams and the quotations hung portraits of "hero pigeons," whose names were often Mercury or Comet or Arrow. And, as with every opening lecture given by Dr. Laufer, so did this one overflow with winged heroes. In 1574, when the city of Leiden was under siege and had nearly been razed and the citizens were contemplating surrender, who was it that brought them the news that help would arrive within two hours? The pigeon. During the time of Queen Marie Antoinette's imprisonment, who passed messages from her to her advisers outside Paris? The pigeon. And during the campaign against Fort Souville at Verdun, who was it that succeeded in taking off above the clouds of poison gas spread by the Germans and transporting a message to the front? Only a French homing pigeon.

He updated the participants on important pigeon-related information from around the world. The English, he told them with a grimace, had trained peregrine falcons to snare enemy homing pigeons. In Germany, he told them with a grave demeanor, a law had been passed requiring all breeders to register and place their pigeons in the nation's service during national emergencies and, in turn, Germany would finance the transport of pigeons for training and competitions. A Canadian homing pigeon named Sunbeam had rescued fishermen whose boat nearly capsized in the frozen waters off Newfoundland. And in Belgium—the world's powerhouse for pigeons and pigeon handlers in spite of a meager population of only four million inhabitants—there were some one hundred thousand registered pigeon breeders. "And there is no clipping the wings on those numbers, *haw, haw haw . . .*"

Several of the participants spoke as well. A tearful pigeon handler from Jerusalem read a heartwarming short story she had written about a pigeon that had become entangled in electrical wires and had reached her destination two months after being dispatched, "walking on the burnt stumps of her legs." A pigeon handler from Kibbutz Yagur read a report filed by an American officer in the First World War: "We awaited news from the battlefield when the pigeon Cher Ami arrived, his body in shreds. The pigeongram he carried said, 'Our artillery is firing on our own troops. Adjust sights or we shall all fall victim.'"

After that someone told about a homing pigeon that delivered a "highly disturbing pigeongram" to the starved citizens of besieged Candia, on the island of Crete: It read EAT ME. This led to a moral discussion. One person shouted out that the story was unbelievable and improbable. Dr. Laufer hushed the gathered crowd and announced loudly, "And now—pigeons in Hebrew poetry!" He asked the Girl to rise and stand beside him to read from a poem he had asked her to prepare, "penned by the famous poet Dr. Shaul Tchernichovsky," who described many varied types of pigeons:

> *These are Egyptians pigeons, and these are called Saxon Monks,*
> *And there are others, the Cropper pigeons;*
> *Like peacocks they puff out their trunks.*
> *The Fantails enhance their fancy tails,*
> *The Jacobins do up their coifs.*
> *A band of Rhine Ringbeaters*
> *Meets with Hungarian ringleaders.*
> *In the corner lovers coo,*
> *Roman Owl Pigeons and Blackhead Moors by the pair;*
> *While Indian Pearl Highfliers can be spotted*
> *As they descend from the air.*
> *And a chick from the family of Priests—do not miss*
> *Nor the Italians, the Syrians, the Swiss.*

This the Girl recited, with great seriousness, a light blush deepening the pink of her skin. Dr. Laufer thanked her and said, "It would appear that the poet forgot to mention here the homing pigeon, noting only the ornamental pigeons"—he could not help himself and called them man-made "monsters"—but a closer reading revealed the Syrian pigeons at the end of the list, "and we have no doubt that the poet was hinting at the prized homing pigeons of Damascus."

Most of the assembled pigeon handlers were adults, and during lunch the Baby and the Girl exchanged glances and pressed their thighs one to the other underneath the table. Though shorter and younger than she, as he would remain to the day of his death, he was no longer bashful—neither with her or others—and even expressed his opinion like a veteran pigeon handler.

The afternoon sessions dealt with protein-enriched seeds versus seeds rich in fats, and with the question of whether the hand-feeding of chicks was liable to imprint a pigeon and prevent her from mating later on. After that they moved on to the problem of smallpox and how to disinfect a pigeon loft during a plague of dysentery, and from there to matters with no solution or resolution: Does the pigeon navigate by using her sense of direction alone or does she remember landmarks? Or perhaps both are right? The Baby dared to speak up in order to point out that the participants were projecting a human perception of maps and directions and compass roses onto pigeons. But perhaps, he said, she is unfamiliar with all of these, understanding one direction only, and its name is "homeward," unaware that humans give this direction other names—sometimes "southward" and sometimes "eastward" and sometimes "north-by-northwestward."

The room fell silent. The Girl flushed like a proud mother. "That is very interesting," Dr. Laufer said. He was reminded of what she had said about the pigeon disappearing from the eyes of the dispatcher as soon as she is seen by the person waiting for her, and suddenly he understood that this love blooming in front of his very eyes was greater and deeper than what he had imagined. But he shook himself free of these thoughts and resumed his role. "We, too, have interesting and beautiful ruminations such as these on occasion, but it is impossible to work thus."

The other pigeon handlers agreed immediately. One should return to the practical questions: What brings the pigeon back to the loft? A longing for home, the trough, the family? Is it fair and right and worthwhile to train pigeons to fly against their nature, at night? Does the pigeon's beak contain magnetic particles? And what function does the swelling on the beak play?

In the evening the Girl took the Baby for a walk on the beach, strolling with him on the promenade and keeping out of sight of several classmates of hers who wished to know who this boy, the stranger, was. She kissed him on his lips, and this time she allowed him to caress every part of her body, but only through her clothing. He showed her how he had learned to whistle, but he asked if they could do it as they had on their first meeting, each one's fingers in the other's mouth.

The next morning the Baby participated once again in the grown-ups' discussion and said it was his dream to hybridize a local species more impervious to heat and parasites and thirst than the European pigeons. The Girl suddenly noted that in the past the greatest world centers for raising pigeons were in Cairo, Baghdad, and India, where the climate was far less optimal than in Liège or Brussels.

Later, during a ceremonious break during which everyone dunked cookies in tea colored yellow from so much lemon, the Baby followed the Girl from the classroom outside to the schoolyard.

"Is this where you go to school?" he asked. He was already planning in his heart how he would verify in which classroom she studied, in which row she sat, which table and which chair were hers.

"No," she said. "Ahad Ha'am is a boys' school."

"So where do you go to school?"

"At Carmel. It's near the zoo."

"I practically don't go to school anymore," he told her. "I spend the whole day at the loft with the pigeons. But I do kibbutz chores and I read books, too."

The Girl told him that the point he had raised about the sense of direction of pigeons was absolutely correct. "It's not just about directions, either," she said. "All she wants is to get home, but we're sure she wants to pass important pigeongrams to the central pigeon loft."

"We *ladies* are sure," he corrected her, and this time when they laughed their eyes locked. They sat down, and he told her about another idea he had had, an idea that could fulfill the dream of all pigeon handlers of every generation: to train pigeons for two-way flight, not just to return home from somewhere but to travel back and forth between two lofts. Such a capability would open new opportunities in pigeon husbandry, he said excitedly. A homing pigeon could make regular trips between a shepherd in the hills and his farm, between journalists in the field and the offices of their newspapers, or back and forth between army units and the high command.

"Between family members," said the Girl. "Or lovers and couples, too."

# 2

THE CONFERENCE lasted three days, and at the end the fat man from the zoo came laden with woven wicker baskets that cooed. Dr. Laufer fished pigeon after pigeon from them, handing them out to the participants and asking them to dispatch them upon their return home. He placed the pigeons brought by the others in the now empty baskets and told them the pigeons would be dispatched two mornings hence.

The pigeon handlers took their leave of one another and returned to their homes and their lofts. Dr. Laufer, whose life among the animals had taught him to comprehend every shudder of an eye and every hue of skin and every twitch of an earlobe, asked the Baby to stay awhile longer to help the Girl take down the pictures and posters and carry the baskets back to the zoo.

Now the two were alone. They took the pictures and mottoes down from the walls, rolling them up carefully so they would not wrinkle, and when they bent over to collect the baskets their heads drew close and touched. All at once they straightened up and their bodies pressed together.

While she leaned over him and planted her lips on his, the Baby took hold of her hips and pulled her body to his own; then—without knowing what he was doing—he lifted the edges of her blouse, so that her breasts were showing, and removed his lips from hers in order to kiss and suckle her nipples.

She trembled and moaned, but her hands descended, and before she could do anything more than grasp hold of him, the Baby sighed and, with the haste of young men, dispatched his seed into her hand. A pang of longing nipped at him even though she was with him. He felt he was both alive and dead. He had lost his strength and his age. And the Girl felt the warm flow between her fingers and a tremor passed through her. Never before had she known how strong she was.

The Baby, embarrassed, went searching for and found a rag to wipe clean his flesh and clothing, and her hand. But the Girl threw the rag to the floor, wiped her hand on his face, pulled him to the floor, and said, "Now you touch me like that, too."

He was a boy, and did not know who was more anxious and who more pleasured, his hand or her loins, her flesh or his, and he wished to know who had bestowed upon his fingers the sense of taste and the ability to see, and although he did not yet understand all the messages his body was sending him, he already wanted to feel everything that she was—not approximately, but precisely. To know the form of this wonder that his hand was caressing and exploring, not only its warmth and its smoothness and its softness, but also to taste it with his mouth and smell it with his nose and see it with his eyes. Would all this be similar to what he was feeling with his fingers?

The Girl took hold of his hand and moved it from her sex to her stomach. "No, that's it," she said. "I can't anymore." They lay for a while alongside each other, astonished by their power and their weakness, and he licked himself from her hand and she from his. They rose to their feet and adjusted their clothes and lifted the baskets with the pigeons. At first, slightly bashful, they walked down Ahad Ha'am Street. Then, smiling in their hearts, they descended the long, moderate slope that led to the zoo.

At the end of the slope there spread before them a sandy field and the remains of an orchard and a few sycamore trees, and at the opposite end the sandstone hillock with the pool and the zoo. These days, when I pass by there going in the other direction, I imagine the wooden planks placed there "before there were so many sidewalks." The Baby did not wish to walk ahead of the Girl, nor behind her. He walked abreast of her, his legs sinking, his heart overjoyed, and already sadness was eating away at him: soon they would part. The Girl would remain in Tel Aviv and he would return to his pigeon loft on the kibbutz.

# Chapter Twelve

## I

THE TELEPHONE RANG. A man's thin voice said that my wife and I
had passed the interview.

"But there's still one small problem that our treasurer would like to
discuss with you," he said, handing the phone to the treasurer, who
cleared his throat grandly; something about this coughing indicated
that a few other people were standing about and listening to the
conversation. The treasurer told me that "there has been a slight misun-
derstanding," and that the village, "after further investigation and consideration and the input of a professional," would require a small
addition to the price that had been set.

"How small?"

"Fifteen thousand dollars; that's what we were told it would take."

"I'll get back to you," I said, and phoned Tirzah.

"Of course," she said. "Their 'further investigation' was that fancy
car your real wife bought for you. We should have come in the junker of
one of my plasterers and not in the security vehicle of the president of
the United States of America."

"So what am I supposed to do now?"

"Phone and tell them that you're calling off the deal. But not right
away. Do it another forty minutes from now. Forty minutes is a particularly annoying amount of time: it's too short for people to go home and
too long to sit around waiting in the office."

"But the house . . ." I fretted. "I want it."

"Don't worry. They'll back down. I'll bet you that fifteen thousand
dollars they asked for. Call back in forty minutes, and remember: don't

get emotional or angry. Remind them that they were the ones who had set the price and we agreed on it, no haggling. Tell them that you've got the money ready and give them until tomorrow to decide. And don't forget that as far as they're concerned, I'm Mrs. Mendelsohn. If things get messed up I can step into the picture."

"But why?" the village secretary said. "You passed the membership-committee interview so nicely. If you don't have enough cash on hand we can always make some sort of arrangement."

"It's not a matter of arrangements," I said. "You set the price and we agreed without haggling. The money is ready, and you have until tomorrow afternoon to return to your original price or else you can find another buyer."

Meshulam, upon hearing the story from his daughter, inc., the next morning, could not hide his satisfaction. "A new Iraleh!" He slapped my shoulder. "Too bad you didn't add one more sentence: 'You folks did not pass *our* membership committee.' But never mind, the point is that now they know who they're dealing with."

And that is exactly the way it happened. They dropped their demand, and the next morning the new Iraleh signed the contract and paid the money in full. Then he took photographs of the house, had them developed in the nearby commercial center, and drove off to show them to his mother.

At the time, she was at Hadassah Hospital, the internal medicine ward, lying in a bed next to the window.

I stood a few moments in the doorway and observed her. Her body was thin and frail. Her bald head was wrapped in a large blue kerchief. She was gazing at the view—the Castel, Radar Hill, Nebi Samuel—then turned slowly toward me.

"Hello, Mother," I said. "New kerchief?"

"Meshulam gave it to me."

She looked at the photos I had brought. "I'm happy. That is precisely the place I was imagining. I see a few pigeons on the roof. If they've nested under the roof, get rid of them and close up the holes. Pigeons in the roof are a nightmare."

"I'm not a very good photographer," I said, "and it's hard in these pictures to see how well the house fits into the landscape. We'll wait until you're feeling a little better and I'll take you there."

She said, "I'm afraid that won't be happening, Yair, but Tiraleh will certainly do a wonderful job on it. You're in good hands."

I was so taken aback that I did not even ask how she knew about Tirzah renovating the house. "You'll get better," I protested, "and you'll see the house before and after the renovations, and you'll come there whenever you want, and you'll hear the wind blowing in the large trees, and you'll sip your glass of brandy facing the view that you pictured. That house is more yours than mine."

But the next day my mother lost consciousness, and three days later she died. Meshulam said it was only right to postpone starting the renovations. "The house can wait. First you should mourn properly. What's important is that she knew you'd found it and that you're in good hands." Then he burst out crying once again. "Since Gershon and Goldie I haven't felt such pain."

We thought to bury her in her city, Tel Aviv, but my mother had left surprising and explicit instructions in her will. She wanted to be buried in Jerusalem, at the top of the hill in the northwest corner of the cemetery. Through his connections, Meshulam took care of matters with the burial society. "This is what she said to me and the lawyer I brought her: 'It's not so that I can look at Tel Aviv but that Tel Aviv can look at me.'"

We sat shivah in Yordad's flat: Yordad, me, Zohar, who arranged for a samovar and cups and cookies. And Meshulam, who brought us food from Glick's kiosk. The Double-Ys, Yariv and Yoav, were given time off from the army and made the apartment seem full of guests even when no one was there. Liora and Benjamin came in the evenings, along with his condolence callers and friends, who told horror stories of doctors' errors. Tirzah did not come. Meshulam passed along a message from her: she is sorry, she loved your mother very much, and the engineer has set up another meeting with her and the surveyors will come after that.

I wondered whether the two men I saw once at my mother's flat would show up as well: the elderly gentleman who asked me about my major in school and the dark-skinned one who limped and drank strong black coffee that he prepared himself as he hummed a funny tune about King Ahasuerus of the Purim story. Instead, callers came to offer their condolences to Yordad: colleagues and former students, patients he had cared for or their children—some of them in gratitude and others to see what lay behind the brass nameplate that read "Y. MENDELSOHN, PRIVATE."

On the last day of the seven-day mourning period a driving, late-season downpour took us by surprise. By the time I returned to Spinoza Street in Tel Aviv with Liora that evening, the streets were awash. The radio reported flooding and a terrible thought took hold of my mind: my mother's fresh grave might have washed down the slope from the cemetery to Soreq Creek.

At Liora's house, listening to the whisper of raindrops—flowing in the gutters, falling on the roof, dripping on leaves in the garden and tin roofs of memory—I envisioned terrible images of severed limbs and tumbling bones. I sprang up from my bed and got dressed. At last I would put to use the new Gore-Tex rainwear and rubber boots waiting for me in a box inside Behemoth.

"Where are you going?" Liora asked from her bedroom.

I told her the truth. I suspected that my mother's grave had washed away in all the rain and I was going to see what was happening.

"What are you talking about? She's buried inside a cement frame."

"You have no idea what these floods are capable of."

"We just came back from there! What kind of story are you making up?"

"You can come with me if you don't believe me," I told her. She would not come. She would not take part in any of my craziness.

"Even neurotic Jewish sons in America don't go to check whether their mothers' graves have washed away in the rain, and believe me, back home in the U.S. we have worse rains and worse mothers than yours."

"But here, the sons are better," I said as I left.

The weather was terrible. The wind was blowing every which way and rain lashed in all directions. Sometimes it slammed the car's roof and sometimes fell nearly sideways. But Behemoth, as determined as its owner, plied along with confidence and paid no heed to the pleas of smaller cars stuck on the roads, making its way through the Ayalon Valley, climbing past Sha'ar Hagai, ascending, descending, and finally making three right turns from the stoplight before the entrance to the city and up into the cemetery.

I got out of the car and ran among the headstones. Rivulets of water flowed on the paths between the graves, but my mother's plot was intact, along with all the wreaths. There was a wreath from Hadassah Hospital and one from Ichilov Hospital, a wreath from the Hebrew University of Jerusalem and one from the Medical Doctors' Association, a wreath from Kirschenbaum Real Estate of Tel Aviv, Boston, Washington, and New York and one from Meshulam Fried and Daughter, Inc. There was a small, white tin plaque, too, still stuck in a mound of mud. Wet and determined and erect, the words RAYA MENDELSOHN were written on it in black oil paint. I circled the grave, checked it out, and returned to Behemoth to phone Benjamin.

"Everything's fine," I announced.

"What's fine? What are you talking about?"

"Mother. Her grave is in order. It's holding up in the rain."

"Where are you, Yair? Did you go back to the cemetery?"

"I was a little worried. This weather, and the grave hasn't been covered in stone yet."

Benjamin asked if I knew what time it was, I told him I knew, and he asked what was to become of me.

I told him that was not the problem, reminding him I had not asked his advice or assistance. I merely wanted to tell him what was happening.

"Even if you didn't ask for advice," he said, "I'm going to give you some. If you're already in Jerusalem, go sleep at Yordad's. It wouldn't hurt you to pay a visit to a pediatrician before you turn in for the night."

# 2

THE SKY CLEARED the next morning. When I arrived at the house I was met by the faces of three surveyors. One was old and lined and weathered, one, about my age, was potbellied and red-nosed, and one was a large, happy, diligent surveyor-in-training, to whom the others would say, "Bring cold water" or shout, "If your pole's drooping, think about Brigitte Bardot!" to which they would roar with laughter.

After they left, the next-door neighbor came out of her house, stuck two pegs in the ground, and drew a long piece of string from one to the other.

"Why don't you put up a real fence?" I suggested.

"No need." She stretched the string and knotted it and straightened up. "Just so they know that right here's the boundary. That way there'll be no issues or problems," she said sharply.

The next day she made her first tour of inspection along the new boundary. "There have already been issues in the past," she shouted when I stepped out of my house and wished her a good morning. "When matters are clear, all is well."

I did not react to her latest claim, but secretly I was surprised by the gap between her appearance and her behavior. She was a young and beautiful woman, not the kind of beautiful that parches your throat or weakens your knees, but definitely the kind that gladdens your soul. Nothing in her smile or her gait or her demeanor gave any indication of the wrath and misgivings nesting in her heart.

I considered for a moment, then told her that according to the blueprints prepared by the surveyors, the string she had set up was not exactly the border, but in fact had nibbled off a bit of her own land. Her husband, who had come out to listen to our argument, could not resist smiling, and the fury of the young wife rose to new decibels of shouting. She was fed up with "all kinds of new people with money" who came to the village and "interfered with our lives."

Her husband said softly, "He's not interfering with you at all, or me either."

This made her even angrier. "Whose side are you on, anyway, his or mine?!"

They returned to their home, and I sat on a large stone and listened to the sounds around me. The rapid-fire shooting was a woodpecker on the trunk of the neighbors' Persian lilac tree. What sounded like the stealthy footsteps of a murderer in the underbrush were actually blackbirds pecking at fallen leaves. The raucous laughter belonged to a large and brilliantly colored member of the kingfisher family—which one, I did not know—and the loudest noises of all were those of the jays, puzzling birds: I am never able to discern whether they are fighting or playing, cursing or gossiping.

The sun set. From the nearby field, high-pitched shrieks arose. I stood up and approached to see a flock of birds on the ground. Their bodies were a brownish-grayish yellow and slightly larger than that of the pigeon, their legs long, and they shrieked like mad and pranced about with all their energy, welcoming the night with a ceremony of dance.

The blackbirds sounded their last alarms, the darkness deepened, and the first howls of the jackals rose from the hill. Suddenly I recalled how we would hear them in Jerusalem, right near the edge of our neighborhood. There was a pack of jackals nearby, and a second would answer them, sometimes even a third, farther off, whose voices could be heard in the space between the other two packs. I asked you why and about what they howled and you told me that they were not like humans, who expend so much energy on nonsense: animals are very logical creatures. There is an explanation for their every behavior, and packs of jackals, you said, announce to one another where they are and where they plan to search for prey. "Otherwise they will spend all night fighting instead of hunting for food." I loved those little nature lessons of yours. It felt to me as though you, too, had had some teacher in your childhood, someone who taught you, someone whose lessons you loved to listen to.

I went back inside the house. The camping mattress lay on the floor, obediently inflated, and I stripped off my clothes and sprawled across it, closing my eyes. Outside, both winds you promised me were blowing: one in the large trees and a different one in the small trees. I drifted off to sleep and awakened again and again, once because of the "small, common, and hairy" owl, whose voice infused me with mystery and magic: the sounds were so uniform, so hollow, and the spaces between them so precise and measured that they brought on a pleasant sort of pain. Another time it was because I was hearing terrifying death rattles. I went outside and walked toward the source of them and found it was the breathing of a barn owl that lived in the attic of the secretariat building. I returned home, lay down, and did not fall asleep. You were right: the thin scratching overhead was pigeons walking about. Meshulam had been right, too: the weak creaking from outside was the teeth of caterpillars in the fig tree. The pigeons would have to be banished, the holes filled, the fig tree uprooted and a new one planted in its place.

Sounds rose from over the boundary as well; nor was I mistaken about them: the neighbors were making love there, the sounds so clear that they must be doing it on the porch or even right in the garden. While he was silent, her moans were like the pleasant sostenuto of a violin as it crescendos, ending not in a loud cry but a small sigh of resignation. They made it easy for me to imagine the pleasantness of the press of her thighs and the smoothness of her neck and the soft sweetness of her sex. Let her draw strings and establish boundaries: a woman who resonated like that under her lover's bow could never be a bad neighbor, no matter how hard that neighbor tried.

The house itself also emitted noises, becoming a sound box, a memory box. Some of the noises were clear and accidental: shutters in the wind, a door banging its lintel. Others were regular and harder to identify or define: perhaps a discussion between bricks doomed to live next to one another their whole lives; or perhaps of other times and people,

old recordings, words uttered and left behind by those long departed—
a man and a woman, the dream sighs of children, a baby's cries; perhaps
light once soaked up into the walls now wishing to escape as a tone.

I listened, I learned, I sorted, I committed to memory. There was no
blaming the neighbors' apartment here. This was your house, breathing
around you, expanding, teeming, contracting, enwrapping. The ground,
which here is not corseted with cement and straitjacketed with asphalt,
shifts in a slow, never-ending dance, while we—the houses, the trees,
the people, the animals—are carried about in its arms, moving on its
thin outer crust.

# 3

EVER SINCE her divorce, Tirzah has had no home of her own. She left
the house they shared to her husband when they split up. "First of all
because I felt sorry for him. And second of all, if you can get through it
without any disputes, so much the better. How many years do we have
left to live? Seven good years followed by seven terrible years? Maybe
only three, like that poor Robert Louis Stevenson you told me about,
who died after finishing building that house of his on the island? So,
should we waste the little we have on property and revenge?"

She scrutinized me to discern whether I was catching her drift. "I
didn't mind him taking the house, making his day. All I cared about was
getting rid of him, getting him out of my sight. I don't want to see him
or hear him or feel him ever again."

"And now?"

Now she did not have a home. She had her car and her rooms: a room
in the Tel Aviv offices, a room in a hotel in Haifa, a room in a hotel in
Beersheba, and a room in the large house belonging to her father in the
Arnona neighborhood of Jerusalem.

"What if you entertain a guest now and then?"

"You can speak your mind, Iraleh. You mean a one-night stand? A
man for a night? A week? Is that what you call a now-and-then guest?"

"You know . . ."

"No. I don't entertain guests now and then. Not for a night and not
for two. It's been ages. Women can live for quite a while without a man,"
she said, then suddenly smiled broadly. "But Meshulam, you'll be surprised to hear, he entertains women sometimes."

"I'm not surprised at all. Where does he sleep with them?"

"He doesn't. They come and then they leave and then the sleeping part he does alone, in Gershon's bed."

"That's strange."

"What? That they don't sleep over?"

"No. That your father sleeps in Gershon's bed."

"Nothing strange about it. Meshulam is the simple type of bereaved father. Apart from attending the annual Memorial Day service at the military cemetery, he doesn't do anything. He didn't even put out one of those albums in Gershon's memory. And that's a pity, because Gershon left behind a few phenomenal chemistry projects he worked on in high school and at the Weizmann Institute summer camp. I suggested to Meshulam that we give out scholarships in his name and he got mad at me. 'My son's buried and someone's going to study and become a professor in his place?'

"Can you understand the guy? He just cries into his handkerchief and tries to make me call him 'Father' instead of 'Meshulam' like I'm accustomed, and he sleeps in Gershon's bed. And that doesn't bother a soul. Not me, not his lady guests, who leave anyway. Not my dead mother. I'd bet it doesn't even bother Gershon that his father is sleeping in his bed. There's enough room for two. So I don't know why it should seem strange to you, of all people."

That is how the Fried home became a hotel, and Meshulam's garden shed, formerly his own private spot, had become his home. At first it had been a tiny room for tools and fertilizers and seeds, then a small, off-limits world with a folding bed and an immersion heater and a sugar container and two teacups. Ever since Gershon, he added a single burner and a small refrigerator and an armchair that knows how to lie back and become a bed, and ever since his Goldie, too, the shed has gone from being Meshulam's private corner to his actual residence. When he gets home from work he goes straight there, rests and reads and prepares himself light meals; then later he lies down, a large handkerchief—the blue of which is lined with faded streaks of salty tears—spread across his face. Only in the evening does he enter the house itself, where he showers and shaves and entertains his lady guests. Afterward, they leave and Meshulam goes to sleep in his son's bed and listens to the drops falling on the tin sheeting outside. "So much for all that nonsense about rooms and roles and names."

# 4

A NEW NOISE awakened me in the morning. I peered out between the spaces in the planks of wood boarding up the window. Two trucks were parked next to the house. Their cranes were unloading huge sacks of sand and gravel, bricks and floor tiles and roof tiles on wooden pallets, flexible and solid pipes in different diameters and colors, screens of various thicknesses, circuit boards and plumbing equipment. Two Chinese workers were pushing a cement mixer to the wall. This was Tirzah strewing her toys across her new playground.

I got dressed and went out to the yard. "Good morning, Iraleh," Meshulam called out to me. "You see, it's a good thing you pruned and cleaned up. Now we'll be able to make you a very nice garden here."

He swaggered, waved his arms, pointed, did what he likes best: told others what to do. "First of all we have to straighten out this slope. We'll put boulders in here to make a wall and we'll bring in three or four truckloads of earth. I've got someone who'll bring deep dirt, doesn't have even a single seed of weeds in it, and it won't cost you a penny because he owes me a favor." He whispered something into his daughter's ear, and I enjoyed the way their compact, sturdy bodies drew close, the intimacy with which the father planted his lips on the daughter's temple, the self-assurance with which the daughter lay her hand on her father's shoulder, stroking him, giving him strength, drawing out his pain.

"I don't want a big wall there," I hastened to state before the two could determine my fate. "I prefer two or three smaller terraces, and I want access for Behemoth from the back of the property."

"A single large wall is better," Meshulam proclaimed. "As for the car, you've got the whole street in front. Why come from behind like some robber from the fields? Anyway, we've got to hurry because after the summer there will be rain and the entire field will be mud and the trucks with the earth won't be able to come in close."

But Tirzah also thought it was a good idea to keep the option of rear access for Behemoth, and she, too, believed that a few small terraces were preferable to one large wall. She suggested I build them myself. "Look at him, Meshulam," she said, pointing at me. "With all the energy this house is pumping into him, isn't it a good idea to take advantage of it while he's got it?"

"I don't have a clue about this, or any experience," I announced.

"You don't need either. It's donkey work that any jackass could handle," Tirzah said. "I'll give you my pickup truck. Go find stones, load them in, bring them, and build them. Your body is like mine; it likes and needs to exert itself. I'll take the terraces off the bill when we do the final accounting."

She advised me, too: a terrace is not a house. It doesn't require a certain kind of stone chiseled in a certain, unified manner. On the contrary: rough-hewn stones of different sizes and hues lend beauty and personality to the terrace. "And remember," she called after me, "the pickup has to be able to get back on the road, so don't overload it and drag it through the dirt."

The pickup truck that Tirzah loaned me was quite different from the car that Liora had bought me. Rougher, tougher, and on rocky terrain it lifts a rear wheel at every opportunity. "But," as its mistress boasted, "absolutely nothing stops it. It'll keep running long after your fancy chariot breaks down going over some step."

I drove it carefully, enjoying the hum of the motor and the stubborn clutch after the smooth automatic gears of Behemoth. My hands grasped the steering wheel in the same place hers did. I felt as if I were wearing an article of her clothing, smelling her scent, imagining the heat of her loins that had been absorbed into the seat and was now rising into me.

Several minutes later, just as I plunged into the blind spot on the other side of the hill, I stopped to poke about in the compartments of the pickup. A person should know exactly who his contractor is, especially if his contractor is a woman. I found a small and shockingly bad collection of songs recorded by military bands, a pair of black sunglasses, clear Vaseline lip balm, a few plastic lighters, a packet of Drum tobacco, a medium-sized Swiss Army knife, a key ring with five keys on it.

"Tell us about yourselves, guys," I told them. "One by one, please."

I open the house she's building for you. I open the Fried home in Jerusalem. I open the offices of Meshulam Fried and Daughter, Inc., and I, the filing cabinet.

"And what about you?"

Silence.

I got out of the pickup and opened the back door. Rolling around on the floor were a hard hat and a pair of worn and faded hiking sandals very different from my own. Three bottles of mineral water, too, all of which had been drunk from, and toilet paper, and rubber boots. A straw hat sat on the seat, along with a digital camera, wet wipes, hand cream, and a number of dog-eared novels, all of which had been translated into Hebrew.

"I can't stand reading books written about us," she told me later. "I prefer reading about other people and lands." She smiled. "That's the only question you have for me after poking around my car?"

Behind the seat I found tow straps with professional red shackles, tie-down ropes, an old army jacket with the name STAFF SERGEANT GERSHON FRIED fading on the lapel, and a pair of work gloves. From there I moved to the back, where I found all the tools needed by a stone thief: a crowbar, a pickax, a second pair of gloves. And then—relief! The fifth key fit a locked metal toolbox that contained a few repair tools, a coffee kit, and a sealed Pelican suitcase. I opened that, too: a clean, perfume-scented dress, pressed trousers, two shirts, two pairs of shoes, toiletries, a small bottle of aftershave, another key, underwear. My heart—because it had relaxed—now contracted even harder. Where do you go for entertainment, Tiraleh? And with whom? When will you wear this dress with me? And this new damned key, what takes place behind its door?

I put everything back in place and shut the case. I continued on my way, at first along a shallow ravine, bouncing along over the metal bars meant to keep cows from straying, then up a moderately sloping hill to its other side, until finally I reached the small, ruined Arab village I had discovered during my wanderings over a map of the area.

All the buildings had been demolished. Some had caved in on their own; others had fallen victim to explosives training conducted by the army. The collecting pool of the spring had been destroyed, but a trickle of water still flowed through a channel that emerged from the thick undergrowth of wild mint and raspberry. All around were piles of stones, here and there half a wall still standing, or a stubborn arch upon which was scrawled the graffiti of soldiers on navigational training missions: YALLI'S TEAM; PLATOON FOR THE SICK, TIRED, AND FED-UP; BORN TO KILL; FLYING TIGER RECONNAISSANCE UNIT. And, as in every such abandoned village, hedges of prickly-pear bushes, bitter almond trees, grapevines crawling on the ground for lack of someone to shape them, prune them, harvest them. Here, too, forsaken fig trees cried out, their leaves drooping and their bloated, unripened fruit bearing witness to the terrible effort of motherhood to pass on the tiniest drops of moisture to the offspring.

Nearby stood several wild plum trees. Their fruit was small and blue and piqued my curiosity. Once upon a time they had been grafted with apricots and cultured plums, but many years had passed since they had last been looked after, and the strong understock had overwhelmed the scions and produced shoots and tiny, sour fruit—not sweet and delicious like the cultured plum, but still tempting to the palate thanks to its strangeness. I picked a few to bring to Meshulam because they looked just like the plums in the picture on his bottles of țuică.

Next, I turned to the stones. The selection was large: cleanly hewn stones and simple fieldstones, stones from nearby and stones from far away. A few I could identify as limestone, which someone must have brought from the coastal region. Several of the stones were quite ancient. Depressions made by hinges or bolts could be detected in some, evidence of the ways of this land: war, exile, people uprooted and banished, stones abducted, moved from one place and time to another. Perhaps I should take my bird-watchers to observe the flight of these migrating stones: stones from temples, from cemeteries, from bathhouses, stones from the catapult and the walkway, stones rolled from the head of a grave or the mouth of a well, stones that covered and walled and fenced, that served as corner or head or threshold or lintel. Stones from oil presses, milestones, upper and lower millstones. Mosaic stones and stoning stones.

Then, after I had finished selecting and loading them, I nearly fell into a large cistern, the opening to which I had not noticed before. I leaned over and peered into the dark void. Two pigeons, two bluish-gray rock pigeons, flew out from it with a startling beating of wings. I leapt backward. The pigeons rose high in the sky and circled slowly, waiting for me to depart.

I tossed a small stone into the cistern. It hit lightly, dryly. The pit was empty; there was no water in it, yet pigeons still flew from its abyss. The beating of the pigeons' wings alarmed their sisters in adjacent cisterns, and they, too, lifted off from their oblivions. The earth, so it suddenly seemed, opened its mouth beneath me and spit out pigeons, more and more of them, and they flew overhead like a cloud of feathered breasts and flailing wings.

Afterward, the pigeons gathered into a large flock, forming an enormous circle with me centered beneath them. And when I left there, they dived and returned to their dovecotes as if sucked into the chasm. I climbed into Tirzah's pickup truck and headed to my new house.

# 5

THE WORKERS HAD FINISHED unloading the materials and equipment. They pulled an old refrigerator off one of the trucks, stood it under the house in the space between the support columns, and plugged it into an extension cord dangling from the window. Next to the refrigerator they set up a cabinet and a table with an electric kettle and a gas burner. A tall, yellow-haired youth filled the refrigerator with vegetables, containers of yogurt, cottage cheese and hard cheese, bottles of beverages, boxes of milk and eggs.

The unpacking completed, Tirzah's loading crew took to its wheels and disappeared. Meshulam hung the building authorization notices endorsed by the local council on the wall, as required. "You see? One phone call by Meshulam saved you a whole mess of running around."

As if on cue the tractor operator reappeared in the yard. He pulled his rubbish cart up to the back of the house, removed from it a thick metal pipe, and hung it from the lemon tree. He struck the pipe soundly and it resounded; the two Chinese workers, the tall, yellow-haired youth, the tractor operator, and another sturdy laborer all lined up in front of Tirzah. Since I did not know what to do with myself, I remained at the side.

"Men," said my contractor, who is a woman, "I have taken you off our big jobs because this fellow needs a place of his own. We're going to make a little Garden of Eden for him here. He'll have a floor and a roof, water and light, grass and trees, birds and animals. He'll have new plumbing, new electricity, windows, doors. We'll reinforce the foundations, we'll plaster and whitewash, we'll build him a small outdoor shower and a large wooden deck on which he'll be able to sit and relax facing the view."

The workers chuckled, nodded in my direction, and entered the house.

"What a speech!" I told her. "Are you sure they understand Hebrew?"

"They don't need to understand Hebrew, Iraleh; that speech was for you. Now let's go inside, because we're going to start soon and you need to be there for the beginning."

Not with anything else—not the signing of the contract with the village, not the transfer of the first payment—was there the decisiveness, the feeling of in-the-beginning, as there was at this moment, the start of the work or, more precisely, the first strike of a heavy hammer against a wall doomed to destruction.

The chosen wall was the western wall of the main room, which faced the view. It had one frightened little window, the dimensions of which expressed its aspiration to remain shut rather than its ability to open. Now both—the window and the wall—had been condemned to vanish. Tirzah said an enormous opening would be ripped out here, beyond which the wooden deck would be built.

Tirzah instructed the sturdy laborer to take up the hammer; then she gave a slight nod of her head and raised her eyebrow in the direction of the wall. The laborer did not spit into the palms of his hands, nor did he rub them together. He grasped the very end of the long wooden handle in order to increase the strength of the blow and swung it over his left shoulder. Like an iron pigeon whose message is its landing, the hammer lifted off, circled the man's head and shoulders, and hit squarely, tearing a hole in the wall.

The house reverberated. For days it had been sensing the commotion, had taken note of Meshulam's profession thanks to his rapping and tapping and his voice, had listened in on my conversations with Tirzah, had watched the surveyors and the engineer and the trucks and the equipment that emerged from them, and it had already prepared itself for what was coming: the slam of the hammer, the pecking of the chisel, the sawing of the disc, the crowbar, the extraction and the shifting and the removal. But none of this reduced the shock it was feeling just then, and the knowledge that the matter would not end with this one strike. A new resident had arrived and he would change the ways of the house—its entrances and exits—and he would re-create its light and its darkness, he would erase memories and footprints and aromas, he would proclaim the establishment of a new relationship between its insides and its outsides.

The sturdy laborer pounded around the first gaping hole, demolishing the bricks in an orderly and systematic manner. And when there was nothing left of the wall but a heap of crumbs and dirt and lumps, the two Chinese workers attacked it with large shovel and heaved it into the rubbish cart put in place below, in the yard, by the tractor operator.

"And there was light!" Tirzah said. "Look how much light there is in your house all of a sudden."

In the same manner, the man pulled down two more internal walls, and with the disc cutter he enlarged the window openings in the external walls. The Chinese workers drained rusted pipes and pulled them from the walls, then did the same with the electric cables, which, now that they were powerless, looked like dead snakes. They removed, too, the old windowsills and doorposts and lintels.

Tirzah said to the tall, yellow-haired youth, "Go down and put a big pot of soup on the burner so we have something to eat for lunch."

"What kind?" he grumbled.

"The kind you like to eat at your mother's house."

"But I don't know how to make her soup."

Tirzah removed the mobile phone from her pocket and handed it to him. "Here. Call her and ask how she makes it."

The youth stepped aside and held a conversation in Russian, during which he wrote copious notes; then he approached Tirzah and told her something, received the keys to her pickup truck along with several bills, and drove off. Less than an hour after his return, a delicious aroma rose from the gas burner below. He had prepared a large, thick pot of soup as his mother had taught him, brimming with potatoes, barley, onion, turnips, carrots, garlic, beef, and bones. He asked Tirzah when she wanted it to be served.

"When it's ready. I'm famished."

And when it was ready the yellow-haired youth struck the metal pipe that the tractor operator had hung from the lemon tree and called one and all to eat their first lunch in my new home.

# 6

THE NEXT DAY Tirzah sent the Russian youth and the sturdy laborer to other building sites of hers, while we remained with the two Chinese workers. "It's us and them to the end," she said. "Except for a few craftsmen who will join us later on."

The two of them climbed to the empty space between the ceiling and the roof tiles. They could be heard sawing and prying. Bits of roofing—

crumbling old plaster held together by rusted iron mesh—plunged downward and raised dust. The pigeons living there and hoping up to that very moment that this was some kind of mistake flew off in a panic. They darted about under the roof tiles, then fled through the new, large window.

I told Tirzah my mother had ordered me to get rid of them.

"She was absolutely right. Get those filthy birds out of here and make sure they don't come back," she said. "We've got to plug up every crack and hole. That's all you need: pigeons on your head."

The removal of the ceiling doubled the open space of the house and filled it with echoes. Tirzah stood a ladder there, climbed it, and walked expertly about on the planks, locating pigeons' nests. At once she destroyed them with the tip of her boot. The spindly twigs, covered with dung, fell to earth along with several white eggs, which splattered on the floor.

"Pigeons," she said, "are very nice when they fly in the air, and even nicer when they bring letters, and nicest of all when served with rice and herbs, but in the roof they are not nice at all. Not here, ladies. Go find yourselves another home."

She came down. "Want to work?" she asked me.

"Okay," I said, "but don't forget I'm no expert. Give me something simple to do."

She broke two floor tiles in the far corner of the room and handed me a crowbar. "Take this guy and pry out the old tiles, then clear them out with the wheelbarrow, along with the refuse from the ceiling."

I enjoyed the way the tiles surrendered, their parting from the floor, the removal of all those feet that had previously walked about in this house. I placed everything in the wheelbarrow and wheeled it to the edge of the room, where at the beginning of the day there had been a wall and where now there was a huge opening toward the view. I tipped the wheelbarrow into the rubbish cart parked underneath and returned for more. Later, I cleaned up with a large pushbroom all the way down to the cement.

"Nice work," Tirzah praised me. "I like this stage of maximum height, from the cement to the roof tiles, no floor, no ceiling. The biggest space possible."

When she finished speaking, Meshulam showed up with a gaunt and sinewy old man whose hands were so broad that it seemed they had been borrowed from some other man.

Tirzah beamed. "This is Steinfeld the tiler, our most veteran employee. I've known him from the time I was born. Back then he was a hundred years old, so you can imagine how old he is today."

In one of his massive hands Steinfeld was carrying a bucket that held a long, flexible, transparent pipe, a small funnel, and a collapsible wooden measuring stick. A thick yellow pencil was stuck behind his ear and a very old schoolbag hung across his back, its leather tattered, its buckles peeling, and its shoulder straps so ancient that it raised the suspicion that he himself had been the pupil who had carried this schoolbag to the first grade.

On one of the walls he drew a small triangle three feet above the cement floor.

"Hold the end of this here, kid," he said as he handed me the pipe.

"He's not an employee, Steinfeld, he's the home owner," Tirzah said. "The Chinese guy over there is the worker."

"The *Khinezer*?" he asked, slipping into Yiddish. "How can I tell him what to do? Which does he prefer, Yiddish or Hebrew?"

He ladled water into the mouth of the pipe he was holding and began pulling it from wall to wall and from room to room and from corner to corner and from opening to opening, skimming the walls and drawing small triangles and shouting in my direction, "Don't move!"

"Do you understand what he's doing?" Tirzah asked me.

"No."

"You're doing the *stichmuss*."

"Now I get it. It's all perfectly clear."

"Don't you remember back in high school, the law of communicating vessels? All those little triangles are exactly the same height. They'll determine the height of everything in the house later on—the floor, the thresholds, the windowsills, the countertops, the windows. Neat, huh?"

"I hope it's accurate, too."

"What are you talking about? The *stichmuss* is the most accurate thing there is! It's not a way of measuring with a ruler or visually or with your hand. It's relative to the floor or the ceiling of the house. It's relative to the world. Isn't it nice to know that the windowsill over your kitchen sink and the sill on your bedroom window are exactly the same distance from the center of the earth?"

"That certainly is nice, yes."

# Chapter Thirteen

## I

THE NAME of the Baby is written on the memorial plaque for fallen soldiers in the Jordan Valley Regional High School, but the truth is, he was a weak student who rarely visited the classroom, and his teachers were constantly scolding him. At fifteen he decided that pigeons interested him more than anything he was learning there, and two years hence, Miriam also informed him she had nothing more to teach him.

Indeed, at seventeen the Baby was already a respected *duvejeck* who attended in-service training sessions and won competitions and hybridized excellent males with female racing champions, and sometimes he would travel to Tel Aviv, either on pigeon business or to meet the Girl, to talk to her, to whistle with her, to touch her in the same manner that she touched him, and to take his pigeons to her and to take her pigeons back with him. At eighteen he announced that it was time for him to enlist in the Palmach.

His aunt and uncle were terribly anxious on his behalf, but Dr. Laufer assured them that the Baby would continue his avocation in the Palmach and, like Miriam, would set up a pigeon loft. "Anybody can light a campfire and shoot a Sten gun and steal chickens," he said, "but how many expert pigeon handlers are there?" He reassured them that their Baby would soon be training and rearing pigeons and, when necessary, dispatching pigeons to central command or providing a battle-bound unit with a pigeon for dispatch.

In anticipation of his enlistment, the Baby went to the kibbutz carpentry shop, and with the help of the carpenter he prepared a one-of-a-kind dovecote he could carry on his back, with four stories—three built of wood and screens, the fourth of tarp sewn with compartments for message capsules, strings, quills, pigeongram forms, mineral powder, medicines, eating and drinking implements for the pigeons, and tea, sugar, and a glass mug for him. He added a curtain to guard the pigeons against rain and the beating sun, and his uncle sewed wide, thick shoulder straps for him.

And this is how he enlisted: in work boots and faded khaki clothing he had received from the kibbutz warehouse and a brand-new *tembel* hat on his head, and in his small suitcase there were clothes and underwear, a sweater and a woolen stocking cap knitted by his aunt, and toiletries and writing implements and a sewing kit, and three pigeons in the dovecote, one of Miriam's and two from Tel Aviv.

Although it was numbingly heavy, he maintained that same gaping, slightly sky-bound look of fascination, that same heavyset body, that same expression of wonder he'd had upon awakening on that very first day the new pigeon loft had been erected next to the children's house. And so it is easy to imagine the reaction he received when he appeared thus at the Palmach tent camp in Kiryat Anavim, near Jerusalem, where he had been sent. There was a huge outburst of laughter; someone called him a "donkey carrying birds" and someone else called him *kelbeleh,* or "calf," just like his aunt had named him; however, this *kelbeleh* had not been uttered in love but in scorn, the smile accompanying it an evil one full of long rat's teeth. Suddenly a guy who had studied two years ahead of him in school appeared and said, "The situation must be pretty bad if the Palmach has started enlisting babies." And so his nickname became known and it stuck to him here, too.

But the Baby took it all in stride. He laid down his belongings, fed and watered his pigeons, and went to investigate the loft in which he would raise the chicks he would soon be receiving from the central loft in Tel Aviv. When he saw it he deemed the loft and its location unsuitable, both for the pigeons and for operational needs. "A homing pigeon must love her home," he said, declaiming the pigeon handler's motto. "No pigeon will want to return to this loft."

He hurried to the carpentry shop and succeeded in persuading the carpenter—an exact duplicate of the carping carpenter on his own kibbutz, in fact just another in a long line of carping carpenters in every carpentry shop on every kibbutz during those times—that he should take a break from his other work and help him build a new loft. The carpenter was a small man with meticulously combed hair and work clothes that were clean and pressed. He did not dare sport a tie there, but he buttoned his shirt all the way up his neck and in the shop he had a large mirror that was far grander than any mirror kept by any kibbutz comradette in her room.

Together, the two built a large loft that would keep the pigeons safe from strong winds and dampness but would still be sun-drenched and full of air, precisely accordingly to what Dr. Laufer had told the Baby: "There are no hard-and-fast rules of loft building, just as there are no hard-and-fast rules in building for human beings. Everything depends on needs and possibilities." The Baby found a quiet, out-of-the-way spot and, with the help of the carpenter, a mule, a cart, and two guys from the Palmach unit stationed there, he transported the loft and set it down facing south. After digging a large, square pit for waste, he washed his hands, took hold of one of the Girl's pigeons, and attached a message capsule to her leg and tied a quill between her tail feathers. The pigeongram in the capsule was intended for Dr. Laufer: "The loft is ready to receive chicks and commence training." The note in the quill was intended for the Girl, and it read "Yes and yes and yes." Yes I love you, yes I miss you, yes I know and remember that you do, too, for in her last missive she had written "No and no," that is to say, No I do not want anyone other than you and no I do not manage to sleep at night.

He raised his hands, let go, and dispatched the pigeon, watching her rise in the sky. At first she darkened and then she melted and disappeared into the blue-gray sky that was the same color as she, and once again he experienced the thrill of this feeling, which persisted even after hundreds and thousands of dispatches, since that day, now receding, when he went with Miriam to the fields and dispatched his very first pigeon, to the day, now approaching, when he will lie in a pool of his own blood and dispatch his last.

# 2

ALMOST NINE YEARS had passed since a wounded pigeon had landed on a Tel Aviv balcony and since Dr. Laufer had come with Miriam and the pigeons to a Jordan Valley kibbutz. The Baby and the Girl had become a young man and a young woman. Miriam had smoked more than three thousand evening cigarettes. The green pickup truck had logged many kilometers and engine hours and years of life and had grown quite old and scarcely capable of ascending from the coastal plain. But Dr. Laufer, in spite of the white that had begun to weave its way through his red hair, remained as full of energy and excitement as ever. He showed up at Kiryat Anavim with the equipment and the chicks and leapt from the pickup truck, his long narrow back stooped, his limbs flailing, the royal or humble *we* in his mouth.

"We brought you a surprise!" he shouted to the Baby, and from inside the pickup truck emerged the Girl, tall and serious and curly-haired, just as blue-eyed and pink-cheeked and fair-haired as she was in his dreams and his memories.

"I came to give you a hand," she said, a blush creeping across her face, her eyes joyful.

His heart stopped. In Dr. Laufer's presence he did not dare touch her, but the Girl leaned her head over his. Their faces drew close, touched, caught fire. Their hands folded and unfolded, did not know where to land.

The carpenter arrived from the carpentry shop and attached the trap doors that had been brought in their frames. Dr. Laufer inspected his work and said, "It is good" and "It is very good," and then, as was his custom, he searched the loft for splinters and nails that might cause injury and slits through which a snake or a mouse could infiltrate. He sealed and tightened and banged with his little hammer and exclaimed, "You thought we didn't see you!" which is what he said when he inspected every new loft.

The Baby and the Girl unloaded the boxes containing the chicks and bags of seed and all the regular loft equipment from the pickup truck. Dr. Laufer dispatched several pigeons he had brought from the central loft, went to pay a visit to the Haganah loft in Jerusalem, and brought pigeons from there—young ones to dispatch from Kiryat Anavim and experienced ones to dispatch from Hulda and even more experienced ones for dispatch from Tel Aviv.

"Every trip must be put to good use," he said, then wished the Baby good luck and disappeared.

The Girl stayed on for two days at Kiryat Anavim. They arranged the bags of seed on raised strips of wood, covered them with dense chicken wire to keep them out of reach of mice, and prepared the identification bands with the month and year of banding—which was also the birth date of the pigeon—and the first letter of the name of the pigeon handler, since it was not safe to write the name of the place or the unit. They fitted the bands to each pigeon's three front toes gathered together, pulled them over the back toe—which had been pressed to the leg—and let go.

After that, the Girl organized the individual file cards of each chick and the breeding cards, which would be filled in when the chicks had matured and were paired off, and she entered the initial information in the flock log.

In the evening, the Baby went to the dining hall and brought back bread and olives. They sat and ate next to the loft. It was a late-summer evening, hot and dry, and, as happens in the Jerusalem hills, cool caresses were woven in with the warm breezes. When they had finished eating they spread a wool army blanket on the ground near the loft and lay down upon it, side by side.

From Abu Ghosh they could hear the first evening calls of the muezzin, the jackals competing and overtaking him as they did every night. The Girl breathed into his neck. "They're so close," she said.

"They're farther away than they sound," the Baby told her.

Several shadows passed by, slipped down to the ravine, disappeared.

"Who were they?" she asked him.

"Guys from my unit. They're on their way to an operation."

They awakened together before dawn. From the wadi below there arose a metallic sound of digging, hoes hitting rock, pickaxes raking stone rubble and clumps of earth.

"What's that?" the Girl whispered.

He hesitated. He thought to tell her it was members of the kibbutz digging planting holes, but instead he told her the truth, that these were his comrades digging graves for those who would not return. He grinned. "I usually dig, too, because I don't go out on operations, but tonight they let me skip duty because of you."

The next day the Girl returned to the central loft. In the Baby's loft there were only the new chicks, which had not yet undergone domestication or training, and he had no pigeon of his own to give her, but she left one of hers with him before climbing into the truck that would bring her back to Tel Aviv.

When the truck disappeared from view the Baby felt more alone than ever before. Suddenly he recalled his mother, who had left him and returned to Europe and was killed in the Holocaust—by this time he understood what the adults had assumed and whispered—and he thought, too, about his father, how he had come to visit him at the kibbutz but could not look him in the eye. And about his father's wife, who had glanced around and said, "What a beautiful place—I wish I could live here . . ." And he recalled himself as well, the day he had said, "Don't bring her here again. If you do, I'll kick you both out."

His heart tightened and grew sad. He went back to the pigeon loft, wondered at how such a bad start had turned so good: had his mother not left his father and returned to Europe, his father would not have remarried and he would not have been banished to the kibbutz and would never have met Miriam or Dr. Laufer or the pigeons or his beloved. Then he shook himself free of these thoughts and consoled himself that from here on there would be no more ups and downs and setbacks, only love for the Girl and the routine of the pigeons. This was good: a daily schedule, a work program, regular chores. These calmed and healed the heart, and he yielded to them gleefully.

He awakened each morning, released the pigeons of his flock for their first flight—which grew longer and longer—and gathered them back to the loft with flags and whistles, then fed, confined, and washed them. At night he dug graves, and the hours he was required to give to the kibbutz he spent in the cowshed and the carpentry shop. Some of the fighters looked down on him, even scorned him: he lost neither friends nor blood, he added no sticks to their bonfires nor took part in their convoys to Jerusalem, and, as they used to joke back then, he neither killed nor was killed even once. The more soulful ones among them, however, regarded him with curiosity because there was something captivating about this short, chubby boy who caused pigeons—even transient ones—to swoop down to him and hover about his head and land on his shoulders.

Dr. Laufer once said at a conference that pigeons never look as fast or determined as when they return home, and they never look as bad-tempered or vicious as when they are fighting for their nest or their mate. The Baby, too, gave a mistaken impression. He still had the small, rotund body of his youth but his self-confidence had grown, and beneath the dimpled elbows and knees and hands that every baby has, his muscles had hardened. He had grown slightly thinner—just like me, when Tirzah had me building my new house—and people who know how to interpret the angle of someone's lips and the expression on someone's face saw on his direction and determination.

And still he maintained his old desire to teach pigeons—which know to fly to only one location—to fly back and forth between two points. Such homing pigeons, the experts told him in wonder, could be found only in India and America, the former thanks to thousands of years of pigeon expertise and the latter thanks to an unending flow of funds.

"And along comes our Baby," Dr. Laufer exclaimed at the pigeon handlers' conference that year, "and succeeds, with no assistance or budget, in training two-directional pigeons, which now maintain regular communication between Kiryat Anavim and Jerusalem."

How had he done it? Well, he'd selected young pigeons whose wings were ready and whose flying feathers had sprouted, and after they completed basic flight training, he taught them that they would receive food at the loft in which they resided but water only at another loft, a portable dovecote marked with a bold color that stood out. This dovecote he gradually moved until the pigeons were eating in Kiryat Anavim and drinking in Jerusalem. And since only six or seven miles separated the two lofts if traveling by air—in other words, only about ten minutes of flight—the pigeons traveled back and forth twice daily, eating here and drinking there, and they transferred reports and instructions from command to command.

Even the dove that returned to Noah's ark, he told his audience, could be seen as a homing pigeon returning to a portable dovecote, one that stood out in its solitude. And he began to plan a large portable loft that could be pulled behind a vehicle and house many pigeons to escort armies into battle. However, at that time he had neither the budget nor the vehicle for such an enterprise, and the roads were unsafe, and the training would be impossible. The matter remained a dream, and the Baby carried on caring for the regular homing pigeons, the ones whose home was with him and the ones from the Jerusalem loft or the central loft in Tel Aviv, and these pigeons waited with longing, thinking of nothing but the screen on their prison and the great skies beyond it and the home beyond that, and they did not know what they were carrying in their wings—a love letter or commands.

# 3

IN THE MEANTIME, the training of a new and especially large group of chicks had been completed at the Tel Aviv zoo, and Dr. Laufer explained to the Girl that these were destined for an important task. War would be breaking out soon and the outposts in the south would be the sole obstacle standing between the Egyptian army and Tel Aviv, so it was necessary to pay visits to all those places and provide them with pigeons that would help maintain communication with central command.

"You will travel to Negba and Ruhama," he told her, "to Dorot and Gvaram and Yad Mordechai, and if possible, to Kfar Darom and Nirim and Gvulot as well. You will need to leave pigeons in every one of those places so they can let us know if, God forbid, they are under siege. And don't forget to tell them absolutely not to let the pigeons out for a flight, because if we are released we will immediately fly homeward, here, to our home in Tel Aviv."

"All by myself?" the Girl asked, astonished.

"A command car has been acquisitioned for your use, along with two young men from the Palmach, which is a lot more than other actions are receiving. One is an excellent driver and the other was wounded in battle, but he is a very good scout and knows the south well. They are responsible for bringing you to all those places and for returning you to Tel Aviv, and you are responsible for handing out pigeons and explaining to people what they must do. In Ruhama and Dorot we have pigeon handlers and proper lofts and you will bring several of their pigeons back with you so that we can send them pigeongrams, and in other places try to catch pigeons in the cowshed. If the distance is not too great there is a chance that an ordinary pigeon will return home. We'll paint two of its feathers yellow and green so they'll know if she has returned."

They prepared the supplies and the equipment; they selected and marked and recorded the pigeons in two identical notepads, one that would remain with Dr. Laufer and the other that the Girl placed in her knapsack. The next morning she woke up, took leave of her parents, and left for the zoo. Her mother cried—"Where are all the boys? Do they have to send girls?"—and her father said only that "they're counting on you out there. Take care of yourself and of the birds."

"Each outpost will receive six pigeons," Dr. Laufer told her. "Four of our own and another that you will get from Shimon, the pigeon handler at Givat Brenner. You surely remember him from the conferences. We've asked him to mark his pigeons with red bands so that at the outposts they will know which should return to each place."

He was silent for a while, then said, "This is a slightly dangerous mission. Please watch out for the young men traveling with you—don't let them get up to any nonsense. And don't forget to take one of the Baby's pigeons so he won't worry about where you've suddenly disappeared to."

The sound of a whistle came from the street. The fat man from the zoo opened the supply gate and a command car carrying two Palmach men entered and moved slowly toward the storeroom. The driver was short, dark, and stocky and reminded her of the Baby but with a tougher, more aggressive look than his; the scout was swarthy and large and walked with a limp. They brought the Girl a long Shinel woolen army coat—the nights were still cold, they told her—and a pistol.

"I don't know how to use this," she said.

"It's really easy," the large one told her. "You put your arms in the sleeves and button the buttons all the way to the top. Like this."

The short one added, "And if you're still cold, pull the collar up."

The Girl grew angry and reddened while the boys shrieked with laughter that frightened the animals. "Don't worry," they told her, "at Givat Brenner we'll take you to a firing range."

Cartons full of equipment and mail were piled into the command car; the fat man from the zoo heaped and tied the boxes containing the pigeons and the feedbags on top. The Girl said good-bye to Dr. Laufer and climbed into the vehicle, sitting on a bench fashioned by the boys from boxes and blankets.

The command car left the zoo and traveled south through the streets of Tel Aviv. That war was impending could be felt everywhere: sandbags stood like fortifying walls at the entrances to buildings. Here and there they passed barricades and barbed wire. Silence prevailed. People in khaki walked purposefully, their faces drawn and contemplative.

At the exit from the city they joined up with several vehicles loaded with supplies that had been waiting for them, and at the first opportunity the little convoy left the pavement and made its way through vineyards and orchards on yellowish-red dirt roads. Here they could see nothing remarkable but signs of spring: wildflowers sparkled, fruit trees gave off sweet scents, birds chirped over their nests, lizards dashed about, butterflies fluttered in the air. An unusually beautiful April reigned supreme, but the boys were constantly busy watching the sides of the roads. The dark, short one who held the wheel had even placed two hand grenades in a small box on his lap, and the large, swarthy one held his Sten gun with two hands while his eyes skittered between the road on the map and the road on which they were traveling. When one of the vehicles in their convoy sank in the sand he commanded his people to lie low in a circle around them, watching and guarding, until the command car could pull it out.

They reached Rishon Lezion, and after passing the winery they parted from the rest of the convoy. The others were traveling to Hulda, while they were heading to Givat Brenner by way of the fields. Shimon, the pigeon handler at Givat Brenner, was happy to welcome the Girl and asked her whether she still managed to meet up with the Baby.

"Whenever possible," she told him.

"Nice young man," Shimon said.

"We ladies would agree," the Girl said, and Shimon laughed.

"Let's just get this war behind us and there will be time for those matters," he said. Then he apologized. "I'm probably sticking my nose in where it doesn't belong. I'll shut up now."

His pigeons were already marked with red bands and waiting in their boxes. Shimon said, "Dr. Laufer thinks only expert pigeon handlers can take proper care of them, but he shouldn't worry. The folks at the outposts won't need to tame or train them—all they need to do is feed them, give them water, make sure they're not sick. All the people down there are farmers; they know how to raise fowl. There's not such a big difference between chickens and pigeons."

"Just don't say that at the next conference," the Girl said. "Dr. Laufer would be very offended."

"I'd recommend that at every one of your stops you find a responsible kid to take care of them," Shimon said. "A kid like that is better than any adult. We know that because we were just like that. You should teach that responsible kid how to send pigeongrams, so that if the children are moved out when it gets too dangerous, like it already has in other places, then they can send messages of encouragement to the parents, who will stay behind to fight. So now, good-bye to you, and good luck."

They passed among broom shrubs snowy with the potency of their blossoms, alongside endless rows of almond trees that had finished blooming, by vineyards soon to flower. The red loam yellowed, the temperature of the air rose, and the boys told her of villages and towns whose inhabitants they needed to beware of, names she was familiar with from headlines in the newspapers: Bureir, El-Barbara, Majdal, Beit Daras.

The short one was a driver nonpareil. Once, a roving band approached from a ravine, shouting and shooting in their direction, and
he hastened to get them out of there, sailing the heavy command car
over the dunes in a most amazing manner. The large swarthy one was a
master of navigation and, more than that, at guessing the right direction to take at every junction. In his knapsack he kept a jar filled with
hamantaschen pastries. "My mother's," he explained. "I eat them all
year round, not just on Purim."

# 4

AND SO THEY TRAVELED, from dry riverbeds to hillocks, from fur-
rowed fields to watermelon patches, from fallow fields to orchards.
They drove then stopped, from outpost to outpost, in a journey that
she would never forget. And so they pushed southward, she and her two
escorts, who did not cease to amuse her with riddles and stories and
songs and with strong, unsweetened coffee, even after they had
watched her dispatch a pigeon from the side of the road and knew her
heart was given to the one in whose loft the pigeon would land.

"He's probably tall and blond and handsome like you," the short one
said.

She laughed. "In fact, he looks like you: small and ugly and dark. But
you're already a young man, while he's still a baby."

"What does he do?"

"Like me: he misses me and waits and takes care of pigeons for the
Palmach."

At each outpost she left behind pigeons and taught what she could
in just a few hours. At each outpost she reminded them that it was forbidden to let the pigeons fly since their home was in a different location. At each outpost she explained to the carpenter how to fix up an
old shed or shipping crate, one that would be large enough for the
pigeons to fly about so their muscles would not atrophy and they would
not grow weak. At each outpost she recommended that they catch a
few stray pigeons around the cowshed and transfer them to a nearby
kibbutz, just to be sure. And at each outpost she found and worked with
a child whose eyes widened and reminded her of herself and the Baby.

In places where there was no convoy they could join, they traveled at
night on their own with the command car's lights off and the engine

low, so low that they could hear the jackals howling and the whisper of the distant sea and the scratching of the pigeon's claws in their boxes as they struggled to clutch the floor of the careening car.

The moon was nearly full. The gold of the sand faded to silver and blue. The large sycamore trees strewn across the area at that time looked like herds of dark animals. Rain fell suddenly, causing the boys to rejoice—the chance of sinking in the sand was less, the large one explained with a mouth dotted with poppy seeds—and when the clouds cleared he showed her a map of the heavens. He knew all the stars and all the mythological figures and all the astrological signs and pointed out Orion the hunter, and next to it, "the big dog," and their neighbor, the "columba," the heavenly pigeon in her tireless flight southward.

"She even has an olive branch in her beak," he said. "But you need a crescent moon to see it, and a telescope helps, too."

At each kibbutz their journey was not forgotten. The three visitors who appeared suddenly, a spot growing bigger and bigger from a distance, then turning into two young men in long coats—one large and limping and wearing a tattered Australian hat and the other, short one in a woolen stocking cap—and a tall girl with a faded pink kerchief on her head, and golden curls, also wrapped inside a Shinel, her face dusty like theirs. The rumor spread. By barks and gusts of wind, from beak to ear, in the mouths of cowshed pigeons. At every outpost people waited for them, the two young men and "the girl with the pigeons" from Tel Aviv.

She handed out her pigeons like a gift giver, like the bearer of verdicts or letters of love or impending death. Never before had she experienced such switches between fear and hope, between worry and security. She felt she had grown up all at once and that she would forever recall this silence, which was more terrifying than the din of war that would follow, and these treacherous roads of sand, so much more pleasant and more dangerous than paved ones, and the rush of air when the two boys deflated the tires so they would not sink and become an easy target. And the two boys themselves, singing loudly to her when they could and humming softly when it was forbidden. And the kibbutz members as they filled sandbags and dug pits and prepared for war on their very homes and tried not to think about who would die or guess who would live.

And mostly she saw and remembered the fighting units waiting at the sides of the roads. People strewn about, walking, chatting, checking equipment, polishing their weapons, sitting around tiny campfires. Some caught a few hours of sleep, others talked about what they had already experienced, and others still argued about what was soon to happen. She saw and she knew that everything she was observing she would never forget.

And after several days she let her thoughts slip to another matter: the large number of letter writers, the ones who put their paper on the hood of the truck or on one knee or on a tree trunk or on the back of a friend, who wrote on another friend's back in turn. More than once they stopped the command car and handed envelopes to her saying, "Put this in a mailbox when you get back to Tel Aviv." She put them inside an empty seed bag and guarded them faithfully. She carried this huge message capsule as it swelled, filling up with requests and commands and fears and longings and children who would be born to some and not born to others, the delusions of returns and encounters, the hopes of parted lovers, the blessings of men about to die. And a great passion for a baby suddenly flooded her belly, along with taboo joy: her Baby was not destined for battle; he would remain with his pigeons, would await her at the loft.

# Chapter Fourteen

## I

"WHY DON'T YOU have a drink?" the elderly American Palmachnik asked me.

"My mother doesn't allow me to drink with strange men," I said.

He laughed. "You're a big boy already."

"Truth is, I don't really enjoy drinking."

"A Virgin Mary for the gentleman and another whiskey sour for me," he told the waiter, indicating his glass.

"If the Baby hadn't been fooling around with those pigeons of his all the time," he said, "he could have been a damn good fighter. Once we even saw him beat someone up. A few of our guys went off to Be'er Tuvia and he asked them to take a few pigeons with them and dispatch them early the next morning."

By ten o'clock the Baby had already begun walking about the loft slightly tense, his eyes turned skyward, watching and waiting. Homing pigeons are capable of traveling at nearly fifty miles an hour or even more, and he was worried. Even when the sun reached the top of the sky they did not return. Nor when it descended; not a sign of them, not even when it set. Nothing.

The next day, too, the pigeons did not come back. When one young pigeon fails to return it can be chalked up to natural selection, an inevitable sifting. But four at once? The Baby's worry turned to anxiety. All four were healthy and strong, daughters of champion mothers and swift fathers, never tardy in any of their training flights. Two even had chicks of their own, an added incentive to return home. Something was amiss; something foul had transpired.

Five days later the men returned. They came to the loft, handed over the forms with the exact time and place and weather conditions of the dispatch, then went to the Palmach tent camp. Something in their prattle aroused his suspicions. He was bothered by the fact that they took no interest in learning when the pigeons had returned and which had arrived first, since on occasion the men would wager on the results, losing a cigarette or earning a square of chocolate. The Baby followed them to their tents, intending to ask them a few more questions. From one of the tents arose peals of laughter. He drew near, listened, and his heart stopped in its place. From bits of conversation he overheard through the flaps of tarp it became clear to him that on the very first evening they had beheaded the pigeons, roasted them over a campfire, and eaten them, one pigeon per man.

The Baby burst into the tent and began pummeling and kicking like a madman. "Murderers!" he shouted. "You fuckers, I'll kill you!" And because there lay hidden, beneath the baby fat and the smooth skin, muscles and fury of astonishing power, several men and ropes were needed to overpower him and secure his arms and legs.

The Baby lay on the ground like a bound lamb, writhing and spitting and shrieking. "Those pigeons could have saved your lives. You're scum! You should have died instead of them! I hope the graves I dig tonight will be yours!"

"It wasn't nice to say that to us," the elderly leonine American said. "We had enough fatalities as it was. The guys got really mad, took a few good swipes at him to make sure he knew the difference between a pigeon and a human being, then dragged him outside and left him there to simmer down."

After they untied him, the Baby returned to the loft to calm himself in the only way he knew how: by writing a pigeongram to his beloved. This time he added a complaint to Dr. Laufer, reporting what had happened. One of his pigeons returned the next day from Tel Aviv; so overjoyed was he that against all the rules he pounced on her even before she had entered the loft. However, the pigeon was not carrying a quill with a letter from the Girl, and the pigeongram in the message capsule had not been written by the veterinarian. It was notification of an impending military operation concerning the transfer of large supply convoys to besieged Jerusalem.

He hastened to the operations officer, a sturdy fellow from Ra'anana, about whom there were many rumors of his bravery and coolheadedness in battle. The officer read the pigeongram and demanded to know why it had been opened. The Baby apologized, told him he had thought it was a personal letter. The operations officer upbraided him: the pigeons were not intended for the swapping of personal letters. But immediately thereafter he removed from a cabinet green U.S. Army battle dress, the kind that fighters had been wearing for quite some time, and said, "This is for you, because you're going to take a few pigeons out with one of the convoys and we wouldn't want you to suddenly catch cold."

The Baby put on the battle dress and the operations officer burst out laughing. "We'll make a fighter of you yet," he said. "The pigeons won't even recognize you by the time you come back." He pointed to the darker spots on the sleeves and breast, where unit and rank badges had once been sewn, and said, "This belonged to an American sergeant. We don't know what his name was or where he fought or whether he's alive or dead. Now it's yours. Watch out for each other."

The Baby pulled the battle dress tight around his body, enjoying the pleasant, enticing feeling that enveloped him at once. Instead of rushing back to the loft he headed for the carpentry shop to get a look at himself in the carpenter's large mirror. The anonymous American sergeant was a large man, and the Baby looked slightly ridiculous. He pondered whether he should ask the kibbutz seamstress to take it in, make it more suited to his size. It was actually the dandified carpenter who said it was not necessary: "That battle dress has already been worn by soldiers in other countries and other wars. See? It has stains that don't come off, maybe even blood and grease, and two patches on the back and the side. Coats like these know how to fit themselves to their wearers."

The carpenter finished making his point and the Baby raced back through the tent camp, ignoring cries of "Looking good" and "Way to go" and "Look what we have here" from the tents, in order to prepare his portable dovecote for the operation.

He was not requisitioned for the first or second convoys, but on April 17, 1948, two weeks before he would fall in battle, a third convoy was organized. He was ordered to bring several pigeons and join the fighters traveling to Hulda. From there he was sent to Givat Brenner, where he met Shimon, the kibbutz pigeon handler, who told him, "Your girlfriend was here a month ago. She took pigeons to the south."

The Baby realized that the pigeongram he had received from her then—"No and yes and yes and no"—had not been sent from Tel Aviv, a fact she had kept from him because she had not wanted to worry him. He looked at the pigeons she had left in Shimon's loft and imagined her fingers on their wings and their breasts. He picked one up in his own hands and was overcome with passion and longing. Shimon said, "Listen, one of our commanders is taking a motorcycle to Tel Aviv and coming back tonight. If you want, I'll talk to him about taking you with him."

The Baby took one of the pigeons he had brought from Kiryat Anavim and slipped it into the pocket of his new battle dress. He went to headquarters and stood by the motorcycle parked there.

"Are you the hitchhiker?" the commander asked when he emerged a short while later.

"Yes."

"Have you ever ridden on a motorcycle before?"

"No."

"Put your hands here and here. Got it?"

"Yes."

"And don't you dare try hanging on to me."

"Okay."

"Let's go. Get on and we're off."

# 2

IT WAS EVENING. The zoo was already closed for the day. The motorcycle stopped by the gate and the Baby alighted. He thanked the commander and they agreed on the pickup time. Then he climbed over the wall of the zoo and dropped to his feet on the other side. The Girl, he knew, would be in the pigeon loft. He hoped she would be there alone.

All around him the animals were noisy and unstill, sounding their growls and shrieks and chirps and roars as they did every evening in every zoo. Sadness, too, prevailed in the zoo, as it did every evening in every zoo. The Baby ran between the cages feeling the curious, hopeful glances of the imprisoned and avoided glancing at them in return.

There was light in the storeroom next to the loft. The Girl was working there, arranging sacks and filing cards and medicines. She heard his footsteps, looked behind her, emitted a cry of joy. They embraced.

"Not too hard. I have a pigeon in my pocket."

She thrust her hand into his pocket and held the pigeon.

"For me?"

"No, for me," the Baby said. "For you to dispatch another letter to me."

The Girl marked the pigeon's leg with a ribbon and placed her in a box at the side. "I'm so happy you're here. How much time do you have?"

"An hour."

"That's all?"

"Tomorrow we're leaving with a convoy to Jerusalem," he told her, "and I'm going out with the fighters. I've got battle dress like theirs, see? It belonged to an American sergeant in World War II." He twirled and laughed.

"Great," she said. "And I got a Shinel. So what? A pistol, too, they gave me, and I practiced at a firing range and went all over the south in a command car."

"And the pigeon you dispatched from there was sent as if you were in Tel Aviv."

"I didn't want to worry you."

"Shimon told me you were at his kibbutz as well."

"I took some pigeons from him, too. They sent me to hand them out at each and every kibbutz."

"And how was it?"

"Interesting. Frightening. Sad. Full of hope, and despair, too. I saw the fighters writing home and I thought how wonderful it is that you are with your pigeons at the loft. What happened that they're suddenly sending you out with a convoy? You don't even know how to shoot a gun."

"I do too, a little, but anyway I won't need to. There will be enough guys around me who do. And stop worrying, I'm not going to battle. I'll be at the rear with the pigeons on my back."

"That's not true. You're like a signalman—you'll have to walk at the head, next to the commander."

She brushed away a tear of acrimony, flushed, kissed him, then drew back. "So, you've come to say good-bye?"

"I came to see you and touch you and talk to you. And also to say good-bye. We had an hour, but because you're arguing with me we only have fifty-two minutes left."

She pressed against him again, pushed her breasts into his body; his thigh found its place between hers, felt the heat of her loins. She took hold of him through his trousers. He sighed, pulled away from her, removed the battle dress. The Girl hugged him and smiled at him with eyes wide open and very close.

"Stroke me," the Baby said. "Touch me and say what you always do: 'Now you touch me like that, too.'"

They entered the pigeon loft, and while he was still unlacing his boots the Girl began kissing the hollow of his neck, between two muscles that descended to his back, and her kisses were warm and long and enfeebling.

"I hate those monkeys," she said. "Look at them—they're watching us like some hooligans on the beach."

She pulled the cords from around the curtains and all at once the cooing of the pigeons ceased. Together they spread an army blanket on the floor and lay upon it, kissing at length. He leaned his chin into her neck and said, "That's you. Your fingers are like the petals of a tulip. I can feel that's you."

She released her grip, brought her hand to her mouth, dripped saliva into the crook of her fingers, and took hold of him again.

"And now?"

"Like the belly of a lizard."

"And now?"

He moaned. "Like a ring of velvet."

"Now you touch me like that, too," the Girl said.

He slid his fingers in between her thighs and she squeezed, stretched, relaxed. Her scent filled the room.

"Let's do it," she said. "All the way. We're not kids anymore. We are people who deliver homing pigeons to the front and who go to battle."

"When I get back from the war," he said.

"I looked at the boys down south," she said, "the ones who gave me their letters to send, and I thought, Who's going to make it home? Who's going to have children, and who isn't?"

"We will."

"Come, my love, let's do it," she said. "Let's make our child right now."

"I'm afraid to do it now."

"Afraid? Of what? What people will say?"

"No way . . ."

"So then what?"

"That if we make love I won't come back."

"Don't talk nonsense."

"Things like that happen."

She pulled away from him, sprawled on her back, breathed. "I want to take off my clothes, be naked. You, too."

They stripped down to their bare skin and lay upon the blanket.

"Hold me, my love," she said. From where was this terror sneaking in? What was this sadness in her heart?

"When I come back from the war," he said, embracing her. "We'll do it then. When you have what to live for you don't die."

And after a short silence and the probing of fingers he said, "I want our first time to be a reuniting, not a parting. At home, on a bed with sheets, not on the floor of a pigeon loft. We've held off this long, we can wait a little longer."

They pressed together with all their might, then pulled slightly apart so that her other hand could join in.

"That's nice," he said.

"What's nice? Tell me exactly."

"That you can do two different things with your hands at the same time."

They giggled, then fell silent, his the silence of preparation and concentration, hers that of curiosity. "I love watching your semen spurt out," she said, and the Baby's entire body trembled, his back arched, he moaned, and he buried his head between her breasts and laughed. "And your laugh. And your scent, just like our first time together. You remember? At the Ahad Ha'am School."

"I remember. Even now I don't understand how it happened."

"You were suddenly suckling my nipples and I touched you and your semen was so new and white," she said, holding up her cupped fingers as if on display. "We haven't been together for a while—look how much there is . . . I could put this inside me and then I would have a child from you."

"Don't you dare!" the Baby said, grabbing her wrist and wiping her hand vigorously on his chest. "We'll make our child after the war. I'll come home alive. We'll make love in daylight, with our eyes wide open. We'll see each other, we'll be inside you, inside me."

"Kiss me," she said. From where this ache in her belly? Who would roll this boulder from her breast?

"And when you're pregnant, I'll shell almonds for you so your milk will be white and the baby's teeth will be, too."

He caressed her stomach; her breathing was ragged. "You touch me like that, too . . ." she said, and the Baby sprawled on top of her, his lips wandering between her nipples, her fingers guiding his, revealing, encircling the delight of her flesh, and she fell mute, then moaned, and her voice rose so that the Baby had to shush her. "Someone on the street will think something is happening to one of the animals in here . . ."

"That wouldn't be wrong," the Girl said. They both stifled their laughter, and she silenced him, grew taut, released, keened, then whispered, "Next time. This war will end, you'll come home, we'll make love with our eyes open, you inside and around me and I around and inside you. We'll hold hands and eyes and we'll be one in the other."

"We'll get family housing at my kibbutz," the Baby said. "And we'll have a child who goes barefoot and gets dirty in the mud."

The Girl did not respond.

"Yes or no?" the Baby asked.

She rose, and when she spread her legs over his body he could see her sex hovering in the darkness above him, puffed and grassy and soft, fair and dark at the same time. And the sight of her was so enticing and beautiful that he sat up and grabbed hold of her hips and placed his lips between her thighs and breathed and kissed and longed to wrap himself inside her and drench himself in her scent and her taste. Again he asked her, "Yes or no? Answer me."

She laughed. "Are you asking me or her?" Her body shook. "Stop . . ." she said, then asked him if he liked her smell, because the attendant in the storeroom had told her that there were boys who said nasty things about a girl's scent.

"The storeroom attendant? She's an idiot! Your scent is wonderful," the Baby said. "Now I'm not going to wash my face or hands until this war is over so that the scent will keep me alive and stay with me every breath I take. Lie down next to me a little while longer; I have to go soon."

She lay down beside him, his right arm under her neck, his left on her waist, his leg between hers, her thigh between his.

"Yes or no?" the Baby asked. "You can't send me off without an answer."

"Yes," she said. "After the war you'll come back, and yes and yes and yes and yes. Yes you and I will make a baby, and yes I love you, and yes I'm already missing you, and yes I will wait."

The darkness deepened. Night sounds from the zoo mingled with people sounds from the city. Far off, a child cried. A horse whinnied at the paddock. A man's shouts could be heard from the direction of Kiryat Meir. The zoo's hyena laughed, and from a distance he was answered by drunken singing in English and the first howls of the jackals, which could be heard—in those days, as you told me—in every house in Tel Aviv.

For several minutes longer they lay there, entwined and silent, listening to the wind in the large sycamore trees and the hum of their own blood in their bodies. Then the Baby pulled away from her and said he had to get dressed, since in only a short while longer the commander would return on his motorcycle to take him back.

"Give me a pigeon, the best one you have here."

She sat up, rolled him onto his back, leaned over him, and kissed him on the mouth. She pulled his clothes near and handed them to him, dressing herself as well.

"I have a wonderful new Belgian pigeon; she finished the course with flying colors," the Girl said. "But Dr. Laufer would never agree to let me give her to you. Not even you."

She reached out to one of the dozing pigeons and took hold of her. "She looks a little delicate, but she's the best female in the country. Last week she was dispatched from Hanita and was back home in two hours and five minutes."

"She's the one I want."

"And what am I supposed to tell Dr. Laufer? Homing pigeons don't just up and disappear. Someone has to steal them and prevent them from returning home."

"That's exactly what you'll say. Tell him I stole her, but promise him she'll be home soon."

"You see this thin line? She's a Belgian, but Dr. Laufer told me that this is a sign that her distant ancestors lived in the sultan's pigeon lofts in Damascus. Take care of her. She really is a fine pigeon."

"It never stops being pleasant," the Baby said, "exchanging pigeons with you. Giving you my pigeon and getting yours."

He stood up and put on his shirt and battle dress. "Can you believe it? There are couples who don't exchange pigeons with each other, don't send letters with them," he said, placing the pigeon she had given him in his pocket. He gave the Girl a quick kiss. "Good-bye, my love. I have to run. See you soon."

Nothing in their embrace made her think this would be their final meeting. Nothing in his kiss told her that she would only ever touch him again in her dreams and imagination. His receding back, his footsteps approaching the gate of the zoo, his oversized battle dress — fairly ridiculous, enraging to tears — the finest pigeon in the country hidden in his pocket, his one hand holding her so that she would not be jostled as he ran, his other hand waving good-bye without turning his head — all these were reassurances that he would return.

The animals had fallen silent, some in despair, others in sleep. The Baby passed the lions and the leopard and the bear, disappeared in the bend just before the turtle pens, and in the place he had been just a moment before the Girl could see the entire from-here-on: the two of them walking the path between buildings at the kibbutz. A child, his facial features as yet unknown but his feet definitely bare, is marching ahead of them, one foot still on the softness of the grass, the other already soiling the hardness of the cement sidewalk with mud, and both feet feeling how wonderful it is to be different from each other. Here is the house, we're home, and here is the door, the key, open the door for Father and Mother and let's go inside. A chubby dimpled hand is on the knob. His eyes ask, Shall I push? Mother will say, "Hello, house. You say it, too." And the house will answer as houses do: with a gentle movement of air, with a smell, with an echo, with a shelf of books, a picture on the wall, a bed, a billowing curtain.

"See you soon," the Girl called out into the darkness. From where this tear crawling down her cheek?

Her right eye was the one — tearing, shutting, in its blindness telling fortunes that the brain did not know and the heart did not accept. It called out, "Don't go!" and shouted, "No and no and no and no!" in the only way an eye knows to shout: by pooling, flooding, spilling over.

# 3

THE SOUND of the motorcycle could be heard, its light weak and groping. The commander told him, "Hold tight, and don't fall asleep."

From Givat Brenner the Baby reached Rehovot, and from there he traveled to Hulda, where he fed and watered the pigeon he had received from the Girl; then he placed her in the dovecote and took her up to Jerusalem in the convoy. In two places they were fired upon. One of the fighters was wounded in the jaw by a bullet that entered through an embrasure. He fell to the metal floor, bellowing, choking on his blood. The Baby grabbed hold of the soldier's gun and returned fire. How odd, he said in his heart: I am not afraid.

Upon his return to the pigeon loft at Kiryat Anavim he reported to the operations officer, who told him, "You passed your baptism by fire. I hear you performed really well." He gave him a pigeongram to dispatch to Tel Aviv. The Baby affixed a message capsule to one of the pigeons from the central loft and to her tail attached a quill in which he announced to the Girl: Yes her lover and her pigeon had arrived safely, and no there is no way of knowing which of them will return to her first.

The pigeon disappeared from his vision at the moment it appeared before the Girl. She unlaced and removed and wrote a response to her beloved: Yes I remember, yes please be careful, no I am no longer angry, yes you and me. She placed it inside the quill, sealed it, attached it, and dispatched the pigeon. The pigeon that the Baby had brought her took off instantly, but the Girl's hands, which after every dispatch remained stretched in the air for a moment, lowered immediately to her lips to stop their trembling. She kept her eyes on the pigeon until she appeared in his. A shiver passed through her; it seemed to her that she was breathing and swallowing his scent. Pain lacerated her gut. Her hands, as wild and independent as a thought, fell from her mouth and clasped her belly.

# Chapter Fifteen

## I

BEHEMOTH CUTS through the Valley of the Cross, passes by the English pillbox inexplicably painted red, and continues up the street. I try to peel away and dispose of the buildings that have been built here since that time and imagine the route the Baby and his comrades would have taken. A rocky slope, olive trees and stone terraces, a donkey trail that winds between small, cultivated plots of land. The fighters pass through, slightly stooped from the weight of their equipment and weapons, but swifter than the eye estimates and quieter than the ear imagines it can catch them. Their belts are in place and tightened, none is weary nor stumbles among them, their legs are already well trained and accustomed to moving at night among rocks and do not need the aid of their eyes to avoid tripping.

On his shoulders the Baby carried his portable dovecote with three pigeons: a female that had only just been paired with a mate from the brigade headquarters loft; a large and irritable male from the Haganah loft in Jerusalem; and his beloved's champion pigeon from Belgium and Tel Aviv. The night and the load sorely limited his maneuverability, not only due to the weight and the darkness but also due to the awe and excitement, and the worry about the pigeons' safety, and the need to consider carefully every step, every turn of the body. He had no experience with this walking, which to the others was their nightly bread. Several times he stumbled and once he nearly took a spill, but the fighter behind him stuck out a long, strong arm and grabbed hold of the frame of the dovecote, helping the Baby regain his footing.

The plan was to continue walking without drawing attention and to crawl up to the monastery itself. However, soldiers of the Jordanian Arab Legion and Iraqi volunteers stationed in the area who had set up ambushes among the rocks opened heavy fire from different directions. There were many, many wounded. The Baby was unfazed, just as he had been several days earlier when the convoy had come under fire on the way to Jerusalem. Still, the dovecote complicated matters and his inexperience slowed him down, so that when the order came to retreat he could barely keep up with his comrades as they hurried down the slope.

The next day the fighters ascended once again to the very same destination. And once again they came under fire. But this time they were closer to the monastery, and they chose to storm instead of retreating. They lost their cover of darkness at once because someone threw a hand grenade and set fire to a barrel of kerosene no one knew was there. The building next to the monastery caught fire and flames lit up the whole area; still, the invaders managed to infiltrate the monastery through a tiny gate in its north wall and organize their defense. They pushed tables against the walls and piled chairs atop the tables in order to stand and shoot from the high, narrow windows of the chapel. The Baby, inexperienced in battle, supported one of the shooters from behind so that he would not fall backward from the blast of the gun.

The monastery came under heavy fire from outside. Cries of the wounded could be heard. The Baby felt a tremor pass through the body of the man he was supporting. The fighter fell from the chair and rolled on top of the dovecote. The pigeons fluttered about in their prison. The wounded fighter bellowed. Feathers scattered. The Baby lifted the dovecote and rushed to find somewhere safe to put it, but then he ran into one of the platoon commanders, and this man rammed the Baby's leg with the tip of his tommy gun and shouted, "Sit quietly somewhere or take up a position and start firing. The only thing we don't need around here is you and your bloody pigeons."

More wounded men were screaming in pain. The Baby found the medic and asked if he needed help.

"I need more bandages and more light," the man said.

The Baby found sheets and tablecloths and tore them into strips. Then he lined up candlesticks with long, holy tapers all around the area in which the medic was working. Outside, the gunfire was neither abating nor weakening. The monastery bell rang and hummed. The medic sighed. "People are dying," he said, "but the bell? Every bullet brings it to life."

Sappers were sent up to the roof but were wounded one after another. The number of injured increased, and their wailing afflicted their comrades. The transmitter was hit and ceased to function and the Baby was certain that any time now he would be asked to dispatch a pigeon, but the platoon commander berated him again. "Are you still here? Look, I have a job for you. There's a shed about a hundred feet from here. It's a little hard to see in the dark, but it's there. Go capture it."

"What do you mean, capture it? How?"

"Don't worry, I'll send a few reinforcements after you. If we stage a counterattack, you people will cover us from there."

"And what about the pigeons?"

"Pigeons? I couldn't care less right now about any pigeons."

"I can't leave them."

Suddenly, the platoon commander smiled. His smile was broad and evil, his teeth long. The Baby knew he had seen those teeth once but he could not recall where.

"No problem," the commander said. "Take your pigeons with you."

The Baby lifted the dovecote onto his back, tightened the shoulder straps, walked over to the doorway, and took a deep breath. Fear flooded his body but so did a pleasant feeling. The platoon commander peered out into the alley between the monastery and the lodgings and told him, "At the end of the alley there's one of their armored vehicles. If you get by it, you're safe. If not, we'll meet up in hell." He shoved him. "Now! I'm covering you. Run in a zigzag! Hurry!"

The Baby dashed outside, stuck near the wall, and ran. He did not run in a zigzag, nor did he crouch; he ran in a straight line and to his surprise did not stumble or get hit. Even though he heard shooting he did not hear bullets whizzing around him like in the stories his friends told. He ran through a transparent tunnel of silence and safety known only to the newest of recruits and the most veteran of fighters, and felt the pleasant green warmth of his battle dress and the weight of the dovecote, which was no longer the nuisance it had been on the ascent to the monastery, providing balance for his back and energy for his feet and making his step lighter. In his heart he imagined that the pigeons on his back had spread their wings and he was flying and being carried on them.

The door of the shed was locked. This was so distressing to him that it took him only one strong kick to break the thin metal bolt. He burst inside, removed the dovecote from his shoulders, and only then realized that his Sten gun was no longer with him. He did not know if it had fallen while he was running or if he had forgotten to take it with him when he left the monastery.

He placed the dovecote on the ground and sat down next to it. My body's jiggling just like Miriam's knee, he thought suddenly, remembering that one night after he had been sent to the kibbutz he had risen from his bed and slipped out of the children's house and lain down on the grass and looked up at the heavens to think about his mother, when all of a sudden he had felt something slide across his legs, and when he looked he saw a snake, one of the large vipers found in the Jordan Valley. He did not budge, did not move in the slightest, but after the snake had disappeared he had begun to shake and his knees were so weak he could not stand up. That was how he felt now, but he was more experienced and knew that this tremor would slough off his fear and quiet his heart.

He sat there calming down, waiting, but no one followed after him, and no one staged a counterattack from the monastery, and no one was coming from the direction that the platoon commander had pointed to earlier. He waited. Time, which evaded every type of measurement at moments like these, passed anyhow. He was afraid to return to the main building, and anyway the commander's order had been clear: sit there and wait. His fatigue and his anxiety increased, and in spite of the noise and the fear and the heat of battle and perhaps even because of them, he fell asleep. When he awakened—with a start, terrorized, thinking, Where am I? Onto what dry land has this dream vomited me? Do they remember over there that I'm here? And what's happening with them?—the eastern sky was already turning a pinkish gray, allowing the eyes to see around a bit. Details came into focus: walls of stone, a small and narrow room. Seedling trays, bags of manure, gardening tools—a hoe, a pitchfork—that told of better times. On the wall, the outline of a thin square of light, a tiny window hidden behind wooden shutters. He rose to his feet and opened the shutters and took a look around. The angle of his vision was too narrow, but his ears told him that the rhythm and the direction of the shooting had shifted. Again he pondered what he should do. Continue to wait? Take the dovecote and return to the monastery? And what if his luck did not hold out as it had when he'd made it there safely? And what if, God forbid, the pigeons were hit. The pigeons were important, maybe even more so than he himself.

Another round hit the monastery bell, the sound sharp and vexing. Another round pummeled the wall of the shed and made a sound like his uncle's fingers galloping like horses on a table. A few days earlier, in the large convoy that had broken through to Jerusalem, the rat-a-tat of bullets on the armored truck had made an entirely different sound from those two. From his little window the Baby could see that there were many more dead and wounded of the enemy at the walls of the monastery. He sat down again, stood again, sat, and stood. He peered out, saw a Palmach soldier ascend to the roof of the monastery and take a bullet in his leg. The Baby heard the shout. Someone—he was young and strapping—rushed over to rescue the wounded man, then returned to the roof and was torn in half by a mortar shell.

Suddenly, the Baby heard different shouts, not of pain but of fury and madness. A door in the corner of the monastery opened and the platoon commander who had sent him to the shed burst into the alley, hollering and cursing and firing his tommy gun. "Die, you shitheads! I'm coming to get you, you bastards!"

The Baby watched as he ran and fired like a madman. He saw the barrel of the machine gun on the armored vehicle swivel in his direction like a sickle. The platoon commander was injured right away. He fell and began to crawl, screaming for help, a red-and-white coil of ropes trailing behind him. Horrified, the Baby realized these were his innards. The armored vehicle did not fire again, just stood at the end of the alley like a large animal testing the torment of his prey, even letting him crawl to a clearing, escorting him with slow, almost caressing, merciful movements of the machine-gun barrel, as if showing the way to its victim: over here, over here, lie down here. Soon Death will make time for you, too. At the moment, he's busy. Calm down. A little patience, please.

When the gun barrel reached the end of its pivot it turned back toward the alley to lie in wait for another victim. The platoon commander lay in a relatively safe place, groaning and cursing. The Baby took action: he hung the dovecote on a thick nail sticking out of the wall of the shed, stepped outside, and ran, crouched, to the wounded man and threw himself down next to him.

The platoon commander began groaning and pleading. "Please . . . please . . . please . . ." The Baby asked, "Please what? Tell me what."

The platoon commander whispered that he was in pain, that he was cold, that he was thirsty—"Bring me water, will you? My throat is so dry"—and he was bleeding, and when the Baby thought he had already died he began talking again, saying he had to stay alive. He fired a round from his tommy gun and shouted, "Come on already, you bastards. And you, move your ass already." Suddenly he began speaking Yiddish, a language that enabled the Baby to identify him: he was the one who had called him *kelbeleh* on the day he'd arrived at the brigade headquarters. Now several times he said, "*Di toybn* . . . the pigeons . . . sorry . . ." and then a few words that the Baby understood, like *mamme, mamme,* but *she,* unlike the monastery bell, which resounded and vibrated after each hit, died out.

The Baby retched and felt slightly better. Now no one knew where he and his pigeons were. He needed to return to the shed, take his dovecote, and get back to the monastery in case one of the commanders wanted to dispatch a pigeon. He took the tommy gun from the hands of the dead platoon commander, slung it across his back, and began to crawl. A bullet whizzed past him and he, afraid of being sighted, froze in his tracks. Then he started again, very slowly, on his stomach and his elbows, his cheek pressed to the ground, careful not to stick out.

# 2

As I HAVE ALREADY explained, at certain times and under certain circumstances the Baby could be firm and determined. His short, chubby body concealed strong muscles and a backbone of steel. And he possessed the power of single-minded concentration, his path unfailingly clear and direct and his will tireless. If he were to see my idle meanderings on the streets of Tel Aviv, he would scold me. If he were to scold me, I could hear him. I know what he looked like, I know about his deeds and his death, I can imagine the touch of his fingers, but I have no idea what his voice sounded like.

After a few feet of crawling, a slug hit his left thigh. He pitched forward, then he rolled, surprised by the strength of the blast. Anyone whose body has never been hit by a bullet—especially when it penetrates to the bone—cannot begin to approximate how powerful it is. His thigh broke near the knee. The Baby released a single shout then stifled the others to come, dug his fingers into the ground, and proceeded to crawl to the dovecote.

His mouth was parched. His eyes teared from pain and effort. His leg dragged behind him like a rag. His trousers were filled with warm blood and his shirt with cool sweat. He drew near a low stone fence and began to gather his strength in preparation for climbing it and in preparation for the pain that would hit him as soon as he dropped to its other, safe, side. He had already managed to grab hold of the top row of stones and pull himself up, but as he lay there considering how he would slide down the other side and how terrible the pain would be, he took another two bullets, which sliced through the old patches on his battle dress and entered his waist and his back.

Moaning, groaning, the Baby slumped to the other side of the fence. None of the bullets had struck a major artery or a vital internal organ, but each had crushed his pelvic bones and torn large exit holes that spurted blood from the front of his body—not the throbbing, artesian eruptions of slit arteries but a strong and unhampered flow.

At this stage, a cannon joined the battle. The Baby heard it and tried to figure out whether it belonged to the armored vehicle or was a field cannon firing from some distance, whether it was trying to hit the monastery or, in fact, his shed—or perhaps it was just firing in any direction with the hope of hitting something by chance. Now he could feel the probing touch that veteran fighters know to sense at times—they after long months of battle, he in his first war—those gentle fingers touching their skin, here stroking the back, there slipping down both sides of the neck, here tickling behind the testicles, there in the hollow of the neck: Death's pleasant foreplay, whereby he prepares his partner to accept him willingly and with love.

In such situations it is a good idea to divide hope into small bits of reality, not to expect a huge miracle at the end of the road but to wish for the grace of the few feet just ahead. In his heart the Baby said that it was all one and the same if he was to die from another bullet or from those that had already hit him, and he understood he was no longer fighting for the monastery or Jerusalem, and not even for his comrades' lives, but for his love of the Girl, and for the child to be born to them after the war. His strength, he felt, was waning, and he wished for nothing more for himself than to return to his dovecote and the pigeon she had given him.

Slowly, in a direct line, pushing with his elbows, his legs dragging behind, his shredded body brushing against the ground and his fingers boring, pulling: to her, to the dovecote, to the pigeon, with Death walking behind him, licking his lips and preparing himself for what was to come.

# Chapter Sixteen

## I

I N THEIR BED, which had become his bed, Yordad lies awaiting his death. He has bad days and he has good days, but this waiting exists in both: on the good days he waits by reading or listening to music, and on the bad days he lies immobile on his back. His body is lean and straight and long, his legs cross at the ankles, a thin and tranquil smile tugs gently at his lips, his hands clasp on his stomach. One of his eyes does not blink, so as not to miss what is being screened on the ceiling. The other eye is shut, so as not to miss what is taking place within.

"This is no good, lying sick and alone all day!" Meshulam exclaimed.

Yordad did not answer.

"And if heaven forbid you should fall? And if heaven forbid something happens to your heart?"

Yordad uncrossed and recrossed his feet. At first his right ankle had rested on his left; now his left ankle was resting on his right.

"We'll set you up with a panic button, we'll get you hooked up to a medical call center, and to me, and to Iraleh, and to anyone else you want. All you'll have to do is push the button and all of us will come in a jiffy."

"Meshulam," Professor Mendelsohn said, "please settle down. A heart attack is no reason to invite guests. I am not ill. I am simply old. Exactly the same as you. If you want a panic button so badly, then install one for yourself."

Meshulam left, returning the next day with the director of the medical call center and one of their technicians, as well as one of his own electricians. Benjamin and I were invited to the installation ceremony, but Benjamin did not come. The idea of installing a panic button is absolutely logical, he told me by phone, and he was certain that Meshulam would have it set up in the best manner possible even without his presence.

Now Yordad had a different reason for refusing. "If I have this buzzer, you won't come to see how I'm doing anymore. You'll all just sit at home waiting for the buzzer to ring."

"That's not true!" Meshulam said, flinching. "If I've been coming three times a week up till now, I'll start coming three times a day. Once to see why the buzzer is buzzing and twice to see why it isn't."

In the end, Yordad acquiesced. The call-center technician connected a microphone and a speaker, and Meshulam's electrician added a double backup system, which relied on a battery and electricity stolen from the stairwell. I asked Meshulam what would happen if someone caught on to the theft, and he said, "In the first first place, it's so little electricity that nobody's going to catch on, and in the second first place Professor Mendelsohn made the worth of the whole building go up, so doesn't he deserve just a few drops of electricity for free?"

"Now Professor Mendelsohn," said the director of the call center, "we're going to stage a simulation of an emergency situation. We're all going to go into the other room and you will stay here as if you are home alone. Please press the button as if, God forbid, you weren't feeling well, and our doctor will answer you through the wall speaker as though he were examining and treating you for real. You will be able to hear each other and speak."

Professor Mendelsohn waved his hand impatiently. He knows what a simulation is, and he certainly knows what emergencies, examinations, and treatments are. All his well-wishers filed out of the room and into the kitchen and the director called out, "Please press the button!"

Nothing happened.

The technician said, "He's not pressing the button."

Meshulam went to the doorway of Yordad's room. "Press, please!"

"But I could hear him in his normal voice," Yordad said, "not through the speaker."

"First you have to press the button, then you'll heart through the speaker."

"Professor Mendelsohn," the director called out again, "please press the button!"

Yordad pressed it. A metallic but pleasant voice answered. "Hello, Professor Mendelsohn. This is your call-center doctor. What seems to be the problem?"

Yordad cleared his throat and said, "In 1964 my wife, Raya, left me and my heart was stricken."

He uttered this in a clear and measured fashion, behind which stood medical knowledge, longing, and frequent repetition. As for me, my legs were melting beneath me.

"I had a small heart attack then," Yordad continued. "I recovered and didn't mention it to a soul except for her. She did not come back to me, and since then my health has been deteriorating."

Meshulam grabbed me tightly around the waist and pulled me in to his short, thick, sturdy body, which was like mine.

"Professor Mendelsohn," the young doctor said through the speaker, "my father was your student many years ago. Please, this conversation is only meant to test whether the equipment is functioning properly."

"This bed, on which I am lying, alone," said Yordad, pursuing his own agenda, "was our bed. When I lie in it I feel very bad, and when I lie in some other bed I feel even worse."

"Why didn't you say so?" Meshulam let go of me and burst into Yordad's room. "I'll bring you new beds right away!"

"Thank you, Professor Mendelsohn," said the young doctor. "The equipment is working. I am ending this conversation."

The director, the electrician, and the technician departed. The cook that Meshulam had found for Yordad appeared, laden with groceries. At that moment I felt useless, since a friend and a cook are far more helpful to Yordad than I.

"Stay for a meal," Meshulam told me. "There'll be kebab and salad within twenty minutes."

"No, I'll leave," I said, thinking I should not have come in the first place. As usual, Benjamin had been right. There are things you need to do with a friend, not with your sons. With a technician, not with family. And there are stories better told to a stranger, through a microphone and a buzzer and a speaker, through wires and panic buttons.

# 2

TWO DAYS LATER I paid him another visit.

"How are you, Yairi? I didn't hear you come in; the panic button didn't ring."

I decided not to explain or correct him.

"How are Liora and the girls?" Yordad asked.

My skin turned to gooseflesh. How had those dead fetuses been reconceived in his brain? How had his mouth given birth to two live girls?

"Liora is fine," I said. Should I remind him of that bird-watching gynecologist who said, "It was a boy," and then, "This boy was a girl"? Should I quote Liora, whose words were no less terrible: "It's the two of us together that's the problem"?

"I have a new joke," Yordad said. "Would you like to hear it?"

"Where do you get these jokes from? Do you have new friends I don't know about?"

"From the Internet. I find them and record them in a notepad."

And he extended a beautiful, white hand to the small table next to his bed, opened a drawer, and removed a notepad. I have already mentioned that Yordad loved notepads and always had a number of them on hand. And just as he classified and separated everything, so too did he divide them up: his patient notepad and his list-of-chores notepad and his ideas notepad, which he would suddenly remove from his pocket to record something that he would conceal with blatant stealth. And although he had become a knowledgeable amateur of computers, he claimed there were situations in which a notepad was quicker and more user-friendly. Now jokes had their own notepad, so that if, heaven forbid, guests should come, he could read them jokes instead of being amicable and conducting a conversation.

"Lots of people are interested in being friends with us," my mother used to tell him. "But you build walls between us and them."

"I am tired," he would say, and "Anyway, you invited people only yesterday," and "I have a headache."

"Those are the kinds of excuses women make, Yaacov."

He would take offense and fall silent, then walk straight-backed down to his clinic.

My mother loved guests and flourished when hosting. She knew how to seat them so that conversation would flow and no one would feel abandoned or out of the loop. She knew who to place near whom and, more important—Meshulam's joke—who to keep away from whom. She recognized the woman who needed to stay near her husband and the woman who would blossom if separated from him. Her eyes sparkled in anticipation of their arrival, her smile shone. Only now, in my new house, many years after she left home and a few months after her death, does it occur to me that she invited guests so as not to remain alone with Yordad.

Pleasant aromas wafted from the refreshments she prepared for guests. There was a sort of simple pastry she was renowned for, small puffs of seasoned dough stuffed with tiny frankfurters. The secret, said mouths astonished into joy, was the sauce in which they were cooked, a sort of "dainty-dainty" sauce, she called it, made of mustard and black cumin, which she had concocted herself.

After my mother left home, Yordad's friends and acquaintances also began to disappear. And he, when his walls of arrogance and isolation had fallen, discovered that behind them there was no one. No enemy, no companion, no battering foe, no knocking guest. There remained nothing but the infrequent visitor: doctors, students, lawyers asking his opinion on issues of medical malpractice, and us: Benjamin, rarely; Liora, who comes to see him whenever she is in Jerusalem on matters of business and they enjoy a conversation together in English; me, who comes whenever I am in Jerusalem on matters of idleness and emotion; and the Double-Ys, his grandsons, who, even today, at twenty, continue their regular entertainment with him, which began when they were babies—a trip through the pages of the large German atlas, the very same atlas he had traveled years earlier with us.

"Come, children," he says to them just as he said to us, "let's take a trip in the atlas to all sorts of lands." And those two enormous twins sit obediently, Y-1 on his grandfather's right and Y-2 on his left, but unlike Benjamin and me, who followed him through deserts and crossed rivers and mountain ranges with him, they stop at their favorite map, the one of food and agriculture. They scan the meat countries and the fish countries, the olive oil countries and the butter countries; they take pity on the puree-deprived and deplore the eaters of tofu and lettuce and seaweed. They spy out land after land, the fat with the lean.

The world is split, Yordad explains to them again: this part eats corn, this part eats rice, and here, in our part, people eat wheat. And they inform him, "Not anymore, Grandfather. Everyone eats everything. We eat corn, too, and different kinds of rices, as well as wheats." And they ask when Yordad's cook will be there, the Romanian laborer whose culinary skills Meshulam discovered and who he then sent to our house after my mother left. He was a young worker when he first came to us, and he has grown old along with Meshulam and Yordad. He cleans the house, too, does the laundry and ironing and shopping, clips Yordad's toenails since Yordad cannot bend down to them anymore, and helps him get in and out of the shower.

Meshulam has warned him not to dare add onion to Professor Mendelsohn's salad, and instead of *mămăligă* and *icre,* Romanian specialties that met with a cool "No, thank you," he learned to prepare *linsensuppe mit wurst*—lentil soup with bits of sausage—and to season potatoes with *schnittlauch* and butter. The Romanian foods he makes include pickled vegetables, *ciorbă,* and *mititei.*

He does not sit with Professor Mendelsohn at the table, although on occasion he will pour the two of them a little *ţuică* as a digestif, and he will stand next to him and say *Salut!,* after which he will clean the kitchen and assist Professor Mendelsohn on his walk outdoors.

Meshulam himself also visits. Three times a week, sometimes more. Even though he has his own key he knocks at the door, gently ("Maybe Professor Mendelsohn is sleeping just now?") but loud enough ("Maybe a lady friend is visiting just now?"), and only then does he unlock the door and enter silently. If Yordad is sleeping, he makes his little "tour of the house": he oils hinges, tests the straps that lift the jalousies ("We're going to have to tighten this little lady"), checks the faucets and outlets ("We're going to have to replace this guy"). And sometimes he ascends to the large apartment upstairs, where we once lived, to see if everything is in order at the renters' place ("So they won't drive Professor Mendelsohn nuts if there are problems up there").

And if Professor Mendelsohn is awake, Meshulam prepares coffee for them both, sometimes pours them each a shot—"Raya loved brandy," they both recall then—and chats with him. Meshulam can talk with anyone about any topic; he makes up for his ignorance with intelligence and curiosity.

I told Yordad I was jealous of this masculine friendship. And after a brief FOR and AGAINST I added, "You know what? I can't help thinking that if Gershon were alive he could have been my friend like Meshulam is yours."

"Gershon died a long time ago," Yordad said dryly. "I would recommend, Yairi, that you find another friend."

"It's not so easy," I said. "At my age people don't make new friends." I told him that wooing a man was far more difficult than wooing a woman because with women "you can send your body on ahead of you, lay your life on the line. With men you have to start with your brains and your heart."

A cloud of dissatisfaction passed over Yordad's face. He gave this terrifying possibility several seconds of consideration, then said, "Yes, Yairi, that is truly an interesting predisposition." And suddenly he added, "I have heard you are building a house for yourself, Yairi."

"I'm not building, I'm renovating," I told him.

"But you have a beautiful home in Tel Aviv."

"The house in Tel Aviv is Liora's. She chose it, she bought it, she designed it. Now I am renovating a home for myself."

"A home of my own," Yordad said, correcting me. He gazed at me and I panicked: Was he interpreting me or quoting you? Was he aware that you had given me money to buy this house? If so, who had told him? Meshulam? You? And if he knew about it, who else did? My brother? My wife?

"Take me there, Yairi. I'm interested in seeing it."

"With pleasure."

"Let's make a date," he said as he pulled a different black notepad from the drawer in the table next to his bed.

"You need a datebook to make plans with me?"

"I am not the idler you and Benjamin think I am," Yordad grumbled. "I have meetings, I still write articles, and every morning I go on the Internet, and there is mail waiting for me from medical journals. I also look for myself there. It turns out I'm still alive. People quote me."

I praised him for his speedy adjustment to using computers and e-mail and word processing.

"It wouldn't hurt you either to move ahead, learn something new," he told me. "All those who stay behind and worship what used to be forget that in that wonderful past half of all children died of disease before the age of five. And what's there to be afraid of with something that makes life so much easier? I download music, Yairi, I go to concerts of Beethoven and Mozart, I attend conferences—"

"What about other composers?"

"There are no other composers. At my age you already know what is good and what is less so."

"Mother loved opera," I said.

"She did not love opera, she loved one opera. Only one: *Dido and Aeneas*. And from that, only one aria, the one successful aria in an opera that is otherwise simply a nuisance."

He began reciting it with solemn proficiency:

> *Thy hand, Belinda, darkness shades me,*
> *On thy bosom let me rest,*
> *More I would, but Death invades me;*
> *Death is now a welcome guest.*
> *When I am laid in earth, may my wrongs create*
> *No trouble in thy breast;*
> *Remember me, but ah! forget my fate.*

"Come, Yairi," Yordad said when he had finished, "let's make a date for our trip."

I took out my datebook, too.

"You see," Yordad said after rejecting the first three dates I suggested, "I am busier than you."

We found a time that was convenient for him, and I suggested we combine our trip to the house with a little journey. "I'll bring some food, we'll sit somewhere pleasant with shade, you'll breathe a little fresh air, and your eyes will be revived by the view."

On the way home I bought a compact disc: Beethoven, not a complete work but a collection of selected bits. That way he would enjoy himself on the way and I would not suffer. I also bought a folding chair in case he accepted my suggestion about parking somewhere along the way and having a bite to eat. And a pillow: perhaps Yordad would get tired and want to doze a bit.

# 3

ON THE APPOINTED DAY I rose and left Tel Aviv early in the morning. When I arrived at Yordad's, I found Meshulam there as well.

"Seven in the morning," I said in wonder. "What, do you sleep here, too?"

"We old guys get up early anyhow, so I come visit. If we don't help one another, who will?"

Professor Mendelsohn made a grand appearance. His thick hair crowned the heights of his head like a silver diadem. Age had not lessened his stature by even an inch; nor had it added an ounce to his weight or diminished the natural elegance and ease of his body.

"Good morning, Yairi." He beamed in my direction. "I am ready. You undoubtedly thought you would have to wait."

"Look at him! As fresh as a palm branch during the Sukkoth holiday. "*Oysgeputst!* Notify the police: Professor Mendelsohn is stepping out of the house, put all the girls behind key and lock!"

He was right. Yordad was dressed in long khaki trousers, perfectly creased, and a soft, pale blue shirt underneath a sand-colored cashmere jacket, with comfortable brown suede shoes.

"Cruisewear!" Meshulam proclaimed. "All he needs is a cravat and he's Prince Monaco!"

He gave a supporting arm to Professor Mendelsohn, who trembled as he descended the four steps. Then Meshulam hastened to bring him his straw hat and walking stick, and when Yordad refused to take them Meshulam handed them to me, to put in Behemoth. In spite of the desire burning in him and apparent in his every movement, he was smart enough not to raise the idea of joining us.

"Did you know that, Meshulam?" Yordad asked. "Yairi is building himself a house, so that he will have a home of his own."

"A very good idea," Meshulam said, feigning innocence. "A small, old house, a few flowers, big trees in the garden. And most important, a view. Iraleh, how is it that you haven't told me? I can help you with the renovations."

He laid a wooden crate next to Behemoth. "This car is comfortable but high. Put your foot here, Yaacov."

Yordad climbed up and seated himself with a soft groan and said, "This car really is comfortable," then fastened his safety belt and settled in. Meshulam circled the car and came to my side. "Don't you tell him I'm involved!" he whispered, then immediately raised his voice. "And take this crate with you, so Professor Mendelsohn can get in and out of the car."

Only then, when Meshulam called him "Professor Mendelsohn," did I realize that earlier he had used his first name. But Behemoth had already begun moving and Meshulam called out, "Drive carefully, Iraleh. Do you hear me? You've got an important passenger with you!"

I decided to leave the city by way of the Jerusalem forest and the village of Beit Zayit in order to enjoy the view. Yordad opened the window, sniffed the pine trees with pleasure, rejoiced at the sight of a gazelle skipping along the terraces beneath the Yad Vashem Holocaust Center.

He was in high spirits. "We used to enjoy hiking around here, your mother and I. We would gather mushrooms. Here, this is the path we would take to reach the elephant boulder. We would walk back in the direction of the bakery and buy a fresh challah bread from the workers."

"We walked this way with her, too," I said, provoking him, "in order to look from far away and remember Tel Aviv."

But Yordad merely smiled. "Yes," he said absentmindedly. "She loved Tel Aviv very much. She loved gladioluses, a little brandy to drink, parsley, and Tel Aviv, of course."

I decided to take advantage of the pleasant atmosphere and dispatched a question into the space inside Behemoth, an intimate space of father and son. "Maybe you remember what side her dimple was on?"

"Whose dimple, Yairi?"

"Mother's. That's who we were just talking about, right?"

Yordad is old, and an old man needs to recognize and exploit advantages when they cross his path.

"She had two," he said. "Two *grübchen*. You know what *grübchen* are, Yairi? Dimples, in German."

Was he pretending? Was he rewriting our history? Had he really and truly forgotten?

"Last time," I reminded him, "you said she didn't have any dimples at all. Another time you said she didn't have dimples in her cheeks but she had one in her chin."

"That could be," he answered, then attacked straightaway. "But if I have already told you all that, why do you two keep asking?"

"What do you mean by 'you two'? Does Benjamin ask you as well?"

"The two of you. You never stop pestering me."

"That's because we can't agree on whether the dimple was on her left cheek or her right."

He fell silent. Just when I was about to lose my patience he spoke up. "It wasn't her left cheek or her right one. She had two dimples at the bottom of her back. Here," he said, thrusting a long, white hand, surprising in its speed and precision, between my right hip and the car seat. His thumb and index finger jabbed both sides of my spine like the teeth of a snake.

"Two. One here," he said, nearly pressing through to my flesh, "and one here, on the other side."

The touch of his hand where the elderly American Palmachnik and the tractor operator with the sickle had touched me silenced and paralyzed me. Yordad, as if wishing to wound me further, said, "I loved kissing those dimples. Sometimes I picture them in my dreams. She was not an easy person, Yairi. Not now, either, when she is no longer here." He fell silent again.

After a few minutes he continued. "We did a lot of bad things to one another. And we fought a lot of battles against each other. But first of all leaving me, then dying in order to beat me? That's too much. For both of us."

We were both silent for a long while, until suddenly Yordad said, in your voice, "I can't anymore." I was horrified, but he smiled at me as if pleased with himself. He fell asleep, and even then, sleeping sitting up, he looked respectable and elegant. Several minutes after waking up he said, "I've grown a little tired from our journey, Yairi. Let's go back."

I protested. "But you wanted to see my home. We'll be there in just forty minutes."

"I'll see it another time. Now I want to go lie down and sleep."

"I'll find us a pretty spot with shade. I brought wine and food, and I have a blanket and a pillow. You can lie down and rest and then we'll continue."

"Another time, Yairi. Now please take me back."

# Chapter Seventeen

## I

A ND WHEN HAD DEATH caught sight of him? When he slipped away from him that first time he ran for the shed? Now, as he drags himself toward it, bleeding into the dust? Or perhaps it was as the Girl had said about the apparition of the pigeon before one who awaits its return: it occurred at the moment the Baby had disappeared from her vision as he rounded the path in the zoo.

Another explosion in the distance and a blow that cracked open the wall of the shed. The Baby crawled into the shed through the breach, groaning and shaking from weakness and pain. He lay still, the roar of battle now a dull, remote din, as though a blanket had been thrown over his head. Draw strength. Don't die yet. Open your eyes. Look around.

Rubble, scattered garden tools, the small dovecote shattered on the floor. It's better that way, thought the Baby; who knows if I would have managed to get to my feet and reach it if it had still been hanging from a nail on the wall. The large male Jerusalem pigeon, half its body crushed, was twitching its last, while the small pigeon from Kiryat Anavim lay next to him. There was no sign on her body of having been hit, but it was clear she was dead. Dr. Laufer had taught Miriam the pigeon handler, and Miriam had taught him, that pigeons are liable to die from fear. "They are like us," she had told him. "They fight, they cheat on each other, they eat with friends, they long for home, and they have heart attacks." The Girl's pigeon was unharmed; in shock, frightened by the tumult, the gunfire, the shouting, and the proximity of the dead and dying pigeons, but quiet and whole nonetheless.

The Baby reached his hand toward the broken remains of the dovecote and withdrew the pigeon handler's equipment, rolled into a scroll. He untied its laces and unraveled it; everything was in place. The pigeon handler likes tidiness, keeps things clean. Here are the goose quills and the empty message holders, the glass tube, the cup, the message pads. Here are the silk strings and the small, razor-edged pigeon handler's scraping knife. Lying on his side, he arranged everything he would need; then he sliced through the strap of the tommy gun he had lifted from the dead platoon commander and let it fall to the ground. It was a good thing he had taken care to whet the knife on a regular basis; it was so sharp that he needed make no effort.

He unzipped his battle dress, slid the blade between his blood-soaked trousers and his skin, and cut the cloth away carefully, working his way to the groin and then left, over his shattered thigh. He peeled the shredded trousers as far downward and to the side as he was able, lowering his gaze to his loins. He sighed in relief: his penis was safe and sound, spotted with blood but unharmed, and in its own way managed to return the Baby's gaze, friendly and abashed. It was short and thick like its owner, crouching now quite nearby two large holes where the bullets had exited his body. Small and timid, his penis was a tunnel-dwelling creature fearful of the light and the cold and the loss of blood.

Thus the four of them remained: the wounded Baby, his healthy organ, the pigeon, and Death, waiting at the side. The pigeon and the penis did not move or stir; Death sent a chilly, pleasant hand to touch him just as the Baby's own hand was touching himself, though neither hand made do merely with wandering, or caresses. Each pressed, lightly: Was the fruit ripe yet? Had the hour arrived?

Not yet; the Baby pushed Death away, then lay sprawled on his back and resumed caressing his organ. There was not enough blood in his body for an erection, but the penis felt the urgent need of his owner as well as his touch, so different from usual, and understood that this was no ordinary form of relief, the kind young men grant themselves with a generous hand; rather, it was something important. He was as young and inexperienced as his master; like him he knew he would die a virgin, like him he grieved, for this is an organ that is capable of rejoicing, so why would it not be able to feel sadness?

The Baby's fingers reached his lips in an attempt to smear them with saliva, for lubrication, and a pleasant feeling, and speeding up the process. But his mouth was as dry as clay and did not produce even a drop. He spilled a bit of water from his canteen into his hand and continued with the task, his fingers simulating the Girl's own fingers as they took the feel of the velvet ring, the tulip bulb, the lizard's belly, but his body signaled to him that time was short and his death whispered to him that the task was great and he would be well advised to cease these pleasant ministrations and return to the plain and ordinary way of men, and his penis, whether from compassion or understanding of the urgency of the matter, managed to stiffen a bit.

The Baby feared that Death would lose patience, and that in this awful race his soul would beat his seed in departing his body. He hoped that curiosity would compel Death to wait until this deed had been completed, and he hurried himself along by conjuring images and feelings that would help him on his way: the Girl's fingers, her pleasant caresses in the place he called "there" and she called "here"—"If he wore a bow tie," she had said, laughing, "it would be right here."

He pictured her body straightening up and her legs parting as she stood over him, her beautiful, puffed genitals floating above his eyes in the dimness of the pigeon loft. He pictured himself, too, rising to his knees and taking hold of her thighs to kiss between them, causing her—and him—to tremble. Her scent returned to his lips and blew new life into his flesh and pooled under his nostrils and lingered in his nose.

And when he felt the miracle occurring, the seed rising in his pipes, not gushing forth but creeping along wishing to ooze out, he leaned on his side, moaning in pain, aimed for the glass cup, and ejaculated. The semen did not spurt, but a small quantity did trickle slowly along. And when this small, white loss joined the larger red loss of blood, the Baby's muscles drained of strength, the heat abandoned his stomach chamber, memory expired in his brain. The laughter he would emit when this moment of release took place between the Girl's breasts had now become a spasmodic smile.

Another squeeze, another drop, the Baby rested. His ejaculation had sharpened his nerves and heightened his pain. But he was happy: the pain would delay Death and grant him a few more minutes. He tilted the cup to the glass tube and helped the flow along with his finger, encouraging his seed to pass more quickly. "Hurry up," he said. "My hands are growing cold, a tremor is lying in wait." He corked the tube and lay flat out on his back. Do not lose consciousness. Do not die yet. There is still work to be done.

All the while the Belgian pigeon watched the proceedings with round, unblinking eyes. First she saw the Baby drag himself inside the shed, bloodied and moaning; then she watched him cut open his trousers and expose himself and perform the same deed that the girl had in the loft. After that he had uncapped the message capsule, placed the tube inside, and closed it, all the while shaking and mumbling. Finally, she watched as the hand that had held his flesh was now extended in her direction. Her heart pounded for him under skin and flesh and feather. By this time he did not know his own body, did not feel what it was he was grasping—her or himself—but the warmth of her body imbued him with strength; his palm sensed the anticipation in her back and wing muscles just like when, in the loft of his childhood, he had taken hold of his very first pigeon.

There was a great peal of thunder. This time a shell had been fired from the cannon mounted on the armored vehicle, knocking over more stones and raising a column of dust. But the Baby was not alarmed. When Death is so close there is no longer anything to fear. Nor was the pigeon frightened; she pulled shut her thin, transparent, auxiliary set of eyelids, which humans do not possess, and prepared herself for her dispatch and strengthened herself for the climb. The Baby attached the message capsule to her leg, groped and dragged himself along the floor as though wafting across his own feebleness, until his head and shoulders and chest and hand had come outside, through the breach in the wall. He stretched out his hand, then slackened his grip, amazed that even now he could feel something of the pleasure there is in every dispatch, and something of the excitement. The pigeon took off in a hurry, as if spurted from the palm of his hand.

Death, who had been waiting all the while, emitted a snort of anger when he understood that he had been duped. But the Baby did not celebrate his victory. He rolled onto his side ever so slightly, unable to summon enough strength to turn over completely, in order to watch his last pigeon rise in the air. Thus he lay, half on his back and half on his side, neither groaning nor moving. From this moment forth the matter was out of his hands. From this moment forth he had to put his trust solely in her: that she would fly straight and true, that she would accomplish her mission, that she would avoid every bullet and arrow and stone, that she would neither become prey nor be tempted, that she would not stop to eat or drink or rest, that she would understand what was contained in the capsule, the likes of which had never before been sent— that is what Dr. Laufer would soon say—throughout the history of homing pigeons worldwide, from its inception until this very day.

Cold gushed from his bones and inundated his flesh. His heart grew tranquil. Am I imagining all this or am I truly feeling it? He gathered his battle dress around himself, covered his loins, and crossed his arms over his chest, and thus, with open eyes, watched the pigeon fly, at first light-colored as she distanced herself, then darker as she ascended, with her soft, puffed breast and strong wings, so beautiful that he craved nothing more than to rise toward her, to hold and kiss her before he died. But he was sprawled on the ground below and she was climbing to the heavens above. Silence prevailed all around him and within, the only sound the rhythmic tap of her wings as they grew distant.

"Homeward," he said to her. "Rise, distance yourself, for there is nothing to see or do here anymore. Do not turn your head, do not look back. Do not fear Death; I am holding on tightly to him. Rise. Rise on high, to the safe, the illuminated, the peaceful, and onward to the distant, to the one who awaits, to the Girl. Fly quickly to those eyes on the watch for her beloved."

The pigeon ascended rapidly. Above the flames, above the smoke, above the gunshots, above the shouts, to the sky blue, the silence. Homeward. To her. Cross the great sea of air that has no borders or sounds but for the whistling of the wind in your feathers and the pulsing of your blood and the shouting of my words on your leg.

# 2

THAT DAY was a typical spring morning in Jerusalem, cool and clear. Lemon trees and jasmine bushes were blooming in the gardens bordering the monastery, changing guard with the evening primrose. The fighters' eyes abandoned their scopes and their fingers the triggers and for a moment everyone looked only at the pigeon. At first she darkened against the light sky and then grew small against the hugeness of the heavens. The flapping of her wings fell silent, and she turned blue-gray until she melted into the blue-gray sky. After the silence, the noise of gunfire and shouting was renewed, the war resumed.

A breeze was blowing. On the slope of the hill, between the edge of the grass and the swings of today, lay the Baby's body, the upper half outside the shed, the lower half within, his body weight depleted by the dripping semen and the draining blood. As he lay thus, partly on his side and partly on his back, he discovered that this gentle wind would suffice. Lightweight and feeble, at first he was jostled about by the breeze like the seed of a ragwort, then he was caught up in it like a feather, and finally he grew stronger, rose into the air, and soared.

In spite of his explicit request and instructions, the pigeon did look back, and seeing that he was gliding along behind her put her mind at ease. Without completing the customary circle in the air that homing pigeons make before establishing their precise direction, without the slightest hesitation, and with the speed and accuracy of an arrow, she headed straight for home. The desert and mountains are behind her, the sea ahead, and a Baby is flying in her wake, a young man in battle dress with torn trousers and dirt on his head. His body is sour with blood but his eyes are open and they see: here is the pigeon and here is the city; there in the distance are yellow and blue strips of sea and sand and down below a village and an orchard, a hill and a ravine. Here is a silvering grove of olive trees and a farmer driving a mule slowly along a path, and there a herd of goats spilling down a slope. Rocks are strewn about a riverbed that had been doused with rainwater the day before, so that now pools of water wink and shine at him from below. The Baby grew excited: here are the Soreq Creek and Mount Castel and Kiryat Anavim. Here are the cowshed, the dining hall, the tent camp of the Palmach. And here, in the valley, the graveyard. Two of his comrades were laboring there, brandishing pickaxes and hoes. The sound of metal on rock reached him on high, so clear and familiar in the cool air. He heard and saw and understood: it was his own grave they were digging.

And here is the pigeon loft he built with that carping dandy of a carpenter. Here is his comrade the poultry farmer who replaced him, opening the doors, and here are his pigeons returning from their morning flight. The white flag has been lowered, the blue one flying now, calling the birds home. The Baby was struck with the fear that perhaps his pigeon, too, would land, but she did not even lower her gaze or slow her wings. She continued her flight—onward, onward—in the only direction the compass of her species shows.

Homeward. Her wings did not stop plying the air, her eyes did not stop searching out and identifying, her heart did not stop pushing and pumping. Above the crooked byways of those who dare not take the straight path. Above the footprints of those incapable of flight. Above the ancient columbaries long since abandoned by their residents. Above the pigeon lofts and the clefts of the rocks that served as their shelters. Above this land-in-miniature where pigeons soar unimpeded through its skies and humans fail upon its stones and fall to earth and return to dust. Homeward. The loft and the womb summon and motion to her, the tiny oars in the semen press upon her from behind.

Odysseus of the Feathered Creatures — and more. Nothing slows her down or makes her land or throws her off course. Not Circe, not Calypso, not the Cyclops. Not the hawk that suddenly swooped, which she dodged by darting and diving. Not the granary, not the seeds that lie forgotten on the threshing floors. Not the laughing whirlpool that invited her to enjoy herself by the cliffs at the entrance to the ravine. Not the tempting waters of a stream: Descend *yonati tamati,* my undefiled dove of innocence, come bathe yourself and drink.

As for the Baby, at times he flew behind her and at times he glided effortlessly alongside her. And sometimes to amuse himself he chanted to the rhythm of her wings: I am dead, I am back, I am flying, I am alive. He had already grown accustomed to the height, was even enjoying it, and flew upside down and climbed and dived. His ears could hear the beating of her wings and the wind whistling between her pinions and the stifled cries of joy and terror from inside the capsule attached to her leg. His nose smelled the sea of air, his eyes watched the land pass by beneath him; how small it is during our lives, he reflected, and how large when we are dead: barren, terraced hills, fields fighting for their lives with a final uprising of green. Yellow flags of victory, spring in retreat.

The hills shrank and grew round, the hillocks flattened. The pigeon flew over a town, caught sight of a white tower standing erect there, recalled that she had seen it in the past, and knew that home was nearby. From this point forward the land began dressing itself more ornately, in wide, man-made garments: the light green of vineyards, the dark green of citrus groves. The air grew warmer and the scent of the blossoms reached the Baby as a final act of grace, as proof: even the dead may rejoice, even they take pleasure, even they remember and are grateful. Here is the golden strip of sand dunes and the blue sea and, in the middle, Tel Aviv. How beautiful she is, he thought: blue and pink and gold. Waves and roofs and sand. Her eyes, her skin, her hair.

All at once the pigeon dived, the Baby scrambling to keep up, and already the sandstone hillock stood out beneath them. The sycamore trees around the edges, the pool of water at the top, the small fenced-in zoo clinging to the flank of the slope. The pigeon swooped down to the loft while the Baby stopped, hovering and watching from afar: he saw the animal cages, and the animals themselves, the ones sleeping and dreaming, the ones awake and alert, the giant turtles, the waterfowl pool, saw too the lions and the bear, and then her, his beloved, rushing outside the loft, her hand raised, her face hope and joy.

The pigeon alighted on the landing board of the loft and pushed her way inside through the trap door. The Girl welcomed her gently, politely, proffering fresh water and grains of hashish. She stroked the bird, removed the message holder from her leg. The Baby watched her pull out the tube and observe it, open it, bring it to her nose. Her mouth dropped open, his name shot out at him. Her shout rent the air. No and no and no and no. But his ears were already deaf. He was dead.

# Chapter Eighteen

## I

THAT MORNING the Girl had requested the simpler jobs: checking the feed bags, cleaning the troughs, scraping clean the floor of the pigeon loft. If a heart heavy with worry is no good for breeding, then it is certainly no good for dispatching pigeons or teaching the young birds, either. In such a state one can even err in filling out the breeding cards.

She was carrying out her chores meticulously and in silence, taking comfort in the routine, when suddenly she heard the rustle of wings right inside her head; so powerful was it that all the zoo animals fell silent and, like her, tilted an ear and an eye and stood frozen, each and every animal in its place. No monkey chattered, no lion roared, no buck grew fearful, and the Girl turned around, rushed outside, and raised her hand and her gaze.

The pigeon descended toward her with such velocity that it seemed to her as though the heavens were parting. For a moment she did not know whether she was looking upon a spirit or a body, a flesh-and-blood pigeon or merely its likeness, but in such cases the body feels and knows and understands before the mind and the senses, and instead of descending from one's head, joy rises from beneath the breast. The pigeon she had given him had returned; he had sent it to her. He is alive. Everything is in order.

The pigeon alighted on the landing board at the southeastern entrance to the loft, pushed open the bars of the trap door, entered the compartment, and stood motionless. The Girl spread and parted the pigeon's tail feathers, her eyes searching for the quills, and when she did not find them she turned to releasing the message capsule attached to the bird's leg.

A surprise. Inside the capsule there was no message, only a corked glass tube. The Girl held it up to the light and saw that there was no note here either, just a few drops of murky liquid. She removed the cork, sniffed the contents, and the happiness of the pigeon's return vanished in the face of astonishment; already her body had comprehended and had turned to stone, her mouth dropped open and shouted, the name shrieked, blasted.

Her knees shook, but her concern for the contents of the tube strengthened her hand. Don't drop it! Don't fall! Mourning and death were postponed; now it was necessary to gather one's wits. Don't give up! She returned the cork to the tube, wrapped it in cotton wool, slipped the tube into the pocket of her shirt, and pressed it close to her body with her hand. That was how she left the pigeon loft, running toward Dr. Laufer's tiny quarters next to the zoo shed.

"What happened?" the storeroom attendant asked her. "I've never seen you like this. Careful, please, you're going to break something. What's with you?"

"A syringe . . . I need a syringe," the Girl stuttered. Her hands were tugging at drawers, rifling through them, knocking things over, when suddenly she screamed, "I need a syringe and I need a spoon! Don't you understand? You're a woman just like I am! Don't you understand what it means when a woman needs a syringe and a spoon?!"

"No, I don't, but if that's what you need so badly all of a sudden then here, here's a spoon. And over here's a syringe," the attendant said, lifting the lid of a metal container on the shelf. "Take it, just sterilized, right here under your nose. What are you shouting for? And what does being a woman have to do with anything? What size needle do you need?"

"No needle, only the syringe . . . Hurry! It's urgent!" The Girl swiped the syringe from the attendant's hand and the spoon from the table and raced out the storeroom.

The attendant called after her: "I've heard of girls who need chocolate right away or a man right away or poetry right away, but a syringe with no needle, and a spoon?"

The Girl did not hear this little pearl of wisdom; she was rushing back to the loft, where she burst in—against all the rules and conventions. She spread an army blanket on the floor and placed a small feed-bag on top of it. She steadied herself with a deep breath and opened the door, releasing a large flock of surprised birds. They burst out and took off for the skies above the zoo, but they did not fly away or rise too high, merely wheeled in wide circles. With four swift tugs she pulled the cords from around the curtains so that heavy flaps of cloth fell across the windows and darkness rose from the floor. She took the tube in hand and removed the cork. As she tapped her finger gently on the side, the Baby's semen dribbled onto the spoon. The Girl drew back the piston, sucking it into the syringe. How much was there? Not more than a few drops.

She stripped off her clothes and lay flat on her back on the blanket, thinking how her last time with him they had been on this blanket, how she had kissed him, hugged him, touched and caressed him, how happy it had made her to bring him such pleasure, and now she was sorry she had not demanded to have intercourse with him, sorry for the semen spilled in her hand. Enough crying! She pulled the small feedbag under her loins and spread her thighs wide. She took the syringe in her right hand, brought the fingers of her left hand to her mouth and moistened them, then thrust them into herself. Again and again she wet her fingers, lubricating herself generously all around and deep inside. Then she held her breath, plunged the entire length of the syringe in, and pressed the piston.

She pressed her thighs together, drew her knees up to her chest, and wrapped both arms around them. There was nothing more she could do, nothing but trust her body and his seed, that it would find its way. She lay that way, her eyes shut, listening to the flux of the semen—down, down, down—as it skirred and dived inside her.

That's right, she said in her heart, travel downward, homeward, in a straight line. A thousand tiny wings were plying her, floating over the depths of her body. Down, lower, to the dark, the safe, deeper inside, inside, inside, to the warm, the living, the encompassing and the moist, we have done our part, now do yours. Push onward, do not look back.

And the semen, as if heeding her voice, hastened and plunged. Homeward. From the skies of death to the depths of life, from the outside chill to the inner warmth, from the whistling of sun-drenched flight to the night-darkened silence of the abyss.

# 2

AFTER A FEW MINUTES passed the Girl parted her eyelids and saw that the pigeon had not fled the pigeon loft with her fellow birds but was standing near her head. They looked at each other, the Girl's eyes moist, the pigeon's round and compassionate, her head cocked in the manner of pigeons when they wish to see better.

"Where did you come from?" the Girl asked.

Pigeons have no way of indicating directions or places; creatures whose eyes are telescopes and whose beaks are compasses and whose longing is a map have no need for such things. Thus, the pigeon's answer was vague, if more poetic than expected and more florid than necessary.

"From the summit of the hill," she pronounced. "From the noise and fire whence the Baby dispatched me ere his death."

"How long did it take you?"

"Forty minutes."

"And the sun?"

"At my back for the length of the journey."

"Forty minutes from the southeast," the Girl said. "You came from Jerusalem."

"So be it," cooed the pigeon. "It is all the same to us pigeons whence we come, so long as we are bound for home." And, feeling important, she added, "I was his last pigeon. I am the last pigeon the Baby dispatched."

The Girl's eyelids grew heavy and exhausted. Large teardrops escaped from beneath them and streamed down her cheeks. Now that the act had been completed she was free to contemplate her beloved's death, not what he had sent her or what she had done with it.

"Tell me what happened," she requested. "Was he carrying you in the dovecote when he was hit?"

"No," answered the dove, "he had left us in a safe place and gone out. A bell rang, thunder pealed, a tongue of fire leapt forth. The world shook and the dovecote fell and broke open. My two comrades were killed, the small one instantly and the large male shortly thereafter. I alone remained, waiting."

She fell silent. She gathered a single kernel from the floor and sipped a bit of water to indicate that she had finished eating, then moved away from the dish and eyed the Girl.

"And what about the Baby?"

"He returned. His skin was flayed and his blood flowing. He came back crawling and moaning."

The pigeon's ceremonious recounting alarmed the Girl. She restrained her tears so that her body would not tremble and disturb the flow of the seed inside her.

"And what did he do?"

"He slit open his trousers and exposed his flesh and did things to his body that you used to do, right in this very place."

Both smiled. The pigeon charmingly so, with a squint, her beak slightly open, and the Girl, her eyes scrunched and tearful, her lips white.

"If he had wings he would have come to you himself, exactly like I did, all purpose and progress and direction and aim. The trickle, the pouring, the closing and affixing of the capsule to my leg. He took hold of me, crawled, dispatched, and expired."

"If I had wings, I would have flown to him and rescued him," the Girl said.

"I was your wings," the pigeon declaimed, "I am the flesh and the soul, I am the breeze of the body and the burden of love, I am wind and strength."

The pigeons that had been flying over the loft now descended and circled it. Perhaps they were hungry and thirsty; perhaps they wished to listen in on the conversation. Several of them perched on the roof while others landed and walked about and cooed on the ground.

"Hush," the pigeon said to them. "Hush. The seed is returning to its nesting place. Be patient."

"Hush," the Girl intoned. "He is returning, he is sailing inside me, soaring. I can feel it."

The pigeons outside flew off again, circling over the loft. The Girl removed the syringe from her body and, without casting a single glance at its empty chamber, let it drop to the ground. Her eyelids shut, her limbs fell limp, her entire body slackened. And that was how Dr. Laufer found her when he came running in several minutes later, panting and sweaty. Half an hour earlier he had seen from a distance the pigeons hovering, neither descending nor ascending, neither drawing near nor departing, merely floating in a circle whose center was clear and singular. He saw and understood that something had happened.

He was no longer a young man, but his fear restored his legs to those of a buck and his imagination infused them with youthfulness. He ran like a madman, hopping over fences, sinking in sandy patches, flailing and gulping and plying forward, shortening the distance to the zoo through backyards, rushing along shouting, "Please, not now, we are in a terrible hurry!" to anyone wishing to detain or protest or stop him. And when he reached the zoo, he did not head for the gate but girded his loins, continued on his direct course, and stormed the wall, climbing over it and dropping down on the other side, where he stood and made straight for the pigeon loft.

He peeled back the flap of the curtain and peered inside, where he saw the Girl lying on the ground. At first he feared she was dead, then discerned that she was sleeping, and only then saw that she was naked. Naked, her limbs sprawled, drying trails of tears shining on her cheeks and drying trails of saliva fading between her thighs. And what was the missing Belgian champion pigeon doing there with her? Why was she sitting by the Girl's shoulder? And what was she watching over?

At once he turned his face so as not to gaze any longer at the Girl's nakedness. He went off to find his gray woolen blanket, the one he used when he needed to sleep on a cot in the zoo while caring for some animal that was ill or giving birth with difficulty. Walking backward, he entered the loft, spread the blanket over the Girl, and departed, closing the door behind him and proceeding to his tiny office, where he found the storeroom attendant, who informed him in an excited whisper that the Girl had gone crazy.

"I mean totally crazy, Dr. Laufer," she said. "I'm telling you, Dr. Laufer, she went nuts. She showed up in the storeroom screaming and you won't believe, Dr. Laufer, what she wanted: a spoon and a syringe, Dr. Laufer, I don't understand what for."

Neither did Dr. Laufer understand the meaning of this, but he— unlike the storeroom attendant—knew the Girl well and comprehended that this was an act not of madness but of purpose. He returned to the pigeon loft and waited outside until the curtains were raised and the Girl—awake and dressed—came out. The Belgian pigeon was perched on her shoulder, and the pigeons that had been flying overhead just a moment before entered the loft and began to eat.

"That is the pigeon that disappeared on us several days ago," he told her.

"The Baby is dead," said the Girl.

"Where? What?" Dr. Laufer shouted. "How could he be dead?"

"And before he died he dispatched this pigeon to me."

"What are you talking about? When did you give her to him?"

"He came to say good-bye to me, to take his leave before going to battle. I gave her to him and he left."

"Before going to battle?" Dr. Laufer exclaimed, feeling the facts land one after the other around him. "What battle? He is a pigeon handler, not a fighter. What battle? And why do you say that he died?"

"This morning he fell in a battle for some monastery in Jerusalem. A monastery with a bell and a cannon . . ."

At this point the Girl burst into heavy, bitter, howling sobs. Dr. Laufer hugged her shoulders, said, "Shhh . . . shhhh . . . shhhh. Who told you he died? What has caused you to say such things?"

"He told me. And the pigeon, too."

"How can a person announce his own death? How can pigeons converse? This cannot be!"

The Girl said nothing.

"And what is it that he sent with her?"

The Girl handed him the open capsule and the empty tube.

Dr. Laufer looked inside. His legs gave way even before he caught the scent. His nose confirmed what his body understood and what his heart had accepted and his mind had rejected. He sat slowly on one of the boxes, clasped the Girl around her thighs, and pressed his head against her belly. His shoulders trembled. His throat constricted.

"Forgive us," he told her. "Please forgive us for crying. We were promised that he would merely raise pigeons, that he would simply set up a loft. But what, in the end, do we know? All we do is heal animals and raise pigeons. What do we understand?"

He stood to his full height and rested the Girl's head on his shoulder, muttering, "And you . . . it is unbelievable. That is why you asked the storeroom attendant for a spoon and a syringe . . . no wavering, no FOR and AGAINST, such a decision . . ."

"It was what I wanted, what he wanted. We talked about having a baby when we last met, a child we would make after the war. And that is what he sent me."

"A miraculous new story," Dr. Laufer said, taking heart, as though the Girl's returning strength was pouring into him. "A story unlike any other in the world history of pigeonry. We shall tell the story at our next convention of pigeon handlers."

# 3

SEVERAL DAYS PASSED, amassed, turned into weeks. Dr. Laufer came to his senses and told nothing to anyone, but at the next convention— which took place half a year later—all the pigeon handlers could clearly make out the Girl's large belly, and the Belgian pigeon that did not leave her shoulder. Three months after that she gave birth to a boy who closely resembled his father, and there is no need to make any effort in guessing his identity.

When the child was six months old his mother brought him to a pigeon handlers' conference. Dr. Laufer photographed her sitting there, the Belgian pigeon on her shoulder, the baby suckling at her breast—Where is that picture now? I wish I knew—and the pigeon handlers were out of their minds with joy. They approached her one after the other, sharing her mourning and her happiness, smiling and wiping their tears.

The Girl nursed her son for a relatively long time—some twelve months or so—and just when Dr. Laufer hinted to her that the time had come to desist ("As veterinarians we understand these things better than pediatricians"), a nearly forgotten guest appeared at the zoo: the boy who had been with her that day on the balcony when the wounded pigeon landed. He was the neighbors' son who had dressed the pigeon's injury and accompanied the Girl to the zoo and brought stale bread and studied Corning's Anatomy and the English dictionary and traveled to America to study medicine in Chicago.

Ten years had passed since then, and they were as long as a hundred in his eyes. There was not a day in which he did not think of her, a night in which she did not visit his dreams. He was no longer a boy; he was a young man for whom the world awaited his choices and deeds. Behind him were a dozen rejected job offers, a dozen failed attempts at persuasion, and four broken American hearts. He had disembarked from the ship in Haifa Port, kissed his proud, excited parents hello, and an hour later, in the taxi en route to Tel Aviv, had asked about the Girl.

"Better you shouldn't know," his mother said. His father said, "We'll talk about it at home," to which his mother added in a low grumble, "The whole city knows. It's a scandal."

They no longer lived on Ben Yehuda Street above the Girl's parents; they'd taken a larger new apartment near Dizengoff Square. He put his luggage in the room his parents had prepared for him and told them, "I'm going out. I'll be back later."

"Where are you going?" his mother called out. "You've only just come back from America and you're already off?"

"I'll only be gone a little while," he said. "I need to see her."

His legs carried him not toward Ben Yehuda Street but in the opposite direction. The fat man collected from him the stale bread he had gathered on the way and allowed him to enter the gate of the zoo, but with a distressed and lowered gaze.

The young doctor entered the zoo, followed the path, and at the pigeon loft he saw the Girl sitting and nursing a baby. His blood hardened in his veins. His flesh turned to wood. The Girl did not notice him because her head was bent in the way of nursing mothers. He managed to withdraw, and there, hidden behind the bend in the path, he regained his strength. He drew near and stood next to her.

"Hello, Raya," he said.

"Hello, Yaacov," Raya said, raising her head.

"You were a girl when we parted, and now you are nursing a baby."

"His name is Yair."

"He's a beautiful child."

"He looks like his father. Had he looked like me he would have been more handsome."

"I've just returned from America. I finished my medical studies there."

"Congratulations."

"You, too. I got home half an hour ago. The first thing I did was come to see you."

"Thank you."

"And where is Yair's father?"

"His father was killed in the war."

"I'm sorry. I didn't know."

Suddenly he felt courageous and could no longer contain or imprison what he had said in his heart all those years when he rose in the morning and when he walked about and when he sat in the university library, the laboratory, the hospital, and when he lay down at night. And the words burst out: "It could be, Raya, that I should have stayed in this country, and instead of going to study medicine in America I should have gone to war here. It could be that I should have accepted Dr. Laufer's offer to work with you here in the pigeon loft. That could be, too. But then he was the one who said I would make a good doctor, and he was right."

"Funny," said my mother, "how Dr. Laufer determined all of our fates. Yours, mine, my baby that lives, and my Baby who died."

She moved me from one breast to the other in a decisive movement, a hurried, terrifying skip from fear to security, and said, "Dr. Yaacov Mendelsohn. It has a nice ring to it."

"I had hoped to forget you, Raya," said the young doctor. "But I couldn't."

She did not answer.

"I sent you seven letters in the first year and ten in the third and another five in the fourth, and then I stopped because you did not respond."

"There was no point."

He sat facing her and said, "I have always loved you, Raya, from the time you were a girl, when you lay reading on your stomach on the balcony, even before that wounded pigeon landed there. Often I would watch you from our balcony above. Once your shirt rose a little and I saw the dimples on your back and from upstairs I closed my eyes and kissed them."

She was silent.

"And that shirt of ours that fell to your balcony on the day the wounded pigeon landed—I threw it there. It didn't fall."

"I thought so."

"And if you ask me what the most important thing I learned in medical school was, I will tell you this: that things can be fixed. Not only bodies. Souls, too. They can be fixed and mended. And in my opinion that is exactly what we need to do now."

She was silent.

"I didn't even know you'd married," he said. "My parents wrote about all sorts of things, but they never wrote that you'd gotten married."

"I didn't," my mother said.

The young doctor took a deep breath. He decided to save all the clarifications and all the surprises for other times and conversations.

"I'd like you to marry me," he said. "And you'll give birth to a girl, I want a daughter, and this boy I will raise exactly as if he were my own."

And so it was, more or less. That is to say, several days later my mother told him, "We agree," though instead of a sister, a brother was born, and Dr. Yaacov Mendelsohn become Yordad, a nickname that suited everyone from every standpoint.

# Chapter Nineteen

## I

"THAT'S THAT," said my contractor who is a woman. "We've torn down and thrown out everything we needed to. Now it's time to build."

"What are you starting with?"

"Usually you put up the inner walls and lay the groundwork for water and electricity. But we're going to start with your outdoor shower."

She called one of the Chinese workers. "Pour the concrete here," she instructed him, "five feet by five feet so there's room for two, with a two-degree depression toward the drain."

"Are you sure this is a good spot?" I queried. "I don't want all the village kids to come and spy on me."

"Don't worry. The Chinese invented noodles, kites, gunpowder, and outdoor showers. They know how to build them so that nobody can see you."

The worker asked something incomprehensible and Tirzah pointed and said, "Have the water drain off to that lemon tree over there. Use a two-inch pipe."

To me she said, "That's all. Now we just have to leave him alone. The Chinese are just like us—it makes them mad to have someone breathing down their necks."

"How did he understand what you said?"

"When we each speak our own language, the music of our speech is normal and our hand movements and body languages are natural, and then we understand each other."

"How could he understand 'a two-degree depression'?"

"What do you mean, how? He's a professional craftsman. He knows it's a two-degree depression."

"So why did you have to tell him?"

"So he knows his contractor understands, too, even if his contractor is a woman. He should respect me."

And that was how the building of my new home commenced: with an outdoor shower. The Chinese worker leveled the earth, built a wooden frame for the pouring of the concrete, laid down a metal net to which he affixed the drainpipe, and mixed and poured and smoothed with long strokes. When the cement had hardened a bit he suggested— smiling cordially, and gesturing naturally—that I sink the palms of my hands in as a memento. I did, then suggested that he do the same. He laughed, refused, walked away, and finally bent down next to me and did as I had asked.

The following day I led a barn-owl tour in the Beit She'an Valley, and when I returned Tirzah announced, "Your shower is ready. Come have a look."

I went to have a look. A narrow path of tiles—"So mud doesn't get in between your wet toes"—led to my new spot, where I found everything one needs for an outdoor shower: a floor and a drain, towel racks, a place to put soap and a scrub brush, even a small mirror—the inspiration of the Chinese worker, who'd guessed what Meshulam and Tirzah had failed to: that I like to shave in the shower, under a light sprinkle and with my face soaped.

"Check to make sure everything works properly," Tirzah said. "So that you don't come complaining to your contractor later."

I turned on the faucet. There was a soft and plentiful outburst of rain—a sharp stream does not suit an outdoor shower—and the water disappeared into the whole in the floor, emerging by the lemon tree.

"The tree is no less happy than you," Tirzah said.

"Why did you choose that one? You could have drained the water off to some other trees."

"That tree deserves it. It gives off a wonderful scent and good fruit," she said. She pushed me toward the worker. "Go thank him. The Chinese are just like us—they like praise and compliments."

I thanked him with warm Hebrew words and natural body movements and he beamed and bowed and smiled. I returned his bow and told him the shower was his to use whenever he wanted. Tirzah came back from her pickup truck with soap, shampoo, hand cream, four new towels, a wood-slat bathmat, a loofah, a small, hard brush for the palms and nails, a razor, and five memorial candles.

"Are you nuts? What are we going to do, shower in mourning?"

"It's nice to shower in the evening with candlelight, and memorial candles don't drip and they don't fall over and they burn for a long time. And anyway, it's nice to enjoy yourself and know that others are dead but you aren't."

# 2

THE SUN SET and Tirzah gave the tractor operator the keys to her pickup truck and told him to take the workers to their lodgings and bring them back in the morning. We were alone.

"Iraleh," she said, "do you want to inaugurate the new shower I built you outside?"

"Tiraleh," I said, "do you want to cut a ribbon and sound the trumpets?"

"No, just shower in it the first time."

"Naked? Outside?"

"You can shower in your clothes if you want, but before you ask any more stupid questions, then yes, with me."

I watched her while she undressed and opened the faucet, stepped under the stream. Her eyes, which were usually a yellow-green, turned blue under the water. She lifted her face to the flow, passed her fingers through her hair, squeezed her locks, pivoted to face me.

"Aren't you joining me?" she asked.

I stripped and stepped under the water with her.

"Ever since Gershon, I haven't showered with you," she said. Two minutes later she turned off the water—"Jerusalemites can't stand watching water flow for no reason"—and began soaping me with great purpose, like you bathe a child: behind the ears, the elbows, the "peepot," the knees, between the buttocks.

"What are you doing?" I chuckled from being tickled and from embarrassment and from pleasure.

"I'm cleaning you, luvey. I'm washing away everything that's gotten stuck to you. Now you clean me like that, too."

Tirzah's body is solid and sturdy. Her skin is naturally dark, not white with suntanned patches. I soaped her up, first hesitantly, then all over:

neck and belly, hands and back. Lengthwise and crosswise, inside and around, front and back. The way I would soap the Double-Ys when they were little and they came to their uncle's house for the weekend. I shampooed her strong, short hair. I crouched next to her and tapped her ankle and she laughed and presented me with one foot and then the other, like a horse being shod. "I'd remembered what a jerk you are but I'd forgotten how sweet you are," she said.

Her hand, behind my back, turned the water on again—just a little bit, so that the flow was not full and solid but rather light showers and heavy drops and random, surprising streams. Our bodies overflowed with joy. Tirzah pressed against me and said, "The thing I remember best is you standing in the window of your apartment and looking at me and how all at once I loved you."

"You were ten years old," I said.

"What do you think, that a ten-year-old girl can't understand what she's feeling?" For a moment she fell silent; then she continued. "There was a time when I thought we were brother and sister, that my father had had some old business with your mother. That really turned me on."

"If we were brother and sister, your father would never have taken such trouble to get us together."

"Don't talk logic to me. I knew we weren't."

The shadows fled. A westerly wind was blowing, a wet and pleasant shiver. Lingering gooseflesh speckled my luvey's skin. Our hands roved and settled. Our eyes, our lips tasted and saw. We embraced. Between her thighs I felt her wetness; she was wet beneath the wetness of the water and hot beneath its coolness.

"Lie on the floor," she said. "Until now we've been showering and playing around. Now we'll inaugurate the shower in proper fashion."

And later, when she rolled over on her back and lay beside me, she informed me that this was how we would inaugurate the new floor and the new roof and the deck and the kitchen, each in its turn. "So that you know it's me building this house for you, and so that the house knows it, too.

"I could have built it in a single week," she said. "I could have brought forty craftsmen here, worked on it for six days, and rested on the seventh. But this isn't the heavens and the seas and it isn't the trees and the earth and the animals. Here it's cement and concrete, it's plaster and loam. Every one of those guys takes days to dry. It's not people, my luvey, and it isn't God: it's the materials that hold up the work."

That was how the thing started and how it continued. And that is the way I remember it now, when the house stands finished and Tirzah has left me and gone away. I remember how she built and inaugurated, stage after stage. How she pointed and said, "Let there be a wall" and "Let there be a window" and "Let there be a doorway" and "Let there be a deck." She built and named, inaugurated and labeled, and moved on to another day.

# Chapter Twenty

## I

THE VILLAGE is a small and stagnant puddle, every stone disturbing the algae that covers it, and Tirzah and I—and the house that is being created—attract visitors and curious onlookers. There are the polite ones; since I have not yet hung the front door, they knock on the doorpost, stick their heads in, and ask, "May I come in?" And there are the rude ones; since I have not yet hung the front door, they appear and, without saying hello, enter my home as if entering their own. They look around the house and the garden with the quick and knowing eye of a marten; they tally the number of bags of cement mixture, the pipes, the ceiling mesh. In seconds they have incorrectly estimated the budget and the scope of the renovations, and as soon as my gaze rests upon them they withdraw to the underbrush.

They do not anger me. I am a recent arrival, while they are the natives. And in such a place—so old and ripe that the trees are already large and the sidewalks are cracked and weedy and scores have been settled and enmities and loves have lulled—someone new is also a threat. His memories and his experience come from different places and he does not know the local order of importance. Such a person is liable to upset tradition. He needs to be sized up.

Former residents of the house have started to show up, too. The rumor has spread and they come. To investigate, to confirm, to negate, to wonder. A man older than I appeared and asked permission to cut a single lemon from the tree. "My father planted it," he said. "That's his fig tree, too. What happened to it? Why don't you take care of it? Look at the holes in the trunk, thanks to you it'll die . . ."

His lips trembled. His eyes skittered, and his mouth, too, from blame to memory: "Those houses over there weren't built yet, and that road was a dirt trail for carts, and my father would walk from there to the junction because buses didn't enter the village back then. Over here he made a little cement trough, the only one in the village, and he would bathe my sister and me in it. Where is it? Did you tear it down? Who gave you permission?" And with that he departed.

A young couple suddenly appeared, too. The woman had lived here for half a year as a child and now, just before her wedding, she wished to show the place to her intended. She wanted him to know what had remained and what had disappeared, what had existed and what had not.

She was young, but the dredging up of memories gave her the countenance of the aged. "There was a swing here," she said, leading him through points of reference that no longer existed. "And this is where we hung laundry . . . there was a little cement trough here that my father dug up and threw out . . . this shed wasn't here back then—there was only space between the columns. This is where we took off our boots and scraped them down in the winter and she would shout at us: Don't drag in any mud . . ."

Suddenly she turned to me. "What, are you making it one big room instead of the small rooms?"

"Yes," I answered shortly.

"Why?"

The young man stroked her neck. His fingers spoke love while his palm grew heavy. His voice was losing patience. "Let's go. We're bothering him."

Still, most visitors come out of sheer curiosity. They wish to see the ne'er-do-well as he vacillates in the midst of the workers, and the woman of valor—since the time of the committee interview, everyone takes Tirzah for my wife—who orchestrates the work and has already been nicknamed "the whirlwind" by the elders.

Some people ask her advice on matters of building: What's your opinion, Liora, on insulation bricks? What do you think, Liora, of prefabs? How about thermal plaster? Heated floors? And what about building with wood, Liora? What do you recommend? Finnish pine? Red pine? Treated? Painted? Exposed?

Some people ask for her assistance—Perhaps your Chinese worker can pop over to our place to fix a little something in the kitchen?—

while others ask if everything is all right, and even offer advice: they know of a shop with fair and reasonable prices where you can pick up a showerhead, a galvanized gutter pipe, Marseilles tiles, Caesarean marble. They also have a cheap and excellent tiler or plasterer or roofer.

Others offer agricultural advice: how to nurse a dying lemon tree, how to get rid of weeds, how to kill the caterpillar still boring tunnels through the flesh of the fig tree. But I have no need for advice when it comes to gardening; Meshulam is very knowledgeable, and since he does not wish to argue with his daughter over matters of construction, he prefers to concentrate on the garden.

I listen to all my guests, try to remain patient and amicable—who else but me remembers my mother's advice to Yordad: be nice to them, it saves time—and for that very same reason I am careful to smile abundantly and answer thriftily.

The rules are clear. I know nothing about them and they, apart from my profession and the lies Tirzah told at our interview, know the same about me. But they know the people who lived in my house previously, the children who grew up there and have since matured. They know the happy occasions that took place there and the painful ones that filled its rooms. Locked in their hearts are the shouts and the laughter, the clinking of forks and glasses, the moans and the sobs that hovered between the walls and flowed out the windows.

"This house could tell many stories," one of them told me, expecting me to ask. When I did not, he said, "Better you shouldn't ask," and departed.

I did not ask. I do not wish to know. I simply did what you told me to: I chose my home as you instructed. A small, old house in an old place. A home lived in over the years. I know nothing about the first occupant, and about the last I know only that he left behind four chickens to waste away of hunger and thirst in their prison. That is enough for me.

My young neighbor, too—the one whose wife drew a dividing string between us—showed up unexpectedly for a visit carrying a large, full bowl of perfectly cubed watermelon. The precise red cubes were so chilled that dew beaded on them. Only a woman who takes care that matters should be clear can cut watermelon so flawlessly.

"A gift from my wife," he said. "How are the renovations coming along?"

"Everything's fine."

Her voice rose, broke in: "Did you give it to him? Don't forget to return the bowl."

He rose to his feet. Nonplussed, he picked up the bowl even though there were still several cubes of watermelon inside. "Well, I'll be seeing you."

"Thank you very much," I called after him. "And send my regards and thanks to your wife."

He turned his face back toward me. "You should know, she's really fine!"

"I do know. It's a little hard to get used to a new neighbor all of a sudden. Tell her that I'm not so bad either."

To myself I added, "And tell her that I hear you two at night and that I am serene and peaceful. A woman who makes love to her husband like she does really is fine."

The local building inspector showed up as well. Young, short, energetic—his eyes were nice and happy, but his smile was evil. Where are the plans? He wants to see the plans. The plans are at the offices of the regional council? Really? So how is it that they didn't show them to him there? Yes, he sees the building permit, but why does the signature appear here and not there? Suddenly the telephone in his pocket rang and he said, "Hello, Mr. Fried," and "I didn't know it was you, Mr. Fried," and "No, there's no need for you to phone the head of the regional council, Mr. Fried," and then he took off.

Mr. Fried's daughter said, "I think Meshulam stands over on that hill with a pair of binoculars and watches what goes on here."

And another inspector turned up: Liora's brother, Emmanuel. Normally I pick him up and drive him around the country on his visits, but this time he appeared by surprise in a taxi.

"Let me introduce you to my contractor," I said.

"Pleased to meet you," said Tirzah.

Emmanuel circled the house, then entered it.

"Watch where you walk," Tirzah told him. "We're laying pipes today."

He had the stooped back and softened step and voice of a born-again Jew, but he was still as feisty and direct in his speech as ever. He said he had wanted to know if the story Liora had told him was true, and when he saw it with his own eyes he wished to know about the costs and the source of the money.

Meshulam, who apparently had spied him through his binoculars, turned up a few minutes later.

"What business is it of yours?" he said. "The money's his."

"Who are you?" Emmanuel asked.

"A friend of the Mendelsohn family. And you?"

"His brother-in-law," Emmanuel said. "Liora Mendelsohn is my sister."

"Friends you choose," Meshulam said, "but brothers-in-law you get without asking. Now I remember. I saw you at the wedding party of Iraleh and your sister. Back then you weren't the tarragon of virtue you are now. You came from America with a pair of snakeskin shoes on your feet and two floozies on each arm."

"How much did you pay for this place?" Emmanuel asked, turning to me.

"Enough."

"And where did you get 'enough'?"

"Listen, I'm going to explain to you where this money came from in a way that you can understand it," Meshulam told him. "This guy bought a Shabbat fish in the market and found a pearl inside it."

I escorted Emmanuel to his taxi. Before settling himself inside it, he warned me: "Just so you know, this house is never going to give you a return on the investment."

"It's not an investment," I told him. "It's a gift."

"From who?"

"From me."

"And that fish was Elijah the prophet!" Meshulam shouted after him. "And why don't you buy yourself something like this, too. It's very healthy to get presents from oneself."

And there were others who came to see the miracle himself: the buyer. Me. The man who, in such difficult times, did not bargain, who paid the full price in one payment and bought himself a wreck that could have been purchased for less. Naturally, those visitors mocked me, but they also locked me in their gaze, studied me, so that they would know how to recognize others like me, so that they would not pass up a similar opportunity.

Don't expect other such buyers, I said in my heart. There is no other person whose mother determined his profession, who introduced him to his wife, and who, during her lifetime, gave him money to buy a place of his own: Take it, Yair, while my hand is warm and I am still alive to give it to you. A home that will wrap you up inside it, protect you, revive you. A home that will build you as you build it, and you will be grateful for each other, and the two of you will heal each other, and you will change each other's roof and floor, and build walls and open windows and doors.

# 2

IN THE MIDDLE of the day, without any prior warning, another guest appeared: Benjamin. He parked behind the workers' pickup truck and shouted, "Yair!"

I came out to him.

"So this is the house everyone's talking about?" he asked.

"Yes."

"Who bought it for you?"

"I did."

"And who's paying for the renovations?"

"Me again."

"Where did you get the money?"

"Do you want the real answer or the answer that will make you feel better?"

He scrutinized me. We had not seen each other since the end of the mourning period for my mother, and the change that the house had brought about in me surprised him.

"You're looking good," he said. "Of course I want the truth. Liora already told me that she didn't give you the money, and she'll be happy to know the answer as well."

"I understand that the two of you are worried."

"Of course we are. Each for his own reasons."

"Meshulam loaned me the money to buy the house," I said. "And Tirzah is renovating it for me as a gift."

"That's what I thought," my brother said, relieved. "But Liora actually had a few different ideas."

"You see," I said, "on the outside you look real slick, but in fact you're pretty gullible. Now do you want to know the real truth?"

His face darkened. "Mother gave it to you?" He fixed her blue eyes on me. "Answer me!" He drew close to me. "And no more tricks. Is she the one who gave you the money?"

"Yes," I said. "A few months before she died. She summoned me, put a check in my hand, and said, Go find yourself a home. A place of your own."

"How big was the check?"

"Not so big. About eight hundred square feet worth. Exactly the size of this house."

"I knew it," Benjamin said. "And I thank you for being frank." Then he added, "That's quite a nice gift. Surprising. Not only for the one who received it but for the one who didn't."

"Absolutely," I said. "Surprising and how!"

"And all along I thought she loved me better," he said, leaning his head toward mine in an aggressively coquettish manner.

"In fact, she did love you better," I said. "That's why I got the check."

Benjamin smiled. And every time I think, How similar he is to you and Yordad. Not only his stature, his coloring, his shape, but also in the elegance of his movement. And with the same joy and gratitude of his clothes, which had the great good fortune of being worn by this handsome body, the shirt clinging to his chest, the trousers hugging his waist: How nice that we are on you and not somebody else.

"You're wrong," Benjamin said. "But what does it matter now? She is dead, and there's nobody to complain to now. The question is whether this is okay with you."

"Completely," I said. "I have no problem with it whatsoever."

"So that's that?" Benjamin asked. "One brother gets a gift that's the size of a house while the other doesn't get a single penny?"

"That was her decision, not mine. And I don't relate to it as money but as a gift. It was compensation."

"No one's to blame that you had a different father," Benjamin said.

"I didn't have a different father. She had a boyfriend who conceived me, but Yordad's the one who raised me. He's my father, and he raised me very well."

"I wonder what he thought about this whole story all these years."

"The thinking doesn't matter. What matters is what you do with it and how you behave. He told her he would raise me as his own son, and that's exactly what he did. He's an excellent father. Too bad all you inherited from him was his outsides."

"In those days it was not at all accepted to have sex with your boyfriend before marriage."

I did not attempt to correct him. I had already said two true things in this conversation, and as Meshulam says, "Telling the truth is very good, but it's not something one should make a habit of."

"She told me everything," Benjamin added.

Everything? Now it was my turn to be suspicious. "What did she tell you?"

"That her friend came to visit her before going to battle and that's when it happened."

A strange pride shone through his voice, the pride of a son whose mother prefers him. There are sons whose mothers give them money, and sons whose mothers open before them the secrets of their hearts. I did not correct him. If that's what you chose to tell him, so be it.

"With regards to the money," I informed him, "your wife and I have come up with an idea that could solve the problem."

Benjamin was both reassured and overcome with suspicion at the same time. "What?" he asked.

"I'll will this house to Yariv and Yoav."

"That's a very nice idea," said my brother after thinking briefly.

"Just don't think it's because of you," I said. "It's because of them. And Zohar, too. You don't deserve such a wife and sons."

"You've changed," Benjamin said. "And it's not only because of the house. I smell love here."

# 3

THE TRACTOR OPERATOR returned. He brought his cart up close to the west wall of the house and went to rest in the shade of the carob trees. The two Chinese workers climbed up to the roof, where they began dismantling the old cement tiles and tossing them to the ground. They continued working by crawling backward, removing and dropping pieces of the roof upon which their knees had rested only moments earlier.

In the afternoon Tirzah returned, followed several minutes later by a white pickup truck with the MESHULAM FRIED AND DAUGHTER, INC. logo. Unlike the first vehicle, this one had no driver.

"That's Illuz, our roofer," Tirzah announced happily. "So punctual!"

The pickup truck came to a stop, the door opened, and an exceedingly thin, exceedingly short man—a dwarf, in fact—alighted. His arms were long and his head large and smiling. He said hello to Tirzah, and with the speed of a monkey he climbed up to the framework of the roof and walked along the cement edges and the wooden beams, investigating and pronouncing judgment: "This one's rotten!" "This one, too." "This stays." "That one needs replacing."

He removed a builder's hammer hanging from his belt and pulled out nails, dismantled and threw away several planks, measured and wrote numbers on the palm of his hand. After that he joined us for a late lunch, dousing his food with a spicy sauce he kept in his bag. He announced that most of the roof was "perfectly fine" and that he would return the next day with his brother and the new materials. Tirzah told him he should take the two workers with him in his pickup truck, sent the tractor operator on his way, and said she wanted to "inaugurate our new non-roof."

"How?" I laughed. I felt it had been a long time since I had last heard myself laugh.

"We'll lie on our backs inside the house and look up at the heavens. We'll see if darkness really falls, as they say, or whether it rises."

We undressed, lay down next to each other. The walls hid us away from human eyes; the gaping roof exposed us to glances from above: those of migrating birds, of pigeons returning home, perhaps even your eyes, if you really are up there.

The greater light set and disappeared; its luminescence faded, then extinguished. First it lost its beingness, then its name. Darkness neither fell nor rose. It was not created all at once, like the light or the sea or the trees or man; rather, it took shape, spread, thickened, and was. The exposed beams of the roof, which previously had stood blackened against the sky, were now swallowed up inside it. The lesser light, that evening merely a narrow sickle, brightened in the west. Exuberant stars shone. Sprawling and naked, holding hands—this too was part of Tiraleh's orchestration—we watched them multiply and make a sieve of the dome of heaven.

Later on, my luvey began caressing me much like she used to when her brother would sit by us, watching and instructing: Touch his peepot, you touch her there, do it like this, I want to see . . .

We snuggled together. We kissed. I pressed myself to her, I growled and gurgled and rubbed up against her body. Tirzah laughed. "Iraleh . . ."

"What?"

"You love me."

Then she said, "We have photos from your wedding party in our house. Mostly you see Meshulam and your parents, but here and there you and Liora make an appearance. She's really beautiful."

I did not respond.

"And one day, about two years ago, I saw her on Ahad Ha'am Street in Tel Aviv. She was leaving a restaurant with a man and woman who looked like they were from overseas. I don't understand what she's doing with you at all."

"And what you're doing with me, you do understand?"

"I feel your mother in you."

"I don't resemble her at all."

"Doesn't matter. Anyway, you and I do resemble each other. And the uglies of the world have to stick together."

"We're not so ugly."

"We're not Medusa and the hunchback of Notre Dame, but we don't exactly turn heads either."

"You do. You're full of light; you shine. You have a beautiful walk and a beautiful butt and long legs and a strong neck. Your nipples are two different colors and your peepot is sweet."

She laughed. "She says nice things about you, too."

"I've seen how people look at you. It's at me they don't."

"A man doesn't need to look handsome; a little bit nicer looking than a monkey is enough," she said, quoting her mother's famous saying. "And maybe that's what Liora likes about you. That every morning her husband thanks God for giving him such a tall and beautiful wife."

"Why do we have to talk about her?"

"Because I want to. Because for once I want to feel what it's like to be really beautiful. To step outside in the morning and experience what a beautiful woman does. To walk down the street every day like she does, from home to the office, like an icebreaker in the North Sea. And not only to have it happen but to know in advance, with absolute certainly, that it's going to."

"Have you been following her?"

"Are you crazy? You yourself told me about how she walks to the office, all the looks she gets from her admirers, the guys who wait for her at the corner. When I was a little girl I saw the expression 'a captivating woman' in a book and went nuts from it. Gershon told me it describes a woman who captures your eyes and causes you to lose your way. My mother told me it had nothing to do with capture but with bewitchment. Meshulam said it didn't matter and it was all the same, anyway."

"Did you share these thoughts with the whole family?"

"Why not? Just like I'm sharing them with you right now. It may say that you're a Mendelsohn on your identity card, but to me and to my father you're a Fried."

Two hours later, while the darkness thickened and the heat remained, we slipped away to the outdoor shower. We bathed and dressed in the light of one of Tirzah's memorial candles—"You see? These candles are great. And you dared to make a face to me about them!"—and later we lit the string of lights strung between the branches of the carob trees and prepared an evening meal of salad, the way they eat it at Zohar's kibbutz: with soft cheese and warm slices of hard-boiled egg and black olives and chopped cloves of garlic. Tirzah laughed when I cracked the shell of the first egg on my forehead—"*Plaff!*"—and the second on hers.

She poured some arak over ice, added sprigs of mint she had found at the edge of the shower's drainpipe. I asked for a sip.

"It's a little strong for you."

"I'll be careful."

"Drink only a little, and slowly. It softens your heart and melts your tissues."

"Not mine."

"That's because the first time you drank you were told to empty the glass in one gulp."

Soft and happy, we sat inside our roofless house, loving and sleeping beneath divinely made heavens and atop man-made cement. Tirzah lay on her stomach, melting a piece of chocolate in her mouth. "Lie on top of me," she said. "I like your weight. It's just right on my body." We fell asleep like that for several minutes, awakened, undressed, and lay face to face, moving slowly and slightly, looking at each other. It is pleasant to lie with a woman you love, and when I inaugurate my new home in such a fashion, my love for my contractor lights up my dark places and moves over my void. Night and morning, day after day, and the creation of the house was coming to pass.

# 4

MY MOBILE PHONE RANG in the middle of the night. The display screen read YORDAD.

"Yairi," he said. "Is Mother at your place?"

"No," I answered, anxious about what would come next.

"If she does show up there"—he sounded relaxed, rational—"tell her—"

I cut him off. "She isn't going to be showing up here. How could you say such a thing? You know she won't be coming here."

"Why not? Have you had an argument? What happened?"

I sat up. "Because she's dead," I called out. "That's why. Don't you remember we attended her funeral?"

My voice had risen, echoing in the empty space. Tirzah stirred next to me. I felt her eyes were open. Yordad said, "Of course I remember the funeral. How can a person forget such a thing? The mourning period, too. A lot of people came—in fact, too many, if you ask me. But if she shows up at your place, Yairi, tell her to enter quietly when she comes home, because if I wake up it's very hard for me to fall back to sleep."

"All right," I said. "I'll tell her to enter quietly."

"Good night, then. I'm going to sleep and you should, too."

I could not sleep. How is it possible to sleep after a conversation like that? I lay sprawled on my back. For a moment I was startled by the missing roof, but at once I took pleasure in the shedding of the black of night in favor of the deep blue that dawn spread before its arrival. Tirzah sat cross-legged at the edge of the blanket and lit a candle. I looked at her, her body naked, the silhouette of her face illuminated. Those shapely lips that had passed over the whole of my body, the fingers that had left no territory unexplored, the shame we did not share then and apparently will never share.

"Did the telephone wake you up?"

"Never mind. I have to leave early to get to a building site of ours up north anyway." She put a kettle of coffee on the gas burner. "I'm not going to make any for you because you can still sleep for another couple of hours."

She stirred and poured and sipped from her mug. "But apropos the conversation you just had, I want to tell you something."

"What?"

"That I went to visit your mother a few days before she died."

I sat up. "I may as well have had coffee. Where did you see her?"

"In the hospital, of course."

"How didn't I see you there? What did you come as?"

"What is that supposed to mean? I came as Tirzah Fried. Meshulam was there. He phoned and said, 'Tiraleh, I'm just leaving Raya Mendelsohn's with the lawyer I brought for the will. If you want to say good-bye, this is probably your last chance.' I told him, 'I want to, but I don't want to run into Iraleh or anyone else from the family.' He said, 'So drop everything and come now. Professor Mendelsohn was already here with Dr. Benjamin, and Iraleh was here before and he wouldn't stop crying and so she got mad at him and he was offended and took off. Now I'm getting out of here and you can be alone with her.'"

"That was nice of him."

"Nice? Sly and clever, for sure. But not nice."

"Sure it is," I said. "Your father is nice and there's nothing you can do about it."

"He's not nice at all. You have no idea how not nice he really is. But the little niceness he has he concentrates on four people, and because you're one of them you think he's really like that."

"Who's the fourth?"

"Himself."

"So then what happened?"

"I got in the car and drove over there. It was night and nobody was around. I guess thanks to your father's connections she'd been given a private room."

"Or thanks to your father's," I interjected.

"She was awake. Very thin and weak, but she recognized me right away. She said, 'Tiraleh, it's nice of you to come visit me. As if you'd sensed I wanted you to.' I said, 'A lot of time has passed, Raya. How are you?' She said, 'Just the way I look.' I said, 'Meshulam said I could come.' She said, 'Are you still calling him Meshulam? Why can't you call him "Father"? He probably misses that terribly since Gershon was killed.' I didn't want to argue with her, because suddenly it seemed like a final wish. I said, 'I'll try to, but I can't promise.' She said, 'If he told you you should come visit me now, that means he sensed you wanted to.' I said, 'And it means he sensed you wanted me to, too.' She said, 'That's right, I wanted you to come.'"

My mother gulped air. She coughed. Tirzah wanted to ask her about me and my life and my happiness and my wife, but she did a FOR and AGAINST and decided against it. My mother said, "We've reached the End of Days: Tiraleh has run out of words!" and she turned her gaze to the window. "Over there in the darkness are the Castel and Bab-el-Wad and Nebi Samuel and the cemetery—they're constantly flying at me, even in the dark. And way out there is Tel Aviv. That's where I came from, but in the end I remained here."

Tirzah held my mother's hand and my mother held hers and said, "You asked me what I was thinking, Tiraleh? Well, I'm doing my last FOR and AGAINST, about what's better for me: to die or to live." Her laughter became a groan and her groan a cough and her cough a spasm.

"That's when she told me you'd found yourself a home and you'd signed a contract, and when you'd been there you'd shown her photographs, and before I could say anything she said, 'So, Tiraleh, maybe this house business will give you two a second chance?'"

"So then you told her you already knew, that you'd been to the house and to the interview committee with me?"

"No," Tirzah said. "I told her, 'I have the impression that you and my father have concocted some sort of scheme, that you two have a story that's above and beyond and predates Professor Mendelsohn saving my brother's life.'"

"There certainly is a story," my mother said. "There is always a story. But no scheme. Just a few things that need fixing, mending. To take care of my baby before I die."

And what is your story, Tiraleh? I asked, as usual not aloud but in my heart.

"I wouldn't be surprised to hear," Tirzah continued, "that Meshulam had given her that money so that she could give it to you and then you and I could meet up again. That's him, your 'nice' friend. When he wants something he knows no bounds. But what do I care? I wanted to meet up with you, and when Meshulam told me you'd found a home I knew right away it might turn into more than just a meeting."

"It's okay with me," I told her. "I wanted to get back together with you, too, and anyway, I'm used to acting in a puppet theater."

"Even if he didn't actually give her the money," Tirzah said, ignoring what I had just said, "I do know that years ago he advised her to put away a *knipele* on the side. A person needs money of his own, especially if this person is a woman. He even invested money for her, too. You know, in the kind of place that people like him invest, where if your investment pans out you make a killing and if it doesn't you need someone like Meshulam to take care of the consequences."

Too many people are touching me, leading me, revealing secrets to me, making plans for me, I thought. Tirzah stood up and said, "In the end, what do we really care? We're not exactly suffering. You have a contractor who is a woman, who sleeps with you and luveys you and isn't cheating you or disappearing on you suddenly in the middle of the job. And I have you. You love me too, Iraleh. I can feel it."

# 5

SHE GOT DRESSED and leaned over me and kissed me on my lips and told me to keep sleeping. I did as she said. The loving and the drinking and the hot night and the infinite, open skies overhead and the story I wished both to sink into and run away from—all these deepened and lengthened my slumber. By the time I awakened the sun had already risen. The tractor operator was standing over me, saying, "Mr. Home Owner, you've got to get up. They're working up there and a plank could come crashing down on your head." On the roof frame above, not one dwarf but two were running about: Illuz the roofer and Illuz his brother, two quick shadows replacing beams.

"No cause for alarm!" they shouted. "We're little, but men like you. No big deal that we saw you without your clothes."

The tractor operator left and Meshulam entered. "Tiraleh's not here?" he asked, pleased. "Very good. Because I want to do something here, too. I want my handprint on this new house, too."

He looked around and told me he would handle the weather stripping, because that was something she probably would not notice. He also mixed mortar and sand in a tin, then cemented and rounded the straight angles between the floor of the bathroom and the walls. "Otherwise, the sealant will crack and there will be dampness here again."

We ate lunch together. Then Meshulam said he would deliver the Chinese workers to their lodgings, "because the house isn't so urgent and pretty soon Tiraleh will be back and you two will want to be alone."

He took them and left. Pretty soon my contractor will be back. We will sit facing the view, we'll talk, we'll fill up with love and happiness. We'll say "And it was good" about what has already been built and we'll mark and we'll inaugurate and we'll give names.

# Chapter Twenty-One

## I

WIND WAS BLOWING among the pine trees of the monastery. Children were playing on an old tank that once stood there but has since been removed. A young teacher flailed his arms this way and that as he told his pupils about the battle that had been fought here and about "the heroes that fell during the War of Independence."

"I have a story to tell you," my mother said. "It will be your story, too. You can pass it on. You can tell it to whomever you want."

To my children, if I have any. To a friend, if I find one. To a woman I love, if she will lie in the crook of my arm. To myself, if none of these will come to be. A story that will not only touch one's intellect and knowledge but will cause the muscles and bowels to contract, will hover and flutter about the valves of the eyes and heart as well.

"A story, and a place of one's own, and air and love, and two hilltops—one on which to stand and the other upon which to gaze— and two eyes for watching the heavens and waiting. Do you understand what every person needs, Yair?"

"Yes," I answered.

A story. Not necessarily about heroism or castles or fairies or witchcraft, but not about petty matters, either. Reality provides us with more than enough pettiness. A story that contains some pain and some confession, some culture and politesse as well, and a dash of amusement and a hint of mystery. And since you are no longer with me, I'll add this as well: this is my story, and I shorten it and lengthen it, I fabricate and confess, I write "my mother" instead of "our mother," even though I have a brother; I fall prey to temptation and conjure up conjectures and guesses. And one more thing I will tell you: you are not the central character of this story. I am. Not you, but your son.

# 2

WE CIRCLED the monastery. "Do you remember," my mother asked, "that we visited this place when you were a little boy? A nun came out from this door and gave us cold water, and you were worried: what would happen to the glasses?"

We returned to the swings. We lingered by the memorial plaque, where above the names of the fallen someone had engraved the following: HERE THEIR LIVES DEPARTED BUT THEIR COURAGE DID NOT. "Well put but untrue!" my mother exclaimed. "When life departs, everything departs. Love and courage and knowledge and memory. You're fifteen years old, Yair; you can already know and understand this."

And she told the story. She told of the wounded pigeon with the YES OR NO? and of the pigeon loft in the Tel Aviv zoo and of Dr. Laufer who used the feminine plural when he spoke and of the neighbor's son who went to America to study medicine and came back and became Yordad and of Miriam the pigeon handler and of the Belgian pigeon and of the Baby's kibbutz aunt and uncle and of his father and his stepmother and his real mother, and of the Baby himself.

"This is where he was killed, and from here he sent his last pigeon before he died, and he was my boyfriend, for whom you are named."

At first I was angry. I thought that if she had not had this boyfriend and if he had not been killed, then I would not have been given his name. I would have taken after my parents, I would have received their fair curly hair and the name Benjamin, and Benjamin would not have been born because they would have had no mistakes to correct.

But when I continued pondering this, another possibility arose in my mind. Now I was angry with Benjamin because he had been born second and had given me his birthright. Had he been born first, it would have been he who looked like a criminal and who would have gotten the name of the dead boyfriend, and I would have been him: light and handsome, with the face of an angel and *goldene* locks. I would have stolen from kiosks and read shop signs on Ben Yehuda Street as they passed by the windows of the bus, and the names of poets engraved on the tombstones.

Meshulam accompanied us on this visit as well. He walked behind us
at a distance only he could calculate. A distance whose smallness was
protection and worry and whose largeness was consideration and good
manners. He walked along making sure that only I could hear, that not a
single word fell to the ground.

I asked, "Did you always have a pigeon of his, and did he always have
a pigeon of yours?"

"Yes."

"And you sent letters to each other."

"Pigeongrams. When we could."

"How many words can you fit onto such small pieces of paper?"

"You'd be surprised, Yair. Sometimes a very short note suffices. Yes
and no, and yes and yes and yes, and no and yes and no."

And she recalled what Dr. Laufer had told his pigeon handlers:
that the ancient Greeks, even before the message capsule was invented,
made do with tinting one of the pigeon's wing feathers in predeter-
mined colors that heralded good news or bad. She also said what
Dr. Laufer had not: that the pigeon itself is a kind of letter. In her
hovering and the fluttering of her wings, in her landing, in the heat of
her body, in the prints of the fingers that held and dispatched her, in
the eyes that watched her until she was seen by the person waiting
for her.

She fell silent. I was already quite familiar with her silences, and I
waited patiently. She had long silences and short ones. She had wide
ones and narrow ones. She had smiling silences and impassive ones. And
then there was the quietest silence of them all, the one that began with
"I can't anymore" and has continued to this very day. I remember, too,
her seasonal insomnia—"From Purim to Pentecost I do not sleep"—
and her daily glass of brandy, and the beautiful song of farewell she
played without cessation on her little gramophone: "More I would, but
Death invades me; Death is now a welcome guest . . ."

Finally I asked her, "So it's really true? From here he sent you a
pigeon, too?"

"Dispatched, Yair. Not sent. It's time for you to know and remember
this."

"From here he dispatched a pigeon to you?"

"Yes. His last one."

"With a letter?"

"Yes."

"What was written in it?"

"Nothing."

"So what did he send you from here? A blank piece of paper?"

"No. From here he sent me you."

And she told the story.

# Chapter Twenty-Two

## I

CEMENT TRUSSES were poured between the beams of the roof, and cement girders around what were to become the windows and doors. Tirzah put up the inner walls and together we inaugurated the two new spaces, the very large one in which I will live and the small one that perhaps I will need one day. She installed and cemented doorposts and lintels, affixed sills to the windows, and said, It is good.

Illuz and his brother stretched tensioned light mesh in preparation for the new Ravitz ceiling. They replaced planks, set down tiles on the roof frame, sealed every opening that might tempt rats or pigeons— and Tirzah said, "It is very good!"

I felt her love for me and my love for her not only when she touched me, not only when she called me "luvey" but also in her building of my house—the way she measured, assessed, gave instructions to the workers, the way the house she was building for me took shape. And when we ate together at the end of the day, and when she went elsewhere and I remained alone.

And sometimes her body and her scent drive me mad and I am flooded by all this love and a spirit of foolishness overtakes me. I press into her like a puppy, nudging and nestling and waggling, grunting and growling, nibbling at her flesh.

And then she laughs and says, "Iraleh . . ."

And I say, "What?"

And she repeats her prognosis: "You love me."

"So?"

"You love me, I can feel it," she says, and the tone of her voice is the tone of other women's voices—anyway, that's the way it seems to me; I have no way of comparing—when they say, "I love you."

# 2

YOAV AND YARIV showed up suddenly as well, large and laughing. "Hello, Uncle Yair. What've you got to eat?"

"Hello, Double-Ys," I said, happy to greet them. "What's up that you decided to come visit your uncle?"

"Dad says that when you die this house is going to be ours. So we came to see the place."

My love for them does not dull the pain I felt on the day of their birth. By chance—or not—I was at my mother's place when my brother phoned from the hospital. I did not hear what he said, but I saw her face beam and I listened as she said, "At last I am a grandmother. Thank you, Benjamin."

The envy that attacked me then was similar to others from the days of my childhood, and my mother was obliged to soothe me with words and ways also borrowed from that period. I shouted, "Why must you do that when I'm here? Why do you have to thank him like that when I can hear you?" And you said, "Calm down, please." I continued: "And what's this 'at last I'm a grandmother' business? Is it my fault that Liora can't give birth to my children? That you're not at last a grandmother thanks to me?" And you said again, "Calm down."

A look of dissatisfaction appeared on your face, but your fingers had already found their own way and were consoling and caressing me. "Please calm down, Yair. Benjamin is my son, too."

I did not calm down, but time did its trick. I discovered that what Yordad had said to you when he asked for your hand in marriage was correct: things can be fixed. Fixed and mended. The years passed and I learned to love my brother's enormous boys. In some measure I even found solace in them for the two fetuses that were not born to me. Like me, the two of them are army medics, although they serve in military clinics at two different bases and are not engaged in course instruction, as I was.

It is not easy raising twins, especially with a partner like Benjamin. When Yoav and Yariv were young, Zohar would ask me to help her out, and on occasion I would take them. I have already said there is affection between Zohar and me, and a number of times I took them for several hours. When they grew older I began inviting them over for weekends. We would play, hike, read. I would tell them stories and dredge up memories.

"Did you know," I told them, "that once there was a zoo right near here? Shall we take a walk and I'll show exactly where?"

"Later. Let's eat first."

"And every evening the neighbors would hear the animals. Imagine, in the middle of the city, roars and shrieks and growls. There was a pigeon loft there, too."

"Who needs pigeons in a zoo? There are enough of them on the street, and Dad says they carry diseases."

Their bodies inclined toward the kitchen. Their necks stretched to bring Liora's giant refrigerator into view.

"What have you got inside that thing to eat?"

"Soon Aunt Liora will be home and we'll all eat together. In the meantime we'll look at the albums."

My finger moved from face to face in old wedding photos. "Who's this?"

"Dad."

"No. That's his father when he was young. They looked a lot alike."

"Who's this?" asked Y-2.

"That's me."

"You don't look like anyone, Uncle Yair."

"I look like me, when I was a baby."

"Here's a meat pie," Yoav said to Yariv, pointing at Yordad's plate.

I told them that Grandpa Yaacov did not like to stand in the line that formed around the casserole dishes and the platters. "Prepare a plate for me, please, Raya," he would say.

They laughed. "So prepare a plate for us, please, Yairi."

I was horrified. "Where did you hear that name?"

"That's how Dad talks to us when we come back from your place. 'Did you have a good time at Yairi's? What did Yairi give you to eat?'"

"That's what he says? Yairi? Really?"

"Yes. But Mom tells him to stop, and that it's not nice."

"Look, there's roast beef. And ribs."

"Then it must be a wedding of the kibbutz uncles."

I flipped the pages. Yairi. It couldn't be Yair or Iraleh or my brother or Uncle Yair. Of all the names, Yairi.

And now the boys were scouting about my new house, and the yard, and the view.

"Very nice place," Y-1 said.

"Cool," concluded Y-2.

"We'll put in a big grill here, and a wood-fired oven over there," said Y-1.

"We'll scarf down pizzas and steak from morning to night."

"And baked potatoes."

"If you don't mind, boys, I am still alive and I have plans to live here another thirty years or so at least."

"We can wait."

# 3

SIGAL PHONED with two matters to discuss: first, Liora's father wanted us to come to America for a family event. It would be taking place during the High Holidays and the airline tickets should be ordered well in advance. When would it be convenient for me to depart and return?

I: "There's no need to order tickets for me. I'm not traveling to any United States."

Sigal: "I'll pass you through to your wife."

Piano music in the background. Other offices have electronic music while you wait. Liora has hired Glenn Gould to play Bach for her fans.

Liora: "What's with you, Yair? What's your problem this time?"

I: "I have no desire to travel."

Liora: "It's not a question of desire, it's a question of good manners and behavior."

I: "I don't like traveling and I'm busy."

Liora to me: "I want a clear answer: are you coming or not?"

I to her: "No."

Liora hung up. Sigal came back on the line with her second matter for discussion. She apologized for the short notice, but several Dutch bird-watchers who had arrived in Israel had requested that I take them on a three-day tour. Beginning the next day, if possible.

Possible? Of course it was possible. Guiding bird-watchers was more pleasant and paid better than ferrying lecturers and actors about. I picked them up from a hotel on Nes Ziona Street in Tel Aviv, very near the Romanian restaurant that is the payback spot for bets between Benjamin and me, and that afternoon we reached the guesthouse I had reserved in the Galilee.

The owner, a tall, thin man, seemed bitter and fatigued. Years earlier he had uprooted a grove of lychee trees and built rooms for rent. For a while his business had prospered. Then later—"With all the troubles in this country"—tourists had stopped coming. "For a while," he told me, "I was forced to rent the rooms out to couples. What can I tell you, it's simply unpleasant. Couples married to other people would come here, you know what I mean?"

"More or less," I answered. To myself I said, If ever I come up to the Galilee with Tirzah, I will stay in someone else's guesthouse.

"Anyway, they've finally fixed up the pond out at the Hula Valley Nature Reserve and they've been spreading corn for the cranes so that they don't eat the chickpeas planted in the fields. So I'm hoping that more people will come for that reason than others."

Not only cranes. Pelicans and cormorants spend time here, and all kinds of geese and gulls and ducks and birds of prey, all of them arriving at dusk for their nightly rest. The skies become spotted with spread wings and beaks calling and shrieking. The pelicans, with their tight and sturdy bodies, go down to the water assuredly, but a moment before touching down they are stricken with an amusing panic, as though they have discovered a malfunction in the landing gear. Their legs thrash and spray water and their wings—especially those of the younger birds— get tangled up. The cranes, with their long legs and outstretched necks, are not swimmers. They land in the shallowest water, first hovering like dancers hanging from strings and only then handing themselves over to gravity and plunging down into the congestion of their congregating friends, a flock that resembles a hundred of the letter *kaph-sophit* printed in your own handwriting.

My excited Dutch tourists stepped out of Behemoth toting binoculars and cameras. One of them, a tall, gaunt old woman, removed from her bag a drawing pad, watercolors, and brushes and sat down to paint the birds with incredible speed and precision. Her friends peered at her drawings, uttered expressions of amazement, and returned to watching the real birds. Bird-watchers constantly share their discoveries with one another by issuing short directives—name of bird, direction, distance—which change from language to language but always keep their sense of urgency. At once, all heads turn, all binoculars are raised. And there is always someone who has come up with a nice catch in his spotting scope. With a gesture of the benevolent victor he invites his colleagues to view his treasure, and in no time a short line forms, polite and grateful, in front of the lens.

Just like the elderly *Vogelkundler*s Yordad had introduced me to, and who had taught me the best bird-watching spots, these Dutch bird-watchers were interested in neither ethology nor ornithology, only identification. Thus, they competed among themselves about who had seen and was familiar with more birds and species. They argued, too: was this a laughing dove or a turtledove, a swamp harrier or a pygmy falcon? More than once their arguments were settled with the help of a spotting scope or a more powerful pair of binoculars, but sometimes the bird under discussion disappeared quickly, or the distinction was particularly difficult to make, as with the common kestrel and the lesser kestrel, especially when the sky was free of clouds. And then the voices rose and the arguments flared.

Very slowly, the sun descended. The mallards lost their sheen, the water silvered, and brown ibises turned black in it. The darkness erased the gray hues in the cranes' wings and, later, the white of the pelicans'. In the end there remained only the last glow from the water and shadows upon it. Then even those were gathered up, and I gathered my own small flock and we returned to our lodgings.

After supper the bird-watchers stayed at the table, comparing their plunder and continuing their arguments. They even tried to get me to join in, wanted me to determine which old vulture—pun intended—was which, and quickly my ignorance was revealed, for which I was even scolded. "It is unfathomable that the guide does not know such elementary things, like the fact that the wings of the steppe eagle are longer than those of the greater spotted eagle." But with me, the more things relate to these small matters—the length of wings, the color of walls, knobs for doors and cupboards—the more likely I am to lose interest in advance. The larger perceptions are enough for me: the height of flight, the arc of the heavens, the beeline, the full press of bodies, the air that fills space and home.

# 4

I ROSE BEFORE DAWN, turned on the samovar set up for us in the evening at the entrance, and awakened my tourists. They wished to see the fowl that had landed in the evening as they took off in the morning. While waiting for them to emerge from their rooms, I filled a large thermos with coffee, removed from the kitchen refrigerator the packages of sandwiches the guesthouse owner had prepared for us and, while it was still dark, we set out for the Hula reserve.

A strong easterly wind was blowing in our direction, raising clouds of dust, bending treetops, and even shimmying Behemoth's heavy nose. At the entrance to the reserve I told them the story of the reclamation of the Hula Lake and its consequences. That is what I always do, and they cluck their tongues, reciting the local words and even jotting some of them down as a reminder. In another week they will be sitting in their local cafés using these exotic words I have taught them—*agur, sharkia, hula, saknai*—with their friends as if they had received them with their mothers' milk, and they will sip beer and pass around their photographs.

The wind and dust caused us to seek refuge in the "Aquarium," a building that is all windows and intended to be an observation point. The door was locked, but the industrious guide—that's me, Mother, your firstborn son—circled the building and found an unlocked window. I slid the glass sideways and invited my charges to enter.

From here on, things happened as if by themselves, like the previous night's events being screened in reverse: the rise of the wake-up cries, the fading of darkness into gray, the clearing of the water so that shadows of the birds are visible on the surface, the further rise of the sun, the beginning of movement. There is no leader or ruler or organizer here, and each bird takes flight when she is ready, and on her own accord and pace. The pelicans heavily, the cranes at first as if dancing in the air, the geese and ducks racing across the water, necks outstretched and clapping their wings. All are trying, failing, hovering, landing, waiting for the sun to grow stronger and heat the air and their muscles.

Slowly, the skies once again grew spotted, filling with movement, wingspans, flapping, noises, and suddenly the mobile phone in my pocket rang, and in spite of the looks of reproach I got from the bird-watchers, I hastened to answer it because on the display screen appeared the name YORDAD.

# 5

YORDAD DOES NOT PHONE often. And certainly not at such an hour. In general, *yekkes* do not wish to be a burden, to make requests from others. And anyway, whenever Yordad needs something he turns to Meshulam Fried. But ever since that conversation and his terrible question—"Is Mother at your place?"—seeing his name on the display screen causes me to worry.

"I am truly sorry for disturbing you, Yairi," he said, his voice perturbed and tired. "I thought long and hard about whether to phone you. You simply must come over here at once."

I excused myself from the bird-watchers and stepped outside.

"I'm up north with a group of tourists. What happened?"

"Someone has been trying to break into my apartment."

"Call the police. Right away!"

"Not now—it's already light outside. It happens at night, every night. Someone presses down on the handle of the door, trying to open it. I haven't been able to fall asleep these past few nights."

"Is the door locked?"

"Of course."

"You're just hearing things," I said, trying to calm him down. "Buildings always make noises. Especially apartment buildings, where there are other residents. And late at night, when everything's quiet, it's enough that some guy on the third floor is flushing his toilet to make you feel certain that someone is trying to break in."

"Excuse me, Yairi, but I am still capable of differentiating between someone trying to break into my home and someone flushing his toilet on the third floor. And in case you're hinting in that direction, I don't have hallucinations, either!"

Slam. Lately he has developed the obnoxious habit that American businessmen have of ending telephone conversations without saying good-bye. I ignored this and phoned him back. I said, "We were cut off," pretending that "the connection is poor from up here." I tried the humorous approach: "Maybe it's Meshulam, checking to see whether Professor Mendelsohn has locked his door before going to bed?"

Yordad's voice sounded pleased to hear from me, as if he had not been angry with me a minute earlier. "I've already asked Meshulam, Yairi. That's the first thing I did."

"And what did he say?"

"He said he would send someone from the firm that provides security to his offices to stand guard outside."

"A good idea."

"A bad idea. This is not the prime minister's residence. You yourself said it: this is an apartment building. I don't need some thug with a pistol in the stairwell."

"Have you spoken to Benjamin about this as well?"

The birds were lifting off. I was encircled by the flapping of wings; the wind roared around me. Still, Yordad's sigh was clearly audible. "There is no point in speaking to Benjamin. He's busy."

"So that's the reason you come to me? Because I'm less busy? I work sometimes too, if by chance you forgot that. At this very moment I'm with a group of tourists. Bird-watchers from Holland. I got up this morning at a quarter to four to show them the migrating birds in the Hula Valley, so I'm a little far away."

"I'm sorry to have bothered you, Yairi. I turned to you because you are my elder son."

That afternoon I drove south with my bird-watchers to our next stop: the Jordan Valley. I made sure that everyone was set up with a room and a meal and I traveled to Jerusalem via the Jordan Rift. At ten-thirty I parked Behemoth on Halutz Street in Beit Hakerem. I removed from the car the handle of the hoe I keep there all the time and the folding chair that has been in the car since the aborted trip with Yordad, and I walked up to Bialik Street through the darkened memorial garden. What would someone who caught sight of me think, a man in his prime carrying a club in one hand and a collapsible chair in the other? Where could he be going? What are his intentions? In fact, there would be no need to make too much effort to guess. This man is the little boy who came down to this garden years ago with his mother. Now he is walking through it on his way to protect the father who raised him as though he were really and truly his own son.

Just as I thought: a MESHULAM FRIED AND DAUGHTER, INC. vehicle was parked outside. I set up my chair in the garden, under the fig tree that had been transplanted there by Meshulam years earlier and that was now a large tree, and I sat in the darkness. From there, no one could see me, whereas I had a clear view of Yordad's front door. Shortly after eleven o'clock the door opened, Meshulam called out, "Good night," locked the door from outside, exited the stairwell, and looked around. What would I say if he spotted me? I would tell him the truth. Meshulam would listen, remove his handkerchief from his pocket, and say, "And who will watch over me since Gershon?" and he would offer to take over for me or keep me company.

But Meshulam did not notice me. He got into his car and drove off. The light was on in Yordad's bathroom. I could hear him coughing and spitting. When people were visiting him he did not cough like that and most certainly did not spit. After that, the light in his bedroom went out and only a small lamp in the kitchen remained lit.

I was sitting like that, bored and weary, when suddenly the light in the stairwell went on. I came to attention, but for naught: it was only Yordad's tenant coming down from the second floor. He removed something from his car, held a brief conversation on his mobile phone replete with stifled giggles, then disappeared back into the stairwell. Twice, people arrived and went up to the top floor. Then all at once I grew tense, because Benjamin had shown up and was standing at the door. He listened, but he did not touch the door handle or ring the buzzer or open the door. I did not move from my hiding place, and my brother departed.

Slowly, the air chilled and grew humid. The passersby diminished and ceased altogether. An after-midnight wind kicked up suddenly, resounding lightly in the small trees and loudly in the large one. From far away came the short and terrible scream of a woman, followed by silence and then barking. Bats circled in the lamplight, catching insects attracted to its glow.

At three in the morning I left. There was light at Glick's kiosk; Mr. Glick was already at work in the kitchen. "If you can hang on five minutes I'll have a samwich ready for you," he called out to me from the window. "Meantime, here's a coffee for you."

I drank it down. Mr. Glick asked, "Make one for Fried's daughter, too?"

I blushed. "I won't be seeing her today," I said.

"That's no good," Mr. Glick said. "A woman like that, every day without her is a waste."

"You're right, Mr. Glick," I said. "All the days without her have been a waste. It was a mistake."

He gave me the samwich. "Don't eat it right away. Give it a few minutes so the tastes inside can mix up together. Since she's a little girl I been telling her that. Tirzah Fried, she's something special. She's not like the others. *Nu,* if you get a move on it before I finally kick the bucket, God willing, then I'll make the food for your wedding."

All the way down from Jerusalem toward Jericho I thought about Yordad, whether or not to tell him about this evening spent in the garden of his building. And then northward bound, in the Jordan Rift Valley, I thought mostly about myself, and my story, and the need for a story in general, and what a man whose story reached its climax before he was even born is supposed to do with himself. Then farther on, near the kibbutz where the Baby grew up, I drove off onto the dirt road on which he had ridden his bicycle with Miriam. I stopped by the abandoned building that had once been a pump house, and my thoughts—in spite of the independence we like to invest them with—moved logically, sanely, from the first dispatch to the last. Only a few pigeon handlers were in attendance at the Baby's funeral. The war had not yet ended, there was still so much work to do, and the roads were dangerous. The father came from Jerusalem. The aunt, the uncle, and Miriam came from the kibbutz. Premature gray was strewn through Miriam's hair. The uncle and the father stood far apart from one another, each one crying in his own fashion, and they did not exchange a single word.

Dr. Laufer and the Girl were there, too. The Girl had difficulty moving and breathing. Every few seconds her mouth gaped and she gulped air in spasms. But the two cells in her womb had already divided and become four, and the four were soon to divide again, later that day, to become eight, then sixteen, then thirty-two, then me, today. Dr. Laufer, the only person apart from her to know, delivered a eulogy, and his feminine *pluralis majestatis,* which never failed to amuse his listeners, this time brought about feelings of horror, because it sounded like the eulogy of a thousand mothers and daughters and sisters and lovers.

One must take advantage of every trip for dispatching pigeons, and each of the pigeon handlers who attended carried a woven wicker pigeon basket with a handle and a lid. At the end of the funeral the pigeons were dispatched, and they soared above the tears and the mourning and the fresh grave. Dr. Laufer said, "This is both a training exercise and a beautiful sight. Perhaps we will make this a tradition at memorial services."

# Chapter Twenty-Three

## I

TOO BAD you were not here today to watch Tirzah's all-star plastering team work on the house you bought for me: a band of Druze men from a single family in Ussefiye, all with broad mustaches and colorful skullcaps. First they built scaffolding on the outer wall of the house; then they climbed up and stood on it, two on the top level and two on the lower level. They rubbed their hands with olive oil to protect their skin, and then they plastered as one and smoothed as one, using exactly the same movements.

"Why four men on one wall?" I asked. "Why doesn't each man take a wall and work on it?"

Tirzah explained that the whole wall needed to dry simultaneously and in the same sun so there would be no differences in the texture or the hue.

They began by throwing plaster at the wall and smoothing it down, this layer intended to seal the cement. On top of that they added a second layer, which they smoothed and evened out by scraping it in circular motions with round handsaws, and then they topped it off with a third layer spread with long, fast rollers. Inside the house they would do the same with a yellowish wash, not white—Tirzah and I do not like white—and the outside plaster was to be covered with a pigmented stucco, the color of which—so Tirzah tells me—is "peach."

A fifth man plastered inside the house. He climbed up and worked from a low and heavy ladder, examining the metal mesh of the ceiling the way you check the strings of a harp, with pinches and tugs. The mesh hummed for him to fill in its empty eyes, and he tossed plaster at it, tossed and smoothed, and when he finished Tirzah said, That's it, that is our ceiling, not the ceiling of someone who lived here previously, and soon the workers will depart and I am pleased to see that you have strength and desire, Iraleh, because we have a double inauguration to do: the ceiling and the stucco.

# 2

THE CHINESE WORKERS spread a layer of sealant on the foundation beneath what was to become the bathroom floor. They laid long plastic tubing in green and black, which they fastened to the floor with handfuls of cement. A plumber and an electrician arrived on the scene to thread pipes and cables through the tubing. And when everything was dry and attached and smoothed and rounded and sealed and fastened and examined, Meshulam turned up with Steinfeld the tiler.

"Hello, Steinfeld," Tirzah called out. "And hello, Meshulam. The weather stripping looks very nice."

Steinfeld was carrying the same old schoolbag on his back, the same bucket in his hand. This time it held a hammer, a spirit level, a putty knife, and a pillow. His mouth continued to spout complaints as though only just then had he finished the *stichmuss* work he had begun several weeks earlier: "You see? This is the tiler's hammer I was talking about; you'll only see it on real craftsmen. No plastic or rubber, like today. The head alone is three pounds of iron for chiseling bumps and angles, and the handle is made of poplar wood for pounding and straightening. The handle's seven inches long, exactly like my *shmekele,* but thicker and softer."

"What are all these tall tales you're telling?" Meshulam said. "They still use your tiler's hammer for the old floor tiles—it's the ceramic tiles they use the rubber hammer for."

"The old floor tiles are prettier," Steinfeld grumbled, "and the measurements of the ceramic tiles are less accurate." He expounded against marble flooring, too, which "makes the new houses look like the bathroom of Rothschild's maid."

"You're the home owner, not them!" he said, turning to me. This pleased Tirzah and Meshulam to no end. "Let the Frieds put whatever they want in their house. For your house, I'm going to bring you the good old-fashioned floor tiles, eight by eight inches."

Tirzah protested. "That makes more tiles, more work, more grouting for the eye to see, and the ceramics machine can't cut them for the wedges at the end."

"Tiraleh, you forget that it's Steinfeld the tiler who's doing the work. There aren't going to be many wedges, and the few there are we'll cut with a disc."

"He doesn't even use a vise when he cuts," Meshulam whispered to me, full of admiration. "The guy's eighty, he holds the tile in one hand and cuts with the other. You'll see it and you won't believe it. When he uses the disc it's like cutting butter with a butcher's wife."

An hour later a truck pulled up and unloaded the tiles. In the meantime, however, a new argument had broken out: Steinfeld insisted on using sand beneath the tiles, while Tirzah preferred fine gravel. She even shared her FOR and AGAINST with me: with sand you could mix in a little mortar powder, which would cause it to stick to the loam better, but its tiny grains transfer moisture from place to place, "and then you have to pull up half the house to figure out where it's coming from."

"I don't like gravel under tiles," Steinfeld complained. "Sand sits quiet. Gravel I can hear like this: kkkhhh . . . kkkhhh . . . kkkhhh . . ."

Tirzah laughed, but this time she did not give in. "First of all, you won't be living in this house. And second of all," she said, pointing to me, "he won't hear the kkkhhh . . . kkkhhh . . . You are the only person in the world who can hear it."

Steinfeld muttered something, then acquiesced, and Tirzah said, "Never mind. You got your way about the tiles and I got mine about what goes underneath. Your victory can be seen, but mine can't."

Meshulam filled with pride. "You see that? You see how she's fighting for you? By the teeth of her skin! By the skin of her nails!"

"That's what makes you happy?" Tirzah asked her father later. "That your daughter, who has built hotels and hospitals and industrial centers and shopping malls and highway interchanges, and who wins battles against all the bureaucrats in the Defense Ministry and the Housing Ministry and the Transportation Ministry hands down, managed to bend Steinfeld the tiler to her will?"

"Don't move!" Meshulam said. "You know you got two gray hairs over your forehead?"

"What's going to be with you, Father? What kind of nonsense have you got running through your head?"

"Oh, that's beautiful. Now I can finally rest in peace."

"It's bad enough that I cry over those gray hairs," Tirzah said. "But you? Put that handkerchief back in your pocket right away!"

"It's not because of the gray hairs. It's because you finally called me 'Father.'"

"Oh, stop talking rubbish. Go on, say it: 'If my Gershon were alive, he would have gray hairs on his head.'"

Steinfeld got angry. "Enough! You're making it impossible to work around here."

He drew a string the length of the room to indicate where the first row should be placed, and the younger of the Chinese workers flattened out the gravel on the exposed concrete. Steinfeld instructed him to pour into the mixing pan the white and the regular sand, the whitewash and the mortar, while he himself added the water.

The Chinese laborer ran the hoe through the mixing pan, chuckling to himself under a barrage of angry shouts issued by Steinfeld. "You see? That's exactly why I didn't want it! There are lumps! Try explaining to the *Khinezer* that the loam has to be as smooth and delicious as chopped liver."

He placed the embroidered pillow he had brought with him on the floor and knelt on it with a groan. The worker brought him a bucket filled with loam. Steinfeld plunged his putty knife into it and tipped a fair amount onto the gravel, smoothing it, then adding a bit more and smoothing it, again. His movements were quick and thrifty, altogether different from his speech and gait. With the end of his putty knife he drew two little lightning bolts, two little z's, in the loam. "That way it won't all spill out the sides. From the pressure it'll fill up the inside and reach everywhere."

After that he placed the first tile, tapped it gently with the wooden handle of the hammer, and with the edge of the putty knife he gathered the leftover loam that had squeezed out from underneath. He set down the spirit level from north to south and from east to west and said, "You see how straight it is? Even if you put a ball bearing on it, it wouldn't budge. Even the pool table of the president of the United States of America isn't as level as the floor I'm building you here."

He smoothed the gravel with the palm of his hand once again and grumbled. "Sand is better!" He placed more loam, smoothed it, drew his little lightning bolts, centered another tile, tapped. His taps were dull and measured and had their own special rhythm, as if he and the house were passing messages to each other like prisoners in their cells. He stroked the two tiles, passed a knowing thumb down the grouting joint, picked up the spirit level again, and placed it atop both tiles.

"A tiler's mistakes are impossible to conceal," Tirzah explained to me. "The electricity and the plumbing hide in the walls and the floor. The builder and the plasterer and the painter all blame each other and cover up one another's errors. But the tiler is exposed, and because of the straight angles and the length of the grouting joints, even an untrained eye sees mistakes at once."

"She's a cheeky girl," Steinfeld growled, "but she understands something about construction."

Some two and a half hours later, when he had finished laying the first three rows, the elderly tiler extended a hand to the elderly contractor and said, "Help me up."

Meshulam grabbed hold of him and pulled. Both groaned from the pain and the exertion. "Now that Steinfeld's laid the first three rows like only he knows how, pretty much anyone can finish up," Meshulam said. To which Steinfeld replied, "What I did for you here not even the government can screw up now. The *Khinezer* can carry on—just make sure he doesn't put rice down there instead of gravel."

I walked outside with him. He looked inside the refrigerator and shouted, "Tiraleh, where can a guy get a piece of herring?"

"Everything's in there," she called back to him from inside the house. "You just have to look."

"And what about a little vodka with the herring?"

"Not during work hours, Steinfeld. Have a beer—that'll do."

Steinfeld found the herring, took out a cucumber and some hard cheese as well, and grabbed some bread, then routed about and drew out a knife from the depths of his schoolbag, spread out a piece of fish, and sat on a chair. His right hand trembled.

"Been doing that for a few years already," he told me. "No doctor's managed to cure it, but it stops shaking when I get down on my knees to go to work." He handed me the cucumber. "Peel it for me, please."

I peeled the cucumber for him and offered to pour the beer into his glass. Steinfeld told me he preferred drinking directly from the bottle. "Everything spills out of my glass. Don't tell Tiraleh, okay?"

After he finished eating and drinking I spread a tarp in the shade of my carob trees and he sprawled out there and fell asleep. Meshulam said to Tirzah, "Give the worker something else to do and we'll continue with the floor for a while." To me he said, "Tiraleh and I have already laid a few tiles in our days, and you can mix and hand us the loam and learn a new profession."

I mixed, I handed, while Meshulam Fried and Daughter, Inc., knelt and laid tiles. Later Meshulam said, "*Nu,* Iraleh, why don't you lay a few tiles, too. It's your floor."

I can still remember the exact location. Even today, several months after Tirzah left me and went away, I can still identify my tiles and her tiles and the invisible impressions our bodies left on the floor.

# 3

BUT AT THAT TIME we were still together, and Tirzah admitted, "Steinfeld was right. The eight-inch tiles really are prettier." And the next day she announced, "Come on, the loam has dried. Let's inaugurate our new floor."

"Don't you want me to spread something underneath us?"

"No. How many couples can say they've made love on the floor they tiled themselves? Lie on top of me, my luvey, I want to feel your weight."

I lay on top of her. Our chests touched, our loins were pressed together, our lips met. We were kneecap to kneecap and our hands were outstretched to the sides, fingers intertwined, as if we had been crucified to each other.

"Let's get completely undressed. We'll feel the heat of our bodies and the cool of the floor."

The setting sun filled the gap torn in the wall on the first day of work, flooding and inflaming the space inside my new home.

"Did you miss me, Iraleh?"

"Yes."

"So here, I've come to you. It's me. I'm here."

"Good."

"And when I wasn't here?"

"When you weren't here, what?"

"Did you miss me then, too?"

"Yes."

"When more?"

"Tiraleh, I saw you only this morning."

"I'm not talking about this morning. I'm not talking about today.

I'm talking about all these years, all the years that have passed since then. Did you miss me then, too?"

"You're a pest."

She laughed. "Are we going to argue? Because if you argumentate me I won't be able to get it up later."

We rolled over. Tirzah's face came to rest above mine, sank slowly into my own. I began to quiver, not only from the pleasure but also from the immediate sharpness of the picture. There are some people whose sensory organs capture reality for them. But with me, my sensory organs mediate between reality and memory, and not every organ in its realm. Sometimes my nose connects sound to image, sometimes my ear feels, my eye recalls aromas, my fingers see.

Tirzah kissed my neck and made it tremble. She lifted herself up a bit so I could see her eyes and her body. Although she had been pregnant and had given birth, her nipples were still small and well defined, the left one pink and the right one mauve. Sometimes she would check them with fingers slightly moist with spittle. "Look at them. I took this one from our sour pomegranate tree and this one from the sweet one."

I never grew tired of thinking about her. Her small breasts, her thick hair, the slight bulge of her belly. Her short, sturdy body, her long legs. Her protruding navel and, below it, the dense darkness that astonished me each time anew, like when we were adolescents, when she laughed and said, "I've got steel wool growing in my peepot!" and, beneath it, the only softness on her body, like a stream running between reeds and rushes.

We caressed each other like Gershon instructed us to when we were young. All the memory cells in our bodies awakened, the ones in the muscles and the skin and the fingertips. Tirzah said, "This is unbearably pleasant."

"What is?" I asked.

"The mixture of us. The me and the you. What we did together once and what we're still going to do."

Her hand, the fingers spread, moved from my waist to my lower back. She signaled me with a press of her hand. Come. Every woman in my body pressed against her brother in Tirzah's. Every cell of my flesh found its mate in her.

# Chapter Twenty-Four

## I

THE NEXT MORNING the Illuz brothers returned and began building me a deck. They dug pits and filled them with cement and stones to support the iron toes that would grip the wooden posts. It took the dwarf roofers three days to finish the deck. They built the floor of planks and ran a railing around it, while overhead they pulled down flaps held by steel cables that gave it the look of a sailboat.

On the fourth night, after we had inaugurated the deck and fallen asleep, I was awakened by a loud sound of breaking and falling. Tirzah did not wake up, and I understood at once what had happened: the fig tree had collapsed. Meshulam had been right. The noise was the fulfilling of the prophecy.

I did a FOR and AGAINST and decided not to get up. It would be better to assess matters in the light of day, since at night things look different than they really are. I lay there listening. Quiet was restored, filling up the void created by the fall, and following it came the usual noises: the blowing of the wind, the distant barking, the croaking of frogs, and finally the hollow, rhythmical hooting of the small owl and the tread of a hedgehog in the undergrowth.

Tirzah neither heard nor knew about any of this. She rose and left before dawn; I woke up an hour later and went out into the yard. The tractor operator had already been there, armed with a small power saw. The branches of the fig tree were lying on the ground, its foliage strewn about. The broken trunk looked like a sack of sawdust split open. Only then did I understand how devastating the onslaught of the caterpillar had been. When he saw that I was awake, the tractor operator started up the motor of the saw and carved up the carcass, loaded it onto his cart, and drove off to dump it into the garbage heap.

That afternoon Meshulam showed up with a potted fig that was already sprouting and blooming.

"You knew. You'd prepared it in advance," I said, not certain whether I was complaining or acquiescing or expressing astonishment.

"Naturally!" he said. "After all, we saw the holes in the trunk that first day you brought me out here. I told you then she would fall."

"That's a pretty big sapling. You got it ready even before you came here that first time."

"Meshulam is always prepared. For the good and the bad. And this is a real fig," he said, "not like the one you had here until now. She'll give you beautiful fruit and she won't abort them like some figs do."

"We're not so young anymore," I told him.

"Who isn't?"

"Don't play innocent, Meshulam: Tirzah and me."

Meshulam was neither nonplussed nor offended. "These days you got doctors at Hadassah who could even get old Methuselah and his wife pregnant."

He went back to his pickup, brought a pickax and a hoe and a pitchfork and another new and strange tool—a long, thick galvanized pipe with the blade of a pickax stuck in the end, the wider side pointing outward.

"This is a planter's tool, Iraleh. You won't find a guy like this in any shop."

He explained that before planting one needs to "think real good" in order to imagine what the place will look like in another few years, "when this little sapling will be a large tree and will need to get along with its neighbors: its plant-neighbors and its building-neighbors and its people-neighbors."

The poplar, for example, cannot be planted near a house—"No way!"—because its strong roots lift floors and sidewalks and get into sewage pipes. The Persian lilac is beautiful and scented but it attracts woodpeckers, and in the end it falls on your head. The ficus makes a mess and attracts flies, "but," Meshulam said, smiling in appreciation, "it sends its roots a long distance and steals water from the neighbors' gardens. That's what I call a good tree."

And fruit trees, particularly apricots and plums, bear fruit all at once, and try picking and washing and organizing pots and jars and standing there making jam. "That's what my Goldie would do every summer. If she was still alive I would argue with her and I would uproot all of those fruit trees of hers, but it's not nice to do something like that when she is no longer around."

We took everything into consideration, we imagined the future, and in the end Meshulam marked a spot by digging his heel into the ground.

"Here!" he instructed me. "You dig a nice pit here, and let a little of your sweat drip in. This is the first tree you're planting in your new home, so let's do it right."

# 2

AT FIRST I PLUNGED the pitchfork into the ground and extricated large clumps of earth. After that I used the hoe, and when the pit was a little deeper Meshulam handed me the iron pipe with the pickax blade.

"Now try it with this guy. You see? Top to bottom, like with the excavator's bar they use in quarries. This way you'll have a nice planting hole, just like a planting hole should be: deep, with straight walls."

I dug and widened and deepened until Meshulam told me it was enough. He filled the hole with water and allowed it to seep in and disappear; then he doused the hole again—"So the tree will have a nice, wet reception." Next he filled the bottom third of the hole with dirt mixed with compost and topped it with time-release chemical fertilizer. "We could use cow chips—they're completely dry and don't smell at all—but never bird dung. Now let's take the sapling out of the pail."

He knelt down and pressed in the sides of the pail all around while I pulled and removed the sapling—"Hold her bottom, too. Got to keep the part with the roots from breaking up"—and then I placed the little tree in the center of the pit.

"Let it lean on your shoulder so you can feel each other's weakness and need. Today she'll lean on you, but soon you'll be sitting in her shade." He raked some dirt into the hole, stepped back, commented that the sapling was lopsided, and had me tilt it gently leftward and pat it into place.

"Put in some more dirt. Don't bury her neck, we don't want any rottiness! Don't tamp it with your feet, you heathen! Don't choke her! This is the first tree you're planting at your new house. Get down politely on all fours and use your hands. A little strength with a lot of gentleness."

The fig tree was in the ground. Meshulam brought three long wooden poles from his pickup. We planted them in a circle around the tree and Meshulam explained to me how to tie them to the dainty trunk. "Use strips of cloth. Rope will cut the bark."

He checked to make sure the cloth strips were loose enough for the sapling to move a bit in the wind. "That causes her to use her muscles a bit. Makes for a thicker, stronger trunk." He stepped back and said, "That's it. She's planted. Now we'll give her a little water, and when we fix up the garden we'll wind a few irrigation drips around her base. In the meantime, visit her every day with a watering can in hand so she learns to wait for you and rejoice when you come. And while you're watering her, take the opportunity to give her a good look. Check her leaves and her bark—that's the way to find out how she's maturing and what her problems are, and she'll know you didn't just plant her and take off, that you're continuing to take care of her."

We sat down beside my new fig tree, me on the ground and Meshulam on the upside-down pail. He lit himself a cigarette and said, "It's a good thing you don't smoke, Iraleh. I want my Tiraleh's fellow to be strong and healthy. And I want to give you another piece of advice, because I don't know if I'll still be around when this tree bears fruit. You were right: I'd already prepared this sapling before you came to me with this house of yours; it's a cutting from the tree Tiraleh likes better than all the rest, one of the green ones with a little yellow in the peel. I'll tell you how you should serve the figs to her: chilled and cut crosswise, not lengthwise, so they look like figs should. You understand what I'm talking about, don't you, Iraleh? Because that's the way you tell her what you want and what you like about her, but politely, without being crass. And with the fig you bring her a little bowl with a tiny bit of arak inside.

"That'll make her really happy," he promised me. "You'll see. She'll be pleased, she'll laugh. A woman likes her man to feel what she wants without having to say so. So don't tell her that I taught you this little trick. Let her believe you understand everything about her on your own."

After pondering briefly, he changed his mind. "You know, if Tiraleh asks you, then tell her the truth. Yes, Tiraleh, it was your father who told me the secret. He wanted me to please you, he wanted us to be together, and he decided to help out a little. And then she'll laugh: So that's it? Every nice thing you do for me I'll wonder if it was my father who put you up to it? And you'll say, No, Tiraleh. Not every nice thing.

This was just the fig. And then she'll ask, Are you sure? He didn't tell you about other things I like? And you'll say, No, Tiraleh, most things that girls like, their fathers don't know about. Come on, let's not talk anymore about him, because now it's just you and me, and what do we care about that old pest anyway? That's what you'll tell her. Now, Tiraleh, we're like Adam and Eve: we're all alone, just you and me. And this is the Garden of Eden we made for ourselves, and nobody's going to drive us out of here."

# 3

AFTER MESHULAM LEFT, I lay on the floor of my house. It was good: in spite of my unabating love for my contractor who is a woman, I found it very pleasant to be alone. The construction was nearly completed, the beams of the roof had been fixed or replaced, the roof tiles laid, the ceiling stood between them and me, Steinfeld's floor tiles underneath my body. The windows and doors had been installed, the countertops and sinks and faucets were in place, the walls were plastered and white-washed. The only things missing were furniture, bathroom and kitchen cupboards, closets. And there were a few spots that needed repainting, and the light fixtures needed to be connected.

I lay on the floor of the empty house looking upward and felt a strange feeling, as though I were lifting off inside it. I do not usually sleep in the afternoon, but this time I fell asleep and at last I dreamt another dream about my mother. Since that last one, in which she had said "Yair . . . ? Yair . . . ?" over the telephone, I had not dreamt of her again. This time I even got to see her.

In my dream I went outside the house, into the yard. Dozens of workers were laboring there, and many guests—some of whom I recognized but most of whom were completely unfamiliar to me—were milling about and chatting. The scent of festive activity filled the air. Several tractors were at work, digging and pulling and swinging about, and one of them, an especially large one with my tractor operator driving it, was carrying an enormous cube of rock that was hanging from the tractor's shovel by the wide straps used by movers. The rock was so heavy that it caused the tractor to tilt dangerously. I wondered: Where's Tirzah? And Meshulam? And where are the two workers? Did they return to China?

I drew near and saw that in the front yard of my home, which leads onto the street, there was a group of people, and you were among them, lovely and alive and happy, wearing one of your favorite dresses from my childhood, the kind you don't see anymore today: a light-colored, wide, flowered cotton sundress with a cinched waist and short sleeves and a rounded collar that seems more generous than it really is and suits even small-breasted women.

Clearly I understood that you were dead—it was as plain to me in the dream as if I were awake; I even felt the astonishment one should feel when dreaming such a thing. But the knowledge and the surprise did not keep me from filling with joy. I said to you, "How wonderful that you came." You hugged and kissed me and said nothing, while I—why, damn it, couldn't I think of anything else to talk about?—repeated, "How wonderful that you came, Mother" and "How beautiful you look," and then the dream dissolved and it was as though it had never happened, the kind of dream that is forgotten as it is dreamt, even before the dreamer gets to tell the person he is dreaming about what it was he wanted to say, and before he has heard the answer.

I did not feel myself awaken, but suddenly I was awake, and the pleasantness inside me in the dream continued beyond it. The twilight and the cool air told me it was evening, that my afternoon nap had gone on too long. I called out, "Tirzah . . . Tirzah . . ." a few times in order to tell her about the dream, perhaps even to boast about it, but Tirzah was not there. Nor were the workers. But I was not alone; I could feel that clearly.

I turned on a light and saw a pigeon. She was sitting on the floor, motionless. My body froze, my hair stood on end. It was a completely plain-looking pigeon: bluish-gray with scarlet legs. A pigeon like a thousand others. Round eyes. Two dark stripes like those of a prayer shawl adorning the wings and the tail.

I let out a scream. The pigeon was startled, too, and she flew about flapping her wings. She slammed against the new ceiling and plunged. She took flight again, hit the ceiling again; then she grew confused and began flying about the room, until finally she landed in a far corner. I was standing at the center of the large, empty space. We looked at each other. Silence fell.

"Where did you come from?" I asked at last.

Pigeons have no way of indicating directions or places. "To you," she answered.

"I do not want you," I said. "Go back to your home."

"I have been flying all day long," the pigeon said. "Please give me rest for the sole of my foot, refuge for a single night."

"Not in this house. Not in my home. Not you."

"I will cower in a dark corner. I shall not disturb you. You will neither see nor hear me. Who better than you could know that pigeons can gather themselves in, vanish—in the wicker basket, in the wooden crate, even in a pocket."

"Now!" I shouted. "Leave at once!"

"The sun has already set," she pleaded.

But I clung to my fury. I felt myself gripping it firmly. "I have closed off all the holes in the roof. I have sealed all the cracks. There is no place for a pigeon here."

"You closed off, dammed up, sealed, yet I am here. A pigeon."

I stood up. The pigeon flew off again around the room, while I leaned down and took hold of one of the planks dropped there by one of the dwarf roofers, and I leapt forward with a sprightliness that surprised even me. I swung at her as if she were a baseball, still airborne. She slammed to the ground, fluttered, fell silent. Her right wing was broken and dangled at an odd angle. Her thin broken bone could be seen whitely through the shredded flesh. She was breathing through her gaping beak. Her eyes were clouding with fear and agony.

"I am the flesh and the soul," she announced, like some ceremonious tape recorder.

"Shut up," I said.

"I am the breeze of the body and the burden of love. I am wind and strength."

I took hold of her, went outside, and in a single movement I decapitated her and hurled her head with all my strength into the darkness. I ripped the down from her belly and her breast and tore the plume from her neck and back. The body, now plucked and exposed, was naked and tiny. Her wing feathers seemed to belong to some other creature. Were it not for the pain it had obviously endured, I would say it even looked ridiculous.

I took the Leatherman hanging from my belt—the next time Liora or Benjamin make fun of me I'll be able to tell them that I finally put my useless equipment to use—opened it and sliced off the tips of the wings and the tail. With a quick slit from the breast to the stomach I bisected the belly and pulled back the sides. All the internal organs—the craw, the stomachs, the intestines, the air pouches, the large heart, the developed lungs—I gathered in my hand, then ripped them out and pitched them.

I went down to the back of the property, turned on the lights strung between the branches of the carob trees, gathered a few thistles and boards, and lit a fire. Within half an hour I had a nice pile of whispering coals. I roasted my pigeon on them and ate her. A strong and pleasant taste of blood filled my mouth. Was it her blood I was tasting or had bone splinters cut the insides of my mouth?

I undressed, lit one of my luvey's memorial candles, and got under the shower she built for me. I rinsed my hands of the blood and my body of all the rest, and when I turned off the water and stood naked, letting the drops fall from my body, I suddenly heard the soft crowing, dripping as well. I lifted my gaze to the darkness and saw nothing. Cranes do not always pass over this area, and the crowing, like the flapping of wings, could be heard not only from the highest heavens but from my deepest depths as well.

# Chapter Twenty-Five

## I

T HE MAN from the electric company installed a new meter. The man from the regional council installed a water meter set to zero. The man from the gas company installed tanks and pipes. The man from the Bezeq telephone company put in telephone lines. The house—a golem whose flesh is bricks and mortar, gravel and sand—felt a flow in its veins and came to life. It stretched its tendons, its windows opened and closed, absorbing light and darkness, views and images. Its beams gave support, its walls partitioned, its front door stands ajar or shut. Tirzah had finished her work.

The house emptied of people. The new phone rang suddenly. I picked it up, slightly surprised, and heard her laughter: "It's me, luvey. Your contractor who is a woman. I'm in the garden, next to the carob trees. I just wanted to inaugurate your new phone line."

Night fell. We ate, showered, entered the house. Tirzah said, "It's already our home, with a floor under our feet and walls around our bodies and a roof over our heads." She noted that my camping mattress was "good for a single fakir, not for a couple of hedonists. It's time we bought ourselves a proper bed."

The next morning I woke up very late. The sun was already high in the sky and the air was filled with the aroma of cut vegetables. Tirzah was squeezing a lemon into her hand, letting the juice drip between her fingers into the salad and tossing out the seeds.

"Finally up? I'm making us the kitchen's first salad." She rubbed her hands together. "I learned to do this from my mother. It's good for the skin and gives the body a nice lemony scent."

While she was tasting and improving the salad, I sliced the bread and the salted cheese she had brought, and I put out plates and knives and forks. "Now that all the other guys are on the table, waiting," Tirzah said, "it's time to prepare the eggs."

We sat on the wooden deck she had built me, eating the first breakfast we had prepared in the new kitchen. Tirzah said, "That's it, Iraleh. All we need now is to buy furniture and get rid of all the tools and the leftovers and the mess, but the work is done, and I have a gift for you." She handed me a small, wrapped box. I opened it. Inside were two keys and a brass plaque that read Y. MENDELSOHN, PRIVATE.

It was autumn. In my luvey's eyes the yellow was waxing and the green was waning. "These are for you," she said. "If you want to give me one key, this is the time to do a FOR and AGAINST and come to a decision."

I handed her one key, and she was happy. I was happy, too, and from the sky came that soft, wandering croaking, which at first enters through the skin, then grabs hold of the tissues, and only then can be heard and comprehended.

"What do you see there?" Tirzah asked as I tented my hand over my upraised eyes.

"Those are cranes. They're flying south to their other room. Look."

"Why are there only three? They usually fly in large flocks, don't they?"

"The large flock will come a few hours from now. These are the scouts. They're looking for a good place to rest and eat. When they find it they'll call the others to land."

The three cranes flew lower, passed over the village. My heart pounded. My brain calculated: Where. When. Then. Now. My stomach contracted to the point of pain. My mouth said, "I have to go, Tirzah."

"Where?" she asked, surprised.

"Tel Aviv."

"Your home is here," Tirzah said. "It's finished. Put the nameplate on the door and try the keys."

"I want to bring Liora here. I want her to see it."

"What for?"

"I want her to know that I've found and bought and built a place of my own."

"She knows all that. She also knows that I'm here. She even sent her brother and yours, those two snakes, to check it out for her."

"I just want her to see it built and finished."

"You don't need victories like those. Don't bring her here. Please, Yair."

My stomach cinched even tighter, but I rose from my place. Tirzah grimaced suddenly, stood up, and ran outside, and when I ran after her I found her bent over and vomiting our breakfast onto the earth of the garden. I placed a hand on her shoulder and she brushed it off and moved away from me.

I began to walk toward Behemoth. Tirzah overtook me in three quick strides and stood in front of me. "Wait a minute. Do a FOR and AGAINST like your mother would have."

"I just want her to see this house. It's not such a big deal."

Tirzah stepped out of my way. I went to Tel Aviv.

# 2

LIORA'S STREET honored me with a parking space. Liora's door opened obediently toward me like the automatic doors at an airport. Liora's alarm system welcomed me in preordained silence. Liora herself was waiting for me, sprawled on her bed, her eyes scanning one of her computer printouts. I took off my shoes and lay down next to her.

"My house is finished," I told her.

"Congratulations. I'm sure Tirzah did a wonderful job."

"There's still no furniture," I said, "but it's got water and electricity and doors and windows and floors for the feet and a ceiling for the head."

"So are you here to say good-bye to this house?"

"I'm here to invite you there. The time has come for you to see it."

"When?"

"Now."

"No good. I have a meeting this evening with clients. Let's call the office and have Sigal find a better time for us."

"It has to be today and we've got to get going now. We'll get there late in the afternoon and we'll stay over until tomorrow so you can see the view."

"So it's also an invitation to sleep over? Is there a bed?"

Her smile slanted her eyes and stole into her voice, but there was no sign of it on her lips.

"There's nothing there yet. We'll take your mattress. Come on, get up. Pack a few things while I load the mattress onto Behemoth."

"But I have meetings tomorrow morning, too."

"Postpone them." And with the sharpness of someone grown strong and thin, someone who has built and has been built, I added, "I've seen you solve bigger problems than this."

She got out of bed, opened her closet, and took out a travel bag while I, moving quickly, expansively, stripped the sheets off the bed. I lifted the mattress and pulled it from the bed and dragged it outside the room. We proceeded down the hallway, me pushing and guiding, it feeling led and angry, and all of Liora's rooms—the morning rooms and evening rooms, the rooms for solitude, the rooms for arguing and treatments and sleeping and making up—watched as we passed, and they threw open doors.

We stepped outside the apartment and slid down the steps one at a time, past each and every startled camera, to the garden and the gate and the street. I pulled and lifted the mattress onto Behemoth's roof rack. I bound it with straps and tightened them, while Liora—who had come down after me, looking gorgeous, perfectly suited to her lightweight, light-colored dress and the travel bag in her hand—regarded me with amusement. Could this be Yair? Where had this sudden vigor come from? This energy?

We drove out of Tel Aviv, swimming in the still-warm summer air now fighting for its life with encroaching winter. We spoke little. My hand, which passed between the seats, touched her own briefly. Her hand, feeling the touch of mine, grasped mine for a moment and held tight. It seemed to me we were passing down an enormous corridor, from one room of the world to the other. A red, setting sun was on one wall and the moon was on the opposite wall, while we were in the middle, the mix that would not work.

The sun disappeared. The moon climbed in the sky. The large, yellow ball became a flat, bluish-white disk. Behemoth turned at the junction, rounded the bends, decided not to approach through the fields this time. The entrance to the village came fast. Right turn at the secretariat building, the giant pine, the birds already settled in for the night. The cypress trees that would have gladdened your heart. Two tended gardens and one that was dry and balding.

Behemoth stopped. I got out, rushed around to the other side of the car, and opened the door ceremoniously. A long, white leg stretched from within, and then another. Liora stood beside me. She looked. The moon shone. Not strong enough to show her the entire view framing the house but enough for her to sense the great expanse beyond.

"It's a pity your mother isn't here. This house would suit her perfectly."

"Yes, it's a real pity."

"How many rooms do you have here?"

"One very large one and one very small, and there's a storage room below."

"Too few."

I pulled the mattress from Behemoth's roof rack, dragged it along the cracked sidewalk, and we passed through the front door into the large room and out to the wooden deck that my luvey built for me.

"Here?" Liora asked. "Outside? Why not in the house?"

"Come on, lie down next to me," I said to her. "I have a surprise for you."

Together we stretched the sheet she had brought over the mattress. She spread her dress graciously, sat down, and sprawled out next to me in one elegant movement.

"So what's the surprise?"

We lay there, two supines, one fair and beautiful and calm and awaiting the unknown, the other short and dark and excited at what was about to come.

We lay there some more. Our eyes grew accustomed to the light of the moon and our hands to each other's, until Liora grew impatient and said, "So, what's happening?" and I answered, "Wait patiently."

And still we lay there. Time passed, was measured in the hollow whistles of the small owl, amassed in the falling of dry leaves from the carob trees, spread out among the jackal's howls from nearby and the lowing of cattle from afar. Then silence fell, a great silence, the soundlessness that precedes the soft din. Overhead, the blackened skies began to fill up, and along with them the body's empty spaces, at first slowly, then more rapidly, with a whisper that could be heard and a movement that could not be seen. The whisper became a flapping and the flapping a chatter and the chatter a conversation. The world filled with syllables and wings, and the darkness rained down voices. The full moon skittered and winked, now hidden, now exposed behind passing shadows.

"Mommy, mommy," Liora said in the whining voice of a baby crane, "are we there yet?"

To me she said, "It's them."

A narrow, twinkling path wound its way down her cheek. Her teeth attested to the sparkle of her smile. And I—in spite of the dubbing she had just done for the cranes, and in spite of my memory of her answer back then, about "Daddy Crane" and "Mommy Crane" and the little cranes that were just old enough to be making their first journey with the flock—I repeated my question about what it was they were discussing.

"Us," she said. "They're saying, You remember, children, the story our forefathers heard from their forefathers and we've told to you? About the couple we saw that night lying in the grass at the kibbutz? Well, here they are again. It's them. Look."

She raised herself on one elbow. Her beautiful head drew near. Her lips parted and I stretched my neck toward her kiss. Her hand passed over my chest and my waist and her loins pushed close to my thigh.

"Hello, you," she said.

My body breathed and responded.

I felt the sickle of her thigh rising and descending until it came to rest on my belly. The cranes had already grown distant. The flapping of their wings was muted, but their soft croaking had not ceased, crossing distance and times. The woman my mother prophesied for me moved forward, opened, arced, returned me into her flesh.

# 3

When I woke up in the morning I saw her. Her long, fair, barefooted body in a pair of jeans and a white shirt, leaning over the railing of the deck, drinking coffee and looking at the view.

I sat up. "Where did the coffee come from? Did you bring the gas burner in from Behemoth?"

"Of course not. The neighbor gave it to me. Very nice young woman. She apparently thinks I'm your lover and Tirzah is your wife."

"She may look good, but nice she isn't."

"What's that over by the carob trees?"

"A shower."

"And you shower outside?"

"You want to give it a try?"

"People will see us."

"The worker who built it is Chinese. They know how to build showers so no one sees you."

"And whose handprints are those in the cement? Tirzah's and yours?"

"Mine and his."

"I don't believe you. One print belongs to a man and the other is a woman's."

"The Chinese have small hands."

I stood up to explain the handprints and show her the view. Before my eyes had even taken in the sight revealed to them, my pointing hand fell and my heart died. The area around my house had been cleared and cleaned and emptied. The tools, the bricks, the leftover tiles, the remains of mortar and sand and iron and gravel, the mixing pans, the pallets, the refrigerator, the table—everything had been collected and removed. The yard had been perfectly raked. Even the small cement mixer had disappeared, most likely had passed in front of us the previous night being towed to another place by a convoy of white pickup trucks with the MESHULAM FRIED AND DAUGHTER, INC. logo.

Tirzah, it appeared, had called in her people from other building sites, from all the intersections she was erecting and bridges she was building. In the time it took me to travel to Tel Aviv and back, every trace and track had been erased. Not even a dollop of cement, a grain of sand, a cigarette butt, a bottle cap. Only a single sheet of tin remained, leaning against the wall of the house near the window.

A familiar rumble started up. The tractor operator arrived, the empty rubbish cart in tow behind him. He stopped, went over to the lemon tree, lowered from its branches the thick metal pipe he had chimed that very first day, and tossed it into the cart.

It resounded loudly. The tractor operator said, "Your contractor left," and he climbed onto the seat and drove away.

# 4

I WENT TO FIND myself a home. I came to it returning, not arriving. Hello, house, I said to it, and it answered me.

I built and was built, I loved and was loved, my soul grew a new skin, a roof, a floor, a wall. I have a wooden deck and an outdoor shower, and time and a story and a view, and a tin to hear the rain during the approaching winter, and two eyes to tent a hand over to watch the skies and wait.

And two weeks ago I received my first letter at my new address. It was a thick manila envelope sent from Leiden, in Holland. That gaunt old Dutchwoman who drew the birds in the Hula Valley had sent me copies of several of her watercolors, including *Birds of the Holy Land* and *Migrating Fowl.*

"In appreciation of the wonderful tour," she wrote me, and in among the pelicans and cranes she had slipped in a surprise: a portrait of me she had done in just a few brushstrokes, without my ever having noticed her doing it. Here I am, a thick, black bird, not migrating but returning, not joining the flock.

"I hope you will forgive my forwardness," she wrote apologetically, but when she was a young woman, she said, in the days when the British still ruled the country, "and you, certainly, were not yet born," she had taken an interest in birds and even then had come to the Holy Land in their pursuit. "I am enclosing four more drawings, from several dozen I did back then, my dear Mr. Mendelsohn. Perhaps you will find them to be of interest, since today it is not easy to find such birds and such views in your country, and that is a shame."

And here they are: vultures crowding around a cow's carcass, a large flock of starlings dotting the eye of heaven, a colorful and joyous band of finches atop tall, dry thistles, and a sole boy sitting on the bench at a railway station, a woven wicker basket on his knees, a pigeon basket with a handle and a lid.

# Where Are They Now?

PROFESSOR YAACOV MENDELSOHN gathered up his computer, his notepads, his panic button, and his books, took leave of his apartment in the Beit Hakerem neighborhood of Jerusalem, and moved into the Fried home in Arnona. Together, he and his Romanian cook take care of Meshulam, who had a stroke and is partly paralyzed.

Professor Benjamin Mendelsohn left the country. He lives in Los Altos Hills in California, where he teaches and conducts research at nearby Stanford University. He rarely visits Israel.

Zohar Mendelsohn went with him to California but after a year there returned on her own. She has opened a café in Ramat Hasharon and, right next door, a successful clothing store specializing in large sizes.

Liora Mendelsohn continues to succeed in business.

Yair Mendelsohn was killed in a car accident some two years after completing the construction of his home. He was on his way from the Hula Valley to pick up Tirzah at a construction site in the Lower Galilee. A truck whose driver had fallen asleep jumped lanes and hit him head-on. Yair was severely injured and died one week later.

Tirzah Fried, who had come back to him several months after she had left him, moved out of the house she had built for him immediately after his death. They had managed to live there together for "seventeen months of love and happiness and one week of horror" — that's how she put it. Now she is involved in a "superficial romance," as she defines it, with an El Al pilot she met one evening at a sing-along.

Yoav and Yariv Mendelsohn were accepted to study medicine at Ben-Gurion University, and they are unexpectedly studious. They often visit the house their uncle Yair willed to them. Yoav's girlfriend joins them there, and all the village children know the place from which to watch the three of them bathing together in the outdoor shower.

The Baby's last pigeon never left the loft again. Dr. Laufer locked her up for the purpose of breeding her, and when she died he stuffed her and placed her on his desk. She disappeared when the zoo moved from Tel Aviv to the safari park in Ramat Gan.

Dr. Laufer himself died in great old age in the Ruhr region of Germany, where he had been invited to lecture and judge pigeon races.

Miriam the pigeon handler rejected several suitors from the kibbutz and the Palmach and at the end of the War of Independence moved to Jerusalem and worked for the Jewish Agency. She never married or had children, but she wrote and illustrated wonderful children's books that were published only in Germany. To her dying day she never revealed her passion and love for Dr. Laufer, either to him or to anyone else. She died in the summer of 1999 of lung cancer.

The Baby's aunt and uncle tried to keep up the Palmach pigeon loft on their kibbutz, but did not manage to raise or train any new homing pigeons. When I visited there in 2002 there was nothing left but a pile of planks, a few troughs, and some screens. One old kibbutz member, who spotted me looking around and making notes, approached to tell me that once there had been a Palmach homing pigeon loft there and that "one of our own boys," who had worked there, had fallen later on in the War of Independence.

"He was what we called 'an external,'" she told me. "He didn't get along so well with the other children, but he loved those pigeons."

"What was his name?" I asked.

"He had some nickname. 'The Boy,' or perhaps 'the Baby.'"

"The Boy or the Baby?"

"What does it matter anymore? He's no longer living, and they buried him somewhere else. We remember, we remember a lot, but who can remember it all?"

Then she cast me an apologetic look. "Quite a few years have passed since then, and in the meantime others have fallen, and how much is possible? Even the pigeons don't visit anymore."

## A NOTE ABOUT THE AUTHOR

Meir Shalev was born in 1948 on Nahalal, Israel's first moshav, and is one of Israel's most celebrated novelists. His books have been translated into more than twenty languages and have been bestsellers in Israel, Holland, and Germany. In 1999 the author was awarded the Juliet Club Prize (Italy). Shalev is also the recipient of the Prime Minister's Prize (Israel), the Chiavari (Italy), the Entomological Prize (Israel), the WIZO Prize (France, Israel, and Italy), and, in 2006, the Brenner Prize, the highest Israeli literary recognition awarded, for *A Pigeon and a Boy*.

A columnist for the Israeli daily *Yedioth Ahronoth*, Shalev lives in Jerusalem and in the north of Israel with his wife and children.

## A NOTE ABOUT THE TRANSLATOR

Evan Fallenberg was born in the United States; he is a writer, translator, and teacher now living in Israel. The recipient of a MacDowell Colony artist's fellowship, he is also the author of the novel *Light Fell*.

## A NOTE ON THE TYPE

The Hoefler Text and Hoefler Titling families of typefaces, designed by Jonathan Hoefler, celebrate some favorite aspects of two beloved old-style typefaces: Janson and Garamond No. 3. Unwittingly, the names Janson and Garamond both honor men unconnected with these designs: Janson is named for Dutch printer Anton Janson, but based on types cut by Hungarian punchcutter Nicholas Kis; Garamond is a revival of types thought to have originated with Claude Garamond in the sixteenth century, but in fact made a century later by Swiss type-founder Jean Jannon. Hoefler Text and Hoefler Titling are published by the digital typefoundry Hoefler & Frere-Jones.

*Composed by Stratford/TexTech, Brattleboro, Vermont*
*Printed and bound by Berryville Graphics, Berryville, Virginia*
*Book design by Robert C. Olsson*